Death Clue
Xitli, God of Fire

TWO CLASSIC ADVENTURES OF

THE *Shadow* ™

by Walter B. Gibson
writing as Maxwell Grant

plus "THE FACE OF DEATH"
a radio thriller by Alfred Bester

with new historical essays
by Will Murray and Anthony Tollin

SANCTUM BOOKS

International Standard Book Number:
978-1-60877-096-0

First printing: November 2012

Series editor/publisher: Anthony Tollin
anthonytollin@shadowsanctum.com

Consulting editor: Will Murray

Copy editor: Joseph Wrzos

Cover and photo restoration: Michael Piper

"Shadow face design" production: Kez Wilson (miscmayhemprods.com)

The editors gratefully acknowledge the contributions of Scott Cranford and Karl Shadow.

Published by Sanctum Books
P.O. Box 761474, San Antonio, TX 78245-1474

Visit The Shadow at www.shadowsanctum.com.

THE Shadow™
Volume 67

CONTENTS

Two Complete Novels From The Shadow's Private Annals

As told to Maxwell Grant

Thrilling Tales and Features

Cover art by George Rozen
Back cover art by George Rozen and Graves Gladney
Interior illustrations by Tom Lovell and Earl Mayan

DEATH CLUE

*One tiny piece of paper which meant nothing—
yet it was the clue to the murders that were
threatening hundreds of innocent lives!*

From the Private Annals of The Shadow, as told to

Maxwell Grant

Book-length novel complete in this issue

CHAPTER I
UNDERCOVER

A GRAY-HAIRED man was seated at a desk in detective headquarters. His face, stern of expression, showed the stolidity that the man had gained through years of service with the New York police.

This man was Inspector Timothy Klein. Grizzled veteran of many battles against crime, Klein, tonight, displayed a determination that showed more than ordinary keenness.

Another man entered the inspector's office. The arrival was younger than Klein; his face, however, carried the same firmness. Stocky of build, swarthy of expression, this newcomer looked like a man of action. He was such. Detective Joe Cardona was recognized as the ace of the Manhattan force.

"Hello, Joe," greeted Klein, solemnly.

"Hello, Inspector," returned the detective. "Been talking with the commissioner?"

"Yes," Klein leaned across the desk and played his heavy fist upon the woodwork. "He wants us to get Strangler Hunn tonight."

"A tough order," remarked Cardona, with a grim smile. "If we were using the dragnet—"

"The commissioner won't see it," interposed Klein. "He claims that it would tip off Hunn. He'd know we were after him."

"Maybe," agreed Cardona. "Every crook that's wanted ducks for cover when the net begins to close. Just the same, it's the only way we could bag Strangler Hunn in a hurry."

"Yes," granted Klein. "We'd also take a big chance on losing him. The commissioner is right, Joe, so far as the best method of getting Strangler is concerned. If he stays in New York, we'll spot him sure. The only trouble is how soon we can get him."

"And he's wanted tonight." Cardona laughed gruffly. "Well, Inspector, I'm here to help you. But we're playing a long, long shot."

KLEIN nodded as he leaned back in his chair. Reflectively, the inspector began to sum up the facts concerning Strangler Hunn.

"He was a bad egg, Hunn was," remarked Klein. "He could have choked a bull with those big mitts of his. When he lost his right arm in that dock fight, it crimped his style a bit."

"Yeah?" Again, Cardona laughed. "Well, Inspector, if he can't strangle a bull any more, Strangler can still knock one cold with that left fist of his. What's more, he can use a .45 with that one hand better than the average gangster can handle a pair of .38s."

"A murderer," mused Klein. "One we've got to get. Easily recognized by that fake arm that always hangs at his right side. The glove he wears on his phony hand is a good enough giveaway.

"Spotted last night. We've been looking for him since. Twenty-five plainclothes men out on the street, looking for Strangler Hunn. In this case, Joe, the undercover system is better than the dragnet."

"It will be," admitted Cardona, "if anybody is lucky enough to spot the guy. But the longer it takes, the more chance there is for a leak. If the newshounds get wise—"

"No reporter knows about Strangler being in town?" Klein's question was a worried one. "If any of them know, we'll have to act quick—"

"It's safe for the present," interrupted Cardona. "Only one reporter's wise. Burke of the *Classic*. He knows enough, though, not to spoil a good story by blabbing in advance."

"Burke was in here just before I came back," remarked Klein. "He talked with Markham.

Coming in later. I guess you're right about him, Joe—he shoots straight. We can count on him keeping quiet."

"I'll talk to him when he shows up," rejoined the detective. "He's probably somewhere near here right now."

IN this surmise, Joe Cardona was correct. Two blocks away from headquarters, a young man of wiry build was entering a small corner store. Spying a telephone booth, he entered and put in a call.

"Burbank speaking," came a voice over the wire.

"Burke," rejoined the man in the booth. "On my way to headquarters."

"Remain there," came a quiet order. "Make immediate report on any new information."

"Instructions received."

Clyde Burke strolled from the store. He had the gait and manner of a newspaper reporter; the completed telephone call, however, indicated that he served in some other capacity. Such was the case.

Clyde Burke was a secret agent of the mysterious being known as The Shadow. Through Burbank, a contact man, Burke and other agents reported to their hidden chief.

The Shadow! Being of mystery, a weird personage shrouded in darkness. He, like the police of New York City, waged ceaseless war against crime. When he appeared in the light, The Shadow invariably used some perfected form of disguise—as Lamont Cranston, as Henry Arnaud, as Fritz the janitor, or as anyone he chose to be. A master of impersonation, he was a masquerader who might show any of a hundred faces—but never his own.

When he appeared in his own chosen guise, The Shadow arrived in garb of black. With cloak of inky hue, its collar upward toward the slouch hat above, The Shadow kept his own visage entirely from view.

When The Shadow swept from the cover of darkness, his blazing eyes were the only tokens of his hidden countenance. Those were the eyes that guided the gloved hands of The Shadow—hands that wielded massive automatics against men of crime.

Clyde Burke had reported to The Shadow. Clyde Burke was on his way to detective headquarters. Clyde Burke knew of the undercover search that was being conducted for "Strangler" Hunn. These facts were productive of a single answer. The Shadow, like the police, was anxious to encounter the one-armed murderer who had returned to New York.

Inspector Timothy Klein had more than a score of detectives on the job. Directing from headquarters, Klein held Cardona in readiness. Similarly, The

Shadow, in his hidden sanctum, was directing a search for Strangler Hunn. But The Shadow needed no man in readiness. He, The Shadow, was ready to fare forth when action might be required.

TEN minutes after his report to The Shadow, Clyde Burke sauntered into detective headquarters. He appeared in the doorway of Klein's office. The inspector recognized the reporter and nodded. Then Klein made a sign to Cardona.

"Hello, Burke," said the detective. "You're keeping mum on this Strangler Hunn business, aren't you?"

"Sure thing," returned Clyde. "Not a line goes in the sheet until you give the word. Got anything new on him, Joe?"

"Nothing yet," replied the detective. "He was spotted last night. There's twenty-five men on the street looking for him."

"You'll give me a break as soon as someone locates him?"

"Positively. If I go out after him, you can come along, Burke. You play the game and—"

Cardona stopped. The telephone bell was ringing. Inspector Klein picked up the instrument from the desk. His face became tense.

"Just now? ... Good." Klein was eager. "Sure he didn't see you? ... Good... Yes ... Stay where you are ... Outside the Melbrook Arms ... Cardona will be there ... Yes, a cordon ..."

The telephone banged on the desk. Inspector Klein, forgetting his usual calmness, registered intense excitement.

"Farlan has spotted Strangler Hunn," he exclaimed. "Saw him going into an apartment house—the Melbrook Arms. Here's the address"— Klein paused to scribble on a sheet of paper—"and Hunn is still in the place. Get Markham, Joe. Get started. I'll have the cordon form."

Cardona swung promptly and left the office. Clyde Burke followed on the detective's heels. Cardona was heading down the corridor to find Markham.

"I'll hit the subway, Joe," called Clyde. "I'll be up there as soon as you are. O.K.?"

"O.K.," returned the detective.

Clyde Burke grinned as he hurried from headquarters. He might have worked a ride with Cardona and Markham in the police car. Cardona, however, would think just as well of him for having passed up that privilege. There was another reason, however, for Clyde's action. The reporter wanted to get back to that same telephone that he had used before.

A BLUISH light was shining upon the surface of a polished table. Its rays, focused downward by a heavy shade, showed only a pair of white hands on the table. One hand wore a sparkling gem of ever-changing hue. It was a girasol, a priceless fire opal.

That gem told the identity of the hands. These were the hands of The Shadow. The light from above was the sole illumination in The Shadow's sanctum, the hidden, black-walled room located somewhere in Manhattan.

A tiny bulb glimmered from the wall. The white hands stretched forward and produced a pair of earphones. A strange, eerie voice whispered from the darkness. It was the voice of The Shadow.

"Burbank speaking," came a quiet tone over the wire.

"Report."

"Report from Marsland," announced Burbank. "Now at the Black Ship. No trace of Strangler Hunn in underworld."

"Report received."

"Report from Vincent. Has finished rounds of listed hotels. No trace of Strangler Hunn."

"Report received."

A pause; then came another statement from Burbank. The quiet voice showed not the slightest tinge of excitement.

"Stand by," declared the contact agent. "New call arriving. It may be Burke."

A longer pause while The Shadow waited. Burbank, in a hidden room of his own, had contact with the outer world. Only he could reach The Shadow by the private line that ran from his station to the sanctum.

The pause ended. The Shadow, shrouded in darkness, listened, while Burbank announced that the call had come from Burke. Then came short, terse statements. After that The Shadow's whisper:

"Report received."

The earphones clattered. White hands slid into darkness. The light clicked out. A soft laugh sounded amid the complete blackness of the sanctum. Weird tones of mirth rose to a shuddering crescendo. They broke with a startling cry that ended with taunting echoes.

The walls hurled back The Shadow's mockery. Hidden tongues seemed to join in the fading gibes. The last reverberation died. Silence joined with blackness. The sanctum was empty.

The Shadow, black-garbed battler, who dealt doom to men of evil, had learned the fact he wanted. Through Clyde Burke, The Shadow had gained the information which belonged to the police.

Strangler Hunn, somewhere in the uptown apartment house known as the Melbrook Arms, would have more than detectives and a police cordon to deal with him tonight.

The Shadow, avenger whom all murderers feared, was on his way to strike!

CHAPTER II
AT THE MELBROOK ARMS

THE Melbrook Arms was an old-fashioned apartment house in the upper eighties. Six stories in height, it formed a square-shaped building that stood across the street from an empty lot.

Automobiles parked in the open space; high rows of signboards against a blank-walled garage beyond—these formed the prospect as viewed from the front windows of the decadent apartment house.

Strangler Hunn had been seen entering the Melbrook Arms. The detective who had spied him was waiting in the parking space across the street. Acting under instructions from Inspector Klein, Detective Farlan was to be in readiness only in case of emergency.

The plainclothes man had done nothing to excite Strangler Hunn's suspicion. Farlan knew that the wanted man was in the apartment house. That was sufficient. Until the police cordon had formed; until Joe Cardona was here to act, all must remain quiet.

While Farlan watched, a lean, stoop-shouldered man came briskly along the sidewalk. This arrival entered the Melbrook Arms. Farlan decided that he must be a tenant of the apartment house. In this surmise, the detective was correct.

Passing through the deserted lobby, the stoop-shouldered man entered the automatic elevator and rode up to the third floor. There he unlocked the door of a front apartment and entered an unpretentious living room. There was a desk in the corner away from the front window. The man seated himself there and pulled the cord of a desk lamp.

The illumination showed the man to be about fifty years of age. His face, though colorless, was sharp-featured; and the furrowed forehead was that of a keen thinker. Reaching into an inside pocket, the man who had arrived in the apartment drew out a small stack of folded papers.

HE spread one of these upon the desk before him. He began to read it in careful fashion, starting his forefinger along the top lines, which stated, in typewritten letters:

> To Mr. Roscoe Wimbledon.
> Confidential Report:
> From MacAvoy Crane, Private Investigator.

The perusal of this document required only two minutes. Reaching to the side of the desk, the stoop-shouldered man brought up an old-fashioned portable typewriter. He inserted the paper, clicked off a short additional paragraph, formed a space and beneath it typed the line:

> Special Investigator.

Removing the paper from the machine he produced a fountain pen and inscribed his own signature:

> MacAvoy Crane.

Pushing the paper to one side, the man at the desk picked up a telephone. He dialed a number and sat with ear glued to the receiver. He was paying no attention to the paper which he had just signed. It lay at the left of the desk, upon the other documents. The unblotted ink was still damp.

"Hello ..." MacAvoy Crane was speaking in a sharp tone. "Hello ... Is Mr. Wimbledon there? ... Yes, this is Mr. Crane ... What's that?... Yes, I can call him in half an hour. Where is he now? ... At a conference in the Hotel Goliath? I see ... National Aviation Board ... Yes... It's important ... If I can't get him there, I'll call you again in half an hour ..."

Pausing, MacAvoy Crane still held the telephone. Hanging up, he set the instrument down impatiently. He reached for the paper which he had signed; pushed it aside and picked up the documents below it. He sorted these; his forehead furrowed in deep perplexity.

Then, with decisive thought, Crane dropped the papers and picked up a telephone book from the floor. He looked up the number of the Hotel Goliath. His finger ran down the page. There was impatience in his action. Evidently he was anxious to get his call through to Roscoe Wimbledon.

The number found, Crane reached for the telephone. He paused. He seemed to be making up his mind whether he should interrupt Wimbledon at the conference or wait until the man had returned home. Then, with a sudden change of plan, MacAvoy Crane again picked up the telephone book. An odd smile showed upon his lips as he began to turn the pages.

SOMETHING crinkled at the side of the desk. Crane swung in his swivel chair. His eyes, upon the desktop, bulged as they saw a huge, hairy hand cover the papers that he had laid there. Looking upward, the investigator found himself staring squarely into one of the ugliest faces that he had ever seen.

A vicious, thick-lipped countenance; glowering eyes beneath bristly brows—these were the features that Crane spied. Gripping the arms of his chair, the investigator began to rise. As he did so, he lowered his gaze. He saw that the intruder was a man with one arm.

The single hand was rising from the sheet of paper on the table. Its clutching fingers were symbols of prodigious strength. A sudden gasp came from Crane's lips. He knew the identity of this unwelcome visitor.

"You—you are Strangler Hunn?" he blurted.

The leering face had thrust close to the investigator. The thick smile on the brutal lips was answer enough to Crane's question. The hand from the table was creeping upward; its fingers seemed like preying claws.

One hand alone! The mate to that fierce talon was missing. One-handed, Strangler Hunn was ready to attempt murder. Crane knew it. With a quick jolt backward toward the wall, the special investigator thrust his right hand to his pocket to snatch forth a revolver.

That was the instant which Strangler Hunn chose for his lunge. The murderer's left arm came up with a vicious sweep. With wide spreading fingers, Hunn made a quick grip for Crane's throat. His hand reached its mark.

Crane writhed as the talon clutched his neck. His left hand rose; he dug his fingernails into Strangler's massive wrist. Out came Crane's right, with a snub-nose revolver. The action was too late.

Clutching the investigator's throat as one might snatch a helpless puppy, Strangler used his single arm to yank the investigator toward him. Then, with a piston-like jerk, he slammed Crane back against the wall.

The powerful blow found full force against the back of the investigator's head. Crane's arms dropped as Strangler yanked him forward and propelled him on a second journey.

This time, the investigator's head bashed the wall with even greater force. Stunned, Crane began to slump. Strangler Hunn still held him upright. All the while, those vicious claws did not once relax their pressure.

A long minute passed, while inarticulate gurgles came from the stunned man's throat. The noise ceased. Only then did Strangler relax his grasp. Crane's body crumpled behind the desk. The light, showed livid welts upon his throat.

Strangler Hunn, his face a study in ferocity, stood in admiration of his handiwork. MacAvoy Crane was dead, another victim of the murderer's terrible strength.

With a snarling laugh, Strangler picked up the papers that Crane had brought to the apartment. The killer looked at each one, then tossed the packet into a metal wastebasket that lay beside the desk. Only one paper remained upon the desk; that was the one which Crane had signed—the report.

THE killer pulled a match from his pocket. He struck it on the mahogany desktop. He set fire to the papers in the wastebasket.

Augmented by a crumpled newspaper that lay beneath, the flames rose rapidly. Strangler shoved the basket away from the desk. He looked at the report sheet.

Running his forefinger along the typewritten lines, the killer stopped at a certain point. His bloated lips formed a triumphant smile. Tearing a sheet of paper from a small pad on the desk, Strangler took Crane's fountain pen and began to make an inscription.

It was evident that the killer could not write well with his left hand. Instead of script, he printed letters in crude and clumsy fashion. The small sheet of paper slipped occasionally as he formed the words; Strangler managed to hold it by pressure of his hand.

This job complete, Strangler dropped the fountain pen and uttered a contemptuous laugh. He tossed Crane's report sheet into the wastebasket, where the paper was still burning briskly.

Then, with vicious action, Strangler kicked Crane's dead body to one side. The murderer began to yank open desk drawers. In one he found a stack of papers that he tossed into the wastebasket without examination. In another, he found several dollars in bills. Strangler pocketed the money.

The room formed a strange tableau. The flames from the wastebasket threw a lurid glow upon the huge, ill-faced murderer who stood before the desk. Reflected light from the wall showed the pale face of MacAvoy Crane, murdered investigator.

All the while, the piece of paper on which Strangler had penned his printed words lay in plain view near the side of the desk. The murderer had not forgotten it. His evil eyes fell upon it; his big hand reached to pluck it from the desk.

Word had reached headquarters too late to save the life of MacAvoy Crane. Strangler Hunn had performed his deed of murder. But while the fiend still gloated, avengers were on their way to find him at this spot.

Before he left this apartment where he had delivered death; before he could make use of the information which he had copied upon a sheet of paper, Strangler Hunn would have other persons to encounter.

Joe Cardona—stalwart detectives—a cordon of police. These were the foemen who would arrive to trap the slayer. But more formidable than all was the hidden warrior who had also set forth to deal with Strangler Hunn.

The Shadow, he who feared no living man, would play his part in the strife that was to come!

CHAPTER III
DEATH TO THE KILLER

"LOOK there, Joe!"

The speaker was Farlan, the detective who stood by the parking space across the street from the

Melbrook Arms. Farlan was pointing upward to the third floor of the apartment house.

Cardona nodded. The police car had driven into the parking space; Joe had alighted; he had found Farlan promptly. Now he was staring at the window which Farlan had indicated. The flickering light of flames was reflected from the inner wall.

"Maybe that's where he is—"

"You stay here," Cardona interrupted Farlan. "I'm going in with Markham. The cordon is forming; send in a crew of men as soon as they close in. I'm going up to get Strangler."

With this, Cardona headed across the street, Markham at his heels. Farlan, stepping forward, wigwagged to a pair of bluecoats at the corner. As the officers approached, a young man swung up and headed toward the door of the Melbrook Arms.

"Hold it," growled Farlan. "Where are you going?"

"I'm Burke of the *Classic*," replied the arrival. "Cardona told me I could tag along. I'm going in."

"Stick here." Farlan drew Burke back toward the parking lot. "See that window? That's where Cardona's gone. We think Strangler Hunn is in the apartment. You might get plugged if you went up there."

Clyde Burke shrugged his shoulders. There was nothing to do but wait. Like Farlan, he stared up toward the flickering light that showed in the third-story window. The policemen were at the entrance to the apartment house. Two detectives had arrived; Farlan now was pointing them into the building.

A trim coupé purred into the parking lot. Keen eyes spied Clyde Burke. They also noted the spot toward which the reporter was gazing. A soft whisper— almost inaudible—sounded from within the car.

The Shadow had encountered a longer journey than had Joe Cardona. He had arrived in time to avoid any trouble with the police cordon; but too late to precede Cardona into the apartment house. His quick brain summed the whole situation in a moment.

Policemen were closing into the parking lot. They did not see the figure that was emerging from the coupé. They did not glimpse the black-cloaked form that moved among the darkened cars toward the wall at the inner side of the lot. Nor did they see The Shadow as he merged with the darkness behind the tall tiers of signboards.

The Shadow was moving upward. He knew that police would be at the rear of the apartment house. He knew that Cardona must now be at the third floor. His one opportunity to gain even a partial glimpse into that spotted room lay in taking a vantage post from across the parking lot.

UP in the apartment, Strangler Hunn had completed his brief process of rifling MacAvoy Crane's desk. The killer paid no attention to the burning papers in the wastebasket. He thought that the flame was too far away from the window to be visible from outside. This assumption was partially correct. Farlan would not have noticed the reflection of the flames had he not been watching the apartment house.

Strangler, himself, was in the alcove where Crane's desk was located. The killer was completely out of range of the window. He was picking up the paper that he had worded. He was folding it clumsily with his single hand; making ready to thrust it in his pocket, when a thump at the door brought him to a standstill.

"Open the door!" came a growled voice. "Open the door!"

Strangler made no move.

"Open in the name of the law!"

Strangler knew the voice. He recognized it as the tone of Joe Cardona. His face took on a ferocious glare. Then came a terrific smash. The door seemed to bulge inward. Another crash; a panel began to splinter.

Raising his hand toward his face, Strangler Hunn gripped one end of his paper between his teeth; he held the other end with his fingers. Clumsiness gone, he tore the paper in half. He placed the pieces together. Another tear. Once more; as Strangler stared at the ripped fragments, the upper hinge of the door broke loose, and the barrier swung inward a full foot.

Springing forward, Strangler emitted a vicious laugh as he let the torn pieces of paper drop from his hand. Downward they fluttered. Strangler saw them waver into the upward licking flames. That was sufficient. The message gone, Strangler yanked a big .45 from his left hip.

The fluttering papers seemed to dance into the licking flames. Strangler had taken it for granted that they would be destroyed. He was heeding them no longer. The flames seemed to catch the pieces individually. Two ragged slips bobbed upward from the rising heat; the flames sucked in one as it wavered on the edge of the basket.

But the last piece, a single portion of the torn sheet, fluttered free. Striking the edge of the metal basket it toppled outward and drifted, unburned, to the floor. Strangler Hunn never noticed it. His eyes were busy elsewhere.

Crash!

THE lower portion of the door shot free. As the barrier caved, the body of Detective Sergeant Markham came sprawling into the room. Had Strangler taken a shot at that door-breaking form, it would have been his last.

For there was another man behind Markham—a

swarthy-faced fellow whose revolver muzzle came into view with promptness. Joe Cardona was covering his pal. This was what Strangler Hunn had expected. The killer's arm came upward.

A bark from the big revolver. A bullet flattened itself in the doorway, an inch from Cardona's ear. The detective fired in return. His hasty shot was wide.

New shots sounded in this duel. Cardona, half protected by the door, was safe. Yet his own shot again was wide.

More shots. The fight was an odd one. Both Strangler and Cardona were shooting left handed. The murderer had no right hand; Cardona could not use his because that side of the door was the only one which gave him cover.

Strangler was a dangerous shooter. It was the protection in the doorway that gave Cardona a break. On the other hand, Cardona's handicapped shots were delivered with a prayer, and Strangler knew it.

It was Markham who had caused the prompt duel. Cardona was engaging Strangler chiefly to save Markham. The detective sergeant had the opportunity to change the balance. He sought to use it.

Rising suddenly from the floor, Markham yanked his revolver and blazed at Strangler. Had the shot been well aimed, the battle would have been ended. But Markham was too hasty. His bullet zimmed the tip of Strangler's left ear. The killer, swinging suddenly, delivered his reply. Markham fell groaning, a bullet in his shoulder.

Strangler aimed a quick shot at the door to ward off Cardona. Then he swung his gun toward Markham's prostrate body. This time the hammer clicked. Strangler's last shot had been used. Luck had saved Detective Sergeant Markham.

Springing forward, Joe Cardona fired his last bullet to stop Strangler Hunn. Just as Joe pressed the trigger, Strangler leaped forward. The bullet missed by inches. Cardona dived to the floor to beat Strangler's leap. He and the killer were after the same object—Markham's gun. The detective sergeant had let the weapon clatter on the floor.

Cardona dropped his own revolver as he clutched for Markham's. But Strangler retained his own big gun; and it served him handily. As Cardona grabbed Markham's weapon, Strangler delivered a sidewipe. Having no right arm to stay him, the killer lost his balance, but he gained his purpose. His swinging revolver dealt a glancing blow to Joe Cardona's head. The detective sprawled upon the floor.

CROUCHING on his knees, Strangler seized Markham's gun. He aimed it promptly toward the

door, where a new detective had appeared. Two shots resounded simultaneously. The detective dropped, wounded; a second man yanked him to the cover of the hallway.

Strangler, edging toward the wall beside the window, gained his feet. The stump of his right arm was against the wall. His left hand was close against his body, holding the precious gun that it had gained.

A hoarse laugh came from Strangler Hunn. The killer saw the way to freedom. Detective Sergeant Markham was wounded and helpless; so was a detective in the hall. One man outside was still in action; Strangler was ready to mow down any ordinary dick.

But for the moment he had a score to settle. Joe Cardona, unarmed, was rising to his feet. The ace detective who had opened the battle was a helpless victim for Strangler's wrath.

With an evil smile upon his twisted lips, Strangler Hunn thrust his huge fist slowly forward. The revolver and the hand that held it moved just past the edge of the window. The hand steadied as the finger rested on the trigger to deliver the murderous shot.

Joe Cardona, almost to his feet, was staring squarely into the revolver muzzle. Certain death was before him. Aid from the door could not suffice; Strangler had covered that spot also.

ACROSS the street, a blackened, huddled shape lay atop the highest advertising sign. Keen eyes could see Joe Cardona by the door of the apartment living room; those same eyes were upon the hand and gun that had come past the inner edge of the window, fifty yards away!

An automatic barked as The Shadow's finger pressed the trigger. A tongue of flame spat from the top of the signboard. As if by magic, that distant hand dropped from view!

JOE CARDONA, facing death, saw Strangler's arm drop as The Shadow's bullet clipped the killer's wrist. The report of the automatic seemed to follow, muffled. Yet to Cardona, the event was miraculous. It was as though a hand from nowhere had delivered the lifesaving stroke.

Cardona was leaping forward to grapple with the slayer. With his single arm swinging like a club, Strangler pounced forward to combat the detective. His hard swing swept the detective aside. Then came two shots from the door.

The detective in the hallway had come to aid. With Strangler bounding squarely toward him, the man had fired point-blank, not knowing that the killer had been rendered helpless.

The Shadow, peering huddled from beyond the

parking space, saw the collapse of Strangler Hunn. He knew that deserved death had been received. The Shadow, once he had crippled Strangler, had refrained from its delivery. The actual death had been scored by an excited detective.

Excitement was reigning in the street. All members of the closing cordon had headed toward the apartment house. Along with the shrill of police whistles and the approaching sirens, The Shadow's lone shot had been mistaken for one from the beleaguered apartment.

Yet The Shadow, with that single, long-range delivery, had turned the tide of battle. He had saved the life of Joe Cardona. He had spelled the end of Strangler Hunn's murderous career.

A soft, whispered laugh sounded from atop the signboard. Then the blackened form descended into the hidden space against the wall. The echoes of The Shadow's mockery became a hollow shudder that died unheard!

CHAPTER IV
CARDONA'S CLUE

CLYDE BURKE, standing by the parking space opposite the Melbrook Arms, had first been figuring out a way to join Joe Cardona within the apartment house. Clyde knew that his reporter's card would not aid him in passing the closed cordon; but he also knew that if he managed to get through the entrance, Cardona would square his action later on.

Clyde had been watching for lack of vigilance on the part of the policemen at the apartment house door. Then the firing had begun. Clyde, spotting the third-story room as the place of action, had clambered to the running board of a coupé to gain a better view.

Like policemen in the street, he had heard The Shadow's shot. Although the report of the automatic had differed from those of the revolvers, Clyde had taken it for granted that the gun had been fired within the apartment.

Firing had ceased. Policemen were piling into the apartment house. Clyde decided that now was the time for his entry. He stepped from the running board of the coupé. He stopped stock-still as he heard a hiss not three feet distant from his elbow.

A sinister whisper—a sibilant tone that Clyde recognized. The Shadow was here—within reach of his secret agent. Clyde did not turn. He knew the source of the sound. It came from within the coupé. The Shadow's agent stood attentive.

"Strangler Hunn is dead." The pronouncement came in a weird monotone. "You can enter. Stay with Cardona. Learn all that has happened."

"Instructions received," spoke Clyde, in a quiet tone. Then, without another word, The Shadow's agent paced across the street to the door of the apartment house.

SHOUTS were coming from above. Word was reaching the men below, informing them that the raid had succeeded. A burly policeman, holding his arm as a barrier to keep Clyde out, suddenly dropped his hand.

"All right," agreed the officer. "They've got the guy. That ticket will let you in now. I couldn't have let you by while the fight was on."

Clyde tucked his reporter's card in the outer band of his hat. Scorning the elevator, he took the steps two at a time until he reached the third floor. A detective came forward to stop him; Clyde pointed to his hat. The man let him by.

Then came another halt. Markham and the wounded detective were being carried to the elevator. Clyde watched them pass. He continued to the open door of the apartment.

Joe Cardona was in charge. Strangler Hunn's body lay sprawled upon the floor. Cardona had drawn back the desk. Clyde turned to gaze at the dead form of MacAvoy Crane.

"Did Strangler get him?" questioned the reporter.

"Yeah," returned Cardona, grimly. "Before we got here."

"Do you know who he is?"

Cardona nodded.

"A private detective," informed Cardona. "Called himself a special investigator. MacAvoy Crane. I knew him."

"Why do you think Strangler bumped him?"

"Revenge, maybe. Crane may have had something on Strangler."

Clyde stared at the wastebasket. The flames had died out. Nothing but charred remainders told of MacAvoy Crane's documents. Cardona poked among the ashes. He shrugged his shoulders while Clyde watched.

Neither the detective nor the reporter saw the tiny bit of paper that had escaped the basket. Cardona raised the metal container as he stooped to study the ashes. When he replaced it on the floor, it went directly over that telltale fragment.

Cardona began a search of the dead men's clothes. He found several dollars in Strangler's pockets; nothing else of consequence. A search of Crane revealed identification cards; no papers of other importance.

CLYDE BURKE, watching the detective, saw every item that was discovered. By the time Cardona had finished this work, Inspector Timothy Klein appeared with a police surgeon.

Clyde listened while Cardona made a brief report. Standing by the window, the reporter heard the first account of the actual fight which Joe had waged with Strangler.

"He was standing right there"—Cardona paused to point toward the side of the window—"ready to plug me, when his arm dropped. I went for him; he broke loose. Parker got him at the door—"

"You mean," broke in Klein, "that he had you covered, but deliberately lowered his gun?"

"Something must have got him," explained Cardona. "Maybe one of my early shots wounded him so he gave out at the critical moment."

"His wrist is shattered," announced the police surgeon, bending over Strangler's body. "A bullet did it."

A sudden recollection came to Clyde Burke. He could hear The Shadow's words, whispered from the coupé.

"Strangler is dead—"

How had The Shadow known it? Why had Strangler dropped his arm, just at the moment when he had been about to slay his hated enemy, Joe Cardona?

"A funny thing," the detective was saying. "I thought I heard a shot from outside just as Strangler's arm dropped. Yet nobody could have fired in from the street. They couldn't have seen Strangler, on account of the angle."

Clyde's gaze turned across the street. The Shadow's agent saw the tiers of signboards. Clyde knew the answer. Posted above the signs, The Shadow, master marksman, had intervened to rescue Joe Cardona.

More than that, The Shadow had saved the lives of others. Strangler Hunn, breaking free, might well have blazed a way of destruction in his mad effort to escape below.

Cardona and Klein were summing up the case. The inspector had been talking with Farlan; the detective now appeared to take a look at Crane's body. He nodded to the inspector.

"Farlan saw this fellow come in," stated Klein. "It is obvious that Strangler Hunn came here to lie in wait for him—probably in that inner room. You say that Crane was a special investigator. He probably did know too much about Strangler. That accounts for the destruction of the documents.

"We've gotten the man we were after. That will suit the commissioner. Your job, now, Joe, is to find out more about Crane. If you can link him up with Strangler, that will clinch this circumstantial evidence.

"Do you hear that, Burke?" Cardona turned to the reporter. "You've got a real story. Play it big. That's how we'll learn about Crane's past—through the newspapers. We don't know who he was working for, but we'll find out quick enough after your story goes in print."

"Count on me, Joe," assured Clyde. "I'm heading for the office right now. This is going to be a story you'll like. What's more"—Clyde was speaking to Klein—"you're going to read about how Commissioner Weston's order was put through pronto."

A broad smile showed on the inspector's bluff face as Clyde left the apartment. Klein was pleased. He knew that he would receive his share of the credit. Both he and Joe Cardona thought of Clyde Burke purely as a representative of the *Classic*. Little did they suspect that their findings would go verbatim to The Shadow before Clyde reached the newspaper office!

FIFTEEN minutes later, Joe Cardona was standing alone in the living room. The bodies had been removed. The police cordon had departed. The detective was preparing to leave.

Glancing at the wastebasket, Cardona scowled as he thought of the documents that had been so effectively destroyed. With an angry snort, the detective delivered a kick to the metal basket. The container rolled over on the floor, spilling ashes on the rug.

Cardona's eyes opened. On the spot where the basket had been resting was a small piece of white paper. Cardona stooped to pick up the fragment. He carried it to the lamp light in the corner. He stared at the crude, poorly spaced letters and figures that appeared upon the bit of paper:

With thoughtful expression, Cardona drew an envelope from his pocket. He inserted the scrap of paper. On the desk, he saw a partly used pad. He noted that a sheet had been torn from it, evidently in haste. He folded the envelope and placed it in his vest pocket. He dropped the pad in a pocket of his coat.

Then to the wastebasket. Scattering ashes with his foot, Cardona peered in search of other undestroyed fragments. He found none. With a shrug of his shoulders, the detective turned out the desk light and left the apartment.

TEN minutes afterward, a strange, grotesque

figure came suddenly into view outside of the deserted apartment. Looming from the stairway, this shape looked like a phantom materialized from night.

A tall personage, clad in cloak of black, his head topped by a slouch hat with turned-down brim, The Shadow had arrived upon the spot where murder had been followed with justly delivered death.

The Shadow merged with darkness as he passed the broken door. The tiny circle of a small flashlight glimmered on the floor. Methodically, The Shadow was beginning a search of his own.

The Shadow had received a full report from Clyde Burke. Presumably, his agent had gained full knowledge of all that Joe Cardona had discovered. Clyde had assured Burbank of that fact. Cardona had departed; The Shadow's turn had come.

The flashlight went through with its searching spots of light. The spots where the bodies had been; the rifled drawers of the desk; these came under full inspection. Next the ashes from the wastebasket.

Here The Shadow saw that nothing could be learned. An old newspaper had furnished the blaze in which Crane's documents had met destruction. Cardona's cursory inspection of the ashes had ended all possibility of noting any burned fragments. The overturned basket stood for what The Shadow thought it to be; an outburst of impatience on the part of Joe Cardona.

The flashlight went out. The Shadow's cloak swished as the mysterious being made his departure. This inspection furnished no additional material to the statements relayed by Clyde Burke. The Shadow could find no new clue.

Fate had played an odd trick tonight. Clyde Burke had left too soon; The Shadow had arrived too late. In the interim, Joe Cardona had made an accidental discovery.

The detective, alone, possessed the single clue that remained to tell of Strangler Hunn's purpose in slaying MacAvoy Crane. Joe Cardona did not know the meaning of that shred of evidence.

Had The Shadow found that torn paper, his keen brain might have divined the meaning of its fragmentary statement: MEN 13. But luck had been in Joe Cardona's favor.

Upon that single clue rested the fate of living men. In Joe Cardona's possession, its existence unknown to The Shadow, the bit of paper might allow the perpetration of further murder.

Two freaks of chance. The paper floating from destruction; its discovery by Joe Cardona—these were to be the forerunners of contemplated crime!

The Shadow, though he suspected further purpose behind Strangler Hunn's murder of MacAvoy Crane, had not yet learned the facts that he required.

Only time and The Shadow's keen ability to ferret crime would enable the master sleuth to undo the harm that had occurred tonight.

A task was rising before The Shadow—a task that would require the intuition of a superman—all because of the clue upon which Joe Cardona had so unhappily blundered!

CHAPTER V
THE SHADOW FOLLOWS

IT was late the next afternoon. Joe Cardona was seated at his desk in headquarters. The detective looked up from a stack of papers to see Clyde Burke at the doorway.

"Hello, Burke," greeted the sleuth. "Great stuff, that story of yours. Thanks."

"Same to you," returned Clyde. "I scooped the town because you let me in on it. That's why I'm here now. Looking for another beat."

"You mean on MacAvoy Crane?"

"Yes."

"No luck, Burke." Cardona's tone seemed dull. "I thought your story would bring us a lot of facts on Crane. It didn't. So far as we've learned, Crane hadn't had an investigating job for three months."

"What of it? Maybe it was before that when he ran into Strangler Hunn."

"Crane's last job,"—Cardona paused to refer to the papers in front of him—"was a six-month assignment for the S.P.C.A. He trekked all over New York City looking into livery stable conditions and checking up incoming shipments of live stock."

"Before that?"

"A job with a credit bureau, finding out about phony collection agencies that never turned in the dough on bad accounts. He was in that work for nearly a year."

Clyde became thoughtful. Joe Cardona studied the reporter; then added a new statement.

"Let me tell you something about Strangler Hunn, Burke," vouchsafed the detective. "He was a tough guy that worked along with a tough mob. They took a beating in the dock fight about seven months ago. That's where Strangler lost his right arm.

"The whole crew scrammed out of town, and it was good riddance. They were tough gorillas, and some of the others were as bad as Strangler. But he was the only one that we had with the goods. He was wanted for murder. That's why we got him."

"The others?" inquired Clyde.

"We haven't seen any of them back in town," returned Cardona. "Strangler was working alone— that's a sure bet. There's a chance that some of his old cronies may be hereabouts. We haven't seen

... They took a beating in the dock fight ...

them, though. But the main point is that we can't hook Strangler with MacAvoy Crane."

"Listen, Joe." Burke became serious. "I'm not so sure that there was a past tie-up between Strangler and Crane. I'm thinking about the present. Maybe Strangler was put on the job to get Crane—to stop him from going through with some investigation—"

"I've covered that, Burke," interrupted Cardona. "Haven't I just told you that Crane wasn't working for the past three months? There's no use worrying about it. We've got nothing yet. More than likely, Strangler went in to rob the apartment. Maybe he had some imaginary grudge. The point is that he killed MacAvoy Crane, and we got him for it."

With that, Cardona went back to a consideration of the papers on his desk. It was evident that the detective was concerned with other matters; that he had tabled Strangler's case for the time.

"So long, Joe," remarked Clyde Burke.

The Shadow's agent strolled from the office. As he reached the street, he became thoughtful. There was something in Cardona's manner that had given Clyde a hunch. The glib explanation of Crane's past activities had aroused Clyde's suspicions.

Entering a store, Clyde went to a telephone booth. He put in a call to Burbank, to inform the contact man of his interview with Joe Cardona. When Clyde reappeared on the street, he headed for the *Classic* office, beneath a dark, early evening sky.

BACK at headquarters, Joe Cardona continued to busy himself with his papers. Half an hour passed. Footsteps sounded in the corridor. Cardona looked up. He saw Inspector Timothy Klein. The official made a sign with his hand and nodded. Cardona arose to follow Klein into the latter's office.

"Burke was here," began Cardona. "I stalled him."

"Good," decided Klein.

"I hated to let him down," growled Cardona, "but it had to be done. Maybe I'll have a chance to treat him better later on. He's a real guy, Burke. That story of his was good for both of us."

"That's true," nodded Klein, "and I can see why Burke showed up here. It's natural for him to think that we've learned something about what MacAvoy Crane was doing. If the information had come directly to me, Joe, Burke might have had it. But it came in to the commissioner, and he wants it kept quiet. I've just been talking with him. He wants you to go along tonight."

"Fine. Did he tell you anymore about the call that came to him?"

"A little. Here is the story, Joe. You remember that Universal Aircraft mess a few months ago—the big swindle that the government uncovered—"

"Sure thing. Jackson Gleek committed suicide. He was general manager of Universal Aircraft. I was up at the morgue when they brought his body in. Then there was another fellow implicated—Lester Drayson, the president. He took it on the lam. Supposed to have made off with plenty of cash."

"That's the case. Well, Joe, the commissioner has just informed me that MacAvoy Crane was investigating the affairs of the defunct Universal Aircraft Corporation."

"I thought that would be a government job!"

"It was. But the federal authorities let down after the receivers for Universal Aircraft sold out to the World Wide Aviation Company. It was the president of World Wide—Roscoe Wimbledon—who put Crane on the job."

"To find out if others were implicated?"

"Exactly. If he can uncover other crooked workers, he can turn the job over to the government. Stolen funds may be recovered. Maybe Lester Drayson planted a lot of dough with other people—"

Klein paused suddenly. A shadow had fallen across the doorsill. Joe Cardona turned to follow the direction of the inspector's gaze. Both men smiled as a tall, stoop-shouldered janitor shambled into view, carrying a mop and bucket.

"Hello, Fritz," greeted Cardona. "On the old job again, eh?"

"Yah," returned the janitor, staring with a dull expression upon his stupid face.

"Keep going," laughed Cardona. "Don't mind us, Fritz. We'll be out of here soon."

The janitor began to work with mop and bucket. Inspector Klein arose from his desk.

"That's about all I know, Joe," he told Cardona. "I wanted you to keep mum on the whole business until I'd seen the commissioner. I can't go along tonight. He's taking you to see Wimbledon."

"Where?"

"At Wimbledon's home. Incidentally, a call came in to Wimbledon's last night. It was MacAvoy Crane who called. He said that he had a report to make. Wimbledon, was out at the time. Crane didn't call again."

"Then those papers—"

"Were probably documents that Wimbledon wanted. They may have contained important information regarding the tangled affairs of Universal Aircraft Corporation."

Inspector Klein glanced at his watch. He turned again to Joe Cardona.

"Better get started, Joe," he ordered. "You've just about got time to get up to the commissioner's before he is ready to leave."

Klein and Cardona strolled from the office. As Joe passed Fritz, the janitor was busy mopping in the corner. Cardona gave a friendly jab against the man's ribs. Fritz jumped away and almost upset the bucket.

"So long, Fritz," laughed Cardona.

"Yah," returned the janitor, stooping to pick up the mop that he had dropped.

FOOTSTEPS faded along the corridor. A few minutes passed. Fritz suddenly ceased his work. Picking up the mop and the bucket, the stoop-shouldered worker slouched from the office. He followed the corridor, made a turn and stopped in an obscure space where lockers were in evidence.

Fritz opened a locker. Then began a strange transformation. Out came a folded mass of black cloth. It slipped over the stooped shoulders. Next a slouch hat settled upon a head. Black gloves covered long hands. Fritz, the janitor, had ceased to exist.

In his place stood, a tall, erect being garbed in black. Impersonating the headquarters' janitor, The Shadow had listened in on the conversation between Inspector Timothy Klein and Detective Joe Cardona!

Informed through Burbank that Clyde Burke suspected concealed facts held by Joe Cardona, The Shadow had come here to investigate. He had arrived before the hour when the real Fritz usually put in his appearance. He was leaving in time to avoid the genuine janitor.

The blackened form glided from the locker. It picked an obscure exit to the street. The Shadow merged with darkness, as a soft, whispered laugh came from his hidden lips.

THE SHADOW next appeared within his sanctum, some ime later. White hands beneath a bluish light were the only tokens of his presence. Those hands were fingering clippings and type-written statements which concerned the scandal that had swept the affairs of the insolvent Universal Aircraft Corporation.

The light clicked out. A soft swish sounded in the Stygian blackness of The Shadow's secret abode. Again, a whispered laugh. The sound died, with fading echoes. The sanctum was empty.

HALF an hour later, a tall, dignified individual alighted from a taxicab in front of the exclusive Cobalt Club. The doorman bowed as he passed. This personage, a gentleman clad in faultless evening attire, was evidently someone of high consequence.

In the light of the club lobby, the arrival's face showed as a keen, chiseled visage, characterized by thin, firm lips beneath a hawklike nose. Strolling across the lobby, the arrival approached a telephone booth and entered. A long, blackened silhouette stretched from the booth across the tiled floor, as the newcomer dialed a number.

"Hello..." The occupant of the booth spoke in an even-toned voice. "Yes ... I should like to speak with Mr. Wimbledon... He is busy? Inform him that Mr. Lamont Cranston has called ... From the Cobalt Club ... I shall call on him this evening..."

The receiver clicked. The speaker stepped from the booth. A thin smile showed upon his firm lips. Parting, the lips seemed to voice a soundless laugh.

This personage who called himself Lamont Cranston was The Shadow. Clubman of wealth, he had entry to the homes of the elite.

As Fritz the janitor, The Shadow had learned that Joe Cardona and the police commissioner were going to visit Roscoe Wimbledon. As Lamont Cranston, The Shadow had arranged a trip to the same destination.

ROSCOE WIMBLEDON—who takes over a defunct air corporation—and a great deal of danger along with it.

Like the police, The Shadow was anxious to learn why Strangler Hunn had murdered MacAvoy Crane. Chance had enabled the law to move first. Joe Cardona had dashed forth last night to fight with Strangler Hunn. Police Commissioner Ralph Weston had today received a call concerning MacAvoy Crane. Tonight, Weston and Cardona were interviewing Roscoe Wimbledon, the man who had hired Crane as an investigator.

The Shadow had chosen to follow. He was taking the trail that the law had opened. Such was his only policy for the present. The time would come soon when he would outstrip the action of the law.

A soft, whispered laugh pronounced that fact with prophetic mockery as Lamont Cranston strolled forth from the Cobalt Club.

CHAPTER VI
AT WIMBLEDON'S

THREE men were seated in the library of Roscoe Wimbledon's palatial New York home. One was Roscoe Wimbledon himself; the others were Police Commissioner Ralph Weston and Detective Joe Cardona.

As he viewed his companions, Cardona was impressed with their appearance. Commissioner Weston, a man of powerful build and dynamic personality, had always held Cardona's regard. Weston's keen face, with firm-set jaw and pointed mustache, marked the commissioner as a man of action.

Yet as he noted Roscoe Wimbledon, Cardona found himself admitting that the aviation magnate was Weston's equal. Wimbledon, a man in his early forties, possessed a powerful virility. Tall, broad of shoulders, with square countenance that marked him a man of achievement, Wimbledon showed the ability to dominate those who came in contact with him.

Roscoe Wimbledon was talking. Weston and Cardona were listening. In short, terse phrases, the aviation man was stating the case in question.

"The Universal Aircraft Corporation," declared Wimbledon, "had orders that aggregated millions of dollars. The concern was a going one. The opportunity for quick but unlawful profit proved too great a temptation to resist.

"The company was pillaged by its officers. The government stepped in to end the swindle. Jackson Gleek, the general manager, committed suicide. Lester Drayson, the president, fled the country. The receivers who were appointed found the affairs of the company in a deplorable condition."

Weston and Cardona nodded. They were familiar with this phase of the situation. They wanted to learn the part that followed. From behind his flat-topped desk, Wimbledon began to speak upon this matter.

"Universal Aircraft," he stated, "had lists of unfilled orders. It was because of that fact that I, as president of the World Wide Aviation Company, advised our directors to take over the defunct corporation.

"Our profit will be slight. Nevertheless, for the good of the industry, it was the proper stand for us to take. When I came to study the books of the Universal Aircraft Corporation, I saw an opportunity that I had not foreseen.

"UNIVERSAL AIRCRAFT, gentlemen, had been robbed of approximately five million dollars. The stealing of that sum could be laid directly upon the work of Jackson Gleek, the general manager. It was obvious, however, that Gleek was merely a cat's-paw. What became of the five million dollars?"

"Lester Drayson must have taken it," answered Weston. "He was the president. His hasty flight after the discovery of the swindle stands as proof against him."

"True," agreed Wimbledon. "Drayson must have gained a share of the spoils. But he was absent from New York during a considerable period while the thefts were being made. He was in Chicago when the exposure broke. He fled from that city. Therefore, I came to the conclusion that there must be others in the game."

"Officers of the corporation?"

"No. Drayson and Gleek were the only two who possessed a real control. I mean lesser men—tools, like Gleek, but smaller. It is my belief, commissioner, that certain men in New York are holding lumps of money for later division with Lester Drayson."

"I see," Weston nodded. "They would get their share, of course. At the same time, they would have to come clean with Drayson, or he could expose them."

"Precisely," announced Wimbledon. "That is why I hired MacAvoy Crane as a special investigator. I set him to work with the purpose of locating former associates of Lester Drayson. Could they be discovered and made to disgorge funds that they may possess, the recovered money can be given to the receivers who handled Universal Aircraft Corporation. They, in turn, might see fit to refund a portion of the purchase price that World Wide gave for the defunct corporation."

There was a rap at the door as Wimbledon finished his statement. The aircraft magnate called; the door opened and a quiet-faced servant appeared.

"A telephone call, sir," the man announced. "It was from Mr. Lamont Cranston."

"Ah!" exclaimed Wimbledon. "Is he on the wire?"

"No, sir," replied the servant. "He said that he would come to visit you this evening. Then he hung up."

"All right, Harkin," laughed Wimbledon. "When Mr. Cranston arrives, inform me at once. I shall see him."

"You are acquainted with Lamont Cranston?" inquired Weston, as Harkin left. "I know him quite well myself; it seems that he is widely acquainted in New York."

"He purchased a special plane through World Wide Aircraft," stated Wimbledon. "That was about a year ago. I have met him several times since then. It is quite droll, the way he told Harkin he would be here. Cranston is very informal at times. A matter of an appointment would never deter him."

Wimbledon smiled as he tapped the desk with his fingers. Then, abruptly, he forgot the interruption and came back to the important point.

"MACAVOY CRANE telephoned me last night," announced Wimbledon. "Harkin took the message. From what Crane told him, the job was done. I believe that Crane had gained the data that I sought.

"Crane did not call again. This morning, I read in the newspapers that he had been murdered by Strangler Hunn; that burned papers had been found in his wastebasket.

"Gentlemen, I am convinced that those papers were the documents which I required. There can be but one reason for the slaying of MacAvoy Crane. Strangler Hunn was hired to kill him—hired as the agent of the swindlers whom I am seeking."

Weston nodded. The theory seemed plausible.

"Either by the men themselves," continued Wimbledon, "or by the kingpin of them all—Lester Drayson. It may be he who chose Strangler to act as the assassin."

"But Drayson has fled the country," stated Cardona.

"Are we sure that he has not returned?" questioned Wimbledon, swinging promptly toward the detective. "He may be hiding. He may have been watching Crane. More than that, he may be trying to negotiate with the very men whom I have assumed were connected with him."

"But you don't know who they could be?"

"No. That was the job I left to Crane. The fact that the papers were destroyed seems proof—to me at least—that Crane had gained the names of certain men. But Crane's evidence has turned to ashes."

"Yes." It was Weston who inserted the grim utterance. "Last night I ordered the capture of Strangler Hunn. The job was done; but the victory was a failure. Had a single paper been recovered from those burned ashes, it might have served us as a starting point!"

"One moment, Commissioner." Cardona reached into his coat pocket and produced a pad of paper. While Weston and Wimbledon stared curiously, the detective brought out a folded envelope from his vest.

"This pad," stated the detective, "was on Crane's desk. You can see that a sheet has been hurriedly torn from it. Here"—he opened the envelope and produced the fragment—"is a piece from a torn sheet. It must have missed the basket when Strangler threw it there.

"Look at those scrawled letters. See how the paper is torn crooked. Do you know what this is? It's something that Strangler Hunn wrote down— something he wanted to get rid of!"

WESTON was examining the torn bit of paper. He passed it over to Wimbledon, who eyed it curiously, and turned it about between his hands.

"I think you're right, Cardona," affirmed the commissioner. "Strangler must have done that crude writing. But what does it mean?"

"Men 13," read Wimbledon. "This is indeed perplexing. Do you think it could refer to something that the murderer discovered in Crane's papers?"

"Yes," asserted Cardona. "From what you've been saying, Mr. Wimbledon, I take it that Strangler may have counted a list of names. If there were thirteen, he might have written that fact for reference."

"Let me see the paper." Weston took it from Wimbledon. "I doubt your theory, Cardona. This scrawl could have been Strangler's work; the man had only one arm, and that was the left one. But I think he would have put the number 13 above the word 'men'—not below."

"A good point," observed Wimbledon. "At the same time, Commissioner, the murderer was in a hurry. He may have marked the word and the number in reverse fashion."

"Possibly," declared Weston. "Furthermore, we have no assurance that this is all the murderer wrote. The wide spaces between those letters and figures; the irregularity of the inscription itself— both indicate that this is but a fragment of whatever message Strangler Hunn was inscribing.

"The value of this clue is slight. It signifies no more than we have already supposed. We know that Strangler may have purposely destroyed the documents which Crane had prepared for you. The fact that he made a memorandum afterward; then destroyed his own notation—well, it supports our theory. That is all."

Weston handed the slip to Cardona. The detective

replaced the fragment in the envelope. He folded the envelope and dropped it with the pad, into his coat pocket.

"Keep that piece of paper, Cardona," ordered Weston. "Later developments may make it of value. Tell no one that you have it. We do not want the news to get out that MacAvoy Crane was engaged in an important work of investigation."

A knock at the door. It was Harkin. The servant spoke to Wimbledon.

"Mr. Cranston has arrived, sir," announced Harkin. "Also Mr. Harlton."

"Tell them to come in," ordered Wimbledon. Then, to Weston: "Lamont Cranston is a friend of yours, Commissioner; Ross Harlton is aircraft technician with the World Wide Aviation Company. We can take them into our confidence should we discuss this matter further."

"With reservations," agreed Commissioner Weston. "It will be quite all right to admit them."

Roscoe Wimbledon arose. Striding toward the door, he awaited the appearance of these visitors who had arrived just too late to hear the discussion concerning Joe Cardona's clue.

ROSS HARLTON—Wimbledon's chief engineer, who faces trouble with his chief.

CHAPTER VII
SEARCHES BEGIN

FIVE men were in the room where three had been before. Lamont Cranston and Ross Harlton had joined the trio in Roscoe Wimbledon's library. To Joe Cardona, the arrivals formed an interesting study.

Joe had met Cranston before. As he watched the millionaire's firm-chiseled face, the detective was impressed by its immobility. Lamont Cranston was smoking a cigarette; the occasional action of placing it to his lips was the only motion that he made.

Ross Harlton, a man in his late thirties, was a keen-faced chap who also made a good listener. Dark-haired, with steady, deep-set eyes beneath heavy brows, Harlton looked the part of an aircraft technician.

"We were talking about the Universal Aircraft mess," Roscoe Wimbledon was stating. "I have told Commissioner Weston that the corporation was pillaged in outrageous fashion. You have been going over the technical end of it, Harlton. What is your opinion?"

"The same as yours, Mr. Wimbledon," replied the technician. "I have paid regular visits to the closed testing grounds on Long Island. The workmanship used in the Universal planes speaks very badly for the reputation which the concern once enjoyed."

"This interests me," declared Weston. "The government handled the investigation; I heard comparatively little concerning the findings."

"Explain the details, Harlton," suggested Wimbledon.

"Universal had been handling some big orders," stated the technician. "Up at the World Wide plant, we wondered how they had managed to underbid us on the jobs. We found out after the swindle was uncovered.

"Universal had built a lot of commercial planes; they followed by taking a series of orders for military planes to be shipped to foreign governments. The hitch came when they completed building a batch of ships for the Paraguayan government. They wanted them down there to use on the Bolivian frontier.

"There was some talk of an embargo. Officials from Washington demanded an exact report on the number of planes that were being sent to Paraguay. This was a government investigation that proved to be a thorough one—too thorough for the Universal Corporation.

"Washington ordered a group of navy aviators to test the Paraguayan planes—just to learn how good they were. They found out. One of the navy men went into a bank; the wing came off the plane and he was killed. That started the trouble.

"Government investigators got a look at the

specifications. They compared the planes. They found that the ships were faulty. They communicated promptly with other purchasers of Universal ships. They discovered that cheap and faulty materials had been used constantly. They learned that an outrageous graft had been perpetrated. They ordered the factory closed. That was all."

"All from the technical standpoint," added Wimbledon. "But the real scandal followed. The government went after Jackson Gleek. He was found dead—a suicide. Someone must have tipped off Lester Drayson. He managed to get out of the country."

"And the status now?" inquired Weston.

"World Wide has taken over Universal," replied Wimbledon. "I mentioned that fact to you a while ago. The faulty planes have been condemned. We are keeping them until the government gives the order to scrap them. The Universal factory will be idle until we receive the word to reopen it."

"I am making a full account of stock on hand," explained Harlton. "I have completed all the statistics. It merely remains to compile the details. That, however, will not be a simple task. It involves many minor points."

"You will do the work here," declared Wimbledon. "Beginning with tomorrow morning, Harlton. I have cancelled all appointments for the next few days. This accounting is important. We shall work on it together."

THERE was a pause. It was Lamont Cranston who took up the conversation. In leisurely fashion, the millionaire removed his cigarette from his lips and spoke in a quiet, even tone.

"This is quite interesting," he remarked. "I came here tonight merely to talk with Mr. Wimbledon regarding a new speed plane that I might like to purchase. I find, however, that he will be busy for the next few days. So I shall postpone the matter.

"I must confess that I am quite surprised to find the police commissioner in conference with Mr. Wimbledon. I knew that Mr. Wimbledon has been negotiating with the federal government; I am somewhat perplexed to find that the local law has also commanded his attention."

It was Weston who responded. The police commissioner chuckled as he turned to face Lamont Cranston. Nodding in approval of the millionaire's keenness, he produced the answer.

"Very few facts escape your notice, Cranston," remarked the commissioner. "Since you are a friend of mine and also are acquainted with Mr. Wimbledon, I see no reason why you should not be taken into our confidence.

"Last night, a private investigator named MacAvoy Crane was slain by a notorious murderer called Strangler Hunn. The killer was shot dead by a detective. Before the fight, he managed to destroy all the papers which he had found in Crane's apartment.

"MacAvoy Crane was in the employ of Roscoe Wimbledon. He was seeking facts regarding the business contacts of Lester Drayson, the missing president of Universal Aircraft Corporation.

"Mr. Wimbledon called me personally to tell me that Crane was in his employ. We hold to the theory that Strangler Hunn was acting under orders to kill MacAvoy Crane and to destroy the documents."

"Quite logical," stated Cranston.

"It is obvious," asserted Weston, "that the man behind the game is Lester Drayson. Therefore, I am ordering a general search for the missing president of Universal Aircraft. If he happens to be in New York, we shall uncover him."

There was emphasis in Weston's tone. Everyone nodded in approval, with the exception of Cranston. The millionaire drew upon his cigarette; blew forth a puff, then asked:

"And if Drayson is not in New York?"

There was no answer.

FOUR men sat silent, expecting Cranston to follow up the quizzical remark. The millionaire did not disappoint them.

"The theory is a good beginning," stated Cranston. "Let us assume that Strangler Hunn was working under orders. But does that prove that Lester Drayson would place himself in position to be captured?

"Quite the reverse. I should imagine that he would stay away from New York. But I can see another possibility. If murder has been used as a means to suppress facts, it might be used again.

"Strangler Hunn—a hired killer. Why not a second paid assassin to carry on the work now that Hunn is dead? Have you any proof that Crane is the only man to be eliminated?"

"No," admitted Weston. "Drayson might want to get rid of others who knew too much about him. You're right, Cranston. The very fact that Crane dug up some information proves that there would be good reason to go after other men."

"Associates of Lester Drayson," stated Cranston. "Have you any idea who they might be?"

"That was the information Crane was after," broke in Wimbledon. "Lester Drayson may have had certain men in his confidence."

"He might have had a private secretary," suggested Cranston. "Do you know of any such man?"

"Yes," affirmed Wimbledon, in a slow, meditative tone. "I believe that Drayson did have a confidential secretary. But I have not been able to learn the fellow's name."

"The province of the police"—Cranston was looking directly at Weston as he spoke—"is to prevent crime as well as to solve it. This death of MacAvoy Crane is of high interest chiefly if it presages further murder.

"From Crane's death, we find three factors. First, a man behind the murder. Second, a hired killer. Third, a possible victim. Let us assume that new murder is being plotted. There are three ways to forestall it.

"First: to find the plotter. Second: to discover the new assassin. Third: to look for the coming victim. You have chosen the first method, commissioner. You intend to look for Lester Drayson.

"I should prefer the second method. Hired killers—like Strangler Hunn—are few and far between. The third method, namely to search for the potential victim, would involve too much time."

Commissioner Weston was smiling. He had risen from his chair; stepping forward he clapped Lamont Cranston on the shoulder.

"You are an excellent theorist," commended Weston, with a friendly laugh. "More than that, Cranston, you have summed this case in creditable fashion. Nevertheless, I still hold to my plan.

"I intend to use the law to uncover the plotter. I shall choose the first method that you suggested. We are going to look for Lester Drayson. He apparently has much at stake. The chances are that he is in New York."

Lamont Cranston had also risen. Like Commissioner Weston, he was ready to depart. His lips showed a quiet smile as he made a final statement.

"If I had the power which you possess, Commissioner," he said, "I should prefer the method which I have mentioned. Look for a potential murderer. Find the man who could fill the shoes of Strangler Hunn."

"No." Weston shook his head emphatically. "Your method would not work, Cranston. The search is on for Lester Drayson."

When Commissioner Ralph Weston and Lamont Cranston had left Roscoe Wimbledon's, they parted on the sidewalk in front of the big mansion. Weston stepped into his car, accompanied by Joe Cardona. Lamont Cranston entered a waiting limousine.

HALF an hour later, a light was shining in The Shadow's sanctum. Papers lay upon the table, beneath the glare. These memoranda concerned the checkered career of Strangler Hunn.

The Shadow, following his belief, was looking for a second choice. He was studying the records of the band with which Strangler had been associated. He was out to find a new killer.

Searches had begun. Commissioner Ralph Weston was invoking the law to hunt for Lester Drayson. The Shadow was looking for the pals of Strangler Hunn. In one sense, both the police and The Shadow were aiming for a single goal.

It seemed possible that more lives were at stake. Men like MacAvoy Crane, men who knew too much, might already be spotted for sudden doom. Perhaps innocent persons were slated to die along with the quarry that a hidden plotter sought!

Until now, The Shadow had followed. This was the time that he had chosen to work ahead. His path had diverged from the one chosen by the law. The grim race against crime had started.

Yet all the while, the law held an advantage that The Shadow did not possess. Once more, fate had tricked the master sleuth. Murder was in the making; that fact seemed evident. Yet the only clue had been sidetracked as a matter of small moment.

The paper that rested in Joe Cardona's pocket. What a valuable bit of evidence it would be, had The Shadow known of its existence. Those letters and figures, that formed the disjointed statement— MEN 13—would have given The Shadow the groundwork for a perfect chance to forestall coming crime.

The Shadow had divined the future. One bit of evidence had alone escaped him. Such was the grim irony that blocked The Shadow's course. For that fragment of an unburned paper was the key to all that lay ahead!

CHAPTER VIII
AGENTS AT WORK

FIVE days had passed. They were days that brought nights of strange activities. Manhunts were in progress. The police and The Shadow were at work upon their respective tasks.

Often had The Shadow sought in higher places while police had scoured the underworld in vain search after crime suspects. This time the situation was reversed. Commissioner Ralph Weston had belittled the suggestion made by Lamont Cranston.

Detectives were roaming through Manhattan, looking here and there for traces of Lester Drayson. They were supplied with photographs of the fugitive. Those pictures showed Drayson's portrait—that of an elderly, gray-haired man with a placid face that showed no trace of criminal characteristics.

Meanwhile, stool pigeons were idle. The badlands were ignored by the law. It was The Shadow who was working there. The master sleuth was trying to place his finger upon some skulking messenger of coming crime.

Stalking the underworld, The Shadow was at times a roving phantom. On other occasions, he appeared in notorious dives, disguised as a sweatered mobster. Frequently The Shadow had played the part of a denizen of scumland. Yet he was not alone in his efforts.

Trusted agents were at work. Cliff Marsland, accepted by mobland as one of their ilk, was spending his time in the hangouts where crooks lingered. Harry Vincent, another capable agent, was a visitor at the flossy nightclubs and old hotels which cash-possessing gangsters were wont to frequent.

Clyde Burke, roving reporter of the New York Classic, was patrolling both types of places; and at intervals, he dropped into police headquarters to chat with Detective Joe Cardona.

IT was evident to Clyde that a search was being made by the Manhattan police. Clyde knew, through The Shadow, that the dicks were after Lester Drayson. But Joe Cardona, wary and taciturn, was stingy with his information. The ace detective never once gave Clyde a tip.

The task which The Shadow had set for himself and his agents was no sinecure. The Shadow knew that any former pal of Strangler Hunn would certainly be laying low. The Shadow, as Lamont Cranston, had given Ralph Weston an idea which the police commissioner had not accepted. That duty performed, The Shadow was working on his own, and his course was preferable.

Weston, had he chosen to look for companions of Strangler Hunn, would have invoked the dragnet. The slowness of The Shadow's present search proved fully that any pal of Strangler's would have dodged that method of capture. The Shadow's work, unhampered by police activities, offered better possibilities.

On this night, the fifth after the conference at Roscoe Wimbledon's, The Shadow chanced to give a fleeting trace of his mysterious presence. Like an apparition, he appeared beneath the lamplight near an obscure corner on the East Side.

No peering eyes were there to see The Shadow's passage. Like a being of a supernatural sort, The Shadow glided toward a darkened space beside a wall. From then on, his course was undiscernible.

The next manifestation of The Shadow's weird presence came within the blackened walls of the sanctum. A bluish light clicked on. The hand that wore the girasol appeared beneath the vivid rays. The other hand joined it. Long fingers handled typewritten report sheets.

These papers listed names and descriptions of the persons. They were memoranda that concerned half a dozen members of the scattered band to which Strangler Hunn had once belonged. They listed toughened mobsters; potential killers who had fled Manhattan.

Had one of these returned? That was the question which The Shadow sought to answer. To date, there had been no indication of the fact. Yet The Shadow was sure that when new murder was required, one of these crooks would arrive.

DOWN in an underworld dive, scattered groups of mobsters were chatting among themselves. Things were quiet in the badlands. This place, the Black Ship, showed very little trace of impending activities in the realm of crime.

Among the patrons was a keen-faced man who sat quietly in a corner. There was something in this fellow's appearance that marked him as a member of gangdom's elite. His features were clearly chiseled. His square jaw showed him to be a fighter. This was Cliff Marsland, agent of The Shadow.

Cliff had once served time in Sing Sing. This had given him a high status in the badlands. Only The Shadow knew that Cliff had taken the rap to save the brother of the girl he loved. All crooks who knew Cliff thought that he had gone to the big house for a crime of his own commission.

Cliff had accomplished much through his reputation. He had become one of the most valued agents in The Shadow's small but capable corps. tonight, as on previous evenings, Cliff was alert in The Shadow's service.

A scrawny mobster strolled into the Black Ship. His ratlike eyes spied Cliff Marsland. The arrival caught a gesture from Cliff. He approached and sat down at the table where Cliff was holding out alone.

"Hello, Bowser," greeted Cliff. "How're things going?"

"Lousy," returned the scrawny mobsman. "There ain't nothin' doin'. I'm on my uppers."

"Not like the old days, eh? Back when you were with the dock-wallopers?"

"Nah. I shook that crew before the big fight. Lucky I did. I might have took a bump."

"Or lost an arm?"

Bowser shifted uneasily. This was a reference to Strangler Hunn. Bowser had been but a hanger-on with the old mob. Cliff knew that Bowser could not be a potential killer. Yet the reference worried the scrawny crook.

"Don't remind me of that stuff, Cliff," pleaded Bowser. "I never did like Strangler. He was the bad egg of the outfit. There was more than one guy found with his throat gagged after Strangler had worked on him."

"Yeah. Strangler was a killer." Cliff's tone was a casual one. "Even after he lost his right mitt, he could still do dirty work. Best gat handler in the outfit, wasn't he?"

"Nah." Bowser was emphatic in his protest. "There was other guys that could sling a rod better than Strangler."

"But none of them had nerve enough to come back to town."

"Yeah? That's where you're foolin' yourself." Bowser leaned over the table. "There's one guy that ain't worried about the bulls. He's around here right now."

Cliff leaned back and indulged in a quiet but contemptuous laugh. The action riled Bowser.

"You think that's hooey?" questioned the scrawny mobster. "Well, it ain't. I seen this guy a couple of hours ago, down by Red Mike's place."

"Maybe you were seeing things," suggested Cliff. "That bum hooch down at Red Mike's is enough to make a fellow see a dead man walk."

"I wasn't crocked," snarled Bowser. "What's more, I didn't make no mistake. I'll tell you who the guy was—Shakes Niefan."

BOWSER spoke as though the statement settled everything. He poured himself a drink from a bottle that a waiter had brought him. He held the glass in his hand and began to wiggle his wrist. Drops of liquor plopped over the glass rim.

"See that?" demanded Bowser. "That's the way Shakes Niefan is. Wobbly—all the time. But that don't mean nothin' when he handles a rod. When he gets tough, he steadies. I've seen him."

Bowser paused to gulp his drink. Then, as he set the glass upon the table, he added:

SHAKES NIEFAN—whose name did not mean that he was shaking with fright. He does the dirty work.

"There ain't no mistakin' Shakes Niefan when you see him. He's here in New York; an' he ain't yellow. He didn't want to talk much; an it's a sure bet he's hidin' out somewhere. But that ain't nothin' against him. The best of 'em hide out when they've got some job on."

"You win, Bowser," laughed Cliff, as he arose from the table. "If Shakes Niefan is back, I give him credit."

"Don't say nothin', though," warned Bowser, clutching at Cliff's arm. "I told Shakes I'd keep mum."

"What do you think I am?" growled Cliff. "A stool?" Then, with a laugh, he added: "Say— maybe you think I'm working for The Shadow! Go on, Bowser. Finish your bottle"—Cliff took a friendly jab at the scrawny gangster's ribs—"and forget it. What do I care about Shakes Niefan?"

Bowser was satisfied. He poured himself another drink when Cliff had left.

But had Bowser followed the man who had left, his qualms would have returned. Cliff Marsland, directly after his departure from the Black Ship, headed for an obscure store a few blocks from the dive.

There Cliff found a corner telephone. Unnoticed, he dialed a number. In a low tone, The Shadow's agent informed Burbank of what he had learned. After that, Cliff hung up and waited. A return call came through in a few minutes. Cliff acknowledged new instructions.

Word had been relayed to The Shadow. In his sanctum, the master who battled crime had learned the news. He had sent back orders. Now his hands were at work. They had put aside all papers except one. That was the sheet which carried data concerning "Shakes" Niefan.

The light clicked out. A hollow laugh sounded in the blackness. It died; echoes faded. Then complete silence. The Shadow had departed. His plan had brought results.

Somewhere in New York was the potential murderer who could fill Strangler Hunn's place. The Shadow had fared forth to begin his own hunt for Shakes Niefan's hideout.

CHAPTER IX
MURDER TO ORDER

AT the time when The Shadow was departing from his sanctum, an elevated train was coming to a stop at a station in the nineties. A huddled man arose from a corner seat and strolled out of the car. He crossed the station platform and descended to the street below.

In the light that came from a drugstore window, this individual presented an odd appearance. His face, though not ugly, showed a hardness that was unpleasant. His lips exhibited a peculiar twitch; his eyes seemed constantly on the shift.

The man was well dressed. He wore a dark hat, a dark overcoat and brown kid gloves. As he raised one hand to unbutton his overcoat, his fingers seemed to falter nervously. Twitching lips—shifting eyes—trembling hand—these marked the man's identity. He was Shakes Niefan, notorious mobster.

Shakes appeared contemptuous of recognition in this obscure neighborhood. He was far from the badlands, and there was no need for over caution. Boldly, Shakes went into the drugstore and entered a phone booth. He dialed a number.

"Hello..." Shakes spoke in a growl. "Yeah. I'm up here ...Ready ... Sure ... I came straight from the hideout ... Yeah. I'll call you later ..."

Leaving the booth, Shakes went to the street. He walked for two blocks; turned left and came to a silent house in the middle of an old-fashioned row. Here Shakes paused to light a cigarette. His roving eyes studied upstairs windows. The place was a private home that had been converted into an apartment.

Shakes sauntered up the stone steps to the high front entrance. The door opened to his touch. The gangster entered a darkened vestibule. He flicked his cigarette out into the street and closed the big door behind him.

By light that came through a glass-paneled inner door, Shakes could read the names upon the wall beside an apartment phone. His lips formed a grotesque smile. His shaking hand reached for the knob of the inner door.

This barrier was locked. Shakes noted that it gave a fraction of an inch. He pulled a jimmy from his pocket and pried at the woodwork. After he had splintered the edge of the door, Shakes managed to pry the latch. He entered; smoothed some of the wood with his gloved hand; then closed the door behind him.

SHAKES headed up a flight of stairs. He reached the third floor. He noted a door at the back. It bore the number 3 D. Quietly, Shakes tried the door. His twisting lips formed a grin as his hand found it unlocked.

Shakes Niefan stepped into a lighted room. It was a small chamber that served as living room and study. In the corner was a lighted lamp upon a table. Shakes noted papers lying there. He approached.

With his left hand, he pulled the glove from his right; then thrust the bare hand in the pocket of his overcoat. His left knuckles rested upon the dusty surface of the table. The glove formed a mark in the dust.

Shakes threw brief, shifty glances toward the papers. All the while, he was concerned with a door that led to another room. Light showed beneath the door.

Reaching out with his left hand, Shakes began to paw over the papers. He shrugged his shoulders; then bundled up the whole batch and thrust the pile into his coat pocket. Standing erect again, Shakes faced the closed door to the other room. His left knuckles, resting lightly on the desk, were twitching in their usual fashion.

Shakes had heard the sound of a moving chair. Now, before he could make a step, the door opened. A tall man in shirt sleeves stopped to stare at the intruder. Shakes gave a sour smile.

"Who are you?" demanded the man who stood in the lighted doorway.

"Just a visitor," returned Shakes. "You're Jerome Neville, aren't you?"

"Yes." The speaker still eyed Shakes. "I'm Jerome Neville. Usually, visitors call this apartment. What's the idea of walking in this way?"

"You'll find out quick enough," retorted Shakes. "I'm going to take a look around this dump, see? There may be something here that I want. If there isn't—"

Neville was staring. He saw that the papers had been removed from his table. He noticed the package sticking from the intruder's pocket.

"A crook, eh?" questioned Neville. "Well, there's nothing here for you. Get going, before I call the police."

"I'm warning you," growled Shakes. "I'm going through this joint—"

Shakes still had his left hand on the table. It was quivering. Neville noticed it. He thought the intruder was trembling from fear, now that he had been discovered. Neville closed a pair of hard fists. He snorted as he saw the nervous twitch of Niefan's lips and the shifty action of the man's eyes.

"Get out!" With that challenge, Neville strode forward. Then, as he saw Shakes still stand his ground, Neville made a furious spring, raising his left hand as a guard as he drew his right back for a powerful swing.

Shakes Niefan tightened. His feet never budged. His left hand steadied hard against the table. His right snapped from his pocket with a quick wrist action that was a motion of only a few inches.

A snub-nosed revolver gleamed in the bare hand. As Jerome Neville's left hand came swinging toward him, Shakes pressed the trigger of his gun. Neville's stroke became an awkward swerve as the short revolver barked.

The tall man collapsed to the floor. Shakes Niefan, steadied, leered at the sprawled body. His shot had been aimed for the victim's heart. It had found its mark. Jerome Neville was dead.

SUDDENLY Shakes awoke to furious action.

Neville's stroke became an awkward swerve as the short revolver barked.

He leaped to the table and ripped open its single drawer. He grabbed the few papers that he saw there and thrust them in his pocket with the ones that he had taken before.

Springing across the dead body of Jerome Neville, Shakes reached the inner room. There he found a bureau. He yanked open the drawers in search of other papers. He found none. The quick search completed, Shakes hurried through the living room.

Opening the outer door, Shakes listened. He could hear subdued voices from below; then came one in a louder tone—the voice of a man.

"I'm going up," the speaker was saying. "It sounded like a gunshot—like it was from Neville's apartment—"

Striding to the head of the stairs, Shakes Niefan raised his right hand and fired his revolver toward the floor below. Shrieks sounded as the zimming bullet dug its way into the wall beyond the bottom step. Women were screaming; a man's heavy footsteps took to flight.

Shakes started downward. He saw a man diving for cover through a door at the front of the hall. He fired a bullet that marked the doorway above the fellow's head. Hurrying to the flight that led to the first floor, Shakes fired another shot.

Then came the dash for the street. The murderer reached it unopposed. On the sidewalk, Shakes whirled as he heard the sound of a police whistle. A patrolman was hastening up from the nearest corner.

The officer saw Shakes. A revolver shot sounded; the bullet whistled by the murderer's head. With quick return, Shakes aimed his own gun and fired. The cop sprawled upon the sidewalk.

There was a car parked across the street. A man was in it, hastily trying to start the motor. Just as the engine rumbled, Shakes pounced up to the side of the car.

"Scram!" he snarled as he swung his revolver.

The man in the car ducked. He went sprawling through the open door toward the curb. Yanking open the nearer door, Shakes leaped to the wheel. He jammed the car into gear and sped down the street.

More whistles sounded. The shot from the sidewalk was bringing a new patrolman. The officer, however, was too late. Shakes Niefan was a block away when he arrived.

From the opened window of the old sedan came flurries of paper fragments. Shakes Niefan, driving from this neighborhood, was making sure that no evidence would remain.

These paper bits, scattering in the wake of the speeding sedan, were the destroyed portions of the documents which Shakes Niefan had carried from the apartment of Jerome Neville.

The murder of MacAvoy Crane had been followed by a similar outrage. Shakes Niefan had proven himself to be the new killer. He was the one whom The Shadow had divined might take the place of Strangler Hunn!

CHAPTER X
THE SHADOW'S CLUE

"WHAT do you make of it, Joe?"

It was Inspector Timothy Klein who put the question. He and Detective Joe Cardona were standing in Jerome Neville's living room. The dead man's body had been removed. Klein and Cardona were summarizing their findings.

"I don't get it, inspector," confessed Cardona. "Here's a murder that looks a lot like the killing of MacAvoy Crane. But there was a motive for Strangler Hunn to kill Crane—at least, Crane was an investigator who may have found out something.

"But this fellow Neville was a refrigerator salesman. So far as we can figure, the only letters and papers that he would have here were ones that had something to do with his business. Yet the murderer grabbed everything."

"It looks odd," admitted Klein.

"I'd like to have a description of the killer," grumbled Cardona. "Those people downstairs ducked for cover. The patrolman was wounded before he had a good look at the guy. The man in the sedan was too scared to even take a glance."

Detective Sergeant Markham appeared in the doorway as Cardona finished speaking.

"We've found the car," declared Markham. "The killer left it down on Seventy-first Street. No papers in it, Joe. The fellow made a getaway."

"That's what I expected," growled Cardona.

"Burke is downstairs," added Markham. "He wants to see you. Shall I tell him to come up?"

"All right."

Joe Cardona rested his chin in his right hand. The detective was recalling the conference at Roscoe Wimbledon's. He remembered the statements which had been made by Lamont Cranston.

Had MacAvoy Crane's death been but the first in a series of plotted murders? Was it connected with this killing of Jerome Neville? These were questions that perplexed the sleuth.

"Men thirteen," mumbled Cardona, half aloud. "Thirteen men. Maybe Crane was one; Neville is two—"

"What's that, Joe?" inquired Klein.

"Just an idea, Inspector," returned Cardona. "I was thinking." He paused; then stared toward the door. "Hello, there, Burke. Later than usual tonight, eh?"

"I wouldn't be," retorted the reporter, "if that dumb cop hadn't stopped me downstairs. He wouldn't even send a message up to you. What's the story, Joe?"

"An unknown killer," stated the detective, "entered here and shot Jerome Neville. The victim was a refrigerator salesman."

"Any motive?"

"None apparent. The killer made away with some papers belonging to Neville. He ransacked the place before he left."

CARDONA looked narrowly at Burke. The detective wanted to see what the reporter's response would be. Cardona nodded grimly as Burke made comment.

"Something like the Crane murder, eh?" quizzed the reporter. "Any link between the two deaths?"

"None," decided Cardona. "That is, none except the circumstances. Go easy on it, Burke."

"All right, Joe. Say"—Clyde's eyes turned toward a telephone on the table—"were there any calls out of the place?"

"None," returned Cardona. "We received a report from the telephone company. We've still got to get a final statement. But it looks like there were no calls."

Clyde Burke put further questions. All pertained to the simple facts of the case. Joe Cardona gave the required data. While this was going on, the telephone bell rang. Inspector Klein answered.

"Chief operator?" he questioned. "Yes ... This is Quadrangle two—four—one—three—eight ... Inspector Klein is speaking. Yes, from headquarters ... Final check-up, eh? Thank you."

The inspector hung up. He turned to Joe Cardona with the announcement: "No calls reported on this wire since last night."

Cardona made the notation for his report. He put down the number: Quadrangle 2-4138. Then he turned to Clyde Burke.

"We don't know who the killer was, Burke," stated the detective. "But it's a cinch he wasn't an amateur. One shot was all he needed to drill Neville through the heart. He wounded the patrolman at long range. He knows his business—this killer."

"As well as Strangler Hunn?" questioned Clyde.

"I wouldn't say that," growled Cardona. "Forget that Crane death, Burke. This is another story. Well—we've got all there is to get. How about it, Inspector?"

"I guess you're right, Joe," agreed Klein, in a rueful tone. "We might as well be going."

The three men left. Clyde Burke separated from Klein and Cardona after they had reached the street. The newspaper man went to look for a telephone—presumably to call the *Classic* office.

SOME time afterward, a figure appeared upon the street opposite the old house in which Jerome Neville had died. A policeman was standing by the front steps. The officer did not see the form that had arrived on the other sidewalk.

For the watching shape was one of blackness—that of a creature who possessed a pair of burning eyes; beyond that, no features which were discernible. When the officer turned to pace a few rods toward the corner, the watching being glided in phantom fashion. Crossing the street, the weird prowler gained the darkness of a space beneath the high stone steps.

The policeman paced by. Silently, the hidden personage began to work upon a basement door. A lock yielded with a slight click. When the policeman paused upon the steps, the low door opened without a squeak. It closed. The dark form was no longer in front of it.

Minutes passed. Into the gloom of Jerome Neville's living room crept a weird, amazing visitor. The table lamp was still burning; its partly shaded rays made the arrival appear as a shrouded creature from the tomb.

The Shadow had come to inspect these premises. He was repeating his previous procedure; the one that he had used at MacAvoy Crane's. First: a report from Clyde Burke, telling what Joe Cardona had discovered. Second: a search by The Shadow himself.

Burning eyes turned toward the table. They spied marks in the dust. Joe Cardona had seen those traces. The detective, however, had passed them up because they showed no hand or finger impressions.

To The Shadow, however, those marks were important. A flashlight gleamed to increase the illumination. It showed blurred marks that faded toward the edges. The Shadow's left fist closed; its black-gloved outline poised above the traces in the dust.

The Shadow's hand began to quiver. It was simulating the action that would have necessarily caused the marks upon the table. A gloved hand—a shaky hand—such was the hand that had rested here.

A soft laugh crept through the room. The Shadow had found the clue he needed. The Shadow knew that Shakes Niefan was back in New York; The Shadow was looking for the slayer who had been a pal of Strangler Hunn.

Here was Shakes Niefan's imprint. The murderer who steadied when crime demanded was the slayer whom The Shadow wanted. Shakes Niefan—no one else—was the murderer of Jerome Neville.

The motive? A hidden plotter? A coming victim? These were questions that could be answered by a swift and direct plan. Shakes Niefan must be found. That was The Shadow's mission.

THE flashlight went out. The phantom shape moved from the living room. The tiny bulb blinked as The Shadow searched the remainder of the apartment. At last, the blinking ceased.

Stealthily The Shadow descended the stairs and passed through the silent house. He chose a rear window as an exit. He merged into thick darkness. His purpose here was finished.

Tonight, The Shadow had found a clue that Joe Cardona had missed. The Shadow no longer followed. He was leading in the race to frustrate crime. Yet still, The Shadow was handicapped. Of the two clues—one at Crane's, the other at Neville's—Joe Cardona had found the most important one.

The cryptic message on the torn bit of paper. Its lettered inscription—MEN 13—still remained unsolved. That was the clue which The Shadow needed. Until he learned of its existence, the master sleuth would be working under disadvantage.

His one course now was to uncover Shakes Niefan. The odds were against a speedy gaining of that goal. In the meantime, new deaths threatened— stark murder which Joe Cardona alone could prevent, yet which the detective could not discern.

Only the keen brain of The Shadow could have spotted the meaning of that cryptic fragment which Joe Cardona was holding unused!

CHAPTER XI
AGAIN THE KILLER

THICK, misty night had descended upon Manhattan. Swirls of fog clung to the pillars of the elevated structure where it cut its way through a shoddy district of the East Side.

Dull blares of steamship whistles came in eerie basso through the drizzly blackness. Close to the river, this district seemed to seep in the waters of the bridge-spanned channel between Manhattan and Long Island.

A skulking man came from the opening of a narrow street. His coat collar was turned up about his neck. His dampened felt hat clung closely to his head. His hands were encased in sticky kid gloves. Quick, shifty eyes looked back and forth. Hands fumbled as they pressed the coat collar closer to the chin.

Shakes Niefan was again at large. The slayer of Jerome Neville had spent the night in his hideout. On this evening, twenty-four hours after his murderous stroke, Shakes Niefan was faring forth on new work of crime.

The killer's footsteps pounded up the stairway of the elevated. Then came the rumble of an arriving train. The elapsing time was just sufficient. Shakes Niefan had caught the uptown local.

Gobs of water dripped from the elevated structure as the departing train made the ironwork tremble. Deep-throated foghorns spelled a melancholy message that carved weirdly through the mist. Then, amid moments of fleeting silence, a strange figure moved from darkness into light.

It was The Shadow. Grotesquely shaped in the glimmer of the street lamps, the mysterious master was crossing the avenue to reach the street from which Shakes Niefan had emerged. Stalking the underworld in person, The Shadow was on the trail of the killer who had returned to Manhattan.

Once again, luck had betrayed The Shadow. By a scant minute he had missed the path of Shakes Niefan. Since his investigation of last night, The Shadow had been visiting the most secluded portions of the underworld. He had been using all his cunning to learn the location of Shakes Niefan's hideout.

Dew-like drops glistened upon blackened cloth as The Shadow's phantom form appeared momentarily beneath a lamp near the entrance of an obscure alley. The figure disappeared from view. Moving through darkness, The Shadow tried the door of a dilapidated house. The barrier resisted. Clicks in the dark were tribute to the skill of The Shadow's pick. The door opened inward.

Gaslight showed a short hall; beyond it an opened doorway to a dully lighted room. A tumble-down staircase was at the left. The front door of the house closed as The Shadow pressed it shut. The gaslight wavered as The Shadow moved up the stairs.

TWO men were seated in the rear room that The Shadow had noticed. Crouched at a table, a bottle between them, they were talking in low, growled tones. Stalwart ruffians, with leering, heavy-jawed faces, these rogues formed the toughest pair of dock-wallopers that had ever graced a Brooklyn wharf.

"What's the matter with this hideout, Pete?" one man was asking. "The bulls ain't never bothered us down here."

"Don't ask me," returned the other. "It ain't our business, Slugger, if Shakes don't like the dump. All I know is that he's scrammed and won't be back."

"He plugged a guy last night," declared Pete. "I guess that's why he ain't comin' back. Changin' hideouts. Well, we got a grand between us—"

"*Sh-h!*" The tone of "Slugger" was cautious as he gripped Pete's arm. "Look at that!"

Slugger was pointing upward to the single gaslight in the room. Pete followed the direction of the other's gaze.

"It wiggled like that when Shakes went out," whispered Slugger, hoarsely. "That means that somebody's come in again—"

"Maybe Shakes is back."

"Not him. He gave me his key."

"Come along."

Pete rose to his feet and gestured to Slugger. A pair of apelike fighters, the dock-wallopers formed a formidable pair as they pulled out big revolvers and crept toward the lighted hallway.

Slugger looked about. He saw no one. He nudged his thumb toward the stairway. Pete nodded. Slugger led the way, with Pete at his heels. Despite their bulk, these huge men moved with noiseless tread as they started for the second floor.

A FLASHLIGHT was glimmering beyond a closed door on the second story. Standing in a dingy room, The Shadow was using the sharp but tiny beam in an inspection of the hideout. Two broken chairs; a tumbledown cot with blankets strewn upon it; these were the tokens of recent occupancy.

There was one discovery, however, which told The Shadow more. The flashlight glimmered on crumpled newspapers. There were three of these; all had been turned to inner pages. The Shadow's laugh came in a bare whisper as the flashlight gave the clue.

The man who had been reading these newspapers had evidently started with front-page stories. He had turned to pages on which the news accounts were continued. In each newspaper, the upturned page carried a runover concerning the murder of Jerome Neville.

The Shadow knew that Shakes Niefan was the killer. He had found this hideout, thinking that Shakes might be here. He had arrived too late. Shakes had gone; but the evidence of his occupancy remained.

Would the killer return? That was the question for which The Shadow sought an answer. The flashlight, as it scoured the room, showed no sign of bags or clothing. The Shadow knew that it would be well to watch this hideout; he also knew that Shakes Niefan's absence was an ominous sign. It could mean that Shakes had fared forth to deal with some new victim.

The flashlight snapped out. The Shadow made no move. His keen ears had caught a sound outside the door. Stealthy footsteps. These might mean the return of Shakes Niefan! The knob of the door was rattling softly. The black cloak swished in darkness. Then came silence as the door swung open.

A flashlight clicked. Its large-circled beam cut a swath through the center of the room as Slugger entered. The big dock-walloper swung his light to form a spreading arc. The cot—the window—then the chairs—these were the objects that the torch revealed.

Slugger's gun moved along with the light. The dock-walloper had finger upon trigger. He swerved the light to the final point—the corner of the room nearest to the open door.

Like an avalanche, a mass of blackness came surging into the path of the flashlight's ray. The swiftness of The Shadow's attack blotted out the glare. The Shadow had made his lunge in time with the swerving light. He was upon Slugger before the startled dock-walloper knew what had happened.

A gloved fist was the weapon that The Shadow used. That clenched hand had the power of a piston rod as it clipped upward to Slugger's jaw. The big dock-walloper was lifted from his crouch. Hurled backward, his arms shot out. Flashlight and revolver went flying in opposite directions.

Pete, standing in the dim hall, saw the effect of The Shadow's rush. To his startled eyes, it appeared that some invisible force had hoisted Slugger upward and stretched him sprawled upon the floor. Pete acted on a moment's notice.

Springing into the darkened room, the second dock-walloper fired blindly. His first shot was in the direction of the window; his next deliveries were made from a hand sweeping to the right. But Pete never dispatched the bullet that might have reached The Shadow.

A hurtling form came in from Pete's right. An arm like an iron bar swung up and struck Pete's wrist. The revolver skied to the ceiling. Pete, staggering back, barely managed to ward off The Shadow's punch. The upswing of his own right arm had given the dock walloper an involuntary guard.

Another punch came forward. Head down, Pete escaped its greatest force. Fiercely, the disarmed dock walloper grappled with the black-clad warrior who had sprung so suddenly from the darkness.

THE SHADOW had sought to avoid gunfire. In this portion of the underworld, a single shot would turn loose hordes of ruffians. The Shadow did not fear such enemies. His purpose was simply to avoid delay in his pursuit of Shakes Niefan.

Hence, The Shadow, as he battled with Pete, was dragging the big dock-walloper toward the hallway. Like a mongoose attacking a writhing cobra, The Shadow had gained a hold that enabled him to sling the big man back and forth. Pete, possessed of hardened strength, was fighting back.

The heel of a gloved hand was pressed against Pete's chin. Staring upward with bulging eyes, the dock-walloper could not see his opponent. The Shadow had pinioned the big man's right arm. Pete's left was swinging wildly in the air.

With an angry snarl, Pete threw all of his brute strength into the fray. As The Shadow pressed his head against the wall, the dock walloper wrested his right arm free. Twisting, he threw a pair of paws blindly toward his foeman's throat.

Long nails ripped the collar of The Shadow's cloak. The Shadow's hand dropped from Pete's jaw. Snarling his triumph, the dock-walloper lowered his chin and fought to clutch the neck that was slipping from his big hands. Then came the turn.

The Shadow had dropped to gain a jiujitsu hold. Pete's hands lost their grip as his huge form was hoisted upward in spite of all its bulk. Braced on the floor, The Shadow snapped himself upward and backward. His odd lunge stopped.

Pete kept on. Like a rock slung from a catapult, the big dock-walloper shot straight forward over The Shadow's head. His clawing hands clutched wildly as his arms spread in a vain effort to stop his fall. The stairway lay dead ahead. Pete's plunge carried him halfway to the bottom before his long dive brought him head first to a projecting step.

The crash was terrific. Striking on head and hands, Pete's big bulk described a bounding somersault that ended at the bottom of the stairway. There the dock-walloper rolled in a sideways fashion and smashed into the wall.

The Shadow was gliding down the stairway. His quick pace carried him across Pete's body. His swift hand yanked open the door. Din came to The Shadow's ears. Running forms were arriving beneath the light at the entrance of the alley.

In this quarter all were foemen unless they announced themselves as friends. The dull light from the opened door was sufficient for mobsmen eager for a fight. A revolver barked from the entrance of the alley. A bullet splintered the door frame.

The Shadow's hands swept from his cloak. Two automatics thundered from the doorway. The gangster who had fired his revolver went sprawling in the alley. Others dived for cover. The Shadow leaped outward, yanking the door behind him. An instant later, his automatics opened a new cannonade.

Mobsters scattered while The Shadow backed swiftly through the alley to the further street. Shouts had risen. Wild shots began. Distant whistles sounded as The Shadow reached the next street.

Scurrying gangsters were coming from another block. The Shadow did not wait for them. Swiftly and unseen, he crossed the street and gained a new passage between two buildings opposite.

Weaving his way into the underworld, The Shadow was taking a roundabout course that would lead him from the badlands. He had shown his skill tonight; but he had not sought the adventure which had been his lot.

For this delay—caused by the chance flicker of a gaslight—had ended all chance to trail Shakes Niefan. The killer had gone his way. New death was in the making!

CHAPTER XII
MURDER AT NIGHT

SHAKES NIEFAN had unwittingly eluded The Shadow. While the gun fray was going on about the killer's discarded hideout, Shakes had reached a new objective. After alighting from an uptown station, he had walked two blocks to make a phone call from a booth in a cigar store.

With receiver wobbling in his unsteady hand, Shakes was talking in the fashion of the night before. Once more the slayer was reporting for grim duty.

"Hello..." Shakes was using his affected growl. "Yeah ... I'm all ready ... Sure ... Last night was O.K. wasn't it? All right ... tonight will be the same ... No, I'm not going back to the old place ... I'm going to keep away from those joints ... Yeah ... Some guys think they're too wise ..."

Leaving the store, Shakes walked westward to an avenue. He went one block north; then turned into a side street. He reduced his pace as he neared a lighted archway that occupied a broad space between two old-fashioned buildings. Shakes noted the inscription on the arch:

BALLANTYNE PLACE

Shakes walked beneath the archway. The space within widened out into a large courtyard. Two-story buildings—old English houses in miniature—flanked the sides of Ballantyne Place.

A secluded spot in the heart of Manhattan, this exclusive section consisted of houses built on the cooperative plan. There were perhaps a dozen residences in Ballantyne Place; each bore a conspicuous number upon its door. Shakes Niefan strolled along until he reached Number 8.

Pausing to light his cigarette, Shakes feigned the part of a chance visitor while he glanced about to make sure that no one was in the quiet court. He noted lights in the upstairs windows of the house at which he stood. He tried the door and found it locked.

The style of the lock was its weakness. A large keyhole offered an easy task. Shakes pulled a ring of skeleton keys from his pocket. On the third trial, the lock opened.

Shakes pressed the door inward. It yielded only a few inches. Pulling the glove from his right hand, Shakes inserted his fingers. He found a chain instead of a bolt. This, again, was a factor in the crook's favor.

The chain would not loosen, but when Shakes brought his jimmy into action, the work was simple. A dull, splintering sound occurred as the wall fastening broke loose. Shakes threw a nervous glance toward the courtyard, then entered.

Closing the door, Shakes began a flashlight inspection downstairs. He found a small living room where the embers of a dying fire glowed from a grate. Desk and table drawers revealed an assortment of papers. Shakes bundled these without further inspection; he tossed them in the fireplace and watched them burn to ashes. With a short laugh Shakes approached the stairs and sneaked upward to the darkened hall above.

THERE was a light beneath the door of a front room. A low, hoarse voice issued forth in frightened tones. Pressing close to the door, Shakes distinguished words:

"This is Hiram Engliss speaking... Number Eight, Ballantyne Place ... I believe that my house has been entered ... Yes ... I could hear someone breaking in downstairs ..."

While his lips formed a fierce, distorted grimace, Shakes Niefan pressed his jimmy into place against the edge of the frail door. He was sure that this barrier was locked. The man within was calling the police. There was no time to lose.

Pausing, Shakes heard the clatter of the telephone receiver. He used the jimmy with full force. A startled cry came from within. Hiram Engliss knew now that danger had arrived.

Woodwork splintered from the door. Another wrench of the jimmy. As Shakes leaned to his work, he heard a window come open; he caught the shout that Hiram Engliss uttered:

"Help!" The man was frantic. "Help! Burglars—"

The door snapped open. Shakes Niefan dropped his jimmy as he plunged forward. His right hand shot to his coat pocket. He was face to face with a pale-faced, elderly man who was turning from the window. Hiram Engliss was holding, an old-fashioned pepperbox—a four-barreled pistol that looked like a honeycomb.

The gun was wobbling in the old man's hand. Hiram Engliss, clad in dressing gown, was ready with a frantic effort to stop this intruder. Wildly, he fired. Even at this close range, the bullet went wide.

Shakes was bringing out his revolver with a hand that shook as much as the old man's. But the murderer lacked the nervousness that had gripped Hiram Engliss. The pepperbox spoke with a puny bark. Again, the aim was faulty.

Shakes pressed the trigger of his stub-nosed revolver. His hand had steadied for the action. His aim had its customary perfection. The old-fashioned gun fell to the floor as Hiram Engliss collapsed.

Shakes Niefan lost no time. He yanked open the bureau drawers. They contained no papers. Turning, Shakes dashed down the stairs. He passed the living room, hurried through the front door and crossed the court.

Shouts came from other windows. Shakes turned and delivered a shot that shattered a pane.

Heads bobbed from view. Shakes reached the street. He saw a taxicab stopping at the opposite curb.

"Scram!" shouted the murderer.

Cab driver and passenger jumped to the sidewalk. Shakes grabbed the wheel and shot the car full speed ahead. A patrolman appeared as the cab reached the corner. Shakes opened fire. The officer ducked for the cover of a doorway. He responded with futile shots as the cab swung around the corner.

Once again, Shakes Niefan had delivered death. The murderer was still ahead of The Shadow's pursuit. The police had shown their inability to cope with his swift ways of killing.

The taxi swung into an obscure block. It came to a leisurely stop as a patrol car sped past. The police were on the way to the scene of death; but the murderer had gone.

Shakes Niefan again wore his evil smile as he alighted from the cab and strolled along the street. Safely away, a new hideout chosen for tonight, he was ready to make his telephoned report concerning the death of Hiram Engliss.

CHAPTER XIII
THE COMMISSIONER SPEAKS

IT was midnight. Inspector Timothy Klein and Detective Joe Cardona were at the scene of crime. Standing in the room where Hiram Engliss had died, they were discussing the facts that they had learned.

The telephone bell began to ring. Inspector Klein picked up the instrument from the table beside the bed. The call was from police headquarters. Cardona judged that from Klein's conversation.

"We've fixed one point," declared the inspector, grimly, as he laid the telephone aside. "They've compared the bullets. The same gun was used to kill both Jerome Neville and Hiram Engliss."

"Which means the same murderer," asserted Cardona. "I saw that right away, Inspector. Those ashes in the living room grate—"

Cardona paused as a man entered the upstairs room. It was Clyde Burke. The detective stared at the reporter.

"No alibi for being late tonight," announced Clyde. "It doesn't matter, though. Looks like I've walked in on something interesting."

"You have," admitted Cardona. "Here's the link you want. You can tell the public that we're after one murderer. The same man killed both Neville and Engliss."

Clyde nodded as he scrawled the item on a sheet of folded copy paper. He was about to put a question when the telephone bell jingled. Again, Klein answered.

"Hello," greeted the inspector. "Yes. This is Midtown nine-one-three-six-two ... Final report, eh?

Only one call out of here tonight? Yes ...We know about that one ... It was a call to the police ..."

"Engliss heard the murderer break in," explained Cardona, to Clyde. "He put in a call for help. The killer must have got him right after that."

"Fingerprints?" inquired Clyde, briskly.

"None," responded Cardona.

"No linkup with the Crane case?" asked Clyde.

"None at all." Cardona was almost savage in his retort. "That's out, Burke. Do you understand? We've got enough trouble without you—"

"All right, Joe." Clyde's easy tone mollified the detective. "Don't worry. I'm not mentioning it. This is enough. How did the murderer get away tonight?"

"In a taxicab," stated Cardona. "Chased the driver and the passenger to the sidewalk. We picked up the empty cab a dozen blocks away. It's the same story. Nobody got a good look at the killer. Of all the dumb clucks—"

KLEIN and Burke turned toward the door as they saw Cardona pause. Like the detective, they recognized the stalwart form of the new arrival. It was Police Commissioner Ralph Weston.

"Have you completed your report, Cardona?" questioned Commissioner Weston, brusquely.

"Yes, sir," replied the detective. "Inspector Klein just received word from headquarters. They say that the bullets—"

"I've heard about the bullets," interrupted Weston. "You take charge here, Inspector Klein. I want Detective Cardona to come along with me. Are you ready, Cardona?"

The detective nodded. Weston turned and started downstairs. Cardona followed. Inspector Klein spoke warningly to Clyde Burke.

"Go easy in your story," said Klein. "Don't play it up about the commissioner being here. I think he's on the warpath. He doesn't like it when we give out too much."

"All right, Inspector," agreed Clyde. "Give me a few more facts and I'll call it a night. I'm due at the office anyway."

Staring from the front window, Clyde saw Weston and Cardona passing through the archway to the street. The Shadow's agent wondered what urgency had brought the police commissioner here. Clyde watched the pair enter the commissioner's car. The vehicle pulled away.

CLYDE BURKE would have given much to have heard the conversation that began between Weston and Cardona. The police commissioner was prompt with the reasons that had made him seek the sleuth.

"Inspector Klein informed me of this Engliss murder," announced Weston. "I linked it right away with the death of Neville. Two killings in two nights. This is more than mere coincidence.

"You will recall, Cardona, that when we discussed the death of MacAvoy Crane, we foresaw a possibility of further killings. That is why we began our search for Lester Drayson.

"Are these deaths—Engliss' and Neville's—an aftermath of Crane's? That is the question which now besets us. We have linked Engliss and Neville to the same killer. Can we go further back?"

"I don't know, Commissioner," admitted Cardona, frankly. "We studied Jerome Neville's case. The man was a refrigerator salesman. He had no enemies. Now comes Hiram Engliss. I've been busy calling his friends; the old man was a retired architect with an innocent past.

"On the face of it, you can't link these killings with the Crane case. Strangler Hunn bumped MacAvoy Crane. Strangler is dead; Crane was a man investigating crime. But here's a new killer—and two victims who don't seem logical persons to be murdered. At the same time—"

"Well?" inquired Weston, as Cardona paused.

"I've got a hunch, that's all," returned Cardona. "I'm still thinking about that slip of paper. Thirteen men—"

"Men thirteen," objected Weston.

"It's the same thing," commented Cardona. "Crane was the first; then Neville; now Engliss—"

Further confab ended. The car had swung a corner past an uptown hotel—the Morrisette. The driver was pulling to the opposite curb. Cardona, for the first time, realized the destination. Commissioner Weston was taking him to the home of Roscoe Wimbledon.

THE servant who admitted the commissioner and the detective was prompt to usher them into Wimbledon's library. There they found the aviation magnate awaiting them. Ross Harlton was with Roscoe Wimbledon. It was evident that the police commissioner had made a telephone call here.

Weston came to business promptly. Taking a chair, the dynamic police commissioner opened his conversation.

"I am here, Mr. Wimbledon," asserted Weston, "to confer with you regarding consequences which may have been the outgrowth of the murder which we previously discussed. When you told me that MacAvoy Crane had served as your private investigator, I advanced the theory that other murders might be forthcoming."

"That is right," nodded Wimbledon. "As I recall it, Commissioner, you accepted my belief that Lester Drayson may have had friends in New York."

"Exactly," agreed Weston. "That is why I instituted a search for Drayson. The hunt is still on; to date it has brought no results. At the same time, however, we considered the possibility that Strangler Hunn had been a hired killer and that another assassin might be employed to continue his work."

"That theory," recalled Wimbledon, "was pressed by a gentleman who had called on me. I refer to Mr. Lamont Cranston. I believe that he suggested looking for the potential killer rather than beginning a hunt for Lester Drayson."

"Yes," agreed Weston. "I remember Cranston's statements. They had merit. Present developments have proven so. I told you, over the telephone tonight, that the police are confronted with two new killings. I am anxious to learn whether or not they are the follow-up of Crane's death.

"Assuming that Lester Drayson ordered the killing of Crane because the man was an investigator into his affairs, it is logical to suppose that Drayson would continue by ordering the murder of others who might have facts about him."

"Quite logical," nodded Wimbledon. He reached for a newspaper beside his desk. "I read of the death of Jerome Neville. Here is the story—in today's *Classic*. What puzzles me, Commissioner, is why a refrigerator salesman should have been slain."

"His place was rifled," interposed Joe Cardona. "Papers taken to be destroyed. Just like the situation at Crane's."

"That is true," said Wimbledon. "What about the case tonight? You told me, commissioner, that a man named Hiram Engliss had been murdered. What was his occupation?"

"Retired architect," stated Cardona. "His living room was rifled. Papers were burned in the fireplace."

"Ah!" Wimbledon became alert. "That is interesting. This does make it look like more than mere coincidence."

"What I want to know," declared Weston, "is whether or not these men could have been friends of Lester Drayson. Have you any record of them, Mr. Wimbledon? Do you know the names of Drayson's former associates?"

"No," returned Wimbledon. "That is why I hired Crane. We had positively nothing to go on, except the knowledge that Drayson probably had confidants. In fact, I thought that Crane might have been looking for a lone man. Now, however, I am ready to believe that there must be more than one."

"What gets me," announced Cardona, suddenly, "is this matter of the papers. We have a good idea why Strangler Hunn burned the documents after he killed MacAvoy Crane. The investigator's reports could have made trouble for Lester Drayson.

"But what papers would the others have? None. If they were secretly hooked up with Drayson, about the only thing they would have had would be money. Drayson could have planted cash with them—"

CARDONA stopped suddenly as Wimbledon raised his hand. The aviation magnate had struck an idea through the detective's words. The same thought hit Cardona as he paused. It was Wimbledon, however, who voiced the theory.

"Papers were destroyed!" exclaimed Wimbledon, as he tapped his desk significantly. "Papers which the new murderer found when he killed Neville and Engliss. But were papers the object of his raids?

"Is it not possible that he found money also? That he may have seized negotiable securities held by these men? Suppose that Jerome Neville and Hiram Engliss were friends of Lester Drayson. Their very obscurity would have made them the right persons to serve as guardians of his stolen funds."

"I get it," declared Cardona, turning to Weston. "There's a game that holds water, Commissioner. Suppose Drayson had planted dough with Neville and Engliss. What would he do? Come back—get his profits—and pay them off.

"But Drayson was a fugitive. These fellows knew too much. He could find a simpler way to get that dough. Bump them off—through some killer—and end all chances of them squealing. You can hire a thug cheaper than you can pay off men who know too much."

There was a pause. Roscoe Wimbledon ended it by turning to speak to Ross Harlton.

"Suppose, Ross," he suggested, "that you go upstairs and resume work on those technical reports. I shall join you after I have ended this conference."

"Very well, sir." Harlton arose, bowed goodnight, and left the library. Wimbledon waited until the door had closed behind him. Then the aviation magnate leaned across the desk.

"That paper which you found at Crane's," he said, cautiously to Cardona. "Has anyone seen it except myself and Commissioner Weston?"

"No," returned Cardona. "I have it here."

The detective reached in his pocket and produced the slip. He placed it on the desk. Weston drew close to examine it with Wimbledon.

"I've got a hunch about that paper," asserted Cardona. "I read it thirteen men, and I figure that three of the lot have gone the voyage. Crane—Neville—Engliss—"

"Not Crane." Wimbledon shook his head. "He was the investigator. His job was to learn the names of all who had been associated with Lester Drayson. It seems incredible that there could have been thirteen. Nevertheless—"

Wimbledon paused thoughtfully as he picked up the torn paper and returned it to Cardona. Then he added:

"The more men, the less each one would have to hold in keeping. Yet thirteen—the number seems too great. There is one way, however, that the theory might be tested."

"How is that?" questioned Weston.

"By making it public," declared Wimbledon. "Lester Drayson is known to be a rogue. It seems likely that he dealt with his associates individually; that one could not know another.

"Bring out the facts. Spread them through the newspapers. Let it be known that murder is still in the making. All who have facts regarding Drayson will come scurrying to you for protection."

COMMISSIONER WESTON tugged at the points of his mustache. Joe Cardona knew why the official was pondering. Weston's cardinal principle was to avoid publicity while the police were concerned with unsolved crime.

"We must wait," came Weston's decision. "Sometimes newspaper reports do more harm than good. We can always use the journals as a final resort; but once we have taken such a step, we cannot withdraw.

"A double hunt is on, Cardona!" Weston pounded the edge of Wimbledon's desk as he turned to the detective. "We shall search for two men: Lester Drayson and the unknown killer. I shall find the latter even if Drayson cannot be had.

"The order is going out. Scour the underworld. Bring in this skulking murderer who has taken the place of Strangler Hunn. Examine the records; give out descriptions of all who knew Hunn in the past."

"The dragnet?" questioned Cardona.

"If necessary," agreed Weston. "There are three ways to work." Unwittingly, the commissioner began to paraphrase the statements of Lamont Cranston. "First: find the plotter. Second: the potential murderer. Third: the victims that are to be.

"We shall use the first and second methods. The third is impossible. Our double system will bring the results that we require."

With this assertion, Commissioner Weston arose. His mind was decided. From now on, the law would not concern itself with the single search for Lester Drayson. Weston was throwing all his power to the uncovering of the unknown murderer whose identity The Shadow already knew.

Though the process might be delayed, eventually the dragnet would close in an effort to ensnare the missing slayer: Shakes Niefan.

Without realizing it, Commissioner Ralph Weston was following the lead of The Shadow!

CHAPTER XIV
FIGURES IN THE NIGHT

INSPECTOR TIMOTHY KLEIN and Clyde Burke had not lingered long at the home of Hiram Engliss. Inspector and reporter had left five minutes after the departure of Commissioner Ralph Weston and Detective Joe Cardona.

Klein had gone directly to headquarters. Burke had headed to find a telephone, ostensibly for the purpose of calling the *Classic* office. Instead of performing that duty, however, Burke had reported to Burbank.

Hence, while Weston and Cardona were still at Wimbledon's a strange figure made its appearance in the secluded courtyard of Ballantyne Place. A blackened shape that moved with gliding tread, The Shadow had come to view the scene of crime.

Unseen, The Shadow entered the house where Engliss had died. His probing flashlight showed the broken fastenings of the front-door chain. It glimmered in the fire place where ashes rested as the crumbled remainders of papers which had belonged to Hiram Engliss.

The same light reappeared upstairs. It revealed the door that Shakes Niefan had jimmied. It swung along beside the bed; across the spot where Engliss had collapsed; then to the telephone on the little table.

The searching circle rested there. A silver disk, the flashlight's beam stayed poised. Then came a click. The light went out. A whispered laugh shuddered through the room. A swish announced the departure of The Shadow.

ONE block away from Ballantyne Place, a dozing taxi driver was startled to hear a quiet voice from the interior of his cab. The driver had not heard a passenger open the door. This fare seemed to have dropped from nowhere. Nodding drowsily, the perplexed driver heard the destination which the quiet voice gave him:

"Hotel Morrisette."

UP near the destination that The Shadow had ordered, Commissioner Ralph Weston and Detective Joe Cardona were at that moment coming down the steps of Roscoe Wimbledon's home. Weston, stopping by the door of his car, began to talk to Cardona.

"You'll get instructions at headquarters," asserted the commissioner. "You'll work with Klein to find this murderer. It's a harder job, Cardona, than finding Strangler Hunn. Nevertheless, I rely on you to perform it."

"Give me time, Commissioner," pleaded Cardona. "I want to get the stools working before we use the dragnet. I may be able to spot the guy before he knows what's up. I'm going after anybody that ever worked with Strangler Hunn."

"In the meantime," remarked Weston, "the search will continue for Lester Drayson. If the man is in New York, we will land him."

"Here's his picture," commented Cardona,

Weston pounded the edge of Wimbledon's desk.
"A double hunt is on, Cardona!"

drawing a photograph from his pocket. "Gray hair—clean shaven—he couldn't grow a beard without it being gray, too."

Weston nodded. He took the photograph and stepped away from the car so that he could hold the picture in the light of a streetlamp. The commissioner nearly jostled against two men who were walking by. Then he began to examine the picture while Cardona looked on.

"So that's Lester Drayson," commented Weston. "I saw this photograph before; but I hadn't analyzed it closely. There's a dignity about the fellow, Cardona. He might change that expression; but otherwise—"

"Gray hair," recited Cardona, "and bushy gray eyebrows. Thirty plainclothes men looking for Lester Drayson. They ought to find him."

A strolling man came between Weston and the light of the street lamp. Weston handed the photograph back to Cardona. The stroller paused a few yards along to apply a match to his cigar. Then he crossed the street and entered the lobby of the Hotel Morrisette.

Commissioner Weston stepped into his car. As Cardona stood by, a taxicab pulled up on the other side of the street. Neither Weston nor Cardona noticed it. The commissioner was repeating his previous remarks with new emphasis. He concluded by giving an order to his chauffeur. The big car pulled away. Cardona watched it depart; then turned and walked away.

ACROSS the street, the taxi driver was waiting for his passenger to alight. He had opened the door of the cab; no one had come out. Impatiently, the driver turned and looked into the back. He pressed the light switch.

The door on the left was ajar, like the door which the cabby had opened on the right. A five-dollar bill was lying on the cushion of the back seat. Otherwise the cab was empty.

The driver reached mechanically as he picked up the ample fare. Shaking his head, he started his cab along the street. His mysterious passenger had vanished as weirdly as he had arrived. The driver did not know that he had taxied The Shadow!

Lurking in the darkness on the street side of the cab, The Shadow had caught the last exchange of words between Weston and Cardona. He had heard the commissioner's repeated demand for action in the underworld. He had detected the utterance of a man's name:

Lester Drayson.

The Shadow had arrived too late to learn more definite facts; but his keen brain had divined the answer. He knew that Commissioner Weston had chosen a double course. The police would follow the plan which The Shadow—as Lamont Cranston—

had advocated; namely, to search for a potential killer as redoubtable as Strangler Hunn.

Gliding into darkness, The Shadow passed along the street. Weston's conference with Wimbledon had ended; there could be no purpose in adopting the guise of Lamont Cranston now that the brief visit was over.

THE SHADOW was not the only watcher who had witnessed the departures of Ralph Weston and Joe Cardona. Stationed just within the lobby of the Hotel Morrisette, a man had waited until the commissioner and the detective had both gone on their way.

Turning, this watcher strolled into the lobby and advanced to the desk. He rapped to attract the attention of the drowsy clerk.

"Key to 614," he ordered. Then, as the clerk produced the key: "Any messages for Martin Hyslop?"

"None," replied the clerk.

The man went to the elevator. He reached the sixth floor and entered Room 614. He turned on a table lamp; then walked over and drew the window shades. There was a large bureau in one corner of the hotel room. On either side were light brackets. The man turned on these lights. He stood before the mirror.

In the glare, the face of Martin Hyslop showed as a rounded visage. Black hair glistened in the light. Thin black eyebrows formed straight lines beneath. Hyslop's upper lip had a heavy black

LESTER DRAYSON—fugitive from the law, sought for constantly.

mustache. His low jaw possessed a forward thrust.

Only this direct light revealed a certain artificiality to Martin Hyslop's countenance. As the man brought his face closer to the mirror, the black hair showed more glisten. The eyebrows, viewed closely by the man who studied his own reflection, gave bare evidence that they had been clipped.

Martin Hyslop relaxed his jaw. That slight action gave the clue. A challenging countenance changed to one of formal dignity. The man stared fixedly; then resumed the forward thrust of his chin. The alteration pleased him. He laughed in surly fashion.

In those brief moments of inspection, Martin Hyslop had given a trace of his real identity. This man who had registered at the Hotel Morrisette was none other than Lester Drayson, the man for whom the law was searching!

As a stroller in the night, Drayson had heard the words between Weston and Cardona. He had seen the police commissioner examining the photograph of a face that Drayson, himself, was trying to disguise!

Lester Drayson turned out the lights. He raised the window shades and stared out into the night. Below, he could see the darkened house where Roscoe Wimbledon lived. A spiteful snarl came from Drayson's lips.

Craftily, Drayson had chosen a bold course. This hotel, just across the street from the home of the man who had denounced him, was the best place in New York for the returned fugitive to use as temporary residence. It was evident from Drayson's snarl that the ex-president of Universal Aircraft felt himself capable of avoiding discovery.

Moving through the darkness of his room, Drayson found the telephone. He waited until an answer came from the clerk below; then he gave a number:

"Carmody five—nine—two—one—three."

Minutes passed. Then came word from the desk: "No answer, sir."

Lester Drayson muttered to himself as he returned to the window. Then his tone changed to a short, grunted laugh. Lighting a cigar, the man who called himself Martin Hyslop sat beside the window and stared out into darkness.

ELSEWHERE in Manhattan, a figure had arrived within the walls of a darkened room. A swish amid blackness; then came the click of a light. A bluish incandescent threw its focused rays upon a polished table. The Shadow had reached his sanctum.

White hands appeared beneath the light. They stretched forward and obtained earphones. A voice came over the wire:

"Burbank speaking."

"Report." It was The Shadow's whisper.

"Report from Marsland," announced Burbank. "All quiet at Shakes Niefan's old hideout. Much discussion about the gunfight that took place. Marsland does not think that Niefan will return."

"Report received."

A whispered laugh came from the darkness as The Shadow thrust the earphones to the wall. The hands produced pen and paper. They began to make notations:

Method One.
Find the plotter.
Police searching for Lester Drayson.

The hand paused. Blue ink dried. The words began to vanish. Such was the way with the ink that The Shadow used. This fluid vanished after drying unless sealed within an envelope. The Shadow used it for communications with his agents. He also employed the special ink for inscribing the thoughts that gripped him when he planned his ways to counter crime.

The hand wrote once more:

Method Two.
Find the killer.
Shakes Niefan has not returned to hideout.
Police search will eventually point to him.

Another wait. The ink vanished, word by word. There was significance in the soft laugh that The Shadow uttered. It seemed to indicate a change of policy. The Shadow had left the first method to the police while he pursued the second. Now that the law had followed The Shadow's lead, the master sleuth was planning another course.

Again the hand inscribed:

Third Method.
Find the next victim.

This time a new laugh throbbed within the black-walled sanctum. The Shadow had chosen a more startling course. Yet it was one that offered high reward should it succeed.

Two men had been slain since Strangler Hunn had murdered MacAvoy Crane. Had The Shadow possessed a clue to lead him to Jerome Neville or Hiram Engliss, he could have saved the lives of those unfortunate victims.

Did new murder lie ahead? The Shadow could combat it by learning who Shakes Niefan planned to slay. The Shadow's task was a grim one; yet this master had a faculty for turning past and present into a foresight of the future!

Jerome Neville.
Hiram Engliss.

These were the names that The Shadow wrote. The names vanished while hidden eyes studied them. Next came addresses. Finally, telephone numbers.

Here The Shadow paused. When the writing faded, he repeated the inscription.

FROM the facts that Clyde Burke had furnished, The Shadow had found a meager clue. Taking two sheets of paper, he wrote the name and telephone number of Jerome Neville on one.

Upon the other sheet, he placed the same data concerning Hiram Engliss.

The papers read:

Jerome Neville, Quadrangle 2-4138
Hiram Engliss, Midtown 9-1362

As each sheet dried, The Shadow inserted it in an envelope before the ink had time to vanish. Then, upon a larger sheet of paper, he inscribed a coded message. He folded this, placed it in the envelope and closed the flap. On the face of the envelope, he wrote the name of Clyde Burke.

This envelope went into a larger one. Using another pen, with a blacker ink, The Shadow addressed the outer envelope to Rutledge Mann, Badger Building, New York City. The inscription dried. It did not fade.

A soft laugh sounded in darkness as the light clicked out. The weird mockery rose to a sinister tone; then faded into shuddering reverberations.

Two deaths—both the work of Shakes Niefan— had given The Shadow opportunity for a chance comparison. Between now and the next night, The Shadow was sure that he would gain facts to aid him in pursuance of his clue.

CHAPTER XV
CARDONA TAKES A TIP

AT nine o'clock the next morning, a chubby-faced man was staring from the window of an office high above Broadway. He seemed to have no interest other than his view of the Manhattan skyline.

This was Rutledge Mann, a prosperous investment broker who had his suite of offices in the towering Badger Building. Leisurely in manner, Mann seemed to have no concern other than the fluctuations of the stock market.

Mann's business, however, was twofold. His brokerage activities, though they brought him comfortable profit, were not his most important job. This office was actually a blind. Rutledge Mann was an agent of The Shadow.

Useful in research, Mann also served as a contact agent between The Shadow and his active operatives. The investment broker delivered important written instructions; he also received elaborate reports which he delivered to The Shadow.

Rutledge Mann turned as he heard a rap at the door. It was the stenographer, coming to announce a visitor.

"Mr. Burke is here," stated the girl.

"Show him in," ordered Mann.

When Clyde Burke had arrived, Mann reached into a desk drawer and produced a sealed envelope. This was the inner packet that had come from The Shadow. Clyde Burke's name had faded from the face of the envelope after Mann had read it.

Clyde received the envelope. He tore it open. Out came a folded sheet of paper; with it, two small slips. Clyde noted the slips first. Then, as their writing faded, he unfolded the paper and perused its coded lines.

Clyde began to nod as he finished reading. His lips formed a slight smile. Rutledge Mann watched the slips go in the wastebasket. The folded paper followed. Its coded message had also disappeared.

"All right," announced Clyde. "I'll be back later in the morning."

LEAVING the Badger Building, Clyde called a taxi. The Shadow's agent ordered the driver to take him to detective headquarters. Arriving at his destination, Clyde went directly to Joe Cardona's office.

"Hello, Burke," growled the detective, as he looked up from a batch of papers. "Nothing new on the Engliss case. I'll let you know when any word comes in."

Clyde smiled as he saw Cardona cover a photograph with a paper. The Shadow's agent knew that a heavy search was due for an unknown killer. It was evident that Cardona did not want the newspapers to know too much at present.

"I'm not looking for a story, Joe," announced Clyde. "That is, I'm not asking you to give me one. I've got an idea—a long shot—and I'll slip it to you if you're willing to go through with it."

"On these murders?"

"Yes."

"Spill it."

"Wait a minute." Clyde was working for effect. "You may think I'm crazy, Joe. But I'm not. I've got a real bet for you; it may mean a lot of trouble; but I've got a real hunch that it may bring a big result."

"I like hunches," nodded Cardona. "Go ahead, Burke. I'll be frank with you—we're ready to take any lead that looks good."

"All right, Joe." Clyde considered. "First of all, there's something funny about these two murders. The same killer got Jerome Neville and Hiram Engliss. That's bad enough; but why should he want to murder either one of them?"

"Do you know why?"

"No. But the murderer worked mighty quick. It's a sure bet, Joe, that he isn't finished. Unless you get started, there'll be another killing tonight—and maybe one on the next night—"

"Cut it, Burke." Cardona was impatient. "You're giving me the jitters. Spring your idea."

"It strikes me," declared Clyde, as he seated

himself in front of the detective's desk, "that there must be some connection between Jerome Neville and Hiram Engliss. But all the facts—their work, their ages, their locations—point against it. We just know this—the same guy bumped both of them."

"Is that all you've got to tell me?"

"No. I've figured that the connection must be there. No matter how slight it seems, you ought to follow any point that the two men had in common. I'll go further than that—you ought to follow half a point, if you can get even that much—"

"And what is it?" interrupted Cardona.

"A number," declared Burke, in a solemn tone. "The number thirteen."

INSTANTLY, The Shadow's agent saw that he had scored an unexpected hit. Clyde had come here expecting to sell Cardona an idea that the detective might reject. Instead, he realized that he had struck home. Cardona's hands were gripping the edge of the desk. The ace was staring eagerly.

"What about it?" came Cardona's question. "What about the number thirteen?"

"Jerome Neville," remarked Clyde, "had the telephone number Quadrangle 2-4138. Hiram Engliss had the number Midtown 9-1362. Write them down, Joe. You'll see that each one contains the number thirteen, as big as life."

"That's right." Cardona was scrawling the numbers on a sheet of paper. "Still, I don't get your idea, Burke. This thirteen business is important, because"—he paused abruptly—"well, because I'm superstitious, I guess. But what can I do about it?"

"I'll tell you," stated Clyde. "It's a long shot and it may seem a crazy one; but if you follow it, you might get somewhere. There are about twelve hundred pages in the Manhattan telephone book. Why not put a dozen girls to work, each with a hundred pages. Better still, two dozen girls, with fifty pages each.

"Let them run down the columns. It's quick work spotting every number that has thirteen in it. With a bunch of typists on the job, you can list the names that the girls get. When you're through, you can eliminate a lot of names—businesses and the like—and the list you have will contain the names of whatever men that killer is still out to get."

Cardona was drawing circles on his sheet of paper. He put a ring around each number 13; then began to tap on the desk with his pencil. He eyed Clyde Burke for a moment; then made a definite effort to curb the enthusiasm that he had shown.

"I'll try this out, Burke," he said. "I'll work it through the telephone company. What you say may be true—but there'll be a lot of names in that list when—"

"What of it?" questioned Clyde. "It's not going to interfere with whatever else you're doing. Tell the phone company what you want—but make sure

you have the list before tonight. If my hunch is right, Joe, there may be other lives at stake—"

"All right, Burke," interrupted Cardona, with a nod. He was trying to indicate that the reporter had convinced him. "I'll attend to that matter. By the way, where do you come in on this? You're looking for a story—is that the idea?"

"You bet I am," returned Clyde. "Say—if this hunch brings results, I'll be sitting pretty with the *Classic* office. You're sure you're going through with it, aren't you, Joe?"

"Leave it with me, Burke."

"If you're not sure you'll have that list by tonight," warned Clyde, "I'll take it up with the *Classic*. They'll make up that list pronto, just to see if the next murder has a thirteen in it. But I figured the idea belonged to you."

"Don't tell the newspaper office!" exclaimed Cardona. "What do you want to do—spoil the story for yourself? I'll take care of this right away, Burke. Positively. Call me up in an hour; I'll tell you when the lists will be here."

CLYDE BURKE smiled as he left headquarters. He had followed instructions from The Shadow. The trump card in The Shadow's game had been Clyde's statement that he would get the Classic to work on the list. That threat had been unneeded. Clyde had delivered it solely for good measure.

Back in his office, Joe Cardona was muttering to himself. In his left hand lay the fragment of paper that he had found at Crane's. The detective was staring at the ragged clue.

"Men thirteen," mumbled Cardona. "Maybe it means men with thirteen in their phone numbers. Maybe—"

The detective lifted the telephone and put in an official call. True to his statement, Cardona intended to arrange the list that Clyde Burke had suggested.

In a corner of the *Classic* office, Clyde Burke was preparing a report for Rutledge Mann. The reporter was including every detail—particularly the point of Joe Cardona's sudden response when he had heard mention of the number 13.

This report was going to The Shadow. Through Clyde Burke, the master sleuth had gained the end he sought. The list that was being compiled for Joe Cardona was actually under preparation for The Shadow!

CHAPTER XVI
THE SHADOW'S LIST

IT was six o'clock when Clyde Burke reappeared at detective headquarters. Despite his nonchalant air, The Shadow's agent was tense. He had a new duty to perform; one that would require greater strategy than the morning's job.

Clyde had given his report to Rutledge Mann. The investment broker had forwarded it to The Shadow through a special mail chute in the door of an empty office. Later in the day, a new message had been brought to Mann by a telegraph messenger.

Clyde Burke had visited Mann to get his new instructions. Clyde had not been surprised at The Shadow's orders. The Shadow had picked the very point that Clyde had noted: the willingness with which Cardona had complied with the request to order the list of names.

The Shadow, however, had seen further than had Clyde. His keen brain had divined that Cardona must have gained a clue. It was Clyde's task now to discuss that subject with the ace detective. Through pleas or threats; through both, if necessary, Clyde must gain the truth from Joe Cardona.

Headquarters was practically deserted when Clyde Burke arrived. A light was shining from the open door of Cardona's office. The detective had told Clyde that he would be there. Clyde found him at his desk. Cardona looked up and delivered a sour smile.

"There's your brainchild," the detective remarked, pointing to a huge stack of papers. "Six copies of the list you talked about. Take a look at one—but don't let it throw you."

Clyde picked up a sheaf of typewritten pages. Despite the thinness of the sheets, the stack was bulky. It was fastened at one end by a massive paper clip. Clyde estimated a hundred pages in the sheaf.

"All six lists here?" inquired Clyde.

"All six?" Cardona snorted. "What do you think that big pile is on the table for? That's just one list you've got there, young fellow. Look at it—three columns to a page—more than a hundred pages."

"I didn't know there would be so many," protested Clyde.

"Neither did I," grumbled the detective. "If I'd known it, I wouldn't have gone in for this cuckoo idea of yours. Do you know how many names there are with the number thirteen somewhere in the phone number? I'll tell you. Ten thousand—and that's a conservative estimate."

"It's a wonder you ever got the list."

"I wouldn't have, if it had been anybody but the phone company. I told them what I wanted; I said I had to have the list. They never called back to tell me how big it was going to be. They put a whole office staff on the job to get the list here by five-thirty. I nearly dropped dead when I saw the size of the bundle."

CLYDE BURKE sat down and lighted a cigarette. He glanced through a few pages of the list that he was holding; then tossed it on the desk.

"There's only one point in your favor, Burke," said Cardona, in a conciliatory manner. "This goofy idea of yours won't stop a murder; but it might lead to some further step. That doesn't help me now, though. If another victim goes the route, it won't help him much just because he has thirteen in his phone number."

Cardona paused glumly. Clyde Burke eyed the detective narrowly. The Shadow's agent saw his opportunity.

"Look here, Joe." Clyde tapped the list that lay near him. "Why did you take up this idea when I suggested it?"

"Why?" parried Cardona. "Because I'm as cracked as you are, I guess."

"That's hokum, Joe," said Clyde, with a grin. "I remember what you said this morning. You pulled the stall that you were superstitious. That's why you took up the matter of number 13. That was hokum, too."

"Do you think so?"

"I know it. There's something you haven't told me about—something you're trying to keep out of the newspapers. You know me well enough, Joe. I'm with you. I'll keep mum on whatever you say. But why not put me straight?"

"Burke," remarked Cardona, seriously, "you've been hunting too much news down in Chinatown. You must have found too many hopjoints. Too bad"—Cardona clucked sadly—"just another reporter gone down the slide."

"Now I know you're stalling." Clyde was emphatic. "Listen, Joe. I've been on the level with you. I gave you an idea, and you took it up. I want to know why you grabbed that thought about the number thirteen. I'm going to find out, because you're going to tell me."

"I am?" Cardona's question was harsh.

"You are," retorted Clyde. "You are—or else—"

"Or else what?" barked Cardona.

Clyde paused. He studied the detective. Cardona's fists were clenched. Clyde had gone beyond the limit. Yet The Shadow's agent remained unperturbed. Clyde had received full instructions. Cardona's challenge had been anticipated by The Shadow. His message had provided the answer that Clyde Burke was to give.

"I'll tell you," declared Clyde quietly. "These lists here on this desk are a story in themselves. The number thirteen makes a corking tie-up. I'm ready to bust it if you bounce me out of here.

"I've got more than a hunch. I know that the number thirteen figures in these murders. You wouldn't have jumped if it didn't. If you don't come clean, Joe, I'm going to shoot this thirteen story for all it's worth.

"Thirteen clue in Neville-Engliss murders. Sleuth turns superstitious." Clyde was staring toward the ceiling as though he pictured headlines there. "Phone company aids police search—"

"Lay off, Burke!" Cardona was on his feet. "You started this goofy idea of—"

"And you went through with it," interrupted Clyde. "You can have the credit."

CARDONA'S dark eyes were ferocious. Clyde met them with a steady stare. Two determined men were face to face. Clyde Burke could see that Joe Cardona was in a fury.

"You can't do this, Burke!" came Cardona's hoarse challenge. "What do you want to do—put me in Dutch with the commissioner? I'm on the trail of murder—I'm no bait for newspaper ridicule."

"I don't see it, Joe," rejoined Clyde. "If this thirteen business means nothing to you, why should you get sore about it?"

Cardona had no reply. He stood glowering, not knowing what to say.

"But if it means something to you," asserted Clyde, in a steady tone, "I'm with you to the limit. On one condition only—that you tell me what it's all about.

"I'm not asking anything unfair. I brought you something that you thought was worthwhile. I don't want to see my theory go in the ashcan. I played fair. You know I always do. And fair play means a fifty-fifty break."

Joe Cardona sat down behind his desk. He nodded thoughtfully. He had received the import of Clyde's challenge. He was weighing the proposition. His capitulation came.

"You win, Burke," declared Cardona, slowly. "I've got a clue that fits in with what you gave me. That's why I rushed these lists. You always have played fair. Do I have your word that you'll say nothing about what I show you?"

"Absolutely," agreed Clyde.

Cardona reached in his vest pocket. He produced a folded envelope. From it, he drew the torn fragment of paper. He placed it on the desk in front of the reporter.

"I found that at Crane's," stated Cardona. "It was under the wastebasket. I discovered it after you were gone."

"Men thirteen," read Clyde. "Say, Joe—this does fit in with my idea."

"Strangler Hunn wrote that," asserted Cardona. "He must have made some notation from papers he found at Crane's. He tore the paper when he knew there was a fight coming."

"After he had killed MacAvoy Crane," commented Clyde. "Say, Joe—just what kind of investigation had Crane been doing?"

"I've told you enough, Burke," growled Cardona. "You wanted to know why I followed up your idea on number thirteen. I've told you. I thought that maybe this piece of paper meant something about thirteen men. After I heard your idea, I decided that I might be wrong."

Clyde nodded. Tactfully, he came back to the subject of the paper alone. Picking up a pad that lay on Cardona's desk, he printed with a pencil.

"It might read something like this," suggested Clyde, as he handed the result to Cardona. "Other words on both sides of men and 13, with the little chunk out of the center of the paper."

CARDONA studied Clyde's inscription. In copy of Strangler Hunn's wide-spaced style, Clyde had printed:

KILL MEN WITH NUMBER 13 TELEPHONES

"That might be it." Cardona shrugged his shoulders as he tore up Clyde's effort and threw the pieces on the floor. "We've got two keys—'men' is one and '13' is the other. But you can guess anything for the rest of it—"

The detective paused. A shadow had appeared at the door. Clyde Burke swung to see who had arrived. It was Fritz the janitor. Cardona grinned.

"Bucket and mop on the job again" was the detective's comment. "All right, Fritz. Start to clean up. We're leaving."

"Yah" was Fritz's dull reply.

The janitor shambled toward the desk. He set his bucket close by Clyde Burke's chair. His head was bent. Joe Cardona did not see the keen light that showed in Fritz's eyes as they spied the paper fragment which lay in front of Clyde Burke.

"That's all," asserted Cardona. He reached over and picked up the bit of paper. "I've answered your question, Burke. If this clue brings any new result, I'll let you in on it—when we're ready to shoot the story. But in the meantime, I'm trusting you. I showed this paper to the commissioner, and he said to keep it out of sight."

"No one else has seen it?"

"No one except—well, no one except you."

"All right, Joe. I'll keep mum."

"You'd better. If anything is said about this chunk of paper"—Cardona was putting the fragment in the envelope—"I'll know who's to blame."

Fritz had slouched to the side of Cardona's desk. He was standing there as Clyde Burke arose. From the corner of his eye, the false janitor saw the reporter pick up the list of names that Cardona had given him for examination.

"Wait a minute, Burke!" Cardona shot a paw across the desk. "You don't get that list!"

"Why not?" questioned Clyde, in a surprised tone.

"You've got no use for it," snorted Cardona. "What's more, it's my idea now. I showed you the clue. I keep the lists."

As Cardona plucked the single list from Clyde's hand, Fritz placed his palm upon the stack of lists that lay at Cardona's side. Neither detective nor reporter saw the single, rolling motion with which the fake janitor coiled a paper-clipped list into a cylinder. Turning toward the wall, Fritz thrust the packet into his overalls.

"I don't get you, Joe," pleaded Clyde. "I'd like to look over one of those lists. Maybe I'd get another idea. I won't show it down at the *Classic* office."

"Nothing doing," growled Cardona. "I know you'll keep quiet about the paper I showed you. But a list like this is something that could lay around. I'm taking these lists up to the commissioner's tonight. Nobody gets a copy until he says so."

FRITZ had stooped beside the desk. He came up with a cluster of torn envelopes that Cardona, who scorned wastebaskets, had chucked on the floor. Thrusting an envelope in front of the detective's eyes, Fritz inquired:

"Any goot?"

"No," returned Cardona.

Fritz dropped the envelope in front of Clyde Burke, turning it over as he did so. He thrust a second envelope in front of Joe Cardona.

"This one," asked the janitor. "Any goot?"

"No!" shouted Cardona. "None of them are any good. That's why I threw them on the floor. Chuck them all out, Fritz."

Clyde Burke was staring at the envelope which Fritz had laid in front of him. On the flap—the side that Fritz had turned upward—was a coded sentence in blue ink. A message from The Shadow!

"List not needed," read Clyde. "Agree to all Cardona asks. Off duty."

The words faded as though an invisible hand had wiped them from the envelope. Clyde was still staring when Fritz turned and picked up the envelope—now blank—to take it away with the others that the janitor held.

Joe Cardona still held the list that he had taken back from Clyde Burke. The detective placed it on the stack that lay beside him. He bundled up the lists and arose from his desk.

"I guess you're right, Joe," remarked Clyde. "I can't do anything with that list—maybe you can. Take credit for it when you talk with the commissioner. If anything comes out of it, the trouble will be worthwhile."

"The commissioner will like the idea, all right," asserted Joe. "He's strong for this deductive stuff. But he's a critical bird, too, Burke. Ten thousand names"—Cardona shook his head doubtfully—"it's an awful lot. Too big a list, Burke. Too big."

Clyde had risen. He paced beside Cardona as the detective started from the office. Clyde preceded Joe through the door. Momentarily, from the corridor, Clyde glanced into the office. Fritz was facing the wall, busy with his mop. Overalls and stooped shoulders were the only impressions that Clyde gained in this parting glance.

Even to his agent, The Shadow's disguise had been perplexing. Clyde Burke, as he walked forth with Joe Cardona, still wondered how that message had come upon the envelope which the dull-faced janitor had picked up from the floor. Clyde had rejected the truth—it seemed incredible—that the supposed Fritz was The Shadow. Yet Clyde had obeyed the message; for it had been in the code that The Shadow always used.

IN Joe Cardona's office, the tall figure of Fritz ceased mopping. The false janitor moved into the corridor and reached his locker. He deposited mop and bucket. He drew black objects from the locker.

Two minutes later, a phantom form glided from the side exit. The Shadow, guised in blackness, merged with the gathered dusk. A soft laugh came from his hidden lips.

The Shadow had seen Cardona's clue. The Shadow had gained a copy of Cardona's list. His strategy had worked, through Clyde Burke's capable following of instructions.

Headed for his sanctum, The Shadow was prepared to combat coming crime. While police were engaged in twofold search for plotter and murderer, The Shadow had chosen the final method as his own.

The Shadow planned to frustrate crime by discovering the next victim whom the killer sought!

Clyde Burke had suggested the making of a list. Cardona had followed the reporter's idea. Ostensibly, the plan was Burke's; apparently, the list was now Cardona's.

Actually, both the idea and its completion belonged to The Shadow. He had supplied the purpose; he had gained the copy that he needed.

Ten thousand names! Such was the list that The Shadow had acquired. With his sight of Cardona's clue, he was ready to put the list in use!

CHAPTER XVII
MOVES IN THE GAME

Two hours had passed. The blue light was burning in The Shadow's sanctum. Upon the table lay a torn fragment of paper. It was an exact replica of Cardona's clue. The Shadow had prepared it from memory:

Beside this reminder lay the stacked up papers of the list which The Shadow had taken from Cardona's office. Long-fingered hands were running down the columns of a final page.

A strange clock rested upon the table. Instead of hands, it showed marked circles which registered the passage of seconds, minutes and hours. Each second seemed to pause as though waiting The Shadow's order to depart. Meanwhile, the hands were finishing their task with untiring swiftness.

Though The Shadow's work was thorough, his rapid study of the listed names had been moving at the rate of one page a minute. Allowing for the time that it had taken for him to reach the sanctum, with brief minutes out for calls to Burbank, The Shadow had reached the finish of his survey in one hundred and twenty minutes.

With the last page checked, The Shadow gathered up the heap and deftly removed four pages. He spread these upon the table. Each page bore a mark—a penciled circle around a chosen name.

One page showed the marked name of Jerome Neville, with the telephone number Quadrangle 2-4138. Another revealed a circle about the name of Hiram Engliss, the telephone number Midtown 9-1362. The Shadow placed these pages aside.

The third page showed the marked name of Dudley Arment, with the telephone number Carmody 5-9213. The fourth also had a marked name: Clement Hessling, Riverview 6-3130.

Earphones clicked as The Shadow drew them from the wall. Burbank's quiet tone came across the wire:

"Burbank speaking."

"Report."

"Report from Marsland. He is at the apartment house where Clement Hessling lives in Greenwich Village. There is a party at Hessling's. Marsland on watch."

"Instructions. Marsland to remain on duty."

"Instructions received."

A pause; then came Burbank's next statement:

"Report from Vincent. He is stationed outside Tewksbury Court. Dudley Arment out of town. Expected back tonight."

"Instructions," ordered The Shadow. "Vincent to remain on duty until nine-thirty. Then to join Marsland."

"Instructions received," came Burbank's final reply.

A map of Manhattan came into view upon The Shadow's table. A long, white finger touched one spot; then another. The Shadow was picking the locations where Clement Hessling and Dudley Arment lived.

IN some remarkable fashion, The Shadow had picked these two men from the entire list of ten thousand. He had narrowed the total number of potential victims to four. Two had already died: Neville and Engliss. Two were still in danger: Hessling and Arment.

During his checking of the list, The Shadow had ordered agents on duty.

First, Harry Vincent to watch Dudley Arment, when The Shadow had selected Arment's name. Second: Cliff Marsland to guard Clement Hessling.

Should either of these possible victims be threatened, a stalwart aide of The Shadow would be there to encounter Shakes Niefan. The Shadow had found no other possible victims, according to his survey of the list. He had decided, therefore, to participate in person.

Why had he chosen Dudley Arment in preference to Clement Hessling? Only The Shadow knew; his soft laugh came in mocking tones as his fingers picked up the torn slip of paper which he had prepared as a duplicate of Cardona's clue.

Of two men, Dudley Arment was the one whom The Shadow intended to visit. Still planning to guard Clement Hessling, he was ordering Harry Vincent to join Cliff Marsland. Two agents would form a better guard than one.

The Shadow's finger pointed to a spot on the map. It marked the location of the Cobalt Club. It moved to the district where Dudley Arment's apartment was located—Tewksbury Court was the name of the big apartment house. This indicated that The Shadow would first travel to the club; then to Arment's uptown residence.

The dialed clock was nearing the hour of nine. Hands folded the map. The light clicked out. The sanctum was in darkness. A swish; then an eerie laugh. The Shadow had departed.

DOWN in Greenwich Village, Cliff Marsland was loitering beside the only entrance to the small apartment house where Clement Hessling lived. The sound of boisterous laughter was coming from opened windows in the second-story front. A party was in progress in Hessling's apartment.

A stroller stopped his pace on the other side of the street. His right hand shook as it raised a match to light a cigarette. The flame revealed the face of Shakes Niefan. Cliff, though he glanced across the street, did not observe the countenance because of the raised hand.

As he tossed the match away, Shakes glanced toward the lighted windows of Hessling's apartment. He heard the revelry. With a scowl, he moved along the street. He turned a corner, entered a telephone booth and made a call.

"Hello ..." Shakes announced himself by his

tone. "Yeah ... I'm down here... The guy's throwing a party ... Listen; what about the other bird? Suppose I go up there tonight and pick this fellow tomorrow ...

"You called his place, eh? I see... No answer... Well, maybe he'll be in when I get there ... Sure... If he isn't there, I'll come back here later on ..."

Shakes left the telephone booth. He sauntered from the store and walked at a rapid pace until he neared an entrance of the Eighth Avenue subway. Shakes descended.

IN his darkened room at the Hotel Morrisette, Lester Drayson, alias Martin Hyslop, was gazing from the window. The glow of his cigar kept flickering as the smoker took quick, short puffs.

Gazing to the street, Drayson saw a limousine pull up in front of Wimbledon's. Two men alighted. One was Commissioner Ralph Weston; the other was Detective Joe Cardona. An impatient growl came from Drayson's throat.

The hiding man sensed danger in this new visit. Well did Drayson know that through Wimbledon he could be brought to trial and convicted for his connection with the Universal Aircraft Corporation. Wimbledon in touch with the police commissioner. This was a repeated token that time could not be lost.

Moving back into the room, Drayson picked up the telephone. He hesitated; then replaced the instrument on the table. After a few impatient paces, he again picked up the telephone and spoke to the clerk below.

"Call that number again," he ordered. "Carmody 5-9213."

The number of Dudley Arment's telephone! While The Shadow and Shakes Niefan, each with a different purpose, were on their way to find if Arment had returned, Lester Drayson was choosing this method to learn if the man had returned home.

There had been a peculiar accent to Drayson's voice, when he had spoken to the clerk. Arment, should he be at home, would not recognize that tone, even though he might know Drayson's usual manner of speaking.

A few apologetic words—a bluff about a wrong number—these would suffice if Drayson chose to conceal his identity. But no need for such measures came. As Drayson waited, the clerk's voice responded with the statement that the number did not answer.

TEN minutes after Lester Drayson had made this futile call, a man appeared at the nearest corner to the towering building known as Tewksbury Court. Shakes Niefan, agent of death, had arrived to seek his newest victim: Dudley Arment.

CHAPTER XVIII
THE RETURN

"THE street is blocked, Mr. Cranston."

The statement came from the uniformed chauffeur in the front seat of Lamont Cranston's limousine. The man was speaking through the lowered window between the front and the back.

"All right, Stanley." The words were in Cranston's quiet tone. "I shall leave you here. Go up to the next street and turn down the further avenue. Wait for me at the corner of this street and the avenue."

"Very well, sir."

As Stanley spoke, the door opened and Lamont Cranston stepped to the street. The action was performed before the chauffeur could alight. As Stanley began to back the limousine, he looked in vain for signs of his master. Lamont Cranston had disappeared upon the darkened sidewalk.

There was a reason for his remarkable departure. A small bag lay in the back seat of the limousine. It was a bag that Cranston always carried in the car. The bag was empty. Entering the limousine as Lamont Cranston, The Shadow had taken cloak and hat from within that bag. In his black garb, he had alighted.

The street was under repair. An unexpected barrier had caused The Shadow to disembark a half block from his goal. This was the street in back of Tewksbury Court. The Shadow had chosen to make his entrance from this direction.

IN the lobby of Tewksbury Court, a young man was seated by a potted rubber plant. This was Harry Vincent, agent of The Shadow. Harry's eyes were roving constantly between two spots; a pigeonhole behind the clerk's desk; the clock above the desk itself.

The pigeonhole bore the number 18 M. That was the number of Dudley Arment's apartment. Mail showed in the pigeonhole, along with a key. That was the sign that Arment had not returned.

The long hand of the clock had reached its lowest point. Half past nine had arrived. Harry's vigil was ended. Rising, The Shadow's agent strolled from the lobby. He had called Burbank fifteen minutes before. He was following new instructions. Harry was to join Cliff Marsland.

Harry had not seen Shakes Niefan enter. He had not been looking for the killer. Harry had been appointed to cover Dudley Arment should the man return. Harry had fulfilled that duty.

The Shadow had arranged a clockwork schedule tonight. Two unforeseen factors had interfered. One was the closed street behind the large apartment house. That had delayed The Shadow, withholding his arrival to the final minute.

The other factor was the clock above the lobby desk. It was nearly five minutes fast. Harry Vincent had neglected to check the time. Hence, an interval occurred between the departure of Harry Vincent and the arrival of The Shadow.

At the very beginning of that interim, a middle-aged man walked into the lobby of Tewksbury Court. He approached the desk. The clerk nodded in greeting.

"Good evening, Mr. Arment," he said. "A pleasant trip?"

"Yes." Arment shifted a suitcase to the floor. "My key, please, and my mail."

Receiving these, Arment picked up the bag and entered a waiting elevator. He was whisked to the eighteenth floor. He walked down a hallway, past the shaft of the service elevator and unlocked the door of his apartment. He entered and turned on the living room light.

The room seemed stuffy. Arment opened a window to an inner courtyard. He recrossed the room and opened his suitcase. He brought out a small packet of folded papers, which he laid upon a table.

Next he unlocked a table drawer, using an oddly shaped key from a ring which he brought from his pocket. He took more papers from the drawer, added them to those on the table and delivered a satisfied smile.

Arment went through the letters that he had received from the clerk. One impressed him. He tore open the envelope and unfolded a sheet of paper. His mouth opened as his eyes stared.

Dropping the letter to the table, Dudley Arment reached for the telephone. His hand stopped before it had gained the instrument. A snarling voice brought the interruption. Arment looked up.

STANDING at the door of an inner room was a man in hat and overcoat. His eyes were shifting; his lips had a twitch. His right hand, shaking with a peculiar wobble, held a snub-nosed revolver.

The intruder had evidently entered before Arment had arrived. The sight of the revolver was disconcerting; the shake of the hand momentarily nullified Arment's qualms. Another glance at the man's face, however, convinced Dudley Arment that he faced a real menace.

"Don't mind these shakes," sneered the intruder. "That's what they call me—Shakes. Shakes Niefan. I don't mind telling you the name. You'll never spill it."

The killer was moving toward the table. Arment, his hands half-raised, was staring. Shakes changed to a circling course. Constantly facing his intended victim, the murderer gained the window and placed his gloved left hand upon the raised sash.

From where he stood, Dudley Arment could view both door and window. He was at one point of an imaginary triangle; Shakes Niefan was at the second; the door marked the third. Instinctively, Arment gazed toward the door.

"Stand where you are," growled Shakes. "There's nobody coming in that door. You latched it when you shut it. You aren't going out that way, either—not until they carry you out."

"What do you mean?" blurted Arment. "Do you intend to kill me?"

"I do," retorted Shakes, with an ugly grin. "With this window down, nobody's going to hear the shot. I'm leaving with those papers of yours—and you'll never tell anybody what they were about."

Shakes had paused in the delivery of this challenge. Again his gloved hand gripped the sash. Arment, in desperation, stared toward the door. A gasp of a different tone came from his lips.

The glass knob of the door was turning. Silently and almost imperceptibly, a motion was in progress. Someone on the other side had inserted key or pick into the lock; the latch was yielding and the knob was acting with it!

INSTANTLY, Dudley Arment realized his error. His gasp had been a tip-off to Shakes Niefan. Had Arment kept silent, all would have been well. The time that Shakes was taking to lower the window might have allowed the door to open.

Now, however, as Arment glanced again at Shakes, the killer was alert. He was staring at the doorknob. His left hand rested motionless upon the sash; his right hand was unconsciously turning its weapon toward the direction of the door. Forgetting Arment, Shakes was preparing for an unknown enemy.

Desperation brought action. With a wild effort, Dudley Arment sought to make up for his mistake. Shakes Niefan was momentarily off guard. That gave the opportunity. With a ferocious leap, Dudley Arment hurled himself across the room to grapple with Shakes Niefan.

The killer turned to meet the onslaught. Arment caught his wrist and thrust it upward. Swinging downward, Shakes delivered a vicious blow to Arment's head. The force of the stroke was hampered by the brakelike pressure of Arment's arm; but the metal of the gun, as it glanced from Arment's temple, had a stunning power.

Dudley Arment slumped. Shakes Niefan threw his left arm about the stunned man's body. Holding the helpless form as a shield, Shakes swung again to meet the menace from the door.

His action was not an instant too soon. The door had opened. Upon the threshold stood an avenging form in black. The Shadow, automatic in his gloved fist, had arrived to thwart the killer!

CHAPTER XIX
INTO THE NIGHT

SIX feet lay between The Shadow and the men by the window. The brief struggle between Dudley Arment and Shakes Niefan had given The Shadow the final moments required for his entrance. Though Shakes had commandeered Arment's body as a shield, The Shadow still possessed a slender advantage.

Shakes, as he was turning toward the door, had chosen the best course for his own protection. He was thrusting his gun beneath Arment's left arm, so that he might fire at the door. Had The Shadow waited for a moment, he would have lost all chance to rescue Dudley Arment. To cope with Shakes Niefan, he would have been forced to fire through Arment's body.

The Shadow knew this. He performed the unexpected. Seizing the short interval which still remained—the moments necessary for Shakes to fire—The Shadow sprang forward in a furious attack.

His left hand, picking the spot beneath Arment's arm, shot straight for Shakes Niefan's wrist. His right, dropping its automatic, caught Arment's body and whirled it from the killer's grasp.

Shakes fired. The hot tongue of the revolver flame seared the face beneath the cloak collar as the bullet blasted upward through the hat brim. The Shadow had turned the aim a fraction of an inch.

All mobsters feared The Shadow; but Shakes, a murderer to the end, forgot his dread. As his right wrist faltered in the viselike grasp, Shakes shot a hard blow with his left fist. It was a stroke that The Shadow could not parry.

The Shadow staggered as the punch landed below the hat brim. Dropping sidewise, he still managed to grip Shakes Niefan's wrist, while his free hand caught at the arm which had loosed the drive.

Shakes sought to deliver another jab. The Shadow's clutch prevented him. With both wrists clamped, Shakes gave a vicious twist. The Shadow's cloaked form went backward against the window ledge. Snarling, Shakes tried to force his enemy through.

The Shadow's left fist relaxed. That action changed the killer's purpose. With right wrist coming free, Shakes snapped backward and swung his gun directly toward The Shadow's hidden face.

THIS was the move on which The Shadow had counted. As Shakes pressed finger to trigger, The Shadow's hand tightened with a new twist. The gun barked. The bullet zimmed past The Shadow's shoulder, into the window frame. Then, as the twist increased, Shakes felt his fingers loosen. His revolver clattered to the floor.

The killer straightened with new fury. As The Shadow twisted sidewise, to avoid the danger of the low-silled window, Shakes launched his body forward with terrific power. Catching The Shadow off balance, he sent the black-garbed warrior sprawling.

The fighters grappled as they struck the floor. Shakes saw a long black arm stretch out to grip the automatic which lay three feet away. With a quick kick, Shakes sent the weapon skidding across the floor, past the spot where Dudley Arment, half-dazed, was raising himself to one elbow.

Then, as The Shadow locked for another grapple, Shakes introduced a trick that he had learned from his old pal, Strangler Hunn. The fighters were half risen; they were equal in their grapple; but The Shadow's back was toward the wall. With a furious thrust, Shakes hurled The Shadow's shoulders forward. The slouch hat struck the wall. The blow, though glancing, was sufficient for what Shakes Niefan wanted.

As The Shadow slumped, with loosening grip, Shakes Niefan wrenched free. He dove for his gleaming revolver, which lay on the floor by the window. Pouncing upon the weapon, he swung as he arose erect. Back to the window, he aimed for The Shadow.

The cloaked fighter had risen to his left knee, with his right arm stretched out as a support. His cloak had been ripped in the struggle; the tattered collar lay across his face. Above it, burning eyes peered from beneath the hatbrim.

His lost automatic still lay beyond Dudley Arment, who, in turn, had weakened and slumped to the floor. Shakes Niefan had been lucky, so far. He was out to kill before The Shadow could renew the struggle. Shakes had his revolver swinging into aim. The Shadow's automatic was far away from reach.

BUT Shakes had not reckoned with The Shadow's methods. Never did The Shadow rely upon a single weapon. Shakes, unknowingly, had played into The Shadow's trap. By freeing himself from The Shadow's grasp, he had given The Shadow a better opportunity than his own.

The Shadow's free left hand was swinging from beneath the folds of the black cloak. Shakes Niefan was too late. Before the forefinger of his steadying hand could press revolver trigger, the blackened muzzle of an automatic belched forth its message of retaliation.

The Shadow's left hand was perfect in its aim. The force of the bullet seemed to send Shakes tottering backward. The killer's arms flung upward. The revolver sped from nervous fingers. Shot close

His right … caught Arment's body and whirled it from the killer's grasp.

to the heart, Shakes lost his balance as he sprawled across the windowsill.

The murderer's body poised; then, helpless and lifeless, it toppled on the brink. Head foremost, Shakes Niefan's dead form went hurtling toward the courtyard, eighteen stories down. Into the darkness of the night, the murderer took the plunge that followed the death which he deserved.

A grim laugh sounded as The Shadow gained his feet. While his mockery whispered through the room, the black-garbed avenger glided forward and regained his first automatic. His burning eyes turned to the table. They saw the letter which Arment had read.

The laugh was repeated. This time, it came in a tone that told new understanding. One glance at the papers on Arment's table: The Shadow knew the story. Gathering letters and papers together, The Shadow turned toward Dudley Arment.

The rescued man was seated on the floor. His hand was pressed to the side of his head. Still groggy from the blow that Shakes had given him, Arment was trying to regain his faculties.

Papers and letters swept beneath The Shadow's cloak. The Shadow stopped and thrust his arm about Arment's body. He raised the stupefied man to his feet. While Arment aided with faltering steps, The Shadow dragged him swiftly into the hall and swung the door of the apartment shut.

The door of the service elevator was open. The Shadow pulled Arment into the car and closed the door. The elevator moved downward. Its drop was neatly timed. Five seconds after the departure of The Shadow and Dudley Arment, a regular elevator stopped at the eighteenth floor. Two attendants hurried to the door of Arment's apartment and began to pound upon it.

FRESH air revived Dudley Arment as The Shadow brought the man to the rear street. Yet Arment was still a bit bewildered. Instinctively, he allowed himself to be led along by this stranger who urged him to more rapid pace.

Eighty feet brought them to the corner of the avenue. Stanley, drowsing behind the wheel, looked up as he heard someone stagger into the rear of the car. Then came Cranston's voice from the darkness. Hearing his master's order, Stanley nodded. He started the motor as the rear door closed.

The window was shut between the front and the back. Dudley Arment, slumped in the comfortable cushions, found himself listening to a whispered voice that spoke in uncanny tones. Dully, Arment nodded his understanding. He clutched papers and letter that were thrust into his hand. Fumbling, he thrust them in an inside pocket.

A gloved hand rested on Arment's shoulders.

The other hand produced a small vial and pressed the bottle to Arment's lips. The rescued man gulped as he tasted a biting, pungent liquor. Then came a burning as new vigor possessed him.

As the car stopped, a hand reached forward and opened the door. Hidden lips hissed their command in a voice that Dudley Arment could do naught else but obey.

"Go! Do as I have ordered!"

Dudley Arment stepped to the curb. His head was swimming; he saw the limousine pull away. Then the dizziness ended. The potency of The Shadow's draught produced a swift effect. Dudley Arment steadied. His hand pressed against his pocket. His lips became firm. He studied his surroundings and nodded as he gained the location. He hailed a passing cab and entered.

The voice of Lamont Cranston was sounding through the speaking tube of the limousine. Stanley nodded and turned at the nearest corner. In the darkness of the limousine, a slouch hat tumbled into the opened bag; gloves fell into the inverted hat; then came the folds of the discarded black cloak.

The limousine took another corner. It rolled past the entrance to the Hotel Morrisette. It drew up in back of Commissioner Weston's big car. The door opened. Lamont Cranston stepped out. He ordered Stanley to await him. He ascended the steps of Roscoe Wimbledon's home.

Lester Drayson, staring from the darkness of his hotel room, observed the arrival of Lamont Cranston. He wondered why this new visitor had come.

Little did the watching fugitive realize what had happened at Dudley Arment's. Lester Drayson did not know that he was soon to learn the power that The Shadow held!

CHAPTER XX
THE FUGITIVE APPEARS

"MR. LAMONT CRANSTON is here, sir."

It was Harkin who made the announcement from the door of Roscoe Wimbledon's library. The president of the World Wide Aviation Company looked toward Police Commissioner Ralph Weston.

"Shall we have Cranston join us?" questioned Wimbledon. "Or shall I have Harkin tell him to wait?"

"Let him come in," decided Weston.

"I sent Ross Harlton to the testing field," stated Wimbledon, as soon as Harkin had departed, "because I did not think it wise for him to be at this conference. Of course, Commissioner, Cranston is a friend of yours, as well as mine. I suppose it is all right for him to enter."

"I think it is," declared Weston. "I remember

that Cranston gave us some excellent suggestions when he was here before. Perhaps, if we take him into our confidence—"

Weston paused. The door had opened. Lamont Cranston, quiet of demeanor and perfect in attire, was standing on the threshold.

"Good evening, Commissioner," greeted the arrival. "I thought I recognized your car outside the house. Good evening, Cardona."

With a quiet smile, Cranston stepped forward to shake hands with Roscoe Wimbledon, who had advanced to greet him. Then, before taking a chair, the visitor inquired:

"I am not intruding?"

"Not at all," asserted Weston. "Sit down, Cranston. Our conference may interest you. We are still on the subject of murder."

"No clues to the death of MacAvoy Crane?"

"Yes—and no. There have been two killings since then. Two men: Jerome Neville and Hiram Engliss have been slain. We fear that a second murderer is at work—following up the evil deed of Strangler Hunn."

"I believed that such might happen," Cranston spoke seriously as he leaned back in an armchair. "I noticed in the newspapers that Neville and Engliss were killed by the same gun. What connection have you found between the two men?"

WESTON glanced toward Cardona. The swarthy detective nodded. The naturalness of Cranston's statement answered a point that Cardona had been making; namely, that the thirteen clue had merit as the only link between two deaths.

"We have very little," stated Weston. "Cardona has noted that both Neville and Engliss had phone numbers that contained the number thirteen. He has obtained a list"—Weston raised a sheaf of papers from his lap—"of all such numbers in Manhattan. Our theory is that other murders are coming; that in this list we have the names of men who are threatened."

"And the list contains how many names?" quizzed Cranston.

"Ten thousand," replied Weston, glumly.

There was a pause. Roscoe Wimbledon shook his head. His attitude showed disappointment.

"Too bad," he remarked, "that Crane did not manage to communicate with me. Too bad that Drayson cannot be brought to justice. This list of names seems too hopeless."

"Ten thousand names." Cranston was speaking quietly. "Number thirteen. Can you tell me this, Commissioner: why did the number thirteen appear so significant?"

"Because it was in both telephone numbers," broke in Joe Cardona.

"So I understand," rejoined Cranston. "But from the importance that you attach to it, I can see that there is something behind it all. Some clue— some document—perhaps an incomplete notation— bearing the number thirteen."

Commissioner Weston stared at the speaker. Then he swung to Joe Cardona.

"Cranston has hit the bull's-eye," declared the commissioner. "If he can do that, he might have something better to tell us if he saw the clue itself. Show him that paper, Cardona."

The detective produced the folded envelope. He removed the paper fragment. He carried it to Cranston. The visitor studied it with interest. The Shadow had viewed that torn bit while guised as Fritz, the janitor. Seeing it now, in the guise of Cranston, he acted as though he had never observed it before.

"That paper," announced Weston, "was found in MacAvoy Crane's apartment. The scrawl—letters and figures wide apart—indicate that it was done by Strangler Hunn."

"The remains, I suppose, of a paper that Hunn destroyed?"

"Probably."

"And something, I assume, that Hunn copied from Crane's papers?"

"That is our assumption."

"Thirteen," mused Cranston. "Part of a telephone number. What do these letters mean above? M—E—N?"

"Something about men," stated Cardona. "Maybe a message like kill men with number thirteen telephones, or something to that effect."

"Write down the names of the two men who were murdered," suggested Cranston. "Put the proper telephone number beneath each name."

Cardona took a sheet of paper from Wimbledon's desk. The aircraft magnate and the police commissioner leaned forward in new interest as Cardona followed Cranston's order. The detective passed the notations to the millionaire. A thin smile came to Cranston's lips.

RISING, Cranston handed the torn bit of paper to Weston. Pointing to it, Cranston said:

"Those letters: M—E—N. Crudely formed and poorly spaced, they might be part of one word. On the contrary, a separation might be intended between them. M, for instance, or E, might end a word. The next letter might begin one."

"Yes," agreed Weston. "At the same time, they could all belong to one word—like 'men'—"

"I am not disputing that," interposed Cranston. "I merely wanted to call your attention to the fact that you have a more complete clue than the mere number thirteen. Look at these names."

He passed Weston the paper that Cardona had just written, with the names and telephone numbers:

Jerome Neville
Quadrangle 2-4138

Hiram Engliss
Midtown 9-1362

"The name 'Jerome,'" remarked Cranston, casually, "ends with the letters M and E. The name 'Neville' begins with the letter N. There you have it. M—E—N."

"Now look below. Hiram ends with M. Engliss begins with E; its next letter is N. Again the same rotation.

"That's it!" cried Weston, excitedly. "Look here, Cardona! The torn paper is explained! Strangler Hunn wrote a name—below it the telephone number!"

"Let me have your list, commissioner." Cranston took the sheaf of papers from Weston. "Yes, it would be a great task to kill off all people in New York who have a thirteen in their telephone numbers.

"But I should judge that we will find very few who have the M—E—N combination in their names. This is a double clue—based on your paper slip, Cardona. One man is wanted by the killers. So they have decided to eliminate all. Evidently they are taking no chances."

Cardona grabbed a copy of the list that was lying on Wimbledon's table. He began to run down the columns—something that Lamont Cranston was already doing.

"We can cut this list down to almost nothing!" exclaimed the detective. "We've got all the names with thirteen. I'm looking for names with M—E—N in—"

"Here's one," remarked Cranston. "Under letter A. Dudley Arment; telephone is Carmody 5-9213."

Writing the name and number on a sheet of paper, Cranston handed the data to Cardona. The detective stared at the information; then jumped to the telephone.

"I'm going to talk to this man Arment," he asserted, as he dialed the number. "I'll be foxy—he won't suspect anything. If he's at his place, I can go over there and find him—"

Cardona paused. A voice was clicking over the wire. Cardona parried with his conversation.

"Hello..." Cardona was planning to fake that he had the wrong number. "Is that you, George? What's that? ... No ... I think I've got the wrong number ... Yes ... You say George is there ... I mean George Jennings... He's there?"

Cardona lowered the phone and held the mouthpiece against his chest. He spoke in a low tone to Weston.

"I don't get this," admitted the detective. "I fake the name 'George'—they say they'll let me talk to him. So I fake George Jennings—they say that's the guy that's there—"

CARDONA broke off. The receiver was clicking. Weston and Wimbledon seemed puzzled. Cranston, making notations on sheets of paper, was unobserved as he enjoyed a quiet smile.

"George Jennings?" Cardona was inquiring. "My name?... Terry Drake ... Yes ... Where am I calling from? Say ..." Cardona's scowl suddenly changed. "Say ... Is that you, Inspector Klein? Yes ... This is Joe Cardona. I had a tip that there was going to be trouble where you are ... Yes ... Yes ... Right. I'll call back."

Cardona hung up. With a grim face, he turned to Weston. The commissioner was staring anxiously, awaiting the news.

"I was stalling" declared Cardona, "and so was Inspector Klein. It looks bad, commissioner. Man shot—thrown out the window eighteen stories into the courtyard. They think it's Dudley Arment. They're trying to identify the body."

"Another murder!" blazed Weston, rising. "The same clue. You're right, Cranston! They're killing innocent men to get the one they want. Neville, Engliss—now Arment—"

"Dudley Arment," interposed Cranston, "is the one the killers wanted. They did not need to murder Jerome Neville and Hiram Engliss."

"Why not?" queried Weston.

Cranston passed him three sheets of paper. On each one, the millionaire had printed a name and a telephone number, using capital letters. The papers read:

JEROME NEVILLE
QUADRANGLE 2-4138

HIRAM ENGLISS
MIDTOWN 9-1362

DUDLEY ARMENT
CARMODY 5-9213

"The name on one line," remarked Cranston. "The telephone number beneath. Probably the address below—that part was destroyed. Even allowing for Strangler Hunn's unique scrawl, it is obvious that Dudley Arment is the man.

"In his name, only, do the figures that form thirteen come directly beneath the letters M—E—N. You can search this entire list"—Cranston was tapping the sheaf which he held—"and you will probably fail to find another name that fills the requirement."

"If Arment has been killed!" exclaimed Cardona.

"It may not be his body that was found in the courtyard," suggested Cranston.

"If Dudley Arment is alive," shouted Weston, as he pounded Wimbledon's desk, "we'll find him. He is the key to all these crimes!"

"Why Arment?" questioned Wimbledon. "I have told you that Lester Drayson is the man in back of it. Why not find Drayson?"

"We shall find both!" announced Weston. "Every man of the force will be searching for them. I'll start the search tonight. Lester Drayson and Dudley Arment—"

"A search will not be necessary," came a sarcastic tone from the door.

Commissioner Weston wheeled to stare at two men who had entered during the excitement. One, with black hair and black mustache, was holding a leveled revolver. The other, middle-aged, was pale-faced as he stood unarmed beside his companion.

Joe Cardona had turned with Ralph Weston. Like the commissioner, the detective was startled. Roscoe Wimbledon was rigid behind his flat-topped desk, his hands spread on the woodwork while he glared at the intruders.

Only Lamont Cranston appeared unperturbed. In leisurely fashion, the millionaire was raising a match to light a cigarette. The sight of the revolver did not trouble him. Like a playwright watching a drama of his own creation, The Shadow was ready to enjoy the coming scene.

CHAPTER XXI
DRAYSON SPEAKS

"WHO are you?"

The challenge came from Commissioner Ralph Weston as he faced the leveled gun. The man at the door had finger set on trigger. The moving muzzle of the revolver warned all to hold their ground.

"I am Lester Drayson." The intruder raised his free hand to brush back his dyed hair. "I am the man for whom you have been searching. I have come to end the search."

"Heed my warning!" countered Weston. "You are wanted for fraud and murder—"

"No more words!" Drayson's fierce statement brought silence. "I am here to speak. Until I have finished, no one can interrupt me. Since I am wanted for murder"—Drayson's lips were scornful—"I promise you that I can shoot to kill. After I have told my story—then you may decide your answer."

Drayson paused to glare in challenge. Every member of the group was silent. Weston and Cardona were tense with suppressed rage. Wimbledon had paled. Cranston's firm-set visage had alone retained its calm.

"I have returned to New York," announced Drayson, in a cold tone, "to find a man named Dudley Arment. I have been living here under the name of Martin Hyslop, at the Morrisette Hotel. I have been evading the law because I have been awaiting Arment's return.

"Dudley Arment was once my secretary. He still served as my confidential man. When the Universal Aircraft scandal broke, I was in Chicago. Arment wired me to flee. I reached Canada. There, I received further word from Arment.

"Jackson Gleek, general manager of Universal, had been working to swindle Universal Aircraft. Falsified books, cheapened materials, faked expenses—all were his work. All the while, he was but the tool. A bigger man than Gleek was behind it. A man who was clever enough to know that by planting the blame on me, he could gain further millions.

"I wrote to Arment. I told him to await my return; to hold the papers which he had; to get more evidence outside of New York. He was not in town when I arrived. I sent another letter to his hotel, telling him where he could reach me."

Lester Drayson paused. Stepping aside, but with revolver still in readiness, he used his free hand to indicate the man beside him.

"This man," he announced, "is Dudley Arment. He has gathered the final documents—papers which will support my story—authentic letters received by Jackson Gleek from the master crook behind a game of crime. He has brought them for you, Commissioner Weston."

AT a sign from Drayson, Arment advanced and handed the documents to Weston. Drayson's gun still pointed its challenge, but the man's eyes no longer followed Weston. They were gazing straight across the room, toward Roscoe Wimbledon.

Joe Cardona shifted his hand to his pocket. Unobserved by Drayson, the detective began to draw a gun. To Weston, who was studying the papers, he mumbled:

"Be ready, Commissioner. I'm going to fire on this guy."

"No, no!" exclaimed Weston, suddenly. He looked up and gripped Cardona's arm. "Don't touch Drayson! These papers prove his story. There is the man we want!"

The commissioner was pointing to Roscoe Wimbledon. The man behind the desk was livid. Afraid to move because of Drayson's gun, he could only scowl in fury when he heard Weston's statement.

"Cover Wimbledon," ordered the commissioner.

Cardona obeyed. Weston turned to Drayson.

"Your case is here," asserted the commissioner, tapping the papers. "We shall take care of Roscoe Wimbledon. You will have the opportunity to testify against him. Deliver up your gun, Drayson."

The man at the door stepped forward and gave

his revolver to the commissioner. Weston tossed it in a chair. Drayson appeared both apologetic and relieved.

"They tried to murder Arment tonight," he explained. "Some unknown rescuer battled with the killer and Arment escaped. He came to me. I had seen your car from my window. The best course was to come here. I feared Wimbledon, however. Had I been unarmed, he might have shot me, before I could explain; hoping to justify himself because the law was seeking me."

"I understand," nodded Weston. "Your course was a radical one, Drayson, but it at least assured you of the hearing that you deserved."

Lamont Cranston was smiling. Drayson had not mentioned that the visit here had been suggested by Arment, who was acting under instructions that his mysterious rescuer had given him. The Shadow had arranged this climax, almost to the detail.

ROSCOE WIMBLEDON had steadied. The exposed crook had feared Lester Drayson's wrath. With Cardona covering him, Wimbledon was not afraid to talk. He blurted forth denouncing statements.

"Forged papers!" was his cry. "Those are the documents that Drayson has brought you. You are treating with a crook, Commissioner. Drayson is a fugitive from justice—a branded thief—a murderer—"

For a moment, Weston wavered. He had been convinced by Drayson's statements. Now he was on the verge of listening to Wimbledon's logic. It was Lamont Cranston who intervened.

"MacAvoy Crane was murdered," came Cranston's statement. "Why? Because he had learned the name of the one man who could aid Lester Drayson. Crane was honest. Had he seen that his investigation led to Dudley Arment's death, he would have spoken.

"So it was necessary to destroy Crane's evidence. It was necessary also to eliminate Crane. Strangler Hunn did that work; acting under orders, he wrote down the only data that he needed—the name, telephone number and address of Dudley Arment, the man whom Crane had learned was Drayson's secretary."

Cranston was speaking to Weston. The commissioner was nodding his agreement.

"Wimbledon hired Crane," resumed Cranston. "Wimbledon ordered Crane's death. That was paradoxical; therefore, it proved deceiving. Strangler Hunn destroyed his own notation. All that was left was the bit of paper that Cardona found as a clue. To whom did you show that paper, Cardona?"

"Only to the commissioner," replied Cardona, "and to Wimbledon here. They were the only ones that saw it, until—"

"Until you showed it to me," interposed Cranston, quietly.

Cardona nodded. He had been about to mention the name of Clyde Burke. Cranston had intervened in time to stop him.

"Wimbledon," asserted Cranston, facing the man behind the desk, "your guilt is proven. Why should any one follow the method of killing men whose names had the letters M—E—N and whose telephone numbers contained the figure 13?

"Only one man would have chosen that method. You are the man—the only one who saw the clue and who recognized its meaning. You blundered when you ordered the deaths of Jerome Neville and Hiram Engliss. I mentioned that fact before Drayson arrived."

"How could I have found those names?" stammered Wimbledon. "Where was I to get the numbers—"

Cranston's tall form was beside the desk. Long fingers gripped a knob. A drawer came open. Cranston's hand pulled forth a stack of papers.

"Here is the final evidence." Cranston passed the crumpled sheaf to Weston. "Wimbledon formed a list of his own. He had four days to work on it between the time that you first came here, Commissioner, and the night when Jerome Neville was slain."

Commissioner Weston was thumbing the papers. Lamont Cranston had guessed aright. This list, like the one that the telephone company had prepared in short order, was formed of names with number thirteen listings.

MORE damaging was an attached sheet which Weston discovered with the sheaf. It bore four names, with telephone numbers. Jerome Neville, Hiram Engliss, Dudley Arment and a fourth that Weston had not known: that of Clement Hessling.

"One more point." Cranston was emphatic with his final statement. "The compilation of this list was a private job; but it would have required the work of two persons to be completed within four days.

"I know now why Roscoe Wimbledon and Ross Harlton went into continued seclusion. Presumably, they were making a technical survey of the affairs of Universal Aircraft. Actually, they were preparing this murderer's list. There's another man you want, Commissioner. Ross Harlton, accessory to the murders of Jerome Neville and Hiram Engliss—"

Lamont Cranston paused suddenly and swung to the door. The others followed his move. Keen ears had caught the sound of footsteps just in time. Standing in the doorway, his face glowering above the barrel of a raised revolver, was Ross Harlton.

Roscoe Wimbledon's accomplice had returned unexpectedly. From the hallway, he had sensed the truth. He was here to thwart the law; here to save Roscoe Wimbledon, the master crook whose schemes he had abetted!

CHAPTER XXII
THE BREAK

THE arrival of Ross Harlton was the final proof of Roscoe Wimbledon's treachery. Lester Drayson, with Dudley Arment's documents at hand, had launched the accusation against the master crook. The Shadow—speaking as Lamont Cranston—had driven home denouncing arguments.

Ross Harlton, here to use force in rescue of his chief, had brought opportunity to Roscoe Wimbledon. The plotting president of World Wide Aviation had no chance to clear his blackened name, but Harlton's unexpected aid offered him a way to freedom.

Of the five men who had cornered Roscoe Wimbledon, only Joe Cardona had a gun in readiness. Warned of danger, the moment that he saw Lamont Cranston turn, Cardona swung to the door and aimed for Ross Harlton.

One prompt shot from the detective's gun could end this attempt at rescue. The Shadow recognized that fact upon the instant. Playing the part of Lamont Cranston, he stood and watched, relying upon Cardona's ability to down the foeman at the door.

Ross Harlton had picked Cardona as the man whom he must meet. He saw the revolver in the detective's hand. Springing inward from the doorway, Harlton swung his gun in Cardona's direction: He was too late to beat the detective to the shot. Cardona fired.

The shot went wide by inches only. Cardona, deviating his aim when Harlton lunged, missed his mark by a scant margin. An instant later, Harlton's gun barked. Cardona dropped, a bullet in his shoulder.

Roscoe Wimbledon was yanking open a drawer at the left of the desk. From it, he was snatching a revolver. Trusting to Harlton for the present, the arch-crook grabbed his gun and sprang for a doorway at the far left corner of the room.

Commissioner Weston was drawing a revolver. He was the second enemy whom Harlton had to face. The murderous technician swung to cover the commissioner. This time the odds lay all with Harlton. His aim was completed while Weston's gun was half way from the commissioner's pocket.

THE SHADOW was acting. The instant that he had seen Cardona drop, he knew what was coming. Yet in this crisis, The Shadow had not forgotten his part—that of Lamont Cranston.

As Cardona toppled, The Shadow sprang forward, directly toward the chair into which Commissioner Weston had tossed Lester Drayson's revolver. As Harlton and Weston swung to begin their savage duel, the long arm of Lamont Cranston swept upward with a rapid aim.

Harlton's finger was on the trigger. It never pressed to send the death shot toward Ralph Weston. The Shadow's delivery was a split-second in advance. Drayson's discarded gun was a puny .32—but The Shadow used it with the same effect as a huge automatic.

The revolver barked. A bullet clipped Harlton's aiming wrist. The technician staggered backward with a cry as his own gun fell from his helpless hand. An instant later, Weston's gun blazed its belated message. Ross Harlton sprawled on the floor, mortally wounded.

In those fractions of seconds, The Shadow had performed a double action. Not only had he fired the shot that saved Weston's life; he was also on the move for the next event in the exciting conflict.

As he pressed the trigger of Drayson's .32, The Shadow dropped sidewise behind the armchair from which he had seized the gun. The act was timely. Roscoe Wimbledon, wheeling from the far doorway, had aimed at the very instant of The Shadow's shot. Wimbledon's gun blazed. A bullet whistled across the chair, past the very spot from which Lamont Cranston's tall form had made its sudden fadeaway.

As Wimbledon stood momentarily bewildered, the figure of Cranston bobbed up erect beyond the chair. The hand that held the .32 swung for new aim, while Wimbledon stood flat-footed in the doorway. The master crook was a perfect target. The Shadow's finger was on the trigger of the revolver.

Then came unexpected aid. Harkin, arriving at the door of the library, was just in time to see Lamont Cranston rising to new aim. With Wimbledon the target, the servant acted to save his crooked master. The Shadow had turned with back toward the door. Harkin, leaping furiously, landed upon his shoulders and clutched wildly at the aiming hand.

The revolver spat flame too late. The servant had destroyed the aim. The Shadow's bullet found its lodging place in the door frame above Wimbledon's shoulder. As Harkin bore Cranston's body toward the floor, Wimbledon, seeing opportunity, aimed low to deliver a return shot.

AGAIN, The Shadow acted. The instant that Harkin fell upon him, the master fighter sought to bring quick end to the attack. His right hand dropped the revolver; it rose, with the left, to grip Harkin by the neck.

Knees on the floor, The Shadow lunged his shoulders forward. Harkin's body described a huge somersault that catapulted him over The Shadow's head. Sprawled, almost in a seated posture, the servant landed on the floor. He was the shield when Roscoe Wimbledon fired.

Just too late to clip the stooped form of Lamont Cranston, Wimbledon's bullet found its mark in Harkin's body. Catching the collapsing servant with his left hand, The Shadow snatched for the gun with his right. Still shielded, he was seeking opportunity for another shot at Wimbledon.

Had Wimbledon held his ground, he would have become The Shadow's prey. Another attack caused the crook to resort to flight instead. While Lester Drayson and Dudley Arment had taken shelter— Drayson in a closet and Arment behind a desk— Commissioner Ralph Weston was turning in response to Wimbledon's shot at Cranston.

Weston opened fire in a hurry. His bullets peppered the doorway. Wimbledon, unable to aim toward two enemies at once, decided to leap for shelter. He slammed the heavy door in back of him. Weston, pounding forward, reached the barrier just as the lock turned.

Two policemen came dashing into the library. Weston's chauffeur had heard the shots. He had given an alarm. The commissioner ordered the bluecoats to take up the pursuit. They hurried in chase of Wimbledon.

While Drayson and Arment, coming from hiding, were giving first aid to Joe Cardona, Weston seized the telephone and put in a call to headquarters. Hardly had he finished with his orders when one of the policemen arrived back in the library.

"He's made a getaway, Commissioner," informed the officer. "Out through the back—he drove off in a car that was parked out there."

"Harlton's car!" exclaimed Weston. He turned to Lamont Cranston, who was examining the wound of the servant, Harkin. "Where can Wimbledon have fled? How can we stop him?"

"Harlton came from the Universal testing field," remarked Cranston. "There are ships there. Wimbledon is a skilled pilot—"

"We'll call the testing field!" declared Weston. "We'll stop Wimbledon before he can take off—"

"The field has been closed," interrupted Cranston. "There are watchmen there; but I understand that the telephone has been disconnected."

"Come along!" Weston seized Cranston's arm. "We'll start there in my car. Call headquarters"— this was to the policeman—"and tell them where I've gone. Order out cars—and planes and—"

EAGER for the chase, Weston dragged Cardona with him. The commissioner was talking excitedly as they reached the street.

"The testing field is out on Long Island!" he exclaimed. "Further than the regular airport. It will take Wimbledon half an hour. Come with me, Cranston—"

The commissioner paused abruptly beside his car. Lamont Cranston was wavering. He had clapped his right hand to his left shoulder. His face seemed pale by the light of the streetlamp.

"What's the matter?" questioned Weston. "Are you wounded, Cranston?"

"Slightly," came the weak reply. "That shot of Wimbledon's—it must have grazed me—"

He stopped; then waved to a uniformed chauffeur. It was Stanley. Leaving Weston, Cranston half staggered toward his own car.

"Go ahead, Commissioner," he called, as he leaned on Stanley for support. "My chauffeur will get me home—or to a hospital—"

Weston hesitated as he saw Stanley aid Cranston into the millionaire's limousine. Two patrolmen were alighting from a car. Weston waved one into the house; he told the other to accompany him.

"All right, Cranston," he shouted. "Take care of yourself, old man. I'm going after Wimbledon."

The commissioner's car shot away. Lamont Cranston's limousine followed a few moments later. A soft laugh sounded from the interior. A firm voice spoke through the speaking tube. Stanley was startled by this evidence of his master's recovery. The chauffeur, like the commissioner, had not detected that the wound had been feigned.

"To the airport, Stanley," came Cranston's order. "Long Island. In a hurry."

Black garments came from the bag. Heavy automatics clicked. The Shadow's laugh came in a weird, reverberating whisper.

The regular airport was nearer than the testing field. Lamont Cranston's private plane was at the airport. The Shadow, despite his delayed start, could be in the air as soon as Roscoe Wimbledon.

While Police Commissioner Ralph Weston was hurrying in pursuit; while orders were out to have police cars take up the chase and for police planes to follow with their own pursuit, The Shadow was turning to a plan of his own making.

Should Roscoe Wimbledon, master of theft and murder, escape the closing meshwork of the law, he would find another foe to bar his path to safety.

The Shadow, relentless when he dealt with men of crime, was on his way to block the arch-crook's flight.

CHAPTER XXIII
ABOVE LONG ISLAND

A COUPE came to a jolting stop in front of a heavy gate. Headlights, cutting a swath through the metal bars, revealed the flat acreage of the Universal Aircraft testing field.

Roscoe Wimbledon had arrived at the destination which The Shadow had declared. Fortune had favored the fleeing crook. Not only had he evaded all pursuit; he had reached his goal before the police had managed to get there.

The automobile horn honked raucously. A sleepy watchman appeared beyond the gate. Again the horn; the watchman seemed to recognize its tones. He opened the barrier. The coupé rolled through.

After closing the gate, the watchman came back to the car. He could not see its occupant in the dark; he took it for granted that Ross Harlton was in the coupé. He climbed on the running board as a hand beckoned.

"Where are the pursuit planes?" came a voice. "Take me to their hangar."

"Who are you?" demanded the watchman. "You're not Mr. Harlton."

"I'm Roscoe Wimbledon," retorted the man at the wheel. "Harlton couldn't come with me. Hurry—show me the hangar."

"Over there, sir. Third on the right."

The coupé started forward. Since government tests had revealed faulty ships, this testing field had been closed. Ross Harlton, technician for World Wide Aviation, had been allowed admission since the new owners had taken over Universal.

Harlton's inspection had been largely confined to the Paraguayan planes which Washington had condemned. It was natural that Roscoe Wimbledon, president of World Wide Aviation, should come here to view the faulty ships.

Yet the watchman could not understand the reason for so late a visit. A second watchman also appeared as the coupé pulled up in front of the hangar. The first man's explanation that this was Roscoe Wimbledon was satisfactory to the second.

"Open the hangar!" ordered Wimbledon. "Show me the plane that Harlton has ready for a test!"

The watchman obeyed. The lights came on. A trim, one-seated plane was ready for flight. Wimbledon snapped another order:

"Bring it out!"

Reluctantly, the watchman obeyed. One of them voiced an objection as he aided in the wheeling.

"You can't go up in this ship, Mr. Wimbledon. The field lights are disconnected. Mr. Harlton can't even make a test until he gets word from Washington—"

"My company owns this field," snapped Wimbledon. "I've received the government permission. I'm testing this ship tonight. Spin the propeller!"

WITH these words, Wimbledon clambered into the plane. He found a loaded machine gun in readiness.

He muttered in satisfied fashion as he examined the controls. This ship, fueled and ready for flight, had been arranged by Ross Harlton. It had been planned to carry two in case of emergency. Wimbledon, alone, was taking it tonight.

"Spin the propeller!"

As the watchmen hesitated on the ground, a whining siren sounded beyond the gate. The lights of a car showed through the bars. Pursuers had arrived.

"Police!" cried the first watchman.

"Say—maybe they're after you—maybe you aren't Roscoe Wimbledon—"

"I'm Wimbledon!" came the snarl. "Spin that propeller."

"You can wait," growled the watchman. "Stay here, Jack. I'll let the cops in. Watch this guy."

"You bet I will, Mac," responded the second watchman. "Beat it to his gate."

Wimbledon arose from the pilot's seat. He clicked a flashlight. Its glare showed Jack's running form. With a growl, Wimbledon aimed his revolver and fired. Jack stumbled to the ground and rolled over, wounded.

"You're next!" snarled Wimbledon as he swung the light on Mac. "Spin that propeller or I'll drill you!"

Raising his hands, the watchman sprang to the front of the plane. He feared Wimbledon's threat. He seized a blade of the propeller. Shots burst from beyond the gate. The range was long; but the fire of the police gave Mac new impetus. They were firing at him as well as Wimbledon. He wanted to get clear of the mess.

The motor roared. Mac leaped aside and flung himself flat upon the ground as the trim pursuit plane started across the testing field.

Wimbledon was familiar with the controls. The ship took off within fifty yards. Going away from the gate, heading into a helpful breeze, Wimbledon was freeing himself from the clamoring pursuit of the police below.

Circling to gain a course, Wimbledon saw lights approaching in the air. A glaring searchlight found the rising monoplane. A police plane was sweeping up to challenge the escaping crook.

Wimbledon opened fire with the machine gun. The drilling sound of the weapon was music above the roar of the plane. Wimbledon snarled gloatingly as he saw the police plane skid into a bank. They had not expected this opposition.

A second police plane was approaching. Again the *rat-tat-tat* of the machine gun. The second ship swerved. Like the first, it was sweeping away to escape the fire. Wimbledon, his hands on the controls, swung to the straightaway course he wanted.

He knew that the police planes would follow. His fire had not crippled them. But he knew also that they could never catch this ship in which he was fleeing. These Paraguayan ships, despite their cheapened construction, had been built for speed. That was the only test which they were sure to stand.

WIMBLEDON and his henchmen, Gleek and Harlton, had agreed that other faults would pass unnoticed until after delivery. In their swindling of the Universal Aircraft Corporation, they had confined their efforts to other points of plane construction. Wimbledon was glad of it now.

Clear air showed a path to safety. Miles from New York, Wimbledon could land at some lonely spot and continue his escape unthwarted. The Canadian border was a possible goal. As the ship sped forward, Wimbledon snarled his elation.

Then came a roar from the left. Wimbledon heard it despite the rumble of his own motor. The beam of a searchlight clipped downward from the sky.

Another ship!

Swooping in from the direction of the Long Island airport, this challenger seemed determined to cut off the fugitive's flight. A swift monoplane, capable of equaling Wimbledon's speed, this was a menace greater than the police who had dropped behind.

Wimbledon opened fire. He realized that it was no use. The daring pilot of the other ship was heading straight for the pursuit plane. Unless Wimbledon took some other action, this suicidal drive would lock the two ships in midair!

FROM his seat in the approaching plane, The Shadow was hurtling squarely into Wimbledon's fire. He knew what the result would be should Wimbledon persist to handle the machine gun. Only seconds remained before the moment when the two ships would join in a double plunge to the ground below. But The Shadow was unyielding in his course. His keen brain told him that Wimbledon would lose his nerve.

A weird laugh sounded from The Shadow's hidden lips. The machine-gun fire had ended. Wimbledon, grabbing the controls, was taking heroic efforts to avoid a crash. The pursuit plane seemed to hurtle in the air as Wimbledon threw it into a sidewise roll to avoid The Shadow's swoop.

The maneuver was successful. The pursuit plane seemed to lurch upward as the nose of The Shadow's ship approached it. Twisting above the attacker, Wimbledon's roll continued as The Shadow passed.

The Shadow banked. Staring from his ship, he could see the finish of Wimbledon's roll. This maneuver, carrying tremendous strain, was more difficult than the stunt which had carried a naval aviator to doom in one of those condemned planes.

Struts snapped as Wimbledon's twist neared its end. One wing of the pursuit plane broke loose from the body of the ship. The other wing remained. Going into a crazy spin, the crippled plane shot downward toward the ground.

The Shadow saw the climax of the plunge. The one-winged plane crumpled as it landed in an open field. Searing flames flared upward as spattered gasoline produced a holocaust. The Shadow's sweeping ship straightened to its course as police planes came zooming toward the wreckage.

Again, a weird laugh sounded as The Shadow's swift monoplane took course back toward the airport. The tones that sounded with the thrumming of the motor were notes of strident triumph.

Roscoe Wimbledon, crook and murderer, had hurtled to deserved doom. His crash was of his own making. He had paid the penalty for his scheme that had brought ill-gotten wealth.

The burning plane was a pyre; The Shadow's laugh a parting knell. The Shadow had dropped the final curtain upon a murderer's career.

THE END

Coming soon in **THE SHADOW #68:**

The Shadow and Margo Lane (in her pulp debut) confront the deadly lightning of Thor, *The Thunder King*. Then, the Knight of Darkness investigates the strange machinations of the Secret Six whose giant sapphire, *The Star of Delhi.* is the centerpiece for serial murders.

Plus **an ORSON WELLES radio classic, "The Witch Drums of Salem"**

INTERLUDE by Will Murray

This volume of The Shadow delves into the Dark Avenger's background as an aviator.

Walter B. Gibson recalled that from the beginning, his initial Street & Smith editor, Frank E. Blackwell, wanted The Shadow to be a pilot.

Gibson recalled, "They had an idea, roughly, of a character they wanted. They wanted him to travel by a fast kind of airplane. He would go to scenes of crimes and things of that sort. They were all just suggestions."

So Walter gave his hero a background as a World War One aviator. During the Great War—as they called it back then—The Shadow received his baptism of fire as an combat ace.

This was first alluded to in the debut novel, *The Living Shadow,* wherein an underworld character makes the following report:

"I seen The Shadow again," said Spotter eagerly. "Down by the Pink Rat. This time I looked for his face. I saw nothing but a piece of white that looked like a bandage. Maybe The Shadow ain't got no face to speak of. Looked like the bandage hid something in back. There was a young guy once who the crooks were afraid of—he was a famous spy in the War—and they say he was wounded over in France—wounded in the face. I think The Shadow is this guy come back—

Several formative Shadow novels suggested that the crimson collar of that sinister black cloak concealed gruesome facial disfigurement, an idea Gibson eventually abandoned without explanation.

The notion of a pilot protagonist made sense in an era when Charles Lindbergh had only recently made the first daring Atlantic crossing by plane. A new breed of flying pulp heroes was emerging, whose exploits were filling the pages of *Wings, Flying Aces, Sky Birds, Zoom* and other ephemeral pulp magazines.

But there were other, more practical considerations for freighting the new crimebuster with such an heroic backstory.

As he developed in those formative years of 1931-33, The Shadow was a creature who haunted the New York underworld. In his guise as millionaire sportsman Lamont Cranston, he lived in New Jersey. Traveling in and around the island of Manhattan was not something one needed a monoplane to accomplish! The nearest landing fields were in Long Island and New Jersey. The best Manhattan had to offer was seaplane terminal on the Hudson River. An airplane would only be an impediment to getting around efficiently.

Over time, Gibson decided that The Shadow's air travel needs could be met by adopting an emerging new technology, the autogiro. Predecessor of the modern helicopter, it could take off and land in confined spaces. Over the years, the Dark Avenger graduated from the basic open-cockpit winged autogyro to the wingless cabin job that best suited most Shadow-style operations, such as landing on flat city rooftops. But for long-distance hops, the autogiro simply did not have sufficient range. So once in a while the versatile Master Avenger trundled out his black monoplane.

Death Clue finds The Shadow bringing this unidentified mystery plane out for a climactic aerial battle over the spires of Manhattan. Here, he gives us an early glimpse of the true man under the ebony cloak, Kent Allard.

That revelation of The Shadow's true identity is still five years in the future. But the skills that made The Shadow a great pilot during his war years and beyond are very much in evidence.

In one memorable 1933 case, *The Shadow's Shadow,* Maxwell Grant sketches in a rough history for the Master Avenger, but without naming him.

The story was recounted by former spy Felix Zubian:

"During the War," continued Zubian, "I learned of the existence of a most remarkable person—one who was presumably an aviator in the air forces of the United States. I heard him called The Black Eagle, because of his penchant for flying at night.

A STREET & SMITH MAGAZINE

THE Shadow

FEB. 1ST NUMBER 1933

10 CENTS

MAGAZINE
TWICE-A-MONTH

THE SHADOW'S SHADOW

Will Murray and Walter Gibson

"On one occasion, The Black Eagle was shot down. His role immediately changed; instead of an aviator, he became a secret agent within the enemy lines. His final coup came when he located and mapped an enemy air base, escaping at the last moment in a plane of the German air squadron, flying in safety back to the American lines.

"After the war, The Black Eagle was still alive. I have often wondered what became of him. Now, I believe I know. He, the victor of a hundred strange encounters on land and in the air, has taken on a new identity. He is known as The Shadow."

As if in confirmation of Spotter's theory, when The Shadow confronts Zubian in their climax, the former's face is revealed. The enemy spy recoils in horror at the undescribed sight—something that happened to other foes upon whom the Master of Mystery bestowed the sight of his uncloaked visage.

No doubt Gibson was inspired by "Lucky" Lindberg's other nickname, "the Lone Eagle," although it might have been just as appropriate if Allard had been known as The Black Bat. When Allard chose to tell his own history in *The Shadow Unmasks*, he referred to his wartime *nom de guerre* as The Dark Eagle. Well, The Shadow would know...

Walter Gibson submitted this story as "The Death Clue" in August of 1933. Under the title, *Death Clew*, it first saw print in the May 15, 1934 issue of *The Shadow Magazine*.

Why the weird spelling of the word "clue"? Street & Smith had a house stylebook, said to be as good as the *New York Times* stylebook. Since S&S went back to dime novel days, they employed it well into the 20th century a number of outdated spellings. "Clew" was one. When S&S purchased the Depression-bankrupt Clayton Magazine chain in 1934, they acquired Clayton's top mystery magazine, 2this led to some consternation:

> When I was hired at Street & Smith, they had a stylebook. Blackwell drummed it into you. Their editorial policy was that everything had to be written accordingly. […] For damn, you had to write d—n. Gray was never grey. Clews was never clues. When we bought *Clues* there was turmoil.

Inevitably, it was decided to adopt the modern spelling.Since Walter Gibson detested the old spelling, and it was so antiquated that 21st century readers are unlikely to recognize it, we've taken the unusual step of modernizing the title. Walter would have preferred it that way. He detested the old spelling.

Xitli, God of Fire continues the return of Kent Allard after a hiatus of more than a year. He had bowed out of the series with *Silver Skull* in 1939, and for a long time it seemed as if Maxwell Grant—not to mention The Shadow—had forgotten he ever existed. Revived in the climactic Shadow Vs. Shiwan Khan story, *Masters of Death* in 1940,

Allard has been transformed from a celebrated aviator to a fading celebrity who now walks with a cane. The Shadow's raconteur now calls him "a forgotten skybird."

Gibson explains the rise and fall of Kent Allard, at least as a public face for The Shadow:

> In the novel titled *The Shadow Unmasks*, the real Lamont Cranston was injured in a British air crash, forcing The Shadow to revert to his true self. That of an aviator named Kent Allard, who had disappeared in a flight over the Guatemalan jungle years before. The Shadow took off secretly for Yucatan and emerged from the wilds with two bodyguards from a tribe of Xinca Indians who had presumably worshipped him as a "bird god" during those lost years, though actually he had been combating crime as The Shadow, all that while. In due course, The Shadow reverted to the Cranston guise but occasionally switched to Allard, one advantage being that he could team with the real Cranston, who by now was familiar with The Shadow's ways and always willing to go along with them. In due course, The Shadow reverted more and more to the Cranston role, so that Allard became almost forgotten. Except on rare occasions when his identity could prove useful in diverting crooks from Cranston's trail. In the opinion of some readers, The Shadow apparently "felt more comfortable when he was Cranston," but perhaps it was the readers who felt that way. Whatever the case, it worked out as intended.

Kent Allard

For all readers ever knew, Allard and his loyal Xinca Indian bodyguards might well have retired to Yucatan. Well, in this story the Dark Eagle does return to the primitive tribe that once hailed him as a White God.

In his promotion of this tale, editor John L. Nanovic focused on the setting, writing, "… we think this is one of the most unusual Shadow novels we've been able to give you thus far. The scene is in New Orleans, which has enough color and background to make any story doubly interesting. Furthermore, Maxwell Grant is familiar with all parts of New Orleans, not just the sections that are visited by tourists, and he can give you this atmosphere as no other writer is able to."

Walter visited the Big Easy every other year or so for short periods, usually in connection with one of his magician cohorts. He went there with the Great Raymond in 1931 and returned in '36 in the company of Blackstone the Magician. During the winters Gibson sojourned in Florida, it was an easy matter to pop over to Louisiana by train or car.

One of the Shadow's most-used cover identities, that of businessman Henry Arnaud, was modeled after New Orleans restaurateur, Count Arnaud Cazanave, whose French Quarter eatery, Arnaud's Restaurant, was (and still is) world–renowned.

"I knew him personally quite well, fifty years ago," Gibson once recounted of the expatriate Frenchman. "He's been written up. I wanted a good name. He was very suave."

New Orleans is a city the Master of Darkness also visited periodically, beginning with *Cyro* and *Mardi Gras Mystery* in 1934 and 1935. This was The Shadow's third recorded visit.

It opens, not in the famous capital of Louisiana but farther south, in Mexico City…. •

A Complete Booklength Novel from the Private Annals of The Shadow, as told to

MAXWELL GRANT

ZONIA

XITLI

god of fire

When the drums of the Aztecs rolled out their monotonous beat, only The Shadow knew it was a message of death!

CHAPTER I
AZTEC DRUMS

KENT ALLARD stood by his window in the Hotel Hidalgo, overlooking Mexico City. He was watching the ever-mysterious transformation that dusk was bringing to the Mexican capital, a change unparalleled elsewhere.

By day, the city had lain basking in a gigantic bowl, its valley rimmed by the surrounding mountains, which included the great peaks of Popocatepetl and Ixtacihuatl. With darkness wiping away those summits, the city alone remained, its lights forming a twinkling carpet patched with areas of blackness.

Mexico City was taking on life. Even the traffic, denoted by moving lights, was moving faster and more steadily. All afternoon it had stalled around the fourteen-acre Zocalo, or Plaza de la Constitución, blocked by a protest parade of school children who disapproved of certain teachers and wanted the government to know it.

Tomorrow, the cab drivers threatened a parade of their own, demanding compensation for the fares that they had lost while traffic was jammed the day before. But in between those daytime problems, Mexico City would enjoy a night of glitter and gaiety, as was its wont.

To the keen eyes of Kent Allard, each new spot of light that appeared below possessed a significance.

The lights were like living things that were being rallied and regimented to fight off night's encroachment. Modern though Mexico City might be, it still lay in the great valley amid the plateau of Anahuac, once the heart of the Aztec empire. Here, until the death of Montezuma, last of the Aztec rulers, had stood the strange citadel of an even stranger race.

With darkness, all the weird legends of the past seemed to close in upon the modern city, creeping down from the time-haunted slopes of the Ajusco Mountains. The Aztecs lived anew, not merely in men's imaginations but in their descendants, the Indians of the mountainsides.

There were nights when the rarefied atmosphere of Mexico City carried distant throbs that were true echoes of the past, yet actual symbols of the present. This was one such evening, and Kent Allard recognized it. When the shrouding darkness thickened to a point where his keen eyes could not pierce it, his acute hearing served him.

From beyond the night-deepened waters of Lakes Chalco and Xochimilco, where remnants of famed floating gardens still drifted, Allard caught the faint thrum of Aztec drums, beating in a steady, gloomy rhythm. Those Aztec drums were bringing

in some message from afar to the capital city, where a barbaric emperor no longer ruled.

They were carrying an old story, those drums; one that had been repeated, at intervals, during several centuries. The throbs were tuning: "*Loot—loot—loot—*" telling that once again hostile searchers had come across some buried treasure, once the property of Montezuma or other Aztec kings, and were taking possession of the wealth.

Centuries ago, such drumbeats would have summoned hordes of Aztec warriors to the scene where the evil was in progress; but the armies of Montezuma existed no more. Though the drum throbs carried far and wide, they were little more than protest.

The bzeating of the drums was a duty passed down through generations, and the news no longer stirred the blood of listeners. Yet Allard was intent when he harkened to the drums.

Had their rhythm changed, he would have known that a long-expected time had come—when surviving Aztecs might rally to a cause far more important than the protection of treasure belonging to a vanished dynasty.

The kings of the Aztecs had perished, and their power with them. But the gods of Mexico merely slept, like the giant volcano, Popocatepetl. Once disturbed, those ancient deities might rise again to rule, and all who acknowledged them would then obey.

There was a knock at Allard's door; as he turned to answer it, the sounds of the drums faded, as though imagination, along with hearing, had been needed to discern them. A Mexican lieutenant in full-dress uniform was at the door.

"Señor Cuzana will see you," announced the lieutenant, with a salute. "He has requested that you come with me, Señor Allard."

THEY rode along streets like boulevards, passing theaters and cafes, through parks where strollers were enjoying the mild evening air. Near the leading park, the Alamedo, the car swung into the Paseo de la Reforma and followed that magnificent promenade to the residence of Señor Cuzana.

There, guided by the lieutenant, Allard was ushered into a salon where three men were seated. One was Señor Luis Cuzana, a bland but friendly Mexican official, connected with the presidential cabinet. The others were Americans, whose names Allard already knew.

One was Graham Talborn, wealthy exporter from New Orleans, who had done much to stimulate trade between Louisiana and Central America. Talborn was tall, affable of manner; so energetic that he seemed youthful, except for his grizzled hair.

The other was James Carland, an oil operator

who had, until recently, held large concessions in Mexico. Carland looked old and haggard, with good reason. For two years he had been fighting to regain his oil interests, which had been outlawed by the Mexican government.

All three—Cuzana, Talborn, Carland—studied Kent Allard with interest. They remembered a time when he had been famous as an aviator; but at present Allard looked as though the world had forgotten him.

Allard was tall, and his gaunt features had a hawklike expression that suited a master of the skies. But his shoulders were stooped, as from weariness; the cane that he had used did not hide his limp, the souvenir of a forced landing some years before.

On Cuzana's table stood the model of a Mayan pyramid, which attracted Allard's eye. Cuzana lifted the top of the model and it came apart in sections, showing interior compartments.

"A replica of the great pyramid at Chichen Itza," he said. "They are building a full-scale reproduction in New Orleans to serve as a permanent Mayan museum."

"We have already built it," corrected Talborn. "The interior of this model represents the arrangement of the new museum, not the ancient pyramid. We are quite sure that the museum will be open to the public in time for the West Indian Exposition."

"Thanks to you, Señor Talborn," acknowledged Cuzana. "The museum could not have been completed, I understand, if you had not supplied the hundred thousand dollars still required."

Carland thrust himself forward; his eyes were tiny, ugly beads that blazed from his haggard face.

"I was the man who promised that money!" stormed Carland. "I could still give my donation, Cuzana, if your government had not robbed me of my oil concessions!"

"I am very sorry. Señor Carland,"—Cuzana's tone was cool—"but the decision did not rest with my department."

"But you could use your influence—"

"I have already used it. Nothing can be done. I tell you, officially, Señor Carland, that you can never hope to regain the concessions. The decision is final."

Carland stared, swaying like a drunken man. Then, steadying, he flexed his features into a sneer. Turning on his heel, he left the salon without bidding anyone goodbye. Cuzana gave a bland shrug, then said in a tone of sincerity:

"I am very sorry for Señor Carland."

"You don't need to be," spoke Talborn promptly. "He bought those concessions for a song and made the most of them while he had them. If he had salted away his cash instead of sinking it in other speculations, he wouldn't have to worry.

"Let me tell you something about Carland"—Talborn's tone became confidential—"that may change your opinion of the fellow. When he announced that he could not pay his promised contribution of one hundred thousand dollars to the museum fund, it naturally worried many people, principally Eugene Brendle, the contractor, who had a lot at stake.

"So Carland went to Brendle and borrowed fifty thousand dollars on very flimsy security. All that Carland gave Brendle was temporary title to a few thousand acres of Louisiana swampland. Naturally, Brendle supposed that Carland would use the money toward the museum fund. Instead, Carland spent it.

"Poor Carland!" Talborn's tone was filled with contempt. "You should say 'Poor Brendle!' He would be down and out if I hadn't saved the situation by donating the money that Carland had pledged but failed to supply."

TALBORN'S denunciation put a new light on the matter. It brought a nod from Señor Cuzana, indicating that he was not surprised to learn of Carland's double-dealing.

"Mexico is better rid of such men," declared Cuzana. "They represent the old regime's faults. They came here at a time when men in power were willing to bargain away the republic's resources to the first person who offered money."

Cuzana was assembling the model pyramid. He put it back in the box where it belonged. Then, unfolding a map of Mexico, he spread it on the table and turned to Allard.

"I have bad news for you, too," said Cuzana, "but it is the sort that I feel sure that you will be glad to hear. You came here, Señor Allard, to superintend a search, by air, for the missing expedition of Professor Darius Hedwin.

"Quite fortunately"—and Cuzana gave a whimsical smile—"the expedition has found itself. As you know, they started from Chichen Itza"—he laid his forefinger on a point in the peninsula of Yucatan—"and started into the interior. For a while we heard from them"—Cuzana's finger was making a curve from Yucatan, downward, then up toward Mexico City—"and then communications ceased.

"The reason, we have learned, was because they expected to arrive here before anyone had cause to worry. But Professor Hedwin decided to stop at the ruins of Cuicuilco, less than twenty miles south of Mexico City. He has been there nearly a week."

Talborn inserted a chuckle as Cuzana finished.

"And all the while," added Talborn, "the professor overlooked the trifling detail of informing us— until tonight, when a messenger came in with word.

However, Mr. Allard, I feel sure that we can use you later in a search for undiscovered ruins as soon as we have raised more funds."

"How soon will that be?"

"Quite soon, I hope," replied Talborn. "For the present, my chief concern is the shipment of the Mayan relics which Professor Hedwin has uncovered. *Senor* Cuzana is making such arrangements so that the usual red tape can be avoided."

Taking the remark as an invitation to leave, Allard shook hands with the others. Cuzana politely conducted him out to the front door, where a car was waiting. There, Cuzana remarked on the fact that Allard had earlier noted: the clarity of the night air in Mexico City.

"Sometimes," said Cuzana, "you can almost imagine that you hear the beat of distant Aztec drums."

Allard's keen ears did hear such throbs. They were coming from the south, the direction of Cuicuilco.

Alone in the rear of the limousine to which Cuzana conducted him, Allard smiled as he rode away. Then, from his lips, came a strange, low whisper, a sinister laugh, which carried anticipation, not disappointment. Allard's business in Mexico City was simply an excuse for his presence.

The laugh marked him as The Shadow—the strange master who hunted down crime, no matter where it might be. His mirth told that The Shadow was on the trail of evil, and had learned its location.

Cuicuilco, close by the town of Tlalpan, had become The Shadow's immediate objective. There, near the very mountains that could be seen by day from Mexico City, The Shadow was to solve the riddle of the Aztec drums!

CHAPTER II
STRIFE BY NIGHT

PROFESSOR DARIUS HEDWIN stood in the glow of a powerful electric lantern, directing a small crew of swarthy men who were hacking deep into a stony passage that was cemented with volcanic lava.

Frail of build, with a face as wrinkled as a mummy's, the professor might have been a Mayan god himself. He looked something like a golliwog, for his dried-up face was topped by a mass of shocky white hair.

Near the professor stood his chief assistant, Andrew Ames. He was young, but his square-jawed face and broad shoulders carried the build of experience. So did his manner as he watched the slaving workers. But his face showed disapproval, which Professor Hedwin noticed.

"Come, Andy!" wheezed the professor. "Drop your moping and take an interest. I am sure that we are about to uncover new relics of Xitli, the forgotten fire god."

"Good enough," returned Andy, "but why can't you do the excavating by day and spend the nights in Mexico City?"

"So civilization lures you, Andy!"

"Not at all, Professor. I'm speaking from the standpoint of common sense."

Hedwin gave a headshake.

"You are wrong, Andy," he said. "These workers prefer to work at night. They sleep in the daytime. That's when they take their siestas."

"Siestas by day," returned Andy, "and fiestas by night. It's one and the same, Professor. They won't work unless you drive them, and that goes for either day or night."

The professor told the workers to rest. He drew Andy aside and began to wag a scrawny forefinger. Andy braced himself for what was coming. He could see the strange gleam in the old professor's eyes. Hedwin was going to confide the same facts that he had spoken a dozen times before.

"Many have found relics of the fire god," whispered Hedwin, "and have believed that a strange cult worshipped that mysterious deity—a cult that began with the Mayas and survived among the Aztecs, even to this day.

"But only I"—the professor drew himself up proudly—"have learned the name of the unknown fire god. I have identified him with Xitli, the volcano which disgorged its mass of lava to cover and preserve the ruins of Cuicuilco."

Andy nodded. It was always wise to humor the professor. Hedwin did not take the nod as a criticism, for he knew that Andy understood the history of Cuicuilco.

By day the two had roamed over the pedregal, the fifteen-mile "stony place" of rough volcanic lava, broken with deep cracks and yawning cisterns. The pedregal, site of the Cuicuilco ruins, told its own story of a volcanic overflow in Mayan times, and would naturally have been attributed to the fire god.

Since the name of Xitli belonged to the volcano, which had become extinct, Andy was quite willing to agree that the fire god bore the same title and that the eruption had been regarded as proof of Xitli's wrath. But he still didn't agree with the professor on the matter of making excavations at night.

"Listen, Professor," argued Andy. "When we left Yucatan, we had a tough road ahead of us. I'll admit it wouldn't have been safe to hit the jungle without Panchez and his guards. But now that we've reached Cuicuilco we don't need them. While we're digging for relics of Xitli, Panchez and his mestizos are roaming the pedregal, up to their old game."

"Their old game, Andy?"

"Sure! They've been hunting for treasure all along, Professor. They know that when the Spaniards put Montezuma in a tight spot, the Aztecs buried their gold and jade near the temples of the ancient gods, hoping that it would mean protection. I'll admit that Panchez and his crowd cleared the jungle for us, but only because the faster we went, the more loot they could find."

Professor Hedwin shook his head.

"When Carland was in charge," he said, "he hired Panchez. When Talborn took Carland's place as financier of the expedition, he said that everything could continue as before. So I kept Panchez—"

"Of course," interrupted Andy. "Good enough, while we were in the jungle. But right now, Panchez and his bunch might as well be in Mexico City looking at a double feature. We're not going to run into hostile tribes of Indians around here."

"You think not?" Hedwin cocked his head wisely. "Haven't you heard the beat of Aztec drums?"

"Yes," agreed Andy. "But what do they mean? Nothing but an old ritual carried on by a lot of Indians who don't do anything more dangerous than weave baskets!"

PROFESSOR HEDWIN turned away. He felt that he had won his point. He ordered the workers to chop deeper into the lava, and his manner told that he intended to ignore Andy entirely. It did not hurt Andy's pride; instead, it was the very thing that he had been hoping for.

Using his flashlight, Andy walked a few hundred yards to the deserted tents that made the headquarters for the expedition. As he expected, he found no sign of Panchez nor any of the mestizo guards. They had all gone to the pedregal again, which explained why some of the professor's workers talked of lights that had danced above Cuicuilco on previous nights.

Such lights, according to tradition, meant places where treasure lay buried under the protection of unknown deities like Xitli. But Andy Ames took a reverse view of the phenomenon. To him, the lights meant Panchez and the mestizo crew. If treasure figured, it would only come into the case should Panchez & Co. uncover it.

In his tent, Andy put fresh batteries in his flashlight and picked up a supply of .38 cartridges to supplement the loaded revolver that he always carried. Then, keeping his light close to the ground, he started for the pedregal in search of Panchez.

Andy hoped to find the mestizo leader engaged in excavating of his own. Such a discovery might convince old Professor Hedwin that Andy's ideas were right.

There was one job that Panchez and his men handled very well: the shipment of all the motley curios and relics, such as the broken pottery and baked clay idols that Professor Hedwin uncovered. The willingness with which the mestizos plowed the jungle with such burdens simply convinced Andy that they also carried baggage that they considered valuable to themselves.

Lights were dancing above Cuicuilco. Andy located them, more than a mile distant, along the rough-surfaced pedregal. He watched the peculiar way in which they dipped and reappeared.

Gun in one hand, flashlight in the other, Andy crept closer to the lights. All the while, he could hear the throb of Aztec drums, louder, closer than The Shadow had heard them in Mexico City.

The lights showed the stooping figures of men, but Andy could not see their faces. Some were pushing heavy sacks out from a cistern hole in the lava. The pit could not have been open when they discovered it, for Andy saw a great, chunky slab lying by the hole.

Four men were straining, as if prepared to push the slab back in place at an order from their leader, who was probably Panchez; but four were not enough. More were coming over to help them.

This was Andy's time for action. Springing forward, he suddenly emerged into the lights, brandishing his gun as he poured an order in Spanish for the prowlers to stop their task.

Like the snap of a whip came a countermanding order from a man back in the darkness. With one accord, the stooping men quit their task and surged toward Andy.

His first shots, delivered in the air did not halt them. Finding the warning useless, Andy fired point-blank, then hurled his revolver at faces that he could not see. Knives were flashing toward him, and Andy's only weapons were his fists, good enough against mestizos if he could use them quicker than the slashing blades.

The surge reached him; with it came a quick-snarled order from the rear. Instead of stabbing knives, Andy received the clutches of a dozen hands that thrust him backward toward the pit. The men at the slab had dropped it; they were joining the onrush.

Shoved to the brink, Andy heard another call. With it, the knives began to flash. Instinct prompted Andy to the only course. As he wrenched free from the gripping hands that had thrust his arms behind him, he twisted back to the pit itself.

In that last instant on the brink, Andy Ames saw blackness that loomed fantastically from overhead. Some monstrous shape that looked like a windmill off its moorings was falling toward Andy and his mestizo foemen. Through the whirling shape, the night stars were blinking in kaleidoscopic fashion.

As knives slashed at the sleeves of Andy's flaying arms, the bulking blackness from above gave him the crazed impression that the pit had inverted itself; that he was actually over the brink and falling into the depths. The pricking knives, too, were forcing him to frantic measures.

Wildly, Andy made a sideward lunge, away from the knives, toward what he thought was the edge of the engulfing hole.

Then his illusion was actuality. Blackness was not surging down upon him; he was plunging into it. His hands had grabbed in the wrong direction; he had lost his balance and was pitching headlong into the yawning hole.

Knives were no longer slashing, nor could he hear the snarls of the mestizos. The receiving blackness was complete, lacking its starry blinks, but only for a single second.

It ended in a crash that brought a great burst of light, then darkness absolute, as Andy struck the bottom of the rocky pit. Fortunately, the fall was shorter than he had supposed, and Andy did not strike headfirst, because he glanced from obstructions on the way down.

But those details were lost to Andy Ames, for the jolt that he received was sufficient to render him senseless.

CLINGING to the brink of the pit, the mestizos were the ones who realized the closer approach of the spinning blackness that Andy had seen. It was almost upon them, a silently descending autogiro, a wingless monster of the air, controlled by the whirl of its horizontal blades as it reached the rough surface of the pedregal, landing less than a dozen yards from the open pit.

By then, the men who had conquered Andy were scattering to safety. They saw the autogiro bounce and expected it to overturn as an ordinary plane would have. But the wingless ship held its own, stopping short with a single turn of its landing wheels.

The ugly shout of Panchez told the mestizos that they had to deal with a human foe, not some prehistoric creature sent here by an outraged Aztec god. Rallying to their leader's cry, the murderous crew surged toward the autogiro.

Two dozen strong, they expected to overwhelm the sky ship and the daring enemy who had landed it on the pedregal. But before they could reach their goal, a figure lunged to meet them. They did not see their challenger; instead, they heard him.

Blackness from blackness: a cloaked shape driving from the giro's center—a fighter who issued a peal of uncanny mirth more weird than the continuing thrum of Aztec drumbeats that seemed to form a musical background with their cadence.

Strange, shivering, that mighty laugh chilled the mixed blood of the startled mestizos, stopping them with upraised knives in their hands. They knew, in that instant, that they were faced with a foe more formidable than any they could have imagined.

They had heard the laugh of The Shadow!

CHAPTER III
PATHS OF DARKNESS

GARBED in a flowing cloak of black, wearing a slouch hat that belonged to his shrouding costume, The Shadow was a living mass of dynamite, quite different from Kent Allard, the taciturn veteran aviator who had flown by autogiro from Mexico City only a short while before.

Though the guise of Allard was his real identity, The Shadow always gave it a weary pose, even to the pretended limp that everyone identified with Allard. Once cloaked, he became a knight of darkness whose challenging laugh was but the spear point of his attack. The Shadow knew that he had startled his foemen almost to confusion; but such did not spell victory.

Once scattered, the mestizos could prove more dangerous than when assembled, unless they first felt the power of The Shadow in physical combat. With that design, The Shadow drove in upon them as silently, as ominously as his autogiro had dropped down from the sky.

His tactics were the opposite of Andy's. The Shadow had two guns, big .45 caliber automatics, but he did not pull the triggers. Instead, he used them as sledgehammers, smashing down the knife blades that flashed in belated style; reaching the owners of those weapons with hard blows that met human skulls.

To Panchez, bringing up the reserves, the scene was one of dark confusion; he could see figures sprawling upon the grimy gray surface of the pedregal; others rolling, stumbling in search of safety. But the center of that human flywheel, the forceful fighter who flung mestizos right and left, was no more than a core of blackness, so evasive that it could only be seen in chance glimpses.

The men with Panchez were armed with carbines. Snarling, the mestizo leader pointed his revolver in The Shadow's general direction and fired a shot to start the carbineers. The clear air echoed with the volley from half a dozen guns; then the reverberations were stirred by a mocking answer: The Shadow's laugh!

Not a single shot had reached the foeman from

the sky, and Panchez alone realized why. He had chosen the foreground near the autogiro as his target, thinking that The Shadow would be wheeling back toward the plane that he had left.

Instead, the cloaked warrior had whisked in another direction, finding some entrenchment on the roughened pedregal.

To Panchez's men, the thing was uncanny. They were dropping away, leaving their leader to guess

The man had stumbled upon The Shadow and was trying to knife him. Two figures came grappling upward from a lava bulkhead against a grayish ledge that showed them plainly. They whirled, and Panchez saw the mestizo sprawl from a hard gun stroke.

But The Shadow, whirling away, was still vaguely visible; moreover, he had lost his refuge behind the volcanic mound. Again Panchez fired, and his

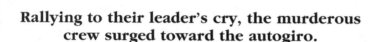

Rallying to their leader's cry, the murderous crew surged toward the autogiro.

where The Shadow had gone; a thing impossible to tell from the elusive laugh itself. Then, from the darkness, came a wild, half-gloating cry, uttered by one of the mestizos who had scattered earlier.

followers began to blast away with their carbines. As before, they were too late, but this time The Shadow answered in kind.

He picked out the marksmen by their gun blasts,

stabbing shots that wounded them in their tracks. It was a system that he had used often in dealing with dangerous foemen, but it did not scatter the present breed of warriors.

Like Panchez, the unwounded mestizos dropped low and began to copy The Shadow's own tactics. Trained to convoy parties through the jungle, this was the very type of battle that Panchez and his tribe liked.

The Shadow was ahead of them, both in shifts

and gunfire, but his moves were so quick that his rapid shots could not take effect.

He had to keep battling while on the go against these sharpshooters, who had demonstrated their skill by very nearly clipping him. Nor could The Shadow change tactics, for he knew that the men with knives had rallied and were crawling in toward him.

Even a trifling wound might mean disaster for The Shadow; and he faced the same fate should his guns run out of ammunition. The knifers would come with their deadly machetes, and backing them, Panchez and the men with carbines would complete the mopping-up process.

But The Shadow had a way to avoid such consequences. Taking a reverse spin as he fired at a carabineer, he went straight for the pit where Andy had disappeared, reaching it while guns were blasting in the wrong direction.

AT the mouth of the pit, The Shadow encountered a rising mestizo who had picked that very refuge after the original fray. Again gunners heard a shout, and aimed in the direction that Panchez pointed out to them.

The volley brought results, flattening a figure that came reeling from the pit. Panchez and his men charged forward.

A laugh greeted them. They had felled their own man, not The Shadow. Instead of shoving his adversary down into the pit, The Shadow had hauled him out and whirled him about as a shield, all in one speedy, superhuman action.

It was The Shadow who held the pit, clinging to the rungs of a crude ladder that Andy had missed in his fall, but which the lurking mestizo had known about and used.

The Shadow's laugh was like a call to action, addressed to unseen fighters who served him. It should have stopped Panchez and his men, making them prey for The Shadow's remaining shots.

But Panchez had come too far; he was beside the huge slab that belonged on the opening of the pit. There he found himself among men who were creeping in with knives.

With one accord, they grasped the big slab. Four of them managed to tilt the huge lava-hewn stone as a shield against The Shadow's bullets, but they could move it no farther, until another arriving pair ducked behind the same shelter. The new hands tossed aside their carbines and helped with the slab.

Overturning, the huge chunk settled into the rough hole, muffling The Shadow's laugh. For the moment Panchez and his crew thought that they had settled their foe permanently, but as they started in the direction of the autogiro, they heard the taunting laugh trickle from a crack beneath the rock. The slab had not fully settled in place.

Panchez ordered a few carbine shots, which was a bad mistake. In answer, fiery stabs came from the crack beneath the slab. In closing the pit partially but not entirely, the mestizos had given The Shadow an effective pillbox wherein he could not only fire, but reload. He was evidently determined to nick any persons who attempted to approach his precious autogiro.

Snarling at first, Panchez changed his tone to glee as he withdrew his men across the pedregal. He was telling them that The Shadow, or *La Sombra*, as Panchez termed him, would simply experience a slow but merciless death, far greater misery than that which bullets could deliver.

"The professor will not know," said Panchez in Spanish. "We will tell him that Señor Ames has gone to Mexico City. Tomorrow the professor will follow, without crossing the pedregal. Later we can return, when La Sombra is too weak to give us battle. We will close the slab and destroy his autogiro."

Quiet settled over the pedregal, though the atmosphere still held the quiver of The Shadow's last laugh. It had carried a strange tone, that mirth—like a signal telling certain men to wait. Then, with Panchez and his mestizos gone, The Shadow's laugh came anew, low-toned, like a summons.

Figures stirred from within the autogiro, two squat shapes that approached the sunken slab. They were Xinca Indians, belonging to a Guatemala tribe which Kent Allard ruled as a white king. He had brought them with him from Mexico City, but had kept them in reserve.

About to summon them when the slab fell, The Shadow had countermanded his order by a laugh of another tone. At present he needed them.

THE Xincas reached the slab, which had required six men to lift. Each Xinca had the strength of two mestizos, as did The Shadow.

While the squat men heaved at the slab, The Shadow provided pressure from below. The rickety ladder groaned, but The Shadow gained the pit edge with his hands and knees and supplied the upward pressure with his shoulders.

The slab tilted away. Emerging, The Shadow turned a flashlight down into the pit, saw Andy's crumpled figure. Alone, he descended and stooped above the unconscious man. Finding that Andy's strong frame had borne the shock without serious injury, The Shadow lifted him up the ladder to the waiting Xincas.

Studying the pit, The Shadow saw that it had been a treasure cache, as evidenced by odd trinkets of jade and gold that still remained in pockets hewn in the walls. But Panchez and his thieving crew had taken the cream of the buried Aztec wealth.

Aided by the Xincas, The Shadow put the slab tightly in place. With the Indians carrying Andy, he traced a course across the pedregal, basing his route on the location of ancient temple ruins where Professor Hedwin would probably be at work.

The procession came upon the camp; ordering the Xincas to wait, The Shadow moved among the tents.

Men were present, evidently some of Hedwin's regular workers, waiting for the next shift. Recognizing that such men were friendly to Andy, The Shadow knew that it would be safe to leave his human burden. He picked Andy's tent by inspecting its belongings, and returned to the Xincas. They took Andy into the tent and laid him on a cot.

Then, with a stealth that the Xincas matched, The Shadow left the camp. Returned to the autogiro, he and his two followers listened to the rhythm of Aztec drums, which continued their unchanged strain.

"*Loot—loot—loot—*"

The same cadence; one of passive indignation. Strange folk of the Ajusco Mountains sorrowed over the loss of wealth long buried by some forgotten Aztec king. But the mountain tribesmen, stirred only by vestiges of old traditions belonging to their ancestors, seemed not inclined to interfere. None had appeared to attack Panchez and the mestizos during the rifling of the treasure cavern.

The Shadow spoke to his two Xincas; silently they acknowledged that a certain mission pertaining to themselves had been fulfilled. They followed The Shadow into the autogiro. Big blades whirred; with a short roll the strange machine took off vertically into the starry night.

Above the roar of the motor that drowned the throb of sullen Aztec drums came the weird crescendo of a parting laugh—The Shadow's farewell to a scene of triumph; a prediction that he would later settle the matter of stolen treasure.

But this strange terrain was soon to bear a new significance. The Shadow had banished crime, only to clear the way for a coming menace that would carry its threat far from the land of the Aztecs!

The very evidence that The Shadow and his Xincas had come to seek, but had not found, was already in the making at the time of their departure!

CHAPTER IV
THE THRONE OF XITLI

THE pounding of drums awakened Andy Ames. They were beating harder, louder than before, in a strange, irregular fashion that seemed tuned to the welling throbs of his aching head. Never had Andy heard them sound like that before, nor had he known them to persist as late as dawn.

Daylight was breaking from across the pedregal, filtering through the palm trees that fringed the camp. Men were astir, babbling excitedly, and the noise of their tongues roused Andy further.

When he demanded the reason for the confusion, Andy received excited headshakes and the pointing of hands. The workers were indicating the direction of Hedwin's excavation, and Andy decided that something must have happened to the old professor. Starting out to find Hedwin, he was passed by more of the excited workers, who were running into camp.

From the night before, Andy could remember a broken chain of experiences that did not seem to make sense. As he recalled it, he had been with Professor Hedwin, watching the workers, who were mostly full-blooded Indians, hack away at the lava passages in the ruins of an old Mayan temple.

Then, as Andy recalled it, he had gone to the pedregal alone. He had been attacked, flung into a pit by men who had been uncommonly like Panchez and the mestizo guards who had been hired to scour the jungle and keep trouble away. How he had gotten back to his tent was a mystery to Andy. There were vague recollections, however, of strange Indians and a man in black.

Maybe he was wrong about the whole thing. The fight might have happened at Hedwin's excavation, not out on the pedregal. Certainly it seemed that the professor was at present in some difficulty, the way his men were deserting him.

Andy found the hewn opening into the old temple. He shouted for Hedwin and was answered by a hollow voice from within, a tone which seemed testy, more than anything else. Entering, Andy used his flashlight to find the chamber where he had last seen the professor.

There he discovered Hedwin, looking more like a golliwog than ever. He was sitting on a squarish chunk of stone that looked like smooth, black basalt.

Apparently the stone had been dragged from some adjoining chamber, for Andy had not seen it the night before. But he saw now that a hole had been chopped into a small secret chamber adjoining this big one.

Hedwin held up a doll-sized figurine of baked clay that reminded Andy somewhat of a Buddha, except that its features were coarse and grinning. He simply nodded, because he had seen similar figurines before.

They represented the fire god which Hedwin claimed the Mayas had worshipped under the name of Xitli. The expedition had picked up quite a few of the statuettes while coming in from Yucatan.

"I was right!" exclaimed Hedwin gleefully. "Xitli *was* the fire god! Look in that chamber, Andy, and you will see a temple of Xitli, complete in every detail"—the professor chuckled—"except one."

Andy looked into the temple and marked the arrangement of it. He saw figurines on crude stone shelves, carved frescoes that represented flame along the walls. At one end of the room was a hewn space that looked like a throne. But nothing was much different from other tiny temples that Andy had seen before, and which Hedwin had identified with the fire god.

True, there were the remains of human skeletons, half buried in the rubble on the ground, but Andy had seen such bones in other excavations. He had particularly expected to find them at Cuicuilco, inasmuch as the ancient inhabitants had been over-whelmed by the lava flow from the volcano Xitli.

"It's just like the temple that you arranged for the new museum," said Andy. "You've been shipping all sorts of fire god relics to Salter so that he can put them in it. Why, you've even sent him masks and costumes of the fire god for his other exhibit rooms."

Professor Hedwin inserted a chuckle, inspired by Andy's mention of Fitzhugh Salter, curator of the Mayan Museum in New Orleans.

"Yes, I suppose that Salter is at his wits' end," Hedwin cackled. "But wait until *this* arrives. Perhaps he will then believe that Xitli was the fire god!"

RISING, the professor indicated the black stone on which he had been seated. Studying the square of basalt, Andy looked into the temple again and saw that the black chunk had formed the seat of the great stone throne.

"This explains it, Andy." Hedwin was tapping the black stone. "Basalt is a form of volcanic rock, aptly suited to such a deity as Xitli. But only the true temple of Xitli would contain the god's own throne.

"Look at the inscriptions on this basalt. They prove its origin, Andy. Deciphered, they say that this stone represents the true Xitli, that this throne is his own. Look at some of those pictures in the temple chamber, where men with torches are bowing to a god crowned with flame. My theory was right. I have proven Xitli to be the fire god!"

Professor Hedwin had raised his voice in such high-pitched triumph that he had to relax. He sat down on the basalt square and began to mop his forehead with a ragged handkerchief. Andy asked:

"What's happened to the workers?"

"The fools!" retorted Hedwin, suddenly remembering that the crew had left him. "They dragged the black stone from the temple an hour ago. When I sat down to rest, they suddenly began to babble. Then they fled."

Hedwin paused. Springing to his feet, he exclaimed:

"I have it, Andy! They feared this stone! It was difficult to persuade them to touch it. When I sat upon the stone, I was actually occupying the throne of Xitli, the fire god. That is why they fled!"

It sounded logical to Andy, although his head was splitting so badly that he could hardly think. Daylight was creeping into the excavation, and with it, Andy still heard the irregular *thrum-thrum* of Aztec drums.

"How long have those drums been beating?" he asked suddenly. "I mean the way we hear them now, with that funny discord."

The professor listened, stroking his dryish chin.

"They began soon after the men fled," he said. "Do you know, Andy, I wonder—" He caught himself. "No, no, it could not be that. And yet—"

"What could not be?"

"The Tribe of Fire. You've heard of it—an ancient group among the Mayas that continued into Aztec times. Men something like the thugs of India, who killed to please the god they represented. Yes, there was such a tribe once. Perhaps it still exists today—the cult of Xitli—"

He broke off suddenly and threw a suspicious glance toward Andy, something that the professor always did when he had voiced his thoughts aloud.

But this time Hedwin's glance seemed cannier than ever. His lips snapped shut like a clamshell; then curved themselves into a twisted smile. Stooping, Hedwin gripped one side of the basalt stone and nodded for Andy to do the same.

The black rock was not heavy, though it needed their combined strength to carry it out through the passages without dropping it. After a brief rest, Hedwin and Andy continued into camp, bringing the stone with them.

Immediately upon their arrival the superstitious workers scattered.

Daylight was full by this time. The discordant strum of distant drums had ended. Andy, too, was beginning to mop his forehead, when he turned to see a man who stared at him with unbelieving eyes.

The arrival was Panchez; the mestizo leader was holding a carbine under his arm. Andy noted that the weapon was shaking, as though it had been imbued with life and was trying to jump from its owner's grasp.

"Well, Panchez?"

At Andy's words, Panchez recovered himself. He decided that ghosts did not rove by daylight, nor did they talk with human voice. Panchez licked his lips, smiled.

"I am glad, Señor Ames," he said, "to find that you are still alive. It was very bad, last night, the fight we have with the *banditti*."

"Along the pedregal?"

"Si, señor," acknowledged Panchez. "We hear you fight them, and we come with carbines. We shoot"—he gestured with his carbine—"and *pouf!*—they run away. But we look for you and do not find you.

"I think, señor"—Panchez had laid the carbine aside and was beginning to roll a cigarette—"that maybe you have gone into Mexico City to tell the police of trouble."

Panchez was lying, and Andy knew it from the way the mestizo had averted his eyes. But there was no use pressing the issue. It was Hedwin's job, not Andy's, to reprimand the guards for any faults. At present the professor was too exuberant about finding Xitli's temple and the throne seat of the fire god to be interested in anything else.

Besides, Hedwin's find meant that the expedition had completed its purpose. Soon the professor would order a start for Mexico City, and men would be needed to carry the basalt stone.

Since the Indian workers would not touch the piece of basalt, that task would have to go to Panchez. When Andy pointed out the stone to Panchez, the rogue nodded and summoned a pair of mestizos, who took up the burden.

WHEN camp was broken, Andy suggested a detour across the pedregal, to which Panchez agreed. His hand ready to reach for his revolver, Andy kept a sharp eye on Panchez's carbine as they strolled along together. He asked Panchez where the trouble had begun, and the mestizo shook his head.

"It is different now, señor," he said. "Day and night they are different. Sometime we make mistake, señor. My men, perhaps, could not tell who you were. You may have mistake *banditti* for mestizos."

Nowhere among the open cisterns did Andy see a cavity that resembled the pit of the night before. He looked for a crack in the lava rock, but failed to find one. The slab had been fitted tightly into place; even Panchez looked puzzled when Andy was not gazing his way.

"What about your men?" demanded Andy suddenly. "You are short-handed today, Panchez."

"Some have been wounded," returned Panchez blandly. "Others, they were killed. You will see them, señor, when we reach Tlalpan, the place where I have sent them."

Arriving at Tlalpan, Andy did see Panchez's corps of cripples; their wounds testified to a larger fight than the one that Andy had made against them. Andy half believed that Panchez and his men had actually encountered bandits, and that he had therewith misjudged them; so he simply congratulated Panchez on having put up an excellent fight.

Later that day a train took Hedwin and Andy to Mexico City, along with a supply of Mayan relics, including the Xitli throne stone, and Andy saw no signs of any luggage belonging to Panchez.

Still, some of the mestizos were not accounted for, and Andy knew that they could have gone ahead with their loot. He decided to forget Panchez and the rest, as he would a bad dream.

Yet, there was something that Andy could not forget, and it belonged in the dream class. Vaguely he could recall brief periods when he had been conscious; after his fall into the pit.

Out of such recollections came a person cloaked in black who spoke in a strange, weird whisper to a pair of squat Indians. Andy recalled a floating sensation, which made him believe that the Indians had carried him into camp at the cloaked rescuer's order.

He was still thinking of that episode when evening came and he visited Señor Cuzana and Graham Talborn. Andy was with Professor Hedwin, who was too busy talking about Xitli to note the broken beat of Aztec drums that seemed to float in from the mountains.

Angry drums, menacing in tone, the same that Andy had heard at dawn, they seemed to spell a message that certain men would surely heed.

Unfortunately, the story of those drums had not yet carried to distant Guatemala, where The Shadow, otherwise Kent Allard, was bidding farewell to the Xinca tribe that acknowledged him as ruler. Wisely, The Shadow did not deny the rumor that worried the Xincas: namely, that the cult of Xitli was about to form anew.

He let his two Xinca servants make the report. They testified that they had been to Mexico with their great white king and had heard the beat of Aztec drums that told of theft alone. They had seen men engaged in such theft, and had watched their powerful chief drive away the marauders.

The robbers had been punished; hence, no revenge was needed. Protection of the stolen treasure was the duty of the Aztecs, not of the Xincas.

But when his servants had finished with their story, The Shadow told them to remain with the tribe when he had gone. They were to be alert, still on the watch for any revival of the Xitli cult.

It was a wise decision on The Shadow's part, considering that the Xitli legend was firmly fixed in Xinca minds. It strengthened The Shadow's authority with the tribe. When he took off in the autogiro, he saw the Xincas gathered about their jungle fire, their arms folded as a token of farewell.

The Shadow's wisdom was to prove twofold. The time was coming shortly when the Xitli rumor was to prove reality. Then would the Xincas more than ever acknowledge the foresight of their ruler,

The Shadow, who had warned them to remain alert, even when the menace of the Xitli cult had seemed to be disproven!

Moreover, they would be pleased because their black-clad chief had left the servants who knew how to reach him and carry such tidings. When that time came, not one among the Xinca tribe would believe that at the time of his actual departure, The Shadow, master of mystery, had in his own mind classed all talk of Xitli as a legend without foundation!

CHAPTER V
THE MAYAN MUSEUM

VIEWED from the window of an arriving passenger plane, New Orleans formed an intriguing sight, a city spread upon a broad plain cut by the curving ribbon of the Mississippi. Toy ships were anchored all along the riverfront, while beyond, the city showed an array of buildings that marked the new town from the old.

New Orleans, however, differed from most American cities. Others were distinguishable by modern skyscrapers, impressive even when viewed from a high altitude. New Orleans lacked buildings that were really tall. A structure of a dozen stories rated high in the Louisiana metropolis.

Perhaps it was quite as well that New Orleans lacked a mammoth skyline. Otherwise, the city's newest landmark, the Mayan Museum, would not have dominated the scene as remarkably as it did.

The museum, built in the form of a pyramid, stood on the outskirts of the city, and its glistening white steps immediately caught the eye. Though only a hundred-odd feet in height, its shape made it appear much greater, and the architectural beauty gained a final touch from the surmounting temple that capped the pyramid.

It was The Shadow's first view of the great stone structure, which had been completed in a rush after a long delay through lack of funds. Other passengers in the same airliner were also intrigued by sight of the pyramid, and they scarcely noticed the hawk-faced traveler with them.

The Shadow was no longer Kent Allard. His hawkish features were fuller, less gaunt. His whole pose seemed leisurely, indolent. His face had a masklike expression that seemed a token of reserve. Actually, it signified a disguise. The Shadow had assumed a different identity, yet one with which he was quite familiar.

He was passing as Lamont Cranston, millionaire globe-trotter, who traveled where whim might call him. Why he had come to New Orleans was something which seemed logically explained as soon as the plane landed.

At the airport, Lamont Cranston was greeted by James Carland, the haggard-eyed oil operator who had so recently left Mexico City, where the government had emphatically ousted him from his concessions.

Carland did not in any wise recognize Cranston as Allard. The resemblance between The Shadow's old face and his new was traceable only in vague fashion, and Carland was not interested in comparisons. As he shook hands with Cranston, Carland failed utterly to guess the significance behind the visitor's slight but inscrutable smile.

The Shadow was thinking of the meeting in Mexico City, where Carland had ignored Kent Allard as a person of no consequence, a broken-down aviator. Here in New Orleans, Carland was sparing no effort at welcoming Lamont Cranston, man of reputed wealth. The contrast gave an excellent index to Carland's nature.

Carland's motto was "cash and carry"; others could supply the cash, and he would carry it. If they ever saw the cash again, it would mean simply that Carland had slipped.

Not that Carland was crooked in the legal sense of the term. On the contrary, Carland was noted for his ironclad methods, as witness his Mexican oil concessions, to which he still argued a valid claim. Carland simply never missed a trick when it lay within the rules of a game called business.

Inviting Cranston into a limousine, Carland began a string of patter as they rode away from the airport.

"I'm glad to meet you, Mr. Cranston," he declaimed. "Glad to meet anyone with vision enough to see the future of rice land in the Mississippi delta. I have thousands of acres of it, the finest land in the world.

"Swampland, some call it"—Carland's chuckle showed contempt—"and that's where they are wrong. It may have been salt marsh once, but today it is covered with rich Mississippi silt, the accumulation of many years. The reeds that grow through the silt simply bind it, and help it to thicken.

"Saltgrass flats? Bah! Two hundred years ago the French called those lands 'trembling prairies,' which proves that they knew the ground was good, although unstable. Modern methods of agriculture weren't known then, Mr. Cranston, but we understand them today.

"Rice can be grown along every bayou and lagoon. Big amphibian tractors, with wheels like paddles, will cultivate the land. We'll have barges moving along channels where now you see only shrimp boats and natives paddling those funny dugout canoes they call 'pirogues.'"

IT was an impressive sales talk, and by the time the car had reached the heart of the city, Carland was tabulating figures to show the big profits from rice that could be brought straight to New Orleans by the water route.

Then, as the car stopped in front of an office building, Carland glanced anxiously at his watch.

"It's well after five," he said, "but I think we shall still find Mr. Brendle in his office. He's a contractor; used to lay roads all over the State. He thinks the rice project is feasible. I want you to meet him, Mr. Cranston."

They found Eugene Brendle in his office. The contractor was a stocky, broad-shouldered man whose concave profile, with bulging forehead and chin, was centered by a very stubby nose. He was the type of man who evidently thought over all decisions, but once having made them, would not alter his final plan.

It happened that The Shadow knew the exact situation between James Carland and Eugene Brendle, for, as Allard, The Shadow had heard it from Graham Talborn, the exporter, while in Mexico City. At present Carland owed Brendle fifty thousands dollars, and the future rice lands—whether salt marsh or rich silt—were the security for the loan.

Evidently Brendle mistrusted Carland, and well he might, for the fifty thousand dollars had not gone to the completion of the museum. Calling the loan when the time came would not help either, unless the delta land proved to be worth fifty thousand dollars, which Brendle appeared to doubt. In his turn, Carland was attempting to convince Brendle that the land was good.

"You're a good judge of property, Mr. Cranston," said Carland, turning to The Shadow. "You know the facts and figures on rice"—glibly, Carland was glossing over the fact that he had just provided Cranston with such information—"and I think you will agree that my land is worth more than fifty thousand dollars."

"As represented, yes," returned The Shadow, in a calm tone that suited Cranston. "Of course, before investing such a sum, I would like to see the land in question."

"And if you found it up to specifications—"

"I would either purchase it or offer to invest in its development."

Carland threw a triumphant look at Brendle, as though Cranston's statement had settled the whole question. Then, like a man slapping a trump card on the table, Carland stated:

"Your offer is a trifle late, Mr. Cranston. I have already heard from Jonathan Dorn, the New York financier, requesting first opportunity to inspect the property. It would not be fair to Dorn to consider any transaction before he arrives."

"How soon will that be?"

"Frankly, I don't know," replied Carland. "Within a week, I hope, Mr. Cranston. If you will be staying in New Orleans that long—"

"I shall be." Cranston's lips formed one of their half smiles. "My hobby happens to be the study of Mayan remains. I hoped that I might get a preview of the exhibits in the new museum before it was open to the public."

Mention of the museum brought a glare to Carland's haggard face. Angrily, he exclaimed:

"I'll have nothing to do with the Mayan Museum! If Graham Talborn had waited, giving me a chance to straighten out matters, I might have regained my oil concessions on the strength of that museum. The Mexican government wanted it completed before the West Indian Exposition; they would have listened to reason while I held the upper hand."

Brendle gave a steady look toward Carland.

"You forget," said Brendle, "that others had much to lose while the museum remained unfinished. Salter, the curator, had his job to think about. Professor Hedwin was nearly stranded, down in Yucatan. I had contracted for materials, and had loaned you fifty thousand dollars—"

Carland's glare had turned to a wince. He interrupted Brendle by clapping the contractor on the shoulder.

"I owe you a lot, Brendle," said Carland. "You're the one friend I had among the whole crowd. The way they deserted me, like rats, when Talborn came along! Don't worry, Brendle. You'll get your fifty thousand dollars, with interest."

"I hope so, Carland."

There was an actual touch of hope in Brendle's tone, inspired, perhaps, by Cranston's interest in the rice fields on which the cash depended, plus Carland's statement that a financier named Dorn had already considered their development.

"Why don't you take Mr. Cranston to the museum?" suggested Carland to Brendle. "Salter will probably be glad to see you, though he wouldn't care to see me. You can call me later, after you've looked over the place."

BRENDLE accepted the suggestion. He closed his office, and they rode to the museum in Carland's limousine. The Shadow and Brendle left the car, and Carland drove away. Entering the museum, Brendle conducted his new acquaintance, Cranston, to the curator's office.

There, they found Graham Talborn, also back from Mexico. Like Carland, Talborn failed to identify Cranston as Allard.

The Shadow also shook hands with Fitzhugh Salter, the curator, a middle-aged man of portly proportions, chubby-faced, and of retiring disposition.

There was a smug touch, however, to Salter's features, that marked him shrewder than his surface showed.

"I'll show you the museum from the bottom up," declared Salter, when he learned why Cranston had come. "That means from the top down, because all our exhibits are on the higher floors. The lower floors are for offices. Come, gentlemen; this way."

They went to the very center of the pyramid, which, on the ground floor, did resemble an office building. The elevators were necessarily in the center, in order to reach the top floor of the tapering structure. They entered an elevator, and Salter took them to the top, where they stepped out to a promenade atop the temple that surmounted the museum.

Daylight had diminished. New Orleans stretched off into the distance, sparkling with lights, a scene that reminded The Shadow of Mexico City, except that here there was no throb of Aztec drums. Yet, somehow, the spell of the past seemed stronger here than in old Mexico.

Like ancient priests who had ruled Chichen Itza, The Shadow and his companions stood beside a parapet from which they could see the spreading steps of the massive pyramid below. It was almost as if the structure itself had been lifted from the ancient city of the Mayas and placed, in all its prime, upon the fringe of a modern metropolis.

This pyramid was, of course, a reproduction; but that only made the illusion more real. The Shadow could sense the spirit of grandeur even more than at Chichen Itza, where he had often visited the ruined temple of the Mayas upon its crumbling mound.

Gazing toward the terraces below, noting the gloom of the low shrubbery that surrounded the museum grounds, The Shadow could almost picture stealthy figures of the past, creeping into this chosen place where a vanished glory had been renewed. The lower darkness, like the blackening sky above, seemed fraught with ominous significance.

Tuned to the unknown, The Shadow possessed a sixth sense that seldom failed him. The very atmosphere was charged with menace of a sort that he had sensed often in the past. Voiceless tongues were crying a message of coming danger that no one else could hear.

Whether it meant evil of an ancient origin, or crime of a modern type, The Shadow could not tell. But his whole being told him to be ready for strange events soon due!

CHAPTER VI
WITHIN THE MUSEUM

FITZHUGH SALTER stood smugly by while the visitors enjoyed the view from the parapet. The curator seemed in no hurry to show them through the museum "from the top down," as he had expressed it. Not until he saw Cranston turn and gaze questioningly in his direction, did Salter suddenly rouse himself.

He bowed his visitors toward the stairs leading down from the roof, and they descended. Darkness greeted them, until Salter found a switch box and supplied lights to the top-floor corridor. The Shadow saw a stairway leading down around the elevator shafts, also the doors of various exhibit rooms.

The doors were locked, but Salter produced keys that opened them. The locks were of a very ordinary sort, which was natural enough, considering that when the museum itself was locked, the whole top floor would be protected.

Many of the Mayan exhibits were already in place, and they formed as large a collection as The Shadow had ever seen.

There were tablets with hieroglyphic carvings that Professor Hedwin had sent from Chichen Itza; great stone rings, four feet in diameter, decorated with intertwining feathered serpents.

In another room were pottery exhibits; also some ancient masks fashioned from such hard substances as turquoise, shell and jet. Salter said they were ceremonial masks, representing such deities as Quetzalcoatl and Tezcatlipoca, but he did not undertake to identify any more of them by name, though there were dozens of the masks.

Passing a rack of costumes, garish and of vivid colors, Salter said that they were of modern manufacture, but that they represented the actual robes used in rituals wherein the masks were also worn. Then, either ignoring, or not hearing, questions, the curator opened the door to a long room that showed an array of statuary, all hewn with stone tools.

They were the gods of the Aztecs: Xochipilli, goddess of flowers; Huitzilopochtli, the war god; his sister, Coyalxauhqui. Stopping to pick up a remarkable life-sized skull of crystal, Salter said that it represented Tezcatlipoca, chief of the Aztec gods. But when they had gone the entire length of the gallery, Salter had at no time mentioned any god of fire.

The answer came when the curator opened the door of a small room that bore a special combination lock, like the dial of a safe. The room was lined with carved slabs of stone; at the far end was a rough-hewn stone, that seemed part of the wall. At the sides of the room, The Shadow saw empty niches.

"The throne room of Xitli, the fire god," spoke Salter, with a smile. "That is, if such a god belonged in the Mayan pantheon. Professor Hedwin believes in such a legend so, to humor his whim, we allowed him to install this throne room.

None of the exhibits have arrived, as Hedwin is bringing them in personally from Mexico.

"According to Hedwin"—Salter's tone carried the slight trace of a chuckle—"a strange cult used to gather in the throne room of Xitli. They were Mayas, and later Aztecs, who accepted a living leader as the incarnation of Xitli. Murder, torture, pillage were not crimes, when Xitli ordered them."

Salter locked the throne room and turned toward the elevators. Politely, he invited Cranston to come back on another day, when more relics would be on display. Many boxes, Salter said, had not yet been opened. Most of them were in the cellar of the museum.

At that moment, Salter was interrupted. He was standing by the door of the elevator, which he had opened, when all the group detected scraping sounds that seemed to filter through the museum. The noise was uncanny, for it was quite untraceable, at first. It was Cranston who explained the riddle.

"Probably from the elevator shaft," he said. "Which might indicate the cellar. You spoke of boxes down there, Mr. Salter."

Salter shook his head.

"It couldn't be the cellar. Do you think so, Mr. Talborn?"

Talborn decided with Salter that the sounds came from a higher floor; but Brendle accepted The Shadow's theory, that the cellar was the source. It was The Shadow who suggested, in Cranston's easy style:

"If we go down to the ground floor, we can trace the sounds from there."

Salter took them to the ground floor in the elevator. As he stopped the car, they listened; the sounds still came from below. Stepping from the elevator, Salter beckoned the group toward his office.

There, he opened a desk drawer and took out two revolvers, after which, he pointed to some canes in the corner and a pair of spears crossed on the wall.

"There are four stairways to the cellar," he said, "each from a corner of the ground floor. I would suggest that we each take a separate stairway and converge on the intruders."

SALTER took a revolver, and so did Talborn. Brendle preferred one of the big spears, while The Shadow, quite indifferently, picked one of the canes. Softly, they started out into the corridor.

The Shadow let the others go ahead. Then, stepping back into the office, he replaced the cane where it belonged.

Opening a briefcase that he had brought with him, the leisurely Mr. Cranston became a man of rapid action. Producing a slouch hat and a black cloak, he put on the garments, then packed a brace of automatics into holsters beneath his coat. By that rapid transformation, he became The Shadow.

Sidestepping from the office, The Shadow became a gliding shape along the dim corridor as he moved toward the outer door. Once he was outside the museum, he vanished. Blackness from the shrubbery blotted out his arriving form. Picking his way through the gloom, The Shadow paced the lower wall of the huge museum.

Somewhere, he expected to find an outside entrance to the cellar, as Salter had termed it, though actually it was a basement, its floor only a trifle below ground level. The museum, according to report, had been built upon a solid square of concrete that served as a permanent foundation.

At the rear of the pyramid, The Shadow came upon the cellar entrance, which betrayed itself by a thin line of light from a sliding door that was not quite shut. Halting, the black-cloaked arrival drew back to a clump of shrubs, finding cover in the darkness, which was now complete except for the whiteness of the museum wall.

The door was sliding open; a man carrying a burlap sack moved outward, past where The Shadow stood. The burden was heavy, even for the husky man who hauled it. The Shadow could not see the man's face, for it was turned away, but his rough clothes and low-pulled cap gave him a thuggish appearance.

The fellow passed the sack to someone in the darkness, then returned to the cellar. Hearing footsteps move away beyond the shrubs, The Shadow decided to look into the cellar first. The man who went inside had closed the door again, but The Shadow worked it open wide enough to wedge through.

A light was glowing in the cellar. Beneath its glare, three men were stooping above a large box, newly arrived from Mexico, working on its half-raised lid. One fist holding a drawn gun, The Shadow placed his other hand behind him and slid the door shut.

He began a slow advance, unnoticed by the stooping men, who failed even to see the stretch of elongated blackness that crept along the floor and into their midst.

A few steps more would have brought The Shadow squarely upon the trio of human rats who were obviously engaged in looting the boxes that Hedwin had sent from Mexico. But The Shadow's unseen command was suddenly broken by a sound from a corner of the cellar.

One of three other invaders, Salter, Talborn, or Brendle, had stumbled while coming down a stairway.

Instantly, the three men by the boxes were up on their feet, one trying to learn which corner the sound had come from, another grabbing for the light, the third turning toward the very doorway through which The Shadow had entered.

All three were armed, and when the third man saw The Shadow, his yell brought the other two about. There were snarls as the light went out; then the sudden bark of revolvers.

Those shots were harmless, fired by men who were spinning, sprawling over boxes under the hard-sledged blows of a human whirlwind. The man who doused the light hadn't given his pals, nor himself, sufficient time to witness the speed of The Shadow's lunge.

Darkness was no handicap to The Shadow, especially when he knew that every figure he encountered was a foeman, deserving of prompt settlement.

The darkness, however, saved the bewildered crooks, as they scrambled for the corners of the cellar, two minus their guns, the third too anxious for flight to try potshots against an invisible target.

The Shadow could not risk shots in their direction, because he heard other sounds beyond and knew that Salter, Talborn, and Brendle were coming into the fray, where they could receive stray bullets.

Only one of them had a flashlight: Salter. The curator used it, somewhat frantically, spreading a beam that he didn't hold in any one place. Each time his light uncovered a crook, Salter shed the glare somewhere else, and the thug went scuttling to cover.

The laugh of The Shadow reverberated through the cellar, bringing startling echoes from the stone-lined room. It told the robbers that surrender was their only course, and they were about to heed it, when new invaders entered. They came from the outer door, which they slid aside, a crew of them with flashlights.

Outlined in the glare, The Shadow furnished gun stabs that brought howls and scattered flashlights. Other guns were blazing from the door, but their shots were wide, spasmodic. In the confusion, the three thugs from the cellar were seeking escape, and blocking off the very marksmen who had helped them.

SUCH were not the only blunders. Salter and Talborn were shooting from their corners, aiming short of the door for fear that some enemies might be diving in upon them. With bullets ricocheting close at hand, The Shadow reversed his course, seeking to fire from a longer, but safer, range.

As he wheeled, the chance sweep of Salter's flashlight showed a bulky man driving in with a big spear. It was Brendle, hoping to head off some of the scattering crooks. The Shadow met him with a charge that sent Brendle backward, his spear clattering away. Seeing Brendle's fall, Salter charged in, shouting to Talborn to join him.

From the floor, Brendle was bellowing for them to stop; that they had made a bad mistake. Salter, by then, was feeling the weight of a fist that carried a gun. He sagged, clutching his jaw, and heard Brendle's shouts. He tried to yell at Talborn, too, but his jaw was too numbed to work.

Talborn was reeling away from The Shadow, when Salter and Brendle reached him. Gone berserk, Talborn began to battle his own friends and gave them a terrific grapple. He had lost his revolver under a slashing blow that The Shadow had given him, and the fact that he was weaponless drove Talborn to greater frenzy.

While three men tumbled around the cellar, they heard The Shadow's laugh again, near the outer door, accompanied by staccato shots that he fired after fleeing crooks. Then the roar of auto motors from a block away told that crooks had maneuvered a departure, due to the chance mix-up that had retarded The Shadow.

The crazed fray in the cellar took a sudden end when another man strong-armed his way among the battlers. Spilled to the floor, Salter found his flashlight and turned it in the direction of grunts and groans.

He saw Talborn lying on the floor, quite subdued by a complacent man who was seated upon the prone fighter. The seated man had Brendle stymied, too. He had gripped Brendle's arm and was holding it behind him, so tightly that Brendle could not twist away.

Groggy though he was, Salter laughed. The man who had pitched him out of things, and separated Talborn and Brendle, too, was the unruffled Mr. Cranston. It seemed that Cranston must have stayed in his own corner, until he realized what turn the fight had taken. He had then proceeded to put his friends in their proper places.

Sheepishly, Talborn and Brendle thanked Cranston for putting them right. Salter, meanwhile, began to examine the boxes. He found them partly opened, and made a checkup of the contents.

The boxes were loosely packed, but none of the Mayan curios were missing, for Salter had a list that he consulted while he made the check-up.

"At least, we managed to get here in time," declared the curator. "Those crooks hadn't finished opening the boxes, when we disturbed them. They have fled, so we might as well go upstairs to my office and inform the police of the attempted robbery.

Lamont Cranston was the last to leave the cellar. He stood alone, with a flashlight of his own, as the others returned up the stairs. With his probing light, The Shadow first studied the corner where he had left his cloak and hat in order to become Cranston again. The garments were out of sight, where he could pick them up at leisure.

Then the light glowed on the boxes. A soft laugh, only a whisper, issued from The Shadow's lips. Fitzhugh Salter had a wrong surmise, as bad as Eugene Brendle's mistaken attack upon The Shadow, or the stumble that Graham Talborn had made, still earlier, while descending the corner stairway.

Intruders had not been *opening* the boxes when The Shadow found them. They had been *closing* those crates from Mexico. In fact, before entering the cellar, The Shadow had seen some sneaking away with the last load of goods that they had bagged.

Nothing was gone from the boxes, according to the list that Salter claimed had come from Professor Hedwin. But the fact still remained that the boxes, loosely packed, could have held a great deal more than the list stated; indeed, had actually held a great deal more.

The Shadow knew what the crooks had stolen. They had picked up Aztec treasure, which Panchez and his mestizos had been gathering all along the route while Hedwin and his expedition were traveling from Yucatan to Mexico City. The treasure had been shipped along with the bonefide Mayan relics intended for the museum.

Who was behind the game, remained a riddle. Whether or not Professor Hedwin had secretly engineered the crooked shipment was a question not yet answered. Conversely, it might be that Fitzhugh Salter was covering the deliveries. Yet, either or both might be innocent, not guilty.

The best way to solve the problem would be to find the men who had carried away the treasure tonight. Such was The Shadow's coming problem, in New Orleans.

CHAPTER VII
CRIME'S NEW CHANCE

LAMONT CRANSTON sat at a writing desk, in his room at the Hotel Montebazan. Another night had come to New Orleans, the fourth since his arrival. From the windows of his corner room, The Shadow covered every angle that he wanted.

In one direction, he could see the city's center; off, far beyond, the white shape of the strange but sightly pyramid that housed the Mayan Museum. In another direction, The Shadow overlooked the French Quarter, otherwise the Vieux Carré, which carried the charm of old New Orleans and was a place where many problems might be answered.

A third outlook showed the Mississippi, with its long curved line of docks. There lay the waterfront, where East met West, with North and South to boot, and the law of human survival prevailed in its rawest form. No city in the United States had a more polyglot waterfront than New Orleans, and The Shadow was quite convinced that the men he wanted would be found there.

The New Orleans police had investigated the attempted robbery at the Mayan Museum, but the belief that the marauders had departed empty-handed made the case an empty one, as well. Hence, the law had practically dropped the matter, leaving intensive investigation solely to The Shadow.

On the writing desk lay a list of names, all of persons who might have been concerned. Gamblers, smugglers, petty racketeers, even former politicians, were on The Shadow's list. He had crossed off names, a dozen and more, until only one remained:

Pierre Laboutard.

It was difficult to class Pierre Laboutard. Some termed him a modern Jean Lafitte, a cross between a smuggler and a pirate, yet a heroic figure who would turn patriotic when occasion called. Such a description exaggerated Laboutard.

He had been a rumrunner in the old days, and later had tried to muscle in on the shrimp fishing industry, to the extent of taking over some fishing shacks from their rightful owners. To save his hide, he had subsequently tipped off Federal authorities to the whereabouts of some gunrunners who were shipping weapons to Central America.

Thus Laboutard, the smuggler-pirate who went patriotic, was, in short, a bootlegger and racketeer who had turned State's evidence. Since then, Pierre Laboutard had faded neatly into the background; but he and his mixed tribe still had to live.

Lately, Laboutard & Co. hadn't been seen, and it was supposed that they had gone back to the bayous. But The Shadow had traced them to the New Orleans waterfront.

Laboutard wasn't in the habit of leaving a forwarding address, but The Shadow, familiar with life along the New Orleans docks, had finally narrowed down the hunt. Tonight, he expected to call on Laboutard; but first, he had another appointment.

Professor Darius Hedwin had arrived from Mexico, Andy Ames with him. Fitzhugh Salter was holding a reception at the Mayan Museum, in Hedwin's honor, and Lamont Cranston was one of the invited guests. Since the event promised some threads to the past that might lead to the future, The Shadow had decided to attend, and look to Laboutard afterward.

Attired in faultless evening clothes, The Shadow reached the museum, where he was introduced to Professor Hedwin and Andy Ames; Fitzhugh Salter was there, of course, and The Shadow also found Graham Talborn and Eugene Brendle.

Affable as ever, Talborn was surrounded by a group of prosperous-looking men, contributors to the museum fund. Talborn's enthusiasm over the museum was quite contagious, and the grizzled exporter was very generous in his statements. Though Talborn was the largest contributor to the cause, he shared the credit with others, much to their pleasure.

A contrasting group acknowledged Brendle as their spokesman. They were men connected with the building trades, who had helped in the construction of the museum. There were architects among them, and craftsmen, and they all received a share of praise from Brendle.

The contractor made it quite plain that he had left many of the details to various specialists, knowing that they were both competent and reliable.

One man was noticeably absent: James Carland. He had been invited, as a matter of courtesy, but no one expected him to appear. There was a slight stir, however, when a girl arrived in Salter's office. The Shadow heard her name buzz through the group:

"Yvonne Carland!"

Promptly, The Shadow gathered that the girl was Carland's niece; that she lived in New Orleans with her uncle. She must have inherited her disposition, as well as her looks, from the other side of her family, for she wasn't a bit like her Uncle James.

YVONNE CARLAND was a brunette, with large brown eyes, and a complexion of a delicate cream that made an excellent contrast to her ruddy, smiling lips. Her features, like her name, denoted the French ancestry of her mother's family, while her voice had a slight touch of the musical Louisiana drawl.

"Uncle Jim wouldn't come," Yvonne told Salter, "and I can't say that I blame him. But I thought you ought to know that we appreciated the invitation, so I up and came myself."

Dropping his smug style, Salter became profoundly polite.

"You are very welcome, Miss Carland," he said. "We feel that your uncle would still be one of us, but for his financial problems. We hope you will assure him on that point."

Yvonne shook hands with Professor Hedwin, who scarcely noticed her during the process. His eyes were far away, as though his thoughts were still in Mexico. But Yvonne's eyes, The Shadow noted, were fixed on someone very close at hand. She had a warm smile, too, for Andy Ames.

"I knew you would come," The Shadow heard Andy confide. "Otherwise, I would have telephoned you, Yvonne."

"Which would have been unwise," the girl returned. "It will take a while, Andy, before my uncle will be in a good humor. He won't hear or speak of anyone who has a thing to do with this museum, except Mr. Brendle."

"Because he owes Brendle money?"

"That's why. It's just good policy with Uncle Jim, to be friendly under such circumstances. Honestly, Andy"—the girl's eyes blazed—"sometimes I hate my uncle."

"You haven't anything on Professor Hedwin," said Andy. "All you have to do is say 'James Carland,' and he erupts like a Mexican volcano!"

Andy's voice had raised a trifle. Hedwin was close enough to hear Carland's name and the reference to the volcano. Instantly, Hedwin's high-pitched voice cackled an interruption to all other conversations.

"James Carland!" he exclaimed. "Why mention the man who tried to destroy all our efforts? He pledged himself to build this museum, and then abandoned us. He used his evil influence on others, too. There was a man from New York, named Jonathan Dorn, who offered to finance my expedition while it was in Yucatan.

"But Carland talked to him and wanted him to put money into rice fields. We heard no more from Dorn. Bah! He was as bad as Carland!

"Don't try to stop me, Salter"—waving his arms, Hedwin pushed the curator away—"because I don't like interruptions. Let me see." The professor's glower became a reflective stare. "What did I intend to tell you? Ah, yes!" Hedwin brightened. "I meant to speak about the volcano: Xitli."

The whole group showed relief as Hedwin changed the subject. They listened, with real interest, while the professor harped upon his theory that the Mayas had identified their fire god with the volcano. Once talking about Xitli, Hedwin became hard to stop.

"Let us go upstairs," he finally suggested, "and I shall show you the prize of this museum—the throne room of Xitli, furnished with the relics that I personally brought back from Cuicuilco."

Riding up in the elevators, the group reassembled outside the throne room. Salter started to turn the combination, but Hedwin pushed him aside. Those two, it seemed, were the only ones who knew the combination to the big strong door.

When he opened the door, Hedwin turned on a

light that gave the room a ruddy glow, symbolizing flame.

THE room contained the curios that Hedwin mentioned. Little images of the squat fire god were in the niches along the walls. Two tablets of stone, with odd hieroglyphics, were on either side of the built-in throne. There were vases and urns about the room, but most important was the seat of the throne itself.

There, The Shadow saw a squarish block of basalt, smooth except for its special markings. He heard Andy telling Yvonne how the professor had unearthed the black stone on the last night at Cuicuilco.

Then, like the rest, The Shadow was watching Professor Hedwin parade across the room, to take his place upon the throne. Seated there, the gray-haired excavator cackled happily.

"I am Xitli!" announced Hedwin. "And you"— he swept his withery hand about the group—"are my followers. Because Xitli had followers"— Hedwin was nodding, wisely—"yes, many of them. The Xitli cult was powerful, and dangerous. It survives to this day, and now its meeting place is in New Orleans, instead of at Cuicuilco!"

Salter was undertoning something to the persons near him. Rising from the throne, Hedwin advanced to the door, demanding sharply:

"What's that you are saying, Salter?"

"I was saying," returned Salter, crisply, "that the Xitli legend as yet remains unproven. This throne room is your whim, Hedwin, not mine."

Hedwin's scrawny hands came up, as though he intended to dig his clawish fingernails into Salter's throat. With a shrug, the curator turned away.

"Come, let us look at the other exhibits," he said. "Then we'll return downstairs, where a buffet supper has been prepared for us."

It was Andy who restrained old Hedwin, for he knew how to humor the professor. Blocking the door, Andy asked Hedwin to identify the various Xitli images in the niches, according to their inscriptions.

Yvonne Carland looked quite interested; so did Lamont Cranston. Finding that he had an audience, the professor roamed the room, picking out the various figurines and stating in what parts of Mexico he had uncovered them.

By the time Hedwin and his present companions rejoined the group downstairs, the old professor was beaming happily, his feud with Salter forgotten, like his outbursts against Carland and Dorn. In fact, Hedwin became deeply interested when he heard Salter tell about the thwarted robbery of a few nights before.

Both Talborn and Brendle supported Salter's description, and all seemed pleased when they saw Cranston nod his agreement to their account. Meanwhile, the guests were making inroads into the buffet supper, and when the story was finished, Professor Hedwin wagged an oyster fork about the group.

"Those robbers were after the Xitli relics, I warrant," declared the professor, solemnly. "But I tricked them. I didn't ship the Xitli remains; I brought them personally, instead. But I am glad, Salter, that you stopped the robbery. By doing so, you saved some very fine exhibits.

"Which reminds me, Andy"—Hedwin turned to his assistant—"another shipment is arriving tonight, on the *Amazonia*. It is the last shipment from Mexico. I think that you should be there when the boxes are unloaded."

"You want me to go right away, Professor?"

"No, not right away." Hedwin threw a smile toward Yvonne. "I would say that an hour from now would be soon enough. They called me at the hotel, to tell me that the Amazonia had docked; but there is no hurry, Andy. No hurry at all."

Rather gratefully, Andy Ames accepted the professor's decision, because it allowed him another hour with Yvonne Carland. But there was one guest in the group who felt that the matter of the *Amazonia* demanded prompt attention: Lamont Cranston.

This was the first that The Shadow had heard of another shipment from Mexico. Its significance was plain.

Since crooks had stolen unlisted contents from boxes in the museum cellar, it was likely that they might intend to repeat the operation. But the museum was better protected than before, and this evening it was thronged with people. Which left the criminals one other choice: a robbery before the boxes were unloaded from the Amazonia.

Unnoticed by the chatting group, Cranston left the museum. Stepping into a car, he drove away, drawing a black cloak around his shoulders. Again, Lamont Cranston had become The Shadow, as was evidenced by his whispered laugh as he placed his slouch hat on his head.

The Shadow was bound for the waterfront ahead of schedule, to look up Pierre Laboutard. If he did not find the so-called pirate at the spot where he expected, there would still be another place to look: the wharf where the steamship *Amazonia* had docked!

CHAPTER VIII
ALONG THE WATERFRONT

BACK from the extensive line of wharves along the Mississippi, the huddled buildings of the waterfront seemed dwarfed and shrunken as they

crouched behind the shelter of the levee, where loomed the steel sheds of the wharves.

There was life throughout that district, as mixed as a score of nationalities could make it, and at nightfall the bulking darkness of the sheds shrouded the menace of the district below, frequently hiding deeds as dark as the night itself.

Only the banana wharves presented activity by night; the chief danger in their vicinity was from tarantulas and tropical snakes that came in with banana shipments. But along the docks where coffee and cotton were unloaded, and near the molasses sheds, menace could exist in human form.

Picking his way past waterfront dives that emitted the babble of many tongues, The Shadow

reached an old storefront that made a forbidding portal. Windows close by betokened watchful eyes, ready to report the advent of any stranger; but no eye could have discerned the cloaked form of The Shadow in that gloom.

Working the door open, The Shadow glided through a pitch-black hallway, down a short flight of steps, to another door that signified a back room. The room was lighted; it contained a crew of rough-clad men, who felt too secure in these preserves to bother about placing a guard on the inner door.

The Shadow was looking in on Pierre Laboutard and his band of thugs. Smugglers, pirates, or mere cutthroats—any of the terms would have suited them. Laboutard, himself, was brawny, hard-faced,

Windows close by betokened watchful eyes, ready to report the advent of any stranger.

and sharp of eye. But the same description applied equally to the rest.

A few were Cajuns, members of the darkish, indefinable race found in the environs of New Orleans. They considered themselves a chosen group, for one of their number was Laboutard's lone lieutenant. Laboutard addressed the fellow as Jaro, and seemed to value his opinions. The rest of the band were largely ex-sailors, of various nationalities.

Laboutard was talking, when The Shadow viewed the meeting through the door crack. The leader's tone came in a forced purr that carried traces of a venomous hiss. Jaro, seated beside Laboutard, saw fit to put in brief comments of his own, supplementing some of the leader's statements.

"Tonight will be one more job," spoke Laboutard. "Like the others, but not at the museum. No. It will be more wise to go to the ship, the *Amazonia*. What matter if we make much trouble? This one will be the last time. A few can go to the ship more easily than many."

"With me," put in Jaro, tapping his chest. "I pick my men." He pointed to the Cajuns. "I take five."

"Then afterward," continued Laboutard, "after all is over, we come back here. I pay you all; maybe more than the price I promise. Then we wait, and do nothing."

Jaro offered an objection.

"First you say there was something more," he reminded. "Some more jobs, for special men, that would bring big money, Pierre."

"Ah, *oui*," recalled Laboutard. "But I have thought it over. I do not like it. To steal, it is easy, even if one have to kill. But to kill for nothing but the pay, is different. It is too foolish."

Jaro looked doubtful on that point, as did several of the others, but Laboutard remained unruffled. He merely made his point more plain.

"One man say steal," he declared, "in a way that nobody find out. We do it, and even with trouble like we have the other night, the police do not bother us. So we can steal more, the same way. Good, eh, Jaro?"

Jaro admitted that it was.

"But another man say kill," added Laboutard, "and when we do, what happen? There will be police everywhere. They ask questions that make trouble for a lot of you, even though they do not arrest for murder."

The ex-sailors caught the point. Some of them would be due for deportation if questioned too closely by the authorities, no matter what the subject.

"So we wait, after tonight," concluded Laboutard, shrewdly, "and then decide what is the best to do. Maybe the man who wish the murder pay for something else. It may be that I know something that he would not like people to hear."

LABOUTARD had made it quite plain that he had two clients: one, who wanted robberies committed and was getting them; the other, a man who desired murder done. In typical fashion, Laboutard was planning a shakedown as an easier way of collecting cash from the second man in question.

The fact that Laboutard had been approached by two different schemers did not strike The Shadow as a coincidence. The simple fact was that Laboutard was the one man in New Orleans best equipped to handle specialized crime. He and his band were the clearing house for such operations.

"I send you, Jaro, to the ship," decided Laboutard. "Go, now, and we can follow. Through the alley will be best for you, while we go out the front. Because maybe you find trouble; but for us, maybe we only watch."

The Shadow took the route through the front door, while Jaro and his squad were sneaking from the back. The cloaked fighter was gone when Laboutard and his reserve crew came sauntering from the front door.

But The Shadow did not pick up Jaro's trail direct. Instead, he took a route of his own to the pier where the *Amazonia* was docked.

The Amazonia was an old freighter that often berthed in New Orleans. Her mixed cargo wasn't the sort that anyone would want to rifle; hence, no pains were taken to protect the ship from boarders. Getting over the rail, The Shadow found a convenient lurking place behind a huge coil of rope, near a hatchway. There, he waited for Jaro and the Cajun squad.

They came on board as stealthily as snakes. Crouching low, they wormed their way to the open hatchway and descended, one by one. When the last had gone, The Shadow moved forward from the rope coil and took a careful look toward the wharf, to make sure that Laboutard and the reserves were not too close at hand.

Then, two guns drawn, The Shadow turned to make his own descent, intending to surprise Jaro and his Cajuns at work in the hold below.

It was a bold plan, but a sure one, considering The Shadow's methods. He had trapped crooks before, below decks, and knew that they did not like it when boxed. Maybe some shooting would be necessary, but it would be in The Shadow's favor.

His shots would alarm the ship's crew and bring them to take over the prisoners. That would leave The Shadow free to greet Laboutard and the reserves, when they made their delayed arrival.

As The Shadow foresaw it, the surprise would strike Jaro and the Cajuns, and there would be no way for them to reverse the situation.

But there was one factor not in The Shadow's calculations: the chance that Jaro and his men might receive a surprise before The Shadow reached them. Such was to happen, for things were happening below deck without The Shadow's knowledge.

Crouched above boxes which they had rapidly opened, the Cajuns were reaching for heavy burlap sacks that Jaro pointed out, when a stir came from deeper in the hold. Low voices seemed to mutter a chant that was anything but human.

Bounding up from a box, Jaro gave a snarl that showed actual fright, for his superstitious nature was aroused. Then, contemptuously, he flung a light into the depths.

The beam showed a sight that froze the band of Cajuns. They were ready to battle man, beast, or reptile, but not the creatures that came clumping toward them. They were men, yes, those figures from the hold, but a sort that could have come from another world. In fact, they did belong to another period.

They were Aztecs, a dozen of them, lineal descendants of the bronze fighters who had ruled ancient Mexico. Chunky-built, with metallic faces topped by sharp-slanted foreheads, they were clad in dusky garb, the hides of jungle beasts.

For arms, they had stone hatchets, which they raised as they advanced. Then, when Jaro reached for a knife as a suitable weapon for a silent fray, the stony Aztecs lunged.

Jaro sprang away, his knife half drawn. The Cajuns followed their leader, frantically trying to get at weapons of their own. Pursued by the Aztecs, who were charging full force, Jaro and his squad went up through the hatchway at top speed, with an impetus that even a superhuman force could not halt.

The Shadow learned that when he tried to stop them. He greeted Jaro's swarming men with a challenging laugh so startling, coming from darkness, that it would ordinarily have made the superstitious Cajuns falter.

Moreover, he was in among them with his guns, swinging to beat them down into the hatchway. But the terror that pursued the maddened tribe numbed their minds to any menace that might lie ahead.

HOISTED high by the mass of crazed men who erupted from the hatchway, The Shadow was swept back on the crest of a human tidal wave. A light from the ship's bridge showed darkish faces and gleaming knives.

Though too wild to recognize The Shadow as the fighter who had battled them in the museum, Jaro's men saw him as an obstacle to their path and tried to hew him down.

Flaying with his arms, The Shadow beat off the knife thrusts, but could do no more. The swirl carried him to the far rail of the ship, where he managed to disentangle himself, though slashing knives threatened to cut his cloak to ribbons. Spinning sideways, The Shadow brought up against a stanchion and landed on his hands and knees.

Jaro was going overboard, and his men were copying his example except for one who had stumbled short, staggered by a gun blow from The Shadow. The luckless Cajun was on his feet as soon as The Shadow, and seeing the cloaked fighter, the fellow came at him. Grappling, they reeled toward the rail, just as the Aztecs reached the deck.

The excitement on the *Amazonia* had been heard by Laboutard and his men, who were lurking far back in the darkness of a shed. Wondering what had happened to his shock troops, Laboutard started forward with the reserves. But another man had already reached the scene. Andy Ames had just come from the museum and was stepping on board the *Amazonia.*

Andy saw The Shadow half across the far rail, a man with a knife poised above him. Andy didn't notice that The Shadow had dropped one gun overboard and had caught the foeman's wrist. Andy was still carrying his revolver, and he used it.

His shot clipped the Cajun. With a howl, the wounded man went over the rail, carrying The Shadow with him.

His gunshot echoed by a splash, Andy heard another sound that whizzed past his ear. Something landed with a choppy noise in a post just behind him. In the dim light of the deck, Andy spied the thrower, a squat man who had come from a hatchway. Remembering the night at Cuicuilco, Andy mistook the Aztec for one of The Shadow's Xincas.

Rather than mistakenly battle a friend, Andy turned for the wharf. Stumbling against the post, he found the object that had driven into it: a stone-headed ax. Yanking the weapon from the post, Andy carried it with him. Hearing a snarly shout from the wharf shed, Andy cut away for cover just as guns began to shoot in his general direction.

Then Laboutard and his mixed reserves were surging on board the *Amazonia*, expecting to find The Shadow milling with Jaro's Cajuns. Instead, they discovered a deserted deck. Like Jaro's crew, The Shadow had gone overboard, and the Aztecs, too, had disappeared.

The strange men from Mexico had sought battle only to keep their presence unknown. Having cleared the deck, they had taken shore leave before the arrival of Laboutard and his reinforcements. So swiftly had they seized their opportunity that even The Shadow, busied with the Cajuns, had failed to see the Aztecs come and go!

CHAPTER IX
TRAIL DELAYED

COMMOTION broke on the *Amazonia* as soon as Pierre Laboutard and his men boarded the ship.

Andy's gunshot had wakened members of the sleeping crew, and the volley that Laboutard's followers supplied completely aroused the sailors. But as soon as they poked themselves in sight, Laboutard ordered gunfire that drove the sailors back to cover.

Laboutard ordered half of his men below to complete the robbery that Jaro had begun. They scurried down the hatchway, and the man who remained on deck began exchanging sniping shots with the barricaded sailors.

All the while, Laboutard was fuming. He knew there would be trouble from the shore, and feared that time would prove too short to complete his purpose.

Things worked to Laboutard's advantage. His men were back in no time, bringing the burlap sacks. Having found the boxes open, they had simply seized the swag. As soon as they arrived, Laboutard ordered a swift trip ashore.

The burden carriers hurried ahead, while Laboutard and the gunners fired shots to keep the sailors of the *Amazonia* in their quarters.

Attracted by the gunfire, two policemen had reached the wharf. They saw the stooped figures of the scurrying men who carried the bags of loot. Shouting for them to stop, the officers hurried forward, firing warning shots as they came.

It was a serious gesture, for they were unwittingly putting themselves in the path of Laboutard's gun squad, which was coming from the boat.

From the next wharf, where he had found shelter, Andy Ames saw the danger. Andy held two weapons: his revolver in one hand, the Aztec hatchet in the other.

He hesitated a mere moment, then flung the hatchet out into the river, where it landed with a choppy *plunk*, its stone head carrying it to the muddy bottom. Waving his revolver, Andy dashed toward the *Amazonia*, shouting a warning to the officers.

"Look out!" he called. "They're coming from the ship, a whole mob with guns!"

Andy didn't give the cops time to doubt. He fired at the gangway of the *Amazonia*, then dropped for the nearest shelter, easily ahead of the return volley that Laboutard's gunners supplied. But Andy's warning wasn't enough.

This was more than a shipside quarrel, which the cops mistook it to be. Laboutard had just committed piracy in earnest, and intended to chop down any blockers who might hold him responsible for the deed.

His roustabouts were joined by Jaro and the Cajuns, who had swum around the ship like water rats, to come ashore. Some were surging en masse, to overwhelm the two patrolmen, who by this time were rapidly retiring; while others, men with knives, were creeping in to wipe out Andy, who couldn't see them against the black side of the *Amazonia*.

Out of that ominous situation came the one challenge that could reverse matters: the laugh of The Shadow!

The black-cloaked fighter had not swum around the *Amazonia*. Instead, he had returned to the deck by way of the anchor chain. He was on the bridge, boldly placing himself where all could see him, confident that Laboutard's close-range fighters could not put up an accurate fire from the comparatively distant wharf.

Having regained the automatic that he had dropped on deck, The Shadow was proving that long range was his forte. His shots were either nicking Laboutard's followers or ricocheting from the concrete at their feet. With his second gun, The Shadow added side shots toward the knifers who were creeping toward Andy.

They were too close to the *Amazonia* to be picked off, but the shots were dangerously close. In scuffling to the wharf edge under the steamship's side, they gave themselves away, and Andy began to blast, glad that his experience at Cuicuilco had taught him to always carry extra ammunition for his revolver.

Laboutard's whole tribe took the quickest course that offered flight. It was every man for himself, with escape the only object, as they scattered everywhere. Laboutard himself was on the run, and Jaro with him, but when they reached the depths of the shed, the pirate chief and his lieutenants shouted for the tribe to rally.

By then it was too late.

The Shadow's timely demonstration had already brought a compact crew to action. The sailors on the *Amazonia* were taking over the vessel's deck, armed with a variety of weapons. They heard The Shadow's laugh, saw the pointing stabs of his flashing guns. They took to the land as readily as the Cajuns had gone for the water.

Crippled members of Laboutard's band tried to stop that surge, and the wharf became a general melee, with everything favoring the sailors from the *Amazonia*. Andy and the officers were coming in to aid, forgetful that Laboutard might rally his remaining men back from the waterfront.

IT was The Shadow who foresaw that complication. Down from the bridge, over the gangway, he was speeding across the wharf, a black-clad avenger whose streaking figure was actually invisible under the gloom of the sheltering shed.

His purpose was to hurl himself as a living bombshell into the cluster that was forming around Laboutard and Jaro.

They were across a street that ran beside a railroad track, and a stretch of light intervened. They spied The Shadow as he reached that last lap and began to scatter, some aiming revolvers, others hurling knives.

Had they remained grouped, The Shadow would have launched into their midst; but since they were scattering of their own volition, he simply went into the next stage of his clean-up.

Wheeling back into darkness, The Shadow jabbed telling shots at flashing guns, shifting his own position with such alacrity that his foemen were belated when they tried to pick his gun bursts as targets.

Nor did The Shadow's mocking laugh give them a key. It could have come from anywhere—or from nowhere.

Laboutard's baffled band was in a tight spot, when a big spotlight suddenly blazed in from a corner. It showed The Shadow, a sleek shape in black, dripping from his trip into the river. Guns began a haphazard tattoo in his direction.

The light was from a police car that covered the waterfront. Its occupants mistook The Shadow for the prime troublemaker, and to add to the complication, other cars were coming up to follow the example of the first. The Shadow's only course was landward flight. As he sped in one direction to elude the revealing lights, Laboutard's fighters fled in another.

Still misguided, the cops in police cars tried to hunt down The Shadow. Those that stopped at the wharf learned of the mistake, but by then the pursuers were too far away. They spotted The Shadow at infrequent intervals as he took to alleyways.

Finally reaching his car, The Shadow managed to get a start to safety, but to avoid a clash with the police, he was forced to drive away from the city's center instead of toward it.

Meanwhile, order had been restored near the Amazonia. Laboutard's cripples had fought to the death; not one remained to name the leader who had ordered them into combat.

Andy Ames explained how he had happened to come to the wharf, and sailors from the *Amazonia* supported him with the testimony that the ship had boxes for the Mayan Museum in its cargo.

Accompanied by a police captain who had taken charge, Andy went on board to examine the boxes. Not only did the shipment appear rifled, but sailors testified that they had seen marauders fleeing with loaded sacks. Nevertheless, the remaining contents of the boxes coincided with a list that Andy had brought from the museum.

It didn't puzzle Andy. He remembered how Panchez and the mestizos had gathered loot on the way from Yucatan. It was plain that they had shipped it with the relics that the expedition had accumulated. Goods for the Mayan Museum had been passed, almost unexamined, by Mexican officials and United States customs officers.

When the police decided that the sacks might have come from elsewhere in the ship's cargo, the men on the *Amazonia* admitted that such might be the case. But Andy was thinking in terms of Professor Hedwin and Fitzhugh Salter, wondering if one or the other could have been responsible for what had happened.

Accompanied by the police captain, Andy returned to the museum. Most of the guests had gone, but the rest were listening to a hectic argument between Hedwin and Salter on the subject of the fire god, Xitli. Graham Talborn and Eugene Brendle were still present; so was Yvonne Carland.

Though Hedwin and Salter seldom agreed on anything, both the professor and the curator were satisfied when Andy announced that the list showed nothing stolen. Hedwin couldn't remember precisely what had gone in various shipments, and Salter declared that all typewritten lists were precise copies of those that Hedwin had sent him.

Hence, Andy's quandary still continued until a new and rather startling element developed. It came when a police car arrived, bringing a darkish, ugly-faced prisoner whose arm was bandaged.

Andy recognized that the fellow must be the Cajun who had grappled The Shadow by the rail of the Amazonia. The man's wound was from the bullet that Andy had triggered.

FISHED from the river by the police, the prisoner was in a mood to talk. He was telling a certain amount of truth because he thought it would be for his benefit and Laboutard's.

The Cajun insisted that he hadn't been on the *Amazonia* at all, but had simply been strolling along the wharf when trouble began. That much was false, but the fellow followed it with facts.

He said that men from the *Amazonia* had started all the trouble; strange men, whose faces looked like copper and whose garments were the rough hides of animals. When he came to the description of their sloping foreheads, there was an interruption from Hedwin.

"Aztecs!" exclaimed the professor, as if quite pleased. "Stowaways from Mexico. Do you know why they are here?" He shot the question at Salter. "They have heard that the temple of Xitli has been restored. My theories are proven!"

"Nonsense!" returned the curator. "Your talk of Xitli is all *fol-de-rol*. I've let you go too far with it, Hedwin, merely because I didn't want to argue."

"What about the mask and robe?" queried Hedwin narrowly. "The costume that you were unable to identify when you put labels on the rest?"

"It is merely an unclassified exhibit," defined Salter. "There is nothing to prove that it represented Xitli. It could belong to any unknown Mayan deity."

Hedwin retorted that there were no unknown Mayan gods, with the possible exception of Xitli. The discussion brought smiles from Talborn and Brendle, who were anxious to see how far it would go. But the police captain wasn't interested in Mayan lore.

"Let's drop this 'X' god," he stormed, "and talk about the Aztecs. They sound phony to me"—he was turning to glare at the Cajun—"and unless somebody else got a look at them, and I mean somebody reliable, we'll count them out."

Looking for someone reliable, the captain noticed Andy Ames and decided that his opinion would do.

"You were there at the start, Ames," he said. "You have already stated that you saw a bunch that looked like Cajuns, along with a crowd of roustabouts. This man"—he nudged toward the prisoner—"and the dead ones at the dock support that statement. But did you see any Aztecs?"

Stolidly, Andy shook his head. He did not feel that he was telling a silent lie. In his opinion, the squat man who had thrown the stone hatchet was a member of some unknown tribe and could not be classed as an Aztec.

Coupled to that was Andy's recollection of the Xincas who had served The Shadow. They fell under Andy's classification of an "unknown tribe." Andy was sure that the hatchet man had come after him by mistake. There had been other mistakes later in the battle at the wharf, and by rectifying one, Andy felt that he was returning a favor to The Shadow.

It never occurred to him that he might be making a greater mistake than all the rest combined, that there had been many stone-faced men on board the *Amazonia*, and that those stowaways, all actual Aztecs, were now loose in New Orleans, forming a murderous flock.

"No Aztecs," decided the police captain. He turned to the Cajun: "Come along, you, and keep your trap shut until you're ready to give us a straight story."

Trucks had arrived with the boxes from the *Amazonia*; all were unloaded and safely stored in the cellar of the museum. Fitzhugh Salter was preparing to close the big pyramid for the night. Ready to leave with the rest, Andy Ames was wondering what had become of The Shadow.

It did not occur to him that The Shadow's trail should rightfully have led back to the Mayan Museum, but that it had been delayed by the interference of the police. Nor did Andy realize that The Shadow was the one person who could have properly judged the statement of the captured Cajun.

This was a time when something that The Shadow had not learned was to prove a hideous factor in schemes of monstrous crime!

CHAPTER X
THE CULT OF XITLI

ALL was quiet outside the Mayan Museum, but the calm itself was so intense that it gave Yvonne Carland the shivers. She pointed to the shrubbery surrounding the pyramid and remarked to Andy that she could almost see the bushes move, as though lurkers were creeping from them.

The comment brought a cackly laugh from Professor Hedwin. He squinted at the bushes, then nodded wisely in support of Yvonne's opinion; but he made no mention of Aztecs.

"Perhaps she is right, Andy," declared Hedwin. "I would advise you to look out for Miss Carland and see her safely home. From all reports, you handled yourself well down at the wharf. If other dangers are abroad, you can protect Miss Carland from them."

With a bow that signified good night, the professor entered a cab and rode away, leaving Andy with Yvonne. Smilingly, Andy asked if he could see Yvonne home. The girl started to nod, then shook her head.

"It wouldn't be best, Andy," she asserted. "My uncle might be up, and he wouldn't like to know that I was really friendly with anyone connected with the recent expedition."

Graham Talborn was standing by. He had heard all the comments. The affable exporter gave a disappointed smile.

"I was going to offer to take you home," he said to Yvonne, "in case Andy did not qualify. But it seems that I am on the blacklist, too. Good night."

Eugene Brendle stepped up when Graham Talborn had strolled away. Brendle offered a prompt solution to the dilemma.

"Come in my car," he told Yvonne. "I'll drop you off at the apartment. If your uncle is watching, he will recognize the car. He doesn't regard me as connected with the museum. I'm only a contractor who couldn't help myself."

Yvonne left with Brendle, and Andy strolled glumly to his car. He took a look at the shrubbery as he drove away and noticed that huddling clumps did seem to move, as Yvonne had suggested. But Andy attributed it to the swing of the car lights.

One man alone remained at the museum: Fitzhugh Salter. The curator was locking the huge front door, and all the while he was wearing a half-smug smile. He glanced sharply about the premises, then walked away on foot. Salter lived in the vicinity of the museum and never used a car.

The stir about the grounds became actual. Squat figures approached the museum itself. Probing along the walls, they must have found secret places of entry, for they gradually disappeared. Then came a half hour of profound calm, until another visitor appeared upon the scene.

He was crouched, and he kept his face well buried in the collar of a light overcoat that was turned up about his chin. If he had come from a car, he must have left it a few blocks away. His tactics were rapid, as well as sneaky. Rounding the corner of the museum, he disappeared.

Within the terraced walls of the great pyramid, creeping men were moving upward by degrees. They were the Aztecs from the *Amazonia*, and they were feeling out their new preserves.

Clever enough to find some secret route that had been left open for them, they were looking for suitable lurking spots in the museum itself, and were discovering them among the passages and rooms of the lower floors. But always their path continued upward.

Only once did the Aztecs pause when the rumble of an elevator told them that someone was ascending more rapidly, passing them on the way. Tightening their grips on the stone axes that they carried, the Aztecs kept on toward their top-floor goal.

Ahead of them, the man with the concealing overcoat reached the exhibit room that held the costumes. He unlocked it quite readily with a master key. With a flashlight, he picked out the unclassified costume that Hedwin had identified with Xitli.

Disposing of his overcoat, he clad himself in the ancient garb. Turning on a light in the inner corridor, the masquerader stepped into the glow.

HE was both hideous and imposing in his new attire. The mask was greenish, composed from bits of jade, but with black lips and eyes formed of jet. His robe was crimson, with streaks of vermilion and dashes of yellow, including varying shades of scarlet and orange.

The whole effect was one of vivid flame, the symbol of Xitli, the fire god.

In fact, the masquerader *was* Xitli—to the Aztecs, when they saw him. Arriving from the stairs, they lowered their stone axes and stood in respectful silence as the fire god addressed them with a hiss. His words, plucked from the vocabulary of the ancient Mayan, pronounced him as the true Xitli.

Then, in case his words did not suffice, Xitli advanced with extended hands which were encased in rough gauntlets that had come with the costume. From one clenched fist he flung a small vial, which cracked on the floor in front of the stolid Aztecs.

There was a burst of dazzling flame that left a quantity of pungent smoke. Their eyes dazzled by the flash, their nostrils stifled by the fumes, the Aztecs drew away with startled babbles. When their sight was clear again, Xitli was gone.

A few minutes passed while the crouching Aztecs waited. Where Xitli had gone was a total mystery to them.

He could have retired along the corridor, or he could have passed right through their midst to reach the stairs. However, their blinking eyes were fixed upon one given spot: the door of the throne room.

It was suddenly swung open from within. The hand that shoved it was withdrawn. Approaching, the Aztecs stared into the room itself, to see Xitli standing beside his throne. His pointing finger indicated the black stone that formed the throne's seat.

As his followers entered the room, giving deep-throated tones of elation, Xitli calmly seated himself upon the basalt slab.

Immediately the Aztecs huddled to the floor. To these descendants of the Xitli cult, whose worship of the fire god had been transmitted down through successive generations, mere possession of that throne established the flame-costumed man as a living deity. Tradition had it that if a usurper sat in the throne of Xitli, fire would destroy him.

Such was the legend of Cuicuilco. Once, so the story ran, a Mayan emperor had taken the throne of Xitli with the approval of his people. The fire god had therewith destroyed the entire city, along with its human ruler, by an overwhelming outpour of green-hot flame and molten rock from the volcanic crater which, therewith, had been named Xitli, in honor of the fire god who controlled it.

Those excavators who worked with Professor Hedwin were men of sufficient Aztec blood to fear the basalt throne slab when they uncovered it. In fact, Hedwin had hazily indicated such facts in a pamphlet which he had written and given to Salter.

Amused by the professor's literary effort, the curator had shown the pamphlet freely. One of Hedwin's "daydreams," Salter had termed it; something that no one could believe.

But these Aztecs accepted such facts, and more. They were of the pure strain that composed the long-smoldering Xitli cult. Presumably extinct, like the crater near Cuicuilco, they had been awaiting the eruption that would bring them back into their own. That time had come, thanks to the green-masked man who occupied the Xitli throne.

Above the mask, Xitli wore a feathered headgear that matched the rest of his barbaric costume. Those feathers had the dye of flame that gave added bearing to the pose of Xitli. By way of

The Aztecs lowered their stone axes and stood in respectful silence as the fire god addressed them.

emphasizing his power, the pretended fire god repeated the trick that he had performed in the hall. He threw another vial and let it burst into flame.

To the untutored Aztecs, who had no knowledge of modern chemicals, the act was some of Xitli's magic. They expected the fire god to disappear; instead, this time he remained.

From the black, frozen lips of his mask he spoke again, slowly, forcing his words, yet making them plain. He was telling the members of his cult that a duty lay ahead.

It was a task that pleased them.

Voices mingled in obedience. Hands gripped stone weapons with new fervor. A wave of Xitli's hand brought his worshippers to their feet. A dozen or more, they were waiting only the fire god's departure before proceeding with the task assigned. They expected another of Xitli's remarkable demonstrations, and he did not disappoint them.

A fling of Xitli's hand, a puff of fire more vivid than the one before. When the smoke cleared, Xitli had vanished. The Aztecs left the throne room and started for the stairs.

When they had gone, Xitli himself appeared surprisingly from the room that they had left. Closing its door, he went back to the costume room and disposed of his flame-hued garb.

Again wearing his muffling overcoat, he descended in the elevator, once more passing the Aztecs, who were taking the slower stairway route.

THE modern Xitli had overlooked one detail. In leaving the throne room open while meeting with his followers, he had supposed that the glare of his chemical flame could not be seen from the windows of the top floor.

He was right, so far as a view from the ground was concerned, because a series of broad terraces intervened.

It happened, however, that an observer was much closer at hand. The Shadow had returned to the museum; desiring to visit its interior, he was scaling the smooth walls at the time the flash came.

The Shadow was using his favorite method for the climb. He was wearing rubber suction cups on hands and feet, squidging those concave disks against the smooth wall that rose from one terrace to the next.

His eyes, looking upward, caught the reflection of the final flash—dim, yet sufficient to tell that something was amiss. The Shadow paused, clinging to the wall; then, on the theory that he might find an inner route from some hidden entrance below, he started downward.

He made rapid progress, for the terraces were only a dozen feet in height, each an easy drop to the one below it.

By the time The Shadow reached the ground, the man from the elevator had gone. But The Shadow's keen eyes picked out the swift-moving figures of the Aztecs who had just come from the pyramid. On foot, The Shadow took up their trail, to find it one of the shiftiest that he had ever attempted to follow.

Had there been less of the Aztecs, The Shadow would have lost them. But with a dozen or more, he was able to gain fleeting glimpses of different natives at sufficient intervals to remain upon their route. It led through dilapidated districts, where houses were thicker, until finally it reached the narrow streets of the French quarter.

There, under a line of balconies, The Shadow found the trail was gone. His only course was to eliminate the places that the Aztecs would have avoided, particularly lighted streets. Choosing alleyways and courtyards, The Shadow soon narrowed down his search, but still he was hunting in the dark.

It was too late to give any sort of alarm that would arouse the neighborhood and bring the police. If the Aztecs were true followers of Xitli, they would hurry whatever deadly work had been assigned to them. Grimly, The Shadow kept to his silent task, yet in the stillness of the alleyways he sensed the ominous.

Death was on the move tonight. Murder insidious, which even the hand of The Shadow might be too late to prevent.

CHAPTER XI
KILLERS BY NIGHT

YVONNE CARLAND wasn't sleepy, though she had gone to bed immediately upon arriving home. The brisk ten-minute ride in Brendle's car had fully roused her by the time she reached the French quarter—Vieux Carré—where her uncle's apartment was located.

The reason Yvonne had gone to bed was because her uncle was asleep when she arrived. She knew that if he awakened and found her still up, he would start to quibble because she had gone to the museum reception.

So Yvonne had undressed in the darkness of her room, to spend the next three quarters of an hour lying in bed, listening to distant sounds of merriment which pervaded the Vieux Carré.

It gradually dawned on her that she hadn't bothered to look at her watch; when she did, she found that it was still early. She began to feel quite foolish at coming home so soon.

Andy had said something about looking up some friends in town. They were all in Yvonne's set, and were probably having a party somewhere. Andy had mentioned it before his visit to the waterfront;

probably he would remember the invitation, if reminded.

Yvonne decided to make a call to Andy's hotel, so she slipped from bed and went to the telephone in the hall.

Cautiously, she called Andy's hotel, but found he wasn't there. She asked if he happened to be in Hedwin's room, and learned that the professor had left word that he wasn't to be disturbed.

Yvonne was debating whether to get dressed and go out, or to return to bed and try to sleep, when her uncle's door opened on the other side of the hall.

Glaring at his nightgowned niece, Carland demanded to know whom she had called. Very sweetly, Yvonne replied that she had heard the telephone bell ring, but that no one was on the wire when she answered.

"Perhaps it was Cranston!" exclaimed Carland. Then, shaking his head: "No; he only had my old address. Bah! What a fool I was to move to this place!"

"I like Frenchtown," replied Yvonne demurely. "It has become quite fashionable to live here, uncle."

"Not when people know you're broke," snapped Carland. "Which I wouldn't be, if I hadn't sunk so much money into that museum. The nerve of that crowd, expecting me to fork over a hundred thousand more after my oil concessions were lost. By the way"—his eyes went sharp—"who brought you home, Yvonne?"

"Your friend, Mr. Brendle," the girl replied. "And if you don't mind, I'm going back to bed and get some sleep."

Again in bed, more wide awake than ever, Yvonne tried to forget the distant music that floated into the courtyard on which the second-story apartment opened. Her system was to concentrate on closer sounds, and she began to hear them, but not in a pleasant fashion.

There were creaks in the hall, strange whispers that Yvonne could not define. Sometimes her uncle paced the hall, muttering to himself, but these sounds were less noticeable. So stealthy, in fact, that Yvonne would not have heard them if her ears had not been more than usually alert.

They were sounds that she finally classed as imaginary, but she still wanted to satisfy her mind about them. She felt that by merely opening the door of the bedroom and glancing into the hall, she could put her worries at rest.

Opening the door, Yvonne looked toward the end of the hall, where a window opened on a little balcony. The window had ornamental bars, and as Yvonne gazed she saw two objects that looked like snake heads come up to the grille. They made a twisting motion, then were gone, so suddenly that Yvonne believed she had imagined it.

She was scared, nonetheless, and when she stood behind the door that she had automatically closed, she listened intently for further sounds. None came, and the silence terrified her.

She opened the door again; seeing the window vacant, she stole toward it. When she arrived there, she gave a horrified gasp.

The things that she had seen were hands, powerful ones. Though they had gone, they had left the evidence of their work. The window bars were lying on the balcony, twisted into pretzel shape. Any hands that could so silently have made a hash of wrought iron must be possessed of terrific strength.

TURNING about, Yvonne saw that her uncle's door was ajar, a dim light coming from it. She felt he ought to know what had happened; that he might be able to do something about it. Still, it wasn't wise to call him; judgment told her to approach his room cautiously.

Not having bothered to put on slippers, Yvonne was able to reach the door very silently. But the moment that she peered through the opening, a total horror froze her.

She saw the same darkish hands that she had viewed before, but this time they were dealing with an object more pliable than iron bars. Those hands were tight-clenched upon a human neck, bringing a face into the light.

Whatever horror Yvonne felt was written tenfold upon the features above those gripping hands. The face belonged to James Carland; it was petrified in death.

The killer's pressure had seemingly bulged Carland's eyes and forced his tongue to its full extension. As Yvonne swayed, the movement enabled her to see the murderer's coppery face, as well as his tawny hands. It was a stony face, yet its very mold seemed one of venom. The man was relishing his evil handiwork as only a savage could.

Memories of her museum visit swept through Yvonne's brain. This man was an Aztec, a member of the Xitli cult that Professor Hedwin had likened to the thugs of India. He was a strangler, whose weapons were his fingers; a fiend inhuman, who served an ancient fire god. Those thoughts came almost in a single flash, and Yvonne's mind was too crowded to think of anything else.

Her scream therefore was involuntary, and louder than any she would have normally given. It must have carried through the outer courtyard and off into the alleyways beyond. Her own vocal effort even startled Yvonne from her lethargy before the Aztec could spring about.

The girl was dashing frantically along the hallway while the killer was still reaching for the stone-headed knife that he wore in his belt.

Yvonne's one hope was to reach the balcony before she could be overtaken.

She managed it so well that she was scrambling through the window before her pursuer reached the hall. But on the balcony, she encountered a new menace.

A figure came over the rail, another of the squat Aztecs, his hatchet already in his hand. Sight of the frail, cringing girl slowed the would-be killer, but only because of his contempt. He was choosing the side of Yvonne's neck, above her shuddering shoulder, as a target for his weapon. The girl's eyes went shut, her lips were gaspless, as she saw the hatchet begin its swinging curve.

The roar that came from the courtyard was indefinable to Yvonne. It was the burst of a gun, accompanied by echoes from the walls about. To Yvonne it sounded as a blast of doom; which it was, but not for her. A whir of air went by her cheek; a lunging body struck the balcony rail beside her.

Opening her eyes, Yvonne saw the floundering Aztec; as she turned her head, she struck against the stone ax, buried deep in the window frame. Then, from the courtyard, she heard a strange laugh that awoke new quivers from the surrounding walls. Yvonne saw her rescuer—a marksman cloaked in black who held a smoking automatic.

Guided by Yvonne's first shriek, The Shadow had arrived in time to turn the course of the Aztec's ax by planting a bullet between the savage's shoulders.

Danger wasn't past. Yvonne remembered the killer inside the apartment. Coming up to the balcony rail, she beckoned frantically to The Shadow. At the same time she saw a ladder extending up from the courtyard, the route that the Aztecs had used for the invasion.

The Shadow was reaching the ladder with rapid strides, but Yvonne feared that he could not possibly arrive in time.

With both hands, the girl grabbed the hatchet in the window frame and tried to tug it free. It came loose and she sprawled backward, half across the rail. She was facing the window, and there she saw her uncle's murderer.

The Aztec saw Yvonne, too, and seemed to gloat at her helpless plight. Off balance, her arms flung apart, Yvonne was so posed that the killer had her heart as a target for his ax.

Again the downward swing of a stone hatchet was beaten by the upward stab of a gun. The Shadow had actually leaped half up the ladder, to thrust the point of his gun between the iron posts below the balcony rail.

The impact of the bullet from his .45 jolted the sturdy Aztec, sending the tawny knife hand high. Again a stone weapon whirled past Yvonne, this time skimming just above her upturned face.

The Shadow was across the rail. Plucking Yvonne from her resting place, he swept her through the window, where she landed, breathless, upon the hallway floor. The stone ax was gone from her hand; she had dropped it over the balcony rail into the courtyard.

She didn't need a weapon while The Shadow was at hand. Still, she could not understand why this black-clad fighter had flung her to safety when the danger was all over.

Then Yvonne saw that danger was not ended.

THE crippled Aztecs were on their feet, both clutching at the cloaked foe who had downed them. A single bullet couldn't finish those stony fighters unless planted in their hearts. Their hatchets gone, they were battling The Shadow barehanded, but their wounds had given them a frenzied power.

The Shadow's gun swings couldn't dent the thick skulls of the stony men, nor was he able to work his muzzle past their warding hands. Hopelessly, Yvonne saw them bend The Shadow half across the rail and thought that no power could save him.

He sagged, then came up with a whip action that quivered his entire form. The snap, to Yvonne's amazement, catapulted one Aztec over the rail. Twisting away from the other's lunge, The Shadow made a cross swing with his gun, hooking the killer underneath the chin.

This leverage sent the Aztec backward, and The Shadow's other arm did the rest. Sweeping up, it lifted the Aztec's legs and tilted the wounded fighter over the rail, where he plunged to join his companion. It was a timely disposal of a troublesome foe, for The Shadow had more by that time.

A third member of the murderous tribe was coming over the rail to the balcony, and Yvonne saw a fourth slanted face on the ladder below. These fighters had their axes, which made The Shadow's chances look slim until he gave them battle. Then he proved that the swing of a stone ax was more to his liking than the clutch of tawny hands.

The Shadow sledged one knife hand with his gun and stabbed the other with a bullet. Borne toward the rail by the man on the balcony, he twisted as he met the one from the ladder, letting one Aztec bear the brunt of the other's drive.

Each was grabbing, one-handed, for The Shadow, and he was wrenching from their combined grasp in a style that this time indicated easy victory.

The fault lay with the balcony rail. It couldn't stand the strain of triple weight. It broke, and the fighters fell from Yvonne's sight, carrying the ladder with them. Like the enemies that he had conquered, The Shadow had gone to the stone courtyard a dozen feet below!

On the balcony again, Yvonne saw The Shadow. He was on his feet, miraculously intact, but he was reeling as he stabbed wild shots, not at four savages, but more than twice that number.

Fortunately, the servers of Xitli had tasted enough of The Shadow's bullets, and supposed that his shots were taking effect. Moreover, they had their crippled companions to look after.

Yvonne saw the Aztecs, making off through a passage on the other side of the courtyard, dragging their wounded with them. The Shadow was staggering after them, blundering into walls and doorways, but still blasting shots that hurried the fugitives along their way.

Dazed from the ordeal, Yvonne regained her senses to find herself back in bed. Andy Ames was standing beside her, waving back police who wanted to question her.

Mechanically, Yvonne told her hazy story of savage fighters beaten off by a foeman cloaked in black—a tale so fantastic that all listeners except Andy believed it the result of Yvonne's strained imagination.

Even Andy had his doubts. He, too, had been rescued by The Shadow, but he couldn't understand about the Aztecs. Grimly, Andy kept his silence, wondering how well The Shadow had fared at the finish of the fray.

Yvonne's final description of The Shadow's staggery departure made it seem that the victor's plight might be worse than that of his conquered foemen.

CHAPTER XII
CRIME'S SEQUEL

LATE the next afternoon, Andy Ames stopped at the Mayan Museum to talk to Fitzhugh Salter. He felt that the curator was the one man who might be able to link events that seemed divided between Mexico and Louisiana.

Andy's suggestion that the men who murdered James Carland might have been Aztecs produced a smile from Salter. The curator summed up the case quite simply.

"You have spent too much time with Professor Hedwin," he told Andy. "Unconsciously, you have absorbed some of his strange notions. His talk of the Xitli cult is quite convincing, of course, and I noticed last night that such men as Talborn and Brendle were impressed by it. Probably the same applied to Yvonne Carland.

"She was distraught by her uncle's death, and her imagination became overworked. Until we have proof that a Xitli cult exists—and I assure you that I shall give the possibility a thorough and impartial study—we must accept the opinion of the police; namely, that James Carland was murdered by local assassins."

Leaving the museum, Andy wondered if he should have told Salter all that he knew. Andy was in a serious dilemma, for he felt that he had put the law on a wrong trail. It went back to last night, when Andy had spiked the testimony of the captured Cajun regarding strange men from the *Amazonia*.

Should he reverse his own statements, Andy would put himself in a serious position, one that might involve actual suspicion on the part of the police, who were not inclined to accept Yvonne's description of the men who had slain her uncle.

It would be better not to talk about the stone hatchet that Andy had thrown into the river, though Yvonne, too, had mentioned such weapons. None of the primitive hatchets had been found in the courtyard outside the Carland apartment, which meant that the invaders must have carried them away.

In fact, Andy himself was doubtful of Yvonne's testimony; not regarding the actual presence of the squat men, but as to their actual number.

From certain facts, Andy was trying to size the whole situation. He knew that The Shadow was in New Orleans; that the cloaked fighter had helpers who looked like Aztecs, but were not. Assuming that the squat man on the *Amazonia* was one of The Shadow's Xincas, Andy naturally presumed that Yvonne had seen men of the same type at the time of her uncle's death.

She could have mistaken them for the killers, and supposed that they were the men The Shadow battled later. But she talked of many, not a mere few, which rather puzzled Andy. He didn't want to fall into the same error as the police, that of regarding Yvonne's story as sheer imagination. But he found himself taking a halfway view of it.

It never occurred to Andy that The Shadow might not have brought his Xincas to New Orleans at all. But Andy Ames did strike upon the theory that the Xincas themselves might be worshippers of Xitli, who had suddenly revolted against their proper chief, The Shadow.

The idea gave Andy qualms, for it brought back the question of last night: how had The Shadow fared after staggering off into the night, as Yvonne had described?

FROM the window of his office in the Mayan Museum, Fitzhugh Salter was watching Andy Ames stroll slowly along the street. The smug curator evidently guessed that Andy was in a quandary, for his smile had broadened by the time Andy was out of sight.

Returning to his desk, Salter began to thumb

through a sheaf of typewritten sheets that pertained to the ancient Mayan language.

These were revisions of an earlier manuscript that the museum had already published. The work engrossed Salter so completely that it was dark when he again looked toward the window. It was time to close the museum, so Salter went out and locked the door, but did not leave. Instead, he returned to his office and drew the window shades down.

To all appearances the museum was closed for the night. Deep dusk was settling when a taxicab stopped at the nearest corner, and a man alighted from it. As soon as the cab had left, the man walked toward the museum and stopped to gaze at the great pyramid. There was still enough light to show his face; it was the withery countenance of Professor Darius Hedwin.

Like probing gimlets, the professor's sharp eyes picked out a tiny crack of light that issued past one of the drawn shades in Salter's office. For a short while Hedwin rubbed his chin; then, giving a cackly laugh, the professor sidled away in stoop-shouldered fashion off into the increasing darkness.

This was a cloudy evening. Tonight the shrubbery was invisible. Only the museum itself could be seen—like ghostly steps, moving up toward the blackened sky. A perfect night for an outsider to approach unseen. Once inside the museum, anyone could prowl at will.

Thus it was not surprising that things occurred, a short while later, on the top floor of the pyramid.

As on the previous night, the flame-robed, green-masked figure of Xitli made a sudden appearance from the room that held the costumes. His casting of a chemical flare was the signal that brought a horde of Aztecs from their hiding places to greet their feathered chief.

This time the door of the throne room stood wide. When Xitli entered and took to his throne, the Aztecs followed at the fire god's beckon.

Xitli questioned them with brief, hissed words. They gave their story of the night before. Xitli sat silent, his eyes glistening through the inlaid jet that formed the eye slits of his mask. The Aztecs waited fearfully, until his hissed voice came again, telling them that what they had done was good.

Evidently Xitli was pleased because of Carland's death; enough so to excuse his followers for their failure to slay Yvonne and their inability to overwhelm The Shadow. Then, in his same forced tone, the fire god spoke new instructions, which the crouching Aztecs accepted as absolute. A fling of Xitli's hand produced a glare that dazzled them; then Xitli was gone.

Stealthily, the Aztecs stole down the stairs, to find the exit that took them out into the night. Later

there was a rumble of the elevator which signified that Xitli, too, had come down from the top-most floor. But the thick darkness outside the museum was too deep to reveal any departure by those who had assembled in the throne room.

The gleam of street lamps a block away did show a pair of squat men moving from the direction of the Mayan Museum. It was fortunate that Andy Ames was not on hand to view that pair. He would have believed that his doubtful theories were actually correct. For the two who passed that light were not Aztecs; they were The Shadow's Xinca servants, mysteriously arrived in New Orleans!

WHILE strange events were occurring near the Mayan Museum, Andy Ames was dining with Yvonne Carland in a private room of the second floor of a French restaurant. They were avoiding discussion of the night before; rather, their talk concerned the future as a relief from the horrible past.

Though Yvonne regretted her uncle's death, Andy knew quite well that she held no sentiment for James Carland. Yvonne's own parents were dead, and it had been Carland's duty to administer the small fund that they had left their daughter.

Yvonne had been living with her uncle not just as a measure of economy, but because she knew that she would have to watch her money as long as he held control of it.

All that was ended; from now on Yvonne could handle her own affairs. She was to inherit Carland's money, too; but his estate consisted largely of debts. They were not the sort that Yvonne would ever have to pay; still, they worried her.

"When Mr. Talborn arrives," declared Yvonne, "I am going to tell him that whatever money is left will go to the museum fund toward the pledge that my uncle did not keep."

"Talborn will be glad to hear it," returned Andy, "if he ever gets here. I wonder what's keeping him? I called him right after I left the museum, and he said he would join us within an hour. But it's been more than that—"

There was an interrupting knock, followed by Talborn himself. Smiling apologetically, the affable exporter explained his delay. There had been some mix-up in a cotton shipment which had forced him to remain at his office. Seating himself at the table, Talborn ordered dinner. His smile faded suddenly when Yvonne began:

"There is something I must tell you, Mr. Talborn. It concerns my uncle and the money he pledged to the museum—"

"One moment, Yvonne," Talborn interrupted. "I think that we should consider that particular subject as closed. None of the men who took over his pledges—that is, persons like myself—felt any animosity toward James Carland. I, for one, could not possibly have been responsible for his death."

Talborn's manner rather shocked Yvonne, particularly as she had not intended to blame him. Knowing what was in Yvonne's mind, Andy promptly intervened by questioning Talborn very bluntly:

"Who do you think might be responsible?"

"I don't know," returned Talborn, "but there were persons whose plans were badly hampered when Carland failed to supply the promised funds."

Andy went hot beneath his collar. One such person might be Fitzhugh Salter, whose job as curator had depended on the completion of the Mayan Museum. Another happened to be Professor Hedwin, who had faced the problem of a stranded expedition in Yucatan. But Andy himself had been with the expedition and could take Talborn's thrust as a personal one.

It was Yvonne who tactfully veered the discussion to safer ground. Quite coolly, she said:

"I was starting to tell you, Mr. Talborn, that I intend to pay my uncle's pledge, in part, at least, from whatever funds his estate provides."

Immediately Talborn became his affable self, but his headshake was a doubtful one.

"A generous offer," he said, "but I doubt that Carland's debts will be covered. You must remember that he owed fifty thousand dollars to Eugene Brendle, in return for which he gave the worthless marshland."

Yvonne's lips tightened. She had to agree that the so-called rice fields were worthless. Too often she had heard her uncle boast of the shrewd deal that he had made when he borrowed the cash from Brendle. He said that if he failed to promote the rice fields, he would let Brendle keep the swampland.

"Mr. Brendle will come first," assured Yvonne. "When I see him, I shall tell him so."

YVONNE hadn't long to wait. At that moment Brendle made an unexpected entrance. The stocky contractor was quite excited and greatly pleased to see Yvonne. He pulled a telegram from his pocket and handed it to the girl.

"For your uncle," said Brendle. "They sent it over to my office. It's from Jonathan Dorn, the man who was going to finance the rice fields. I've been looking all over town for you, Yvonne."

The telegram stated that Dorn was arriving on his yacht that evening and would expect Carland to meet him. The yacht was to dock on Lake Pontchartrain, in the northern section of New Orleans. Quite obviously, Dorn had not heard of Carland's death.

"We should see Dorn at once," insisted Brendle. "It means a lot to both of us, Yvonne. If he really

intends to finance the rice lands, he might pay more than fifty thousand dollars—"

"Or less," put in Talborn. "But don't worry, Brendle. Whatever comes from the property will go toward paying the money that Carland owed you."

"I'm sorry," apologized Brendle. "I only thought—"

"We know what you thought," interposed Talborn. "Carland stuck you with those swamp acres, Brendle, and you want Yvonne to help you get rid of them."

"An outrageous accusation, Talborn."

Andy arose, to come between the pair. As he urged Brendle toward the door, Andy supplied a statement that soothed his own feelings as much as Brendle's.

"Don't worry about Talborn," Andy told Brendle. "At least you stand to be a loser because of Carland's death. So Talborn can't put you in the class of a suspected murderer, as he did with me."

As he turned back to look at Talborn, Andy noted a surprised expression on the man's face, as though Talborn, for the first time, realized that Andy belonged in the same category as Salter and Hedwin.

Yvonne was rising from her chair; she ignored Talborn as she went through the door. Both Andy and Brendle followed, leaving Talborn to his own accusations.

"We'll go to see Dorn right now," declared Andy as they started down the stairs. "We'll put the proposition to him squarely and see if he wants to buy those rice fields."

It didn't occur to Andy that others might already be on the way to visit Jonathan Dorn; men whose ways were dark and deadly, whose propositions were those of primitive law.

CHAPTER XIII
FIENDS OF THE FLAME

NIGHTLIGHTS and the sounds of evening were puzzling to The Shadow as he stared toward the windows of his hotel room. He could not understand the lights at all, for he expected daylight. He could recall a battle, which he had followed up with an incomplete pursuit. Then he had dragged himself away to rest; and, considering his weariness, he should have slept past dawn.

But it was still night, and, more puzzling still, he was wearing his black cloak, a most serious oversight.

It wasn't good policy for Kent Allard to return to a hotel room in Mexico City, clad in a garb that might create a panic among superstitious employees. It would be understandable, perhaps, if this happened to be New Orleans and The Shadow had assumed the character of Lamont Cranston, which in itself preserved his actual identity.

Suddenly the answer broke through. This *was*

New Orleans. Mexico City was a thing of the past, despite the fact that The Shadow had battled Aztecs quite recently. Yes, this was New Orleans; even though the city lights were still confusing, sounds told The Shadow where he was. He could hear the calliope of a river showboat wheezing out its ceaseless music.

Rolling from the bed, The Shadow moved unsteadily toward a mirror. His cloak dropped from his shoulders, the slouch hat fell from its folds. Finding a light, The Shadow turned it on and looked at his face. He saw the hawkish features of Lamont Cranston, not the gaunt face of Kent Allard.

The Shadow laughed, his low tone mirthless. He was Cranston for the present, but he could not recollect his recent adventures. Pressing his hand against the side of his aching head, The Shadow began to understand..

He had taken a fall during the fight and must have received a brain concussion. He knew the effects from old. Fortunately, the result was wearing off.

Then, as The Shadow turned from the mirror, his head whirled anew. He couldn't be Cranston; he must be Allard, because, facing him, were two stolid Xincas who stood like patient sentinels.

Those Xincas served Kent Allard, not Lamont Cranston. Their very presence caused The Shadow to stare from them to the mirror, doubting his own eyes, until the Xincas spoke.

They were using their own language, which The Shadow understood, telling him of new drumbeats that had penetrated to their remote domain in Guatemala, carrying the tale that the cult of Xitli was again alive. These two Xincas, The Shadow's own servants, had smuggled themselves to New Orleans, to bring their chief the news.

As the Xincas spoke, The Shadow recalled that he had given them such an order. But he had expected to contact them at another hotel, where he went daily, as Allard. Not having found him there, the Xincas, through ways peculiar to themselves, had managed to trace The Shadow in his guise of Cranston.

The Shadow was thinking clearly, rapidly, by the time those facts had been recounted. He opened the door of the hotel room, found a newspaper in the hall. It wasn't today's newspaper by The Shadow's calculation. It was tomorrow's!

Therewith, The Shadow realized that he had spent a full twenty-four hours in a semiconscious state. Hours that should have been devoted to further investigation, for the newspaper headlined the mysterious murder of James Carland.

Scanning the columns, The Shadow learned how far the police had missed the truth, for Yvonne's description of the hatchet killers was scarcely mentioned. Turning the pages to read the final paragraphs

of the murder story, The Shadow came upon a minor item that most eyes would have missed.

It simply stated that the yacht *Miramar* was to arrive at Lake Pontchartrain; but the news was weighty to The Shadow. He knew that the *Miramar* belonged to Jonathan Dorn, with whom Carland had dealings.

Considering the riddle of Carland's death— namely, why he had been slated for murder—The Shadow found a partial answer. The menace which doomed Carland might now apply to Dorn!

Seizing hat and cloak, The Shadow bundled them across his arm. Followed by the Xincas, he went down a stairway, out through an obscure exit from the hotel, to the almost deserted parking lot where he kept his car.

A few minutes later, The Shadow and his companions were whizzing northward along Canal Street, the wide, main thoroughfare of New Orleans.

It was better than a tip-off to police headquarters, that pace set by The Shadow. Traffic whistles shrilled as the car roared by, its mad speed forcing other vehicles to the curb. Attracted by the whistles, police cars took up the chase, until it seemed that half the New Orleans force was on The Shadow's trail.

But the cloaked driver outraced them, even slackening at times, to make sure they did not lose his course. The threat that loomed ahead was one wherein The Shadow might need all the aid that he could muster.

ABOARD his yacht, the *Miramar*, Jonathan Dorn was seated in his cabin, going over letters that he had received from James Carland. Hearing a knock at the door, Dorn covered the correspondence, and testily demanded: "Who's there?"

The door opened and a pale secretary inserted his face. He was hesitant when he saw the glower on Dorn's heavy-jowled features. The secretary was greatly in awe of Dorn; ordinarily, he would have retired at the financier's growl.

"I'm busy, Nevil," boomed Dorn. "Don't you remember my order? I told you not to disturb me until Carland arrives."

"But it's about Mr. Carland—"

"What about Mr. Carland? Have you heard from him? Isn't he coming here this evening?"

"No, sir." For once, Nevil was firm. "I think you'd better read this, Mr. Dorn."

He advanced and placed a newspaper on Dorn's desk. When the financier read the headlines that concerned Carland's death, he broke into a fit of rage, which he directed toward Nevil, who was the only person available.

"Get out!" stormed Dorn. "I'll call you when I need you. What does it matter to me, if Carland is dead?" He paused, while Nevil darted through the door. Then, almost to himself, Dorn added: "Perhaps it proves—all these."

By "all these," Dorn meant the letters that lay on his desk. He began to handle them again, as if they were priceless documents. He was stroking his chin, smiling to himself, half pleased, half doubtful, when the door opened again.

Dorn did not hear it, for his attention was attracted by the sound of sirens that were coming toward the lakefront, where the yacht was docked.

The door closed with a *click*. Dorn turned about angrily, expecting to see Nevil. Instead, his jowlish face froze itself, agape, as his eyes viewed three intruders. They were men with faces as stony as the crude hatchets which they carried; squat men with sloping foreheads; savages attired in jungle garb.

With a sharp cry, Dorn came to his feet. He was grabbing for the desk drawer where he kept his revolver; with the other hand, he was seizing the precious Carland correspondence. Dorn's fingers did not even grasp the handle of the drawer. The Aztecs had released their hatchets with short, choppy swings.

The stone weapons buried their crude cutting edges deep into Jonathan Dorn. One ax found his skull, another his neck, while the third drove to his heart.

As Dorn sprawled, scattering the sheaf of letters, the Aztecs bounded forward in rubbery fashion and tugged their weapons from the victim's body.

Dorn's death, at least, was merciful, for it was very swift. Each of the axes had struck with sufficient force to kill him. But the Aztecs were not yet through. Ignoring the arriving police sirens as things which could not concern them, they produced small, bomb-like objects and flung them against the desk.

These were new weapons, provided by their master, Xitli, and the effect exceeded the expectations of the Aztecs. The objects were actually bombs, of an incendiary type, that broke instantly into gushing flame, which spurted throughout the cabin.

By the time the Aztecs were safely through the door, Dorn's body was the center of a miniature inferno. Fiery tongues gulped the Carland letters and ignited the desk, threatening to dispose of its contents, also.

Racing for the yacht's deck, the Aztecs encountered Nevil and members of the crew, who had heard the roar and now saw the raging flames that issued from the cabin. The wild chant of the Aztecs, the anthem that marked them as servants of Xitli, did more than drown the cackle of the flames. It brought a horde of other stony men into sight, from lurking spots about the deck.

Nevil and the other unfortunates were diving for shelter that they could not find, with members of the murderous tribe close after them, when a mighty taunt was delivered from the forward deck, rising to a challenging crescendo that made the Aztecs halt.

They had heard that mirth the night before. It signified a lone foeman, the only one in all their experience who had out-dealt them in their game of quick-delivered death.

The laugh of The Shadow brought vengeful howls from the Aztecs. The followers of Xitli remembered those of their tribe that they had carried from the battle of the night before. Nevil and the others were forgotten.

AS a barrage preliminary to their attack, the Aztecs flung more of the incendiary bombs. The Shadow wheeled back to cover as the deadly shells broke and spewed flame everywhere. Leaping for the gaps, the Aztecs were upon him with their axes, but swift though their swings were, the stabs of The Shadow's guns could not be beaten.

Wild savages sprawled, their hatchets flying wide. The Shadow had beaten off the brunt of that attack, but he knew the wily ways of the Aztecs. Other men of Xitli had reached the superstructure of the *Miramar*, and were poising for long throws. They looked like howling demons amid the flames which they had produced—great sheets of fire that now enveloped the yacht.

The Shadow's only refuge was the bow of the boat. He reached it ahead of flying axes. The axes cleaved the deck behind him and stayed there, waiting for men who were coming, with long leaps, to regain them. Against that horde, even The Shadow's guns were not sufficient; but his reinforcements had arrived.

Police were on the dock, shooting at the savage demons who were clearly outlined by the flames. Some of the Aztecs jolted in midair, sprawled on the deck when they struck it. The Shadow, coolly picking targets, was handling the foemen that the police bullets missed.

Though Dorn was dead, The Shadow had saved Nevil and the crew of the *Miramar*, for they had dived overboard to escape the hell-heat that now possessed the yacht. With his own guns, backed by those of the deploying police, The Shadow had his chance to exterminate the tribe of Xitli. All that saved the murderous Aztecs was the thing of their own making: the fire that raged along the deck of the *Miramar*.

Even the power of Xitli did not grant them immunity from flames. They gave up their thrust toward The Shadow and left the yacht in two directions, some diving to the water, others leaping for the dock. Even the bullet-riddled members of the band were capable of fight. Seeing them coming, still alive, the police wisely dropped away, hoping to clip them as they passed.

Then the Aztecs were gone, beyond the revealing range of the flames. With fire sweeping toward him, The Shadow dived from the bow of the *Miramar* and disappeared into the lake. The police controlled the scene, but their work consisted of simple task; that of helping Nevil and the crew of the *Miramar*, who were floundering in the lake.

Farther along the shore, in the sheltering darkness of a pier, The Shadow came dripping from the water, to find his Xincas waiting. They had started to the aid of their chief, only to be driven off by the flames. Not wanting to be mistaken for Aztecs, they had wisely slid from sight of the police.

From a car which had arrived amidst the strife, other witnesses watched the burning of the *Miramar*. One was Eugene Brendle; he was gasping as he viewed the scene. To Brendle, this meant the death of Jonathan Dorn, a man he had never met.

Brendle was declaring something very obvious: that the death of Dorn must be connected with the murder of Carland; that both crimes were certainly the work of an enemy who had a double grudge against both victims.

To Yvonne Carland, the horror of the scene was almost as great as the terror of her uncle's death. Yet, through her numbed brain drilled the thought that at last her story of strange hatchet men would be believed, for those very creatures had tonight revealed themselves amid the flames.

Most stunned of all was Andy Ames. His theories were utterly destroyed. He knew that he had been mistaken during the battle on the *Amazonia*; that Yvonne had been entirely correct in her description of the strife at the apartment.

The men with hatchets were not the fighters who served The Shadow, for Andy had seen the cloaked warrior engaged in combat with the Aztec throng.

From somewhere, vaguely, came the strident tone of a departing laugh. It told that The Shadow, alone, could solve the riddle of the Aztecs, just as he had proven himself the one opponent who could make them taste defeat!

CHAPTER XIV
MINIONS OF MURDER

MORNING spread terror throughout New Orleans. The destruction of the *Miramar* and the death of its owner, Jonathan Dorn, presaged the beginning of new, and more fearful, events.

The city was in a state of siege against a horde within its gates. Even by daylight, persons feared to walk through parks or isolated areas, dreading the menace of squat killers—strange, stony-faced men who might have come from Mars.

All day, the police were searching for the Aztecs. They did not use that term to describe the assassins; the police simply called them "hatchet killers." By evening, announcement was made that the search had been narrowed to the riverfront; though a rather large area, nevertheless, the news allowed people to breathe more easily.

The waterfront was always a section where anything might happen, and sooner or later, the law could find any culprits who were hiding there. But it didn't occur to anyone to question why the police were so sure that the Aztecs were near the river. The simple answer was that the police had not uncovered the killers anywhere else.

It had not occurred to them that the Aztecs might be living in the colossal new Mayan pyramid that dominated the New Orleans skyscape. There had been trouble at the museum a while before, but since then, the place seemed amply protected. More important, in police estimate, was the episode of the *Amazonia*.

The police now believed the testimony of the captured Cajun: that squat men of an unknown race had started the battle on the docked steamship. Hence, the waterfront was the place to look for them.

At dusk, Fitzhugh Salter stopped at the Hotel Luzane, where Professor Hedwin was a guest. Salter tried to call Hedwin's room, but learned that the professor was asleep and could not be disturbed. Hedwin, it seemed, had picked up the Mexican custom of taking a siesta every afternoon.

With a smug smile, Salter left word that he was dining out, and would call the professor later.

But Salter did not go to dinner; instead, he returned to the Mayan Museum. There, in furtive fashion, the curator unlocked the big front door and stole into his own preserves, like a prowling thief.

Despite his stealth, Salter was observed by a watcher across the street—a stooped man, who repressed a cackly laugh. The watcher was Professor Hedwin.

Waiting until a chink of light appeared from Salter's office window, Hedwin crept into the thickened darkness in a fashion much stealthier than Salter. Hedwin was using a system that he had learned while traversing Mexican jungles, where safety often depended upon complete stealth.

Meanwhile, Andy Ames and Yvonne Carland were dining together, a third person with them. The third person was Eugene Brendle, but the contractor was not having dinner. Instead, he was talking about the deaths of James Carland and Jonathan Dorn.

"We are both losers, Yvonne," declared Brendle, moodily. "Whoever had it in for your uncle and Dorn, certainly hurt us, too. Evidently, all the correspondence concerning the rice land was lost when the yacht burned."

"But I have to raise fifty thousand dollars,

somehow," insisted Yvonne. "I owe you the money, Mr. Brendle."

"Your uncle owed it to me," corrected Brendle, "and after all, he did give me security, though I was a fool to take it. So I'll have to bear the brunt of it, Yvonne. Next week, when the money comes due, I'll simply become the owner of a lot of salt grass that nobody wants."

"Won't someone else buy it?"

"I don't think so. Your uncle used some sales pressure on Cranston, but I think it was just talk. What's more, I haven't seen Cranston since that reception at the museum."

Glancing at his watch, Brendle arose. He went to a telephone in the corner of the private dining room and made a call, but received no answer.

"I was to meet Talborn, for dinner," he said. "Both of us were sorry about our little quarrel. But I can't seem to get hold of him. He was supposed to be home, but he isn't. Well, I suppose I'll find him at one of his many hangouts. Looking for him will give me an appetite."

When Brendle had gone, the conversation shifted. As they finished dinner, nearly an hour later, Andy and Yvonne began to discuss The Shadow. Both were agreed that the black-cloaked fighter was the one person who might uncover the missing Aztecs. In that surmise, they were one hundred percent correct.

AT that precise moment, The Shadow was entering the top floor of the Mayan Museum, coming down from the roof promenade. He could hear the low chant of voices.

Placing his suction cups beneath his cloak, he advanced to the door of the throne room. The door was ajar; peering through the crack, The Shadow saw a most singular sight.

On the throne, occupying the basalt stone, sat the living figure of Xitli, the fire god. In the foreground were the Aztecs, as numerous as the night before, despite the fact that The Shadow had considerably thinned their ranks, in battle. The answer was that more members of the Xitli cult must have arrived from Mexico.

The meeting was coming to its end, and apparently it had been a brief one, otherwise Xitli would have ordered the door of the throne room to be locked.

The throned masquerader had given his Aztecs new instructions for this evening; their chant, which The Shadow understood, was merely their way of saying that the commands of the fire god would be obeyed.

With an automatic wedged through the crack of the door, The Shadow was preparing to end the cult of Xitli by proving that the fire god was very human; a fact that a single bullet would establish. But he wanted Xitli alive, and therefore was taking very careful aim toward the flame-robed figure. The Shadow's exactitude proved fortunate for Xitli.

Just as The Shadow was ready to squeeze the trigger, Xitli gave a gesture with one hand. Something struck the stone floor of the room; there was a vivid spurt of flame. The dazzle blinded The Shadow, as it did the Aztecs. When he obtained a clear view of the throne, Xitli was gone.

The Aztecs were coming from the throne room. Still blinking, they did not see The Shadow. He drew rapidly away, to the door of an exhibit room. His eyes were keen again, but the Aztecs also had regained full vision.

Battle, at this time, would be fruitless. To meet the Aztecs on their home ground, where they could dive for every cranny and fling stone axes from cover, would mean odds much to The Shadow's disadvantage, with no chance of finding the master murderer who ruled this cult in the guise of Xitli.

Having work ahead, the Aztecs moved toward the stairway, and The Shadow followed. To all appearances, Xitli had gone ahead of the stony-faced tribe. At present, the Aztecs were the persons to be followed, as on that night when they had murdered Carland.

But whatever the crime that Xitli had designed for this evening, with the Aztecs as the perpetrators, The Shadow intended to block it.

The trail led down through the museum cellar, where the Aztecs drew away a loosened block and exited through a grating on the ground level, a few feet above.

There were numerous gratings around the museum; they led to drainage pipes that carried water away from the foundation of the pyramid. The Aztecs had simply used the grating in reverse; whether Xitli had loosened the stone for them, or had left the task to his followers, was something of less importance than the fact that the secret route existed.

As before, The Shadow kept close behind the Aztecs, after he, too, had used the grating as an exit. But tonight, the trail was much more certain, because The Shadow called in two waiting aides to help him.

Those two were the Xincas, and they were right in their element. Not only could they move as craftily as the Aztecs; they looked like the squatty men, and could approach very close to them, since the Aztecs mistook them for companions.

Thus, when stretches of light forced The Shadow to remain behind, the Xincas carried through. One followed the Aztecs; the other waited for The Shadow. At no time did the trail show signs of breakage. The amazing thing was the destination. The Aztecs chose the very area where they were being hunted: the waterfront!

POLICE were on hand in plenty, but the Aztecs filtered right through the loose cordon. In the main, they chose alleys; but at intervals, they scaled low roofs. They formed as insidious a swarm as any that The Shadow had ever hunted; coppery men, who moved with the stealth of reptiles and, moreover, resembled snakes in the hissed signals that they exchanged.

At last, the Aztecs reached their goal. They became a close-knit cordon around the doorway of an old, forgotten frame house that was squeezed among other buildings. The door was evidently the rear entrance to the house, and to cover it, the Aztecs chose various vantage spots.

Some lay in the shelter of a little fence; others crouched in an alley. The rest were on top of adjacent sheds, from which they could fling axes with increased effect.

The Shadow drew the two Xincas to a deserted house, pointing them to a low roof. Taking their positions, they produced arrows and short, thick bows.

The Xincas were deadly with such weapons, and their present duty was to be ready with a barrage against the Aztecs, should it be necessary to cover The Shadow's advance. There was enough light, fringing the yard that the Aztecs watched, for the Xincas to pick out the hatchet-armed fighters.

Then, along the darkness of the ground, The Shadow entered the death yard, alone. Entry was easy, for the Aztecs were watching the rear of the frame house. Approaching the door, however, was a feat requiring all The Shadow's skill.

He had to move with the trickling effect of cloudy smoke; and did. His black figure was as flitting as the shadowy motion of the wavering palm trees near the door that he sought.

Inch by inch, it seemed, The Shadow blotted the darkened door itself, and gradually eased his way inside, muffling the very creaks of the woodwork with the folds of his enveloping cloak.

He was inside, the door closed behind him; next came a passage to a room where he heard voices. The Shadow approached, and peered at faces that he had seen before.

Pierre Laboutard was in conference with his motley band; this was their new hideout, and Laboutard, backed by Jaro, was assuring them that they had nothing to worry about. He didn't consider it good policy even to lock the door, or place guards about.

"Perhaps the police find us," suggested Laboutard. "If they do, what can it matter? Like many other people, we are staying away from trouble. So we wait, and say nothing. But if the police do not find us, so much the better."

Laboutard's comments brought approving nods. His men weren't asking him about the "other job"

that they had once discussed. They had done enough crime in the past to be particular about the present. As for the future, it would have to wait until the Aztec scare was ended.

A jangle sounded from a side room, reached from the hall where The Shadow stood. Drawing back, The Shadow waited while Laboutard went alone to answer the telephone. He saw the crafty look on Laboutard's face, listened while the man talked to someone who had called. There was a light in the little room, and through the crack of the door The Shadow observed a tightening of Laboutard's expression.

"Ah, *oui*," said Laboutard. "They have been done, those things you wish, but not by me. So you wonder why I call, eh?"

The Shadow recognized that Laboutard was referring to the murders of Carland and Dorn, tasks on which he had hedged. The man who wanted those murders done had found a better way. He had taken advantage of the Aztecs, and made himself their ruler.

Laboutard, at this moment, was talking to the mastermind who called himself Xitli!

OBVIOUSLY, Laboutard knew who Xitli really was, and had sent him word to call this number. Smoothly, Laboutard was planning a shakedown. He wanted hush money from the master plotter who styled himself Xitli. Naturally, Laboutard wasn't putting it too bluntly. His words were actually purred.

"You promise me that I could kill those men"— Laboutard was referring to Carland and Dorn— "and while I wait, *pouf!*—I find it is already done. It is not fair that you should forget me, after we make the bargain."

His face shrewd, Laboutard listened to Xitli's reply. Evidently Xitli was not willing to pay for work that the Aztecs had done in place of Laboutard's men. But the wily Laboutard expected such refusal.

"But I tell my men so much," insisted Laboutard. "I tell them everything *m'sieu'*, about those men you say for us to kill. Everything, *oui*, except *why* you wish such murder."

A brief pause; then Laboutard added, cunningly:

"You think I do not know why you wish murder? Ah, you are very foolish. You should remember that I come from the bayou, where I paddle many places in my pirogue. I see many thing while in my canoe. I learn—Ah, you understand?"

Triumph gleamed on Laboutard's shrewd features. He was driving home the very point he wanted. But there were things that Laboutard could see, and learn about, without making another trip to the delta of the Mississippi. Things right here in New Orleans, which were happening right around him.

Shadowy patches were creeping in upon

Laboutard, climbing onto the wall beside him. Suddenly startled, Laboutard remembered his old enemy, The Shadow. He wheeled from the telephone and gave a sharp cry of alarm.

But it wasn't sight of The Shadow that caused Laboutard's consternation. The Shadow was still away from view, beyond the hallway door. Other figures had caused the creeping blackness.

Pierre Laboutard was enmeshed by a half circle of Aztecs, chunky warriors who had come in from the windows of this room while Laboutard was busy at the telephone. They were menacing him, with their raised hatchets, as if waiting a signal to bury the weapons in their victim.

From the dangling telephone receiver that Laboutard had dropped came a harsh, significant chuckle: the tone of Xitli!

CHAPTER XV
LINKS IN CRIME

FACED by the horrendous Aztecs, Pierre Laboutard showed frantic changes of expression that told a story which needed no words. Peering from the doorway, waiting with leveled gun, The Shadow could read the entire tale. It summed to this: Laboutard knew too much.

Xitli had foreseen that Laboutard would try a shakedown, demanding cash for silence regarding the motives of, as well as knowledge of, the man who had ordered the deaths of Carland and Dorn. So Xitli had postponed his telephone call until his Aztecs were on the ground. The jangle of the telephone bell had been the signal for the squat killers to creep in upon Laboutard.

At that moment, The Shadow could have taken toll among the Aztecs. But to do so would have been sure death for Laboutard. Other Aztecs had crept in from the windows, to support the ones who held Laboutard encircled. The newcomers were watching the door, and would handle matters from that direction.

So The Shadow waited in the darkened hall, preserving Laboutard's life for the simple reason that Laboutard was the one man whose testimony could prove the identity of Xitli.

Numbly, Laboutard groped for the telephone receiver and found it. Then, in gasps, he was pleading over the wire, promising anything if Xitli would spare him. The Shadow had foreseen that Xitli would give Laboutard a chance to beg; otherwise, the Aztecs would have struck down their victim without waiting.

"Ah, *non*!" gulped Laboutard. "I did not mean that I would ever talk. I meant that because of things I know, I thought that I could be useful to you... Ah, *oui*, I can do anything you ask, and my men will

help ... *Non*, they do not know why you wished murder. None know, I swear it; not even Jaro!"

The plea seemed to bring results, for Laboutard's voice returned to normal, as did his expression. Then:

"You think I work for someone else?" queried Laboutard. "That I take something from the museum, and from the Amazonia?... Very well, I say I have done those things. I take treasure from the boxes, and no one find out... Oui, I do it for the man you name, and he has given me the pay ...

"Ah, very good!" Laboutard's tone showed his approval of Xitli's cunning. "You wish me to rob the man who has the treasure ... Why not? If he do not watch it, he should lose it ... We go and take it, right away, and bring it wherever you say ..."

This time, the pause was longer, and Laboutard showed a trace of worry.

"You wish to know the place?" he queried. "But if I take my men there, it should be enough—"

Xitli's tone came harsh, from the receiver. Hearing it, Aztecs shifted forward. The edges of their hatchets actually grazed Laboutard's neck. There was no more argument from Laboutard.

"I tell you where!" he exclaimed hurriedly. "We put all the treasure in the old Monseca crypt ... *Oui*, the one that stands in the corner of the little cemetery, but which no one ever use ... Very good. I send my men with Jaro, and I bring these men of yours ..."

Xitli must have spoken more instructions, for Laboutard gingerly passed the telephone receiver to one of the Aztecs. Hearing the voice of Xitli, the Aztec gave a guttural reply. He pointed Laboutard toward the door; but when Laboutard moved in that direction, two Aztecs closed in beside him.

They stopped Laboutard when he reached the hall, where The Shadow, by then, was deep in darkness near the stairway. Laboutard called for Jaro; the lieutenant poked his face from the rear room. He didn't see the Aztecs; they were still in the doorway of the side room.

Laboutard ordered Jaro to go to the Monseca crypt and pick up the treasure. Jaro began to sputter something.

"Do what I say!" stormed Laboutard. "Take it all to the old truck, and leave it. Where it goes later, is my business. But it means more pay for all of us."

That was good enough for Jaro. He told the men in the rear room to come along.

Meanwhile, the Aztecs were drawing Laboutard back into the side room. They had closed the door when Jaro passed. Nor did Jaro and the entire crew encounter The Shadow.

He avoided them by moving a short way up the stairs. As soon as the last of them were gone, The Shadow crossed the hall and reached the side room.

The door came open a trifle. An Aztec peered

out, to make sure that Jaro's men had left. The Aztec did not see The Shadow, for the cloaked watcher had edged toward the rear room.

But the moment the Aztec pressed the door tight shut, The Shadow sprang forward. Grabbing the doorknob, he slashed the door inward and came upon the Aztecs with a sudden laugh of challenge.

At that moment, the stony men were surrounding Laboutard, waiting while one of their number talked to Xitli on the telephone. An order was coming across the wire, one that Laboutard should certainly have understood by this time.

His own men gone, Laboutard, surrounded by Aztecs, was definitely on the spot. The Shadow was actually coming to his rescue!

THE Aztecs were no longer worried about the door. That was why The Shadow's entry came as a surprise, and brought them all away from Laboutard.

Reversing his spin, The Shadow was back into the hall, blazing shots while stone hatchets came flying past him. It was life for Laboutard, if the fellow had shown sense enough to dive for a window.

Instead, Laboutard yanked out a revolver and drove for the hall, shooting vain shots that he hoped would reach The Shadow!

Like whippets, the Aztecs were after him. Those who still had hatchets used them on Laboutard's skull, felling him on the way. The rest were plucking up their weapons from the places where they had lodged. To make it worse for The Shadow, the door from the yard clattered open, showing a pair of waiting Aztecs, cutting off retreat.

With Laboutard dead, The Shadow had no reason to wait. He made for the outer door in one long dive, disregarding the fact that the two blockers were already lunging toward him, their hatchets swinging.

The lunges became sprawls, even though The Shadow lacked time to use his automatic. With a bound, he was across his flattened foemen, who were writhing on their faces, each with an arrow projecting from the center of his back. The Shadow's Xincas had picked off the murderous men who threatened their chief.

Whirling across the yard, The Shadow avoided other hatchets that were flung from sheds. Again, he owed his life to his bow-and-arrow specialists. Their quivers handy, the Xincas were quick to *twang* fresh shafts, that downed the hatchet throwers before any could complete a proper hurl.

Then, his Xincas with him, The Shadow was away in his car, leaving the field to police who had been attracted by the shooting. He knew that the officers would not encounter any Aztecs. Having finished Laboutard, Xitli's followers would prefer departure, taking their wounded with them.

MEANWHILE, Jaro and his men were well on their way to the Monseca crypt. They had lost no time in getting away from the waterfront, where there were too many police to suit them.

Far from earshot when The Shadow attempted the rescue of Laboutard, Jaro and his mixed crowd had no idea of what had happened in the hideout.

The Monseca crypt answered the description that Laboutard had given Xitli. It was a mausoleum of a type very common in New Orleans, and it stood in a corner of a small cemetery that was slated for removal.

The Monseca family had built the crypt, but had shortly afterward emigrated from New Orleans. Never visited, the empty mausoleum made an excellent place for the storing of secret treasure.

Approaching the crypt, Jaro and his men found it unlocked, which did not entirely surprise them. Laboutard had been paid for storing the stolen treasure there, and it was never Pierre's policy to double-cross a client.

Even Laboutard's recent dealing with Xitli was not a departure from custom, for Laboutard, by his own system of reasoning, felt that he was the one who had been betrayed in such matters as the murders of Carland and Dorn.

Knowing nothing of Laboutard's game, nor his death, Jaro and his company entered the crypt and began to stack the heavy sacks that they found there. They had been at work only a few minutes, when a guard reported that someone was approaching.

With drawn knives and guns, the invaders waited. As they heard the door swing open, then shut, they used their flashlights.

In the glare stood Graham Talborn.

Obligingly, Jaro hung an electric lantern from the wall, so that Talborn could see the faces of the crowd. Talborn promptly recognized them, but the exporter did not show his usual affable manner. Instead, he demanded sharply:

"Where is Laboutard?"

"He is coming later," rejoined Jaro. "Maybe he is at the truck, waiting until we bring the sacks."

"Did Laboutard send you here?"

Jaro nodded, in answer to Talborn's question. Eyes narrowing, the exporter looked around the group. Seeing that Jaro had them quite under control, Talborn addressed the lieutenant.

"When I hired Laboutard," stated Talborn, "I had to let him know my game: that I was secretly bringing in treasure from Mexico with the shipments to the Mayan Museum. Later, you men found out the full facts. It seemed best to tell you, so that you would be careful never to injure me by mistake."

"That is right," agreed Jaro.

"So it means," continued Talborn, "that you actually worked for me. Any order from Laboutard, regarding this treasure, would have to come from me."

Again, Jaro nodded.

"But I did not tell Laboutard to bring you here tonight," asserted Talborn. "This is his own idea, and it means just one thing. He is trying to double-cross me, although I have paid him in full. If he will do that to me, he will do the same to you!"

The argument bore weight with Jaro. It promised him the opportunity that he had long wanted: to supplant Laboutard as chief of the motley organization. Too long had Laboutard been letting Jaro do the heavy work; the lieutenant had remained loyal, purely because he knew that Laboutard was reliable. Talborn's words put an end to Jaro's shreds of esteem toward Laboutard.

Naturally, Jaro did not guess that Laboutard had made a deal with Xitli, under stress; that otherwise, Pierre would not have double-crossed his former employer, Talborn. Even had he known it, Jaro would hardly have rejected his present opportunity. Looking among his men, he studied their faces to see how they stood.

Of a dozen, about a third were Cajuns, who would side with Jaro under any circumstances. The rest of the crowd, beachcombers and roustabouts, were all riffraff who might do anything. Certainly, Jaro could persuade some of those waterfront rats to see things his way. He decided to sound them out.

"You hear what Talborn says," began Jaro. "Pierre has double-crossed us. Maybe"—he threw a wise look at Talborn—"Pierre didn't pay us all we had coming to us before. If we can't trust Pierre—"

A HOLLOW tone interrupted from the rear of the crypt. Jaro and his men turned; like Talborn, they stared in awe at the figure that had stepped into sight from beyond a heap of sacks.

Certainly, their challenger was powerful. His very appearance proved it. The startled men were viewing Xitli, the ominous fire god, attired in his full regalia.

Green mask, flame-hued robe, vivid headdress, gave the masquerader the appearance of a living monstrosity, a creature who, for all the viewers knew, could have been created by the very atmosphere of the crypt. The hollow tone of Xitli's voice seemed, in itself, a proof that he was something more than human.

Partly muffled by the mask, deepened by the walls of the crypt, the voice did hold an unearthly resonance. To the majority of those who heard them, the words of Xitli were commands that could not be ignored.

"It was I who gave the order!" pronounced Xitli. "The treasure is to be removed. As for that man"—

Xitli pointed toward Talborn—"he is to be taken, also. As for reward"—the tone was scoffing—"I can pay far more than Talborn can ever offer."

Xitli's final words were a mistake. He should have made his rule one of threat, rather than promise. Xitli won out, so far as Talborn was concerned, for men surged promptly in Talborn's direction despite Jaro's appeals for them to wait. But Xitli left himself wide open, should anyone supply a stronger threat.

One came.

The walls of the crypt re-echoed to the fierce crescendo of a mighty laugh, that promised death to any who laid a hand on Talborn. Flung in from the outer darkness by a challenger whose might was known, that sinister mockery brought shivers to men of crime.

Amid the echoes, they saw the very being who had countered Xitli's orders—a black-cloaked fighter whose eyes burned from beneath the brim of a slouch hat, as he wheeled into the crypt to prove his mastery.

The Shadow!

The muzzle of The Shadow's automatic was pointed toward Xitli. One tug of his finger would have ended the masquerader's career. Such demonstration was sure to cow Jaro and his riffraff, who, even now, were at odds among themselves.

Talborn saw the situation; to him, it promised life. He was ready to bear the blame for his own crimes, if The Shadow won. Talborn's one fear was that some of Jaro's men might intervene in Xitli's behalf. Madly, Talborn tried to prevent such disaster.

Springing from hands that made no effort to clutch him, Talborn lunged toward Xitli, shouting for others to follow. His mad rush put him straight in front of The Shadow's gun. As Xitli shifted one way, The Shadow made a sidestep to get new aim at him. But Xitli's hand had already made a fling.

Glass crackled on the crypt's floor. There was a burst of flame that dazzled all but The Shadow, whose cloaked arm was half across his face. A .45 thundered its reply to Xitli's fire bomb, but The Shadow had been forced to swing too wide.

Xitli was gone, down behind the protecting sacks, and the crypt was becoming a scene of chaos.

TO Jaro's men, the great spurt of fire meant that Xitli was more powerful than The Shadow. Knowing that Xitli favored crime, whereas The Shadow fought it, they took sides with the fire god.

Even Jaro and the Cajuns sprang for The Shadow, who was trapped in their midst. Xitli's promise of reward now carried the stronger force. One against a dozen, The Shadow seemed doomed.

He would have been, could the attackers have managed to find him. But the very blast of fire with which Xitli had sworn in new followers was the thing that worked against them. Still blinded by the flare, Jaro's men were stabbing knives, shooting revolvers at everything that looked black.

They were making victims out of treasure sacks and the niches in the wall, but they couldn't find the one target that they wanted: the cloaked fighter who was slugging through the midst of them, delivering the mocking laugh they hated, that came from every side, gathered by the crypt and flung upon their eardrums in a fashion that made them think they fought a horde of Shadows.

Xitli saw the muddle that he himself had caused. Like The Shadow, he was undazzled, and took advantage of it. Unable to reach The Shadow in the midst of the fray, Xitli skirted the battle and reached the crypt door, while The Shadow was flinging off fighters in order to get at him.

From a corner where The Shadow had thrust him, Talborn saw Xitli. Though Talborn's eyes were viewing black spots, too, he couldn't be mistaken about the vivid flame-hued costume.

Talborn lunged, half blindly, not noticing the glint of a revolver that Xitli had scooped up from the floor. Xitli fired, point-blank; then made a frantic leap to outside safety, just before The Shadow managed to break loose and aim his way.

Leaping across the dying figure of Talborn, The Shadow issued from the crypt. He saw Xitli going through a gate, where figures that looked like blocks of stone were lunging in from gloom. Fading for the crypt wall, The Shadow fired at the lunging figures and sprawled a pair of Aztecs, as their hatchets rebounded from the wall.

Only Jaro had managed to follow The Shadow. Out from the crypt, he saw the black blot against the marble wall. Savagely, Jaro sprang, intending to bury his knife in The Shadow's back.

Halfway to his target, he was halted short by a pair of Xinca arrows, that came from different angles and crossed points in Jaro's heart.

Xitli was gone, the remainder of the Aztecs with him. Wails of sirens told that police were coming.

With a strange, low laugh that sounded like a mirthless knell, The Shadow effaced himself in darkness, accompanied by the silent Xincas who had aided him in triumph.

CHAPTER XVI
CRIME BRINGS CALM

FACTS of the fray at the Monseca crypt left New Orleans aghast. That battle was a thing comparable to the greatest events in the city's history. Mere rumors were nothing, compared to the actual discoveries that the police made when they took over the scene of battle.

The truth about Graham Talborn came out. In taking charge of the museum fund, Talborn had raised the hundred thousand dollars that James Carland had failed to supply, but in so doing, Talborn had proven himself as smart as Carland, if not smarter.

As the new benefactor of the Mayan Museum, Talborn had gone to Mexico City, not to dispute about oil concessions, as Carland had, but to arrange the shipment of Mayan relics, which he had managed very nicely.

So nicely, that Talborn had found it child's play to bring in the treasures that Panchez and the mestizos found while with the Hedwin expedition, and planted in among the relics.

Naturally, Talborn had bought out Panchez. He had bought out Laboutard, too, to handle matters at the New Orleans end. Talborn was the one who had mussed things badly during the museum robbery, helping Laboutard to get away. After that one close call, he had shifted activities from the museum; hence, the final robbery had taken place on the *Amazonia*.

Startling enough in itself, the exposure of Graham Talborn was small when compared with the mystery of the strange opposition that had been raised against him. He had, to all appearances, met up with Xitli, the fire god that Professor Hedwin talked about!

None other than Xitli could have brought Aztecs to New Orleans. Aztecs who had murdered James Carland and Jonathan Dorn; who had later slain Laboutard, and then wiped out Jaro and the whole crew, along with Talborn.

Such, at least, was evidence; for dead Aztecs had been found not only at Laboutard's hideout, but near the Monseca crypt. Besides, there were wounded men, members of Laboutard's band, who claimed that they had seen a fiery figure who matched Hedwin's description of Xitli.

There was talk, too, of The Shadow, which proved that he had played an important part. Having seen The Shadow at the burning of the yacht *Miramar*, the police agreed that the cloaked fighter had again been the deciding factor; but that this time, he had handled two factions at once. However, the police were puzzled by finding certain Aztecs who had been felled by arrows, instead of bullets.

They discussed that point with Fitzhugh Salter, on the afternoon following the fray at the Monseca crypt. Salter received detectives in his office at the Mayan Museum, but he was not much help. The curator could not at all understand the arrows.

"Talk to Professor Hedwin," he suggested. "He is better informed on Mayan ethnology than I am, or at least he thinks so. Of course, he will probably attribute this trouble to Xitli, the fire god. I would prefer that you obtain his opinions first. Meanwhile, I shall study the subject, and let you know when I have more to offer."

THE detectives found Professor Hedwin in his room at the Hotel Luzane, where he had just awakened from an afternoon nap. As Salter had predicted, Hedwin promptly plunged into the subject of Xitli and the cult of the fire god.

"It is quite obvious that the cult revived itself," declared Hedwin. "I should have known that it was coming"—he shook his head reflectively—"when I heard the beat of Aztec drums at Cuicuilco. Mr. Ames will tell you the same"—Hedwin gestured to Andy, who was seated near him—"and how the drums disturbed us."

"They disturbed me," said Andy, "but you didn't particularly notice them, Professor. You were too busy digging up the throne of Xitli."

The professor threw an outraged look at Andy, then turned to the detectives. He examined stone hatchets that they had brought, and took a look at the mysterious arrows.

"The modern remnants of the Aztecs sought vengeance against Talborn," decided Hedwin, "because he was responsible for the thefts committed by Panchez. That is why they revived the Xitli cult and came to New Orleans. Unfortunately, they also identified Carland with the thefts, and slew him first. They killed Dorn next, because they thought that he was in it, too.

"In attacking Talborn, they met with opposition from Laboutard's men. I cannot give the exact details, since I know nothing about criminal investigation. But I can help you regarding these arrows. They are the sort used by certain primitive tribes in Guatemala. Therefore, I would say that certain natives, unfriendly toward the Xitli cult, also came to New Orleans.

"You speak of a mysterious avenger called The Shadow. Perhaps he employed those tribesmen who were unfriendly to the Xitli cult. That would account for his remarkable success, as well as the finding of the arrows."

It sounded logical to the detectives, and to Andy, too, inasmuch as he knew of The Shadow's Xincas. In fact, many things, particularly the fray at the *Amazonia*, were clearing themselves in Andy's mind. He had struck upon the fact that the Aztecs must have come to New Orleans first; the Xincas later.

There was something else that occurred to Andy. He expressed it to Hedwin, after the detectives had gone.

"About the Xitli cult," remarked Andy. "Since it is active again, right here in New Orleans, wouldn't the members meet in that throne room at the museum?"

Professor Hedwin darted a sharp look toward Andy, then gave a withery smile, accompanied by a headshake.

"I doubt it," he said. "You must be careful, Andy"—Hedwin's hand fell on Andy's shoulder—

"or they will accuse you of harboring absurd notions, like myself. Why should clumsy detectives tramp through the throne room which I so carefully arranged? No Aztecs have been reported around the Mayan Museum."

Nodding his agreement, Andy remarked that he was going out to dinner with Yvonne. He went down to the lobby, where he ran into the detectives. He guessed what was on their minds before they spoke it.

"We'd like you to do a favor for us," said one. "Stay with Professor Hedwin, and see what he does. It's for his own good, Mr. Ames. He's a trifle eccentric—"

"If you mean that he didn't like Carland or Dorn," interrupted Andy, "I'll agree with you. Carland left our expedition high and dry, and Dorn didn't help us out as we expected."

"Then you think that the professor—"

"I think he's all right. To prove it, I'll do exactly what you want. I'll go up and chat with him, and sound him out on the whole Xitli business."

RETURNING to Hedwin's room, Andy told him that he had called Yvonne, but that she was out. He began to talk about Xitli and the throne room. Hedwin was right, in Andy's opinion, about keeping the police away from the place; still, as Andy put it, a visit to the throne room might be a very good idea, later.

"A very good idea," decided Hedwin, with a nod. "It might even be that someone is masquerading as Xitli. Look, Andy!" He picked up a small statue of the fire god from among his curios. "Here is Xitli, himself. How cunning his features are!"

With an upward sweep, Hedwin drew the statue from his outstretched palm. The thing was hollow, and it left an object behind—a small revolver, which gleamed from Hedwin's hand. As Andy gave an instinctive shift, Hedwin cackled gleefully. Laying the statuette aside, he pocketed the gun. Then:

"I think I shall call on our friend Salter," declared Hedwin, "and learn what he really thinks about Xitli."

The professor went out, and Andy grabbed for the telephone. He knew that the detectives had left the lobby; hence, they wouldn't be there to stop Hedwin. Andy had to call someone, so he chose Yvonne, whose phone number was in his mind. The girl answered Andy's call promptly. In a tense voice, he told her:

"Professor Hedwin just left the hotel. He's going to the museum to talk with Salter. I want you to call Salter and tell him. Then call—"

Before Andy could add "the police," a chuckle interrupted. It came from the door of the room, where Hedwin was standing with the revolver. The professor gestured for Andy to drop the receiver on its hook, which Andy did, glad that Hedwin had not heard him mention Yvonne's name.

Then, keeping Andy covered, Hedwin picked an odd-shaped chain from among the Mayan relics in the room. With a deft sweep, he linked Andy's wrists in the primitive handcuffs.

"So you came back to spy on me," Hedwin clucked. "Very well; we shall put a stop to it! Your ankles next"—he applied another chain, that bound Andy's legs—"and, finally, this!"

The final object was a looped thong, with a metal ring through its knot. Hedwin threw the noose over Andy's head and twisted the ring, thus tightening the loop. The thing was much like a garotte, and a few more twists would have choked Andy; but Hedwin was kind enough to stop it just before the strangulation point.

"Breathe carefully," suggested the professor, "and slowly. But if you try to shout, what happens will be your own fault. I shall see you later, Andy"—Hedwin's cackle reached a high, gleeful pitch—"after I have finished what I intend to do."

Again, Hedwin walked from the room, and soon afterward the telephone began to ring. Andy knew that Yvonne was calling back, but he was forced to listen grimly. At least, Andy decided, Yvonne was safe from harm. She had probably called Salter, and was wondering who should be called next.

Andy was half right.

FROM the hotel where she had been residing since her uncle's death, Yvonne had called Salter, but without an answer. She was calling Andy, to tell him so.

Receiving no reply, Yvonne hung up. Deciding that Andy might have gone to the museum himself, Yvonne went out and called a taxicab. She rode to the Mayan Museum.

It was dusk, and the great pyramid loomed forbiddingly against the last touches of sunset. Yvonne went to the door and found it open; but when she arrived at Salter's office, it was closed. A note on the door stated that the curator would return in fifteen minutes.

Pondering, Yvonne wondered if Salter could still be in the museum. She thought of the exhibit rooms on the top floor.

Walking to the elevators, Yvonne found one open. The car was of the automatic type, and a sudden impulse seized Yvonne. Entering, she pressed the button to the top floor. Smoothly, the elevator carried her to her destination.

Salter wasn't on the top floor, but the exhibit rooms were still open, with the exception of Xitli's throne room.

Wandering from room to room, Yvonne was gripped with a shuddery feeling. The light was getting dimmer, and the statues in the gallery looked like living figures. So did the costumes in the next room, for they were hung from racks. Deciding that the hall was better, Yvonne started through a doorway, then halted in real fright.

Squatty shapes were moving through the hall. They were alive, and very real. From the primitive costumes that they wore, Yvonne identified them as Aztecs, the murderous members of the Xitli cult known to be at large in New Orleans. Frantically, she groped back toward the costumes, expecting to hear padded footsteps follow.

No footsteps came. Evidently the Aztecs were staying in the corridor. Perhaps they were gone, leaving a clear path to the elevator. But Yvonne was afraid to venture out among killers who might recognize her from the night when they had invaded her uncle's apartment and slain him.

A sudden hope struck her.

She had evaded the Aztecs that other night, up until the time she screamed. She might be able to do it again, if she used real stealth. As for recognition, there was a way to avoid it. Among the costumes were primitive dresses worn by Mayan maids, that resembled the very garb of the Aztecs.

Finding one, Yvonne kept deep behind the racks and hurriedly disposed of her modern garb, putting on the Mayan costume, instead. It wasn't a very elaborate outfit. Skirt and tunic formed one piece, and there were slippers shaped like moccasins. Yvonne decided to dispense with the headdress that went with it, because the Aztecs wore none.

With pounding heart, she crept out through the corridor, which had grown darker. A dim glow greeted Yvonne as she passed a corner; it was the light from the open elevator. No Aztecs were in sight, but the chance to reach quick refuge made Yvonne forget her stealthy tactics. She started a quick dash for the elevator.

Her haste betrayed her. Squatty men popped out from lurking places and overtook her before she could reach her goal. Yvonne held back a scream; knowing that it might be recognized; and her silence proved salvation.

Instead of drawing stone hatchets, the Aztecs merely suppressed her struggles. They bound her, hand and foot, with thong-like cords that they wore as necklaces with their deer-hide costumes. Quite solemnly, the Aztecs carried Yvonne to the door of the throne room and rested her upon the floor.

They began a low-pitched babble, in which Yvonne identified a single word: "Xitli." It chilled her more than the coldness of the stone floor, for it meant that the rumors concerning Xitli were actual. Someone, Yvonne was certain, must be masquerading as the fire god.

Murderous captors had spared Yvonne's life, only that her fate might be decided by Xitli, the fiend of flame!

CHAPTER XVII
TRAILS LEAD HOME

ABOUT the time of Yvonne's capture by the Aztecs, two men were having dinner together in a hotel dining room. One was Eugene Brendle, and the stocky contractor was more talkative than usual. He had found the man he wanted to see: Lamont Cranston.

Brendle was discussing real estate. He had the title deeds to Carland's delta land and was going over them in detail, calculating the price per acre and talking about the possibilities of rice production.

As Brendle warmed to the subject, Cranston listened, his features remaining quite immobile. At last, Brendle shook his head and leaned back in his chair.

"It's no use, Cranston," he said. "Carland was a promoter, while I am not. He sold me on the idea that this land was worth the fifty thousand that he wanted to borrow; but after I gave him the money, I was no longer sure.

"I've been telling you things that Carland told me. I've been more conservative in my statements than he was, but at that, I've overstepped myself. There is only one way to learn if rice can be grown on this land. That way is to try it."

The first semblance of a smile appeared upon Cranston's lips. Brendle was encouraged.

"I know what you have been thinking," he admitted. "You suppose that I am trying to dispose of a white elephant—and you are right. But I am not actuated because of my own interests; at least, not entirely. I am thinking of Yvonne Carland.

"She insists upon paying her uncle's debt, and she cannot possibly do it. But she is determined enough to try, and for years to come, she will be thrusting dribs of money upon me. Even worse, Yvonne intends to marry a man as determined as herself: Andrew Ames. He will consider it a debt of honor, too.

"If I could write the whole thing off, by getting rid of the property for the amount I loaned Carland, I would be satisfied. But I can't keep trying to convince you that you ought to buy. I've merely given a rosy picture of the proposition, and the rest is up to you."

For answer, The Shadow drew a checkbook from his pocket. In Cranston's leisurely style, he wrote out a check for sixty thousand dollars and handed it to Brendle.

"That covers the loan," he said, "with ten thousand dollars over, which I expect you to pay to Yvonne Carland, after deducting interest. If this property was good enough to interest Jonathan Dorn, it is satisfactory to me."

"I hadn't looked at it that way!" exclaimed Brendle, in a tone of surprise. "I was thinking purely in terms of James Carland. But you are right, Cranston. Dorn intended to buy—" Brendle paused, gave his head a rueful shake. "Or did he?"

"Carland claimed that he did."

"Not precisely. Carland said that Dorn was willing to finance the rice project. But frankly, Cranston, it is impossible to rely on anything that Carland stated. However, you have offered a solution to the problem."

Folding the title deeds, Brendle placed them in his pocket. Then, picking up the check, he tore it into small pieces. He expected Cranston's face to register surprise; but it did not. Nevertheless, Brendle felt that there must be some puzzlement on Cranston's part; inwardly, at least.

"Our best plan is to leave the proposition open," explained Brendle. "If you wish, you can give me a letter stating that you value the property at sixty thousand dollars, which you evidently do, and that you are willing to buy. That, in turn, should satisfy Yvonne regarding her debt to me.

"We can then proceed to have the land inspected from a marsh tractor. If it proves suitable for planting rice, I shall gladly sell it to you at the price named. In fact, I can sign a contract to that effect. With a clause, by the way, stating that any amount in excess of fifty thousand dollars will go to Yvonne Carland."

Therewith, Brendle proceeded to draw up a memorandum stipulating the terms. He made two copies, and handed one to The Shadow. Brendle emphasized the point that the contract would specify the sale of rice land, not salt marsh, which automatically protected Cranston.

"If you see Yvonne," Brendle added, "you might show her the memorandum, Cranston. If I told her, she would simply think that I was trying to eradicate the debt. She mistrusted her uncle—of that, I am sure—and this Talborn business must have worried her, too.

"Think of it, Cranston! Only last night, I was looking everywhere for Talborn, wondering where he had gone. All the while, he must have been watching that precious crypt where he had stored a quarter million in smuggled treasure."

DINNER ended, both men left the hotel. The Shadow went to his car and blinked a signal with a little flashlight. It brought no answer, which meant that the Xincas had gone. Their departure was in keeping with The Shadow's plans. A soft laugh came from his lips.

Driving from the parking lot, The Shadow thought

over the case of Graham Talborn. The police had appraised the treasure, and the estimate given by Brendle, a quarter million dollars, was about correct.

It would have been all profit for Talborn, too. Being in the export business, he could have shipped his spoils far and wide. Much of the treasure was pure gold or fine jade, which could always find a market.

Again The Shadow laughed.

Not only had he balked Talborn, but he had spoiled the game for Xitli before the masquerader could acquire Talborn's treasure as his own. But the crimes of the self-styled fire god were by no means settled. The Shadow did not share the increasing popular opinion that Xitli's main purpose had been to obtain the loot that Talborn secretly possessed.

Behind the machinations of Xitli lay a larger game, something concerning Carland and Dorn.

One person might, unwittingly, be able to supply proofs that The Shadow needed. That person was Yvonne Carland. It would be easy to talk with the girl and subtly urge her to unravel the past. As Cranston, The Shadow would start proceedings by telling Yvonne that he proposed to buy the rice lands.

Yvonne wasn't at her hotel when The Shadow stopped there. He called Andy at the Hotel Luzane, but received no answer. Next The Shadow tried Professor Hedwin, again with no success. He finally decided to go to the Hotel Luzane. There he learned that Hedwin had gone out, but that the clerk had not seen Andy leave.

It struck The Shadow as rather curious that one should have been noticed, the other not, particularly as the clerk's desk was directly opposite the elevators and the lobby quite small.

The Shadow went upstairs; he tried Andy's door with a special key and found the room empty. Then, as a matter of routine, he went to Hedwin's room.

Gargly sounds greeted the opening of the door. If ever eyes had expressed welcome, they were Andy's when they saw Cranston in the doorway. With a speed quite unusual for Cranston, The Shadow released Andy from the Mayan chains and removed the strangling thong. After feeling his throat and finding he still had one, Andy gulped his story.

"The professor has gone haywire!" he said. "He went to the museum, and didn't trust me enough to take me along. I can't exactly blame him, because he guessed that I was spying on him—something that the detectives asked me to do.

"It's the Xitli stuff again. The professor can't think of anything else. Sometimes I wonder—" Andy caught himself, urged by a fading loyalty toward Hedwin. "I'm wondering about Yvonne. She was on the telephone when the professor grabbed me. You don't think that she went to the museum, too?"

Andy wasn't merely changing the subject; he was really anxious about Yvonne. Calmly The Shadow told him not to worry, and suggested that they go to the museum, which suited Andy.

Riding in Cranston's car, they made a rapid trip, and to Andy's delight they found it open, with a few lights on the ground floor.

Starting in through the museum door, Andy felt himself restrained by Cranston's grip. He heard the calm tone of his companion:

"Wait, Andy. Suppose we enter quietly and look things over. Professor Hedwin does not trust Fitzhugh Salter. He may have treated Salter as he did you."

THEY moved quietly toward Salter's office, where, again, Cranston's hand drew Andy back. From a turn in the dim corridor they saw the door of Salter's office. Two men were standing there, shaking hands. One was Salter, the other Hedwin; they seemed on the best of terms.

"I owe you an apology, Salter," Hedwin was saying. "I thought that you might have stressed the Xitli story and thereby caused me inconvenience. I was annoyed, of course, when the police came to the hotel."

"As I was, when they came here," returned Salter. "So I reserved comment until after they talked to you, Professor. We agree on one thing, Hedwin"—Salter was smiling pleasantly—"and that is that neither of us care to be disturbed."

Hedwin came shambling toward the outer door, apparently engrossed in his thoughts. But his eyes took on a keen light when he heard a slight slam behind him, indicating that Salter had gone back into the office and closed the door.

Hedwin did not see Cranston or Andy; they had drawn toward a deep corner of the corridor. But they saw what Hedwin did next.

Turning about, the professor tiptoed past Salter's office toward the elevators. As soon as he had turned a corner, Andy started forward. The Shadow let him follow as far as Salter's office. There, the gripping hand asserted itself again.

Deftly, without the slightest trace of noise, The Shadow turned the knob of Salter's door. Opening it a crack, he motioned for Andy to listen.

Salter was on the telephone. He was calling police headquarters. They heard him requesting detectives to come to the museum. Coolly, Salter was telling them that he had obtained new facts concerning Xitli, the fire god.

Perplexed, Andy looked toward Cranston, who was silently closing the door. The Shadow pointed toward the outer door. More puzzled than ever, Andy came along.

"Wait here" was Cranston's suggestion when they stood on the outside steps. "When you see the police arriving, go into Salter's office and be there when they come. Let Salter do the talking, and learn all you can."

With that The Shadow strolled away. Andy watched Cranston's figure enter the parked car and decided that his friend intended to wait there. It happened that the car was too obscure to allow Andy a view of the cloaked shape that emerged.

Clad in black, The Shadow was skirting toward the museum, totally unseen by Andy. Nor did the watching man hear the low, sibilant whisper that came from somewhere near the shrubbery. In answer to that call, two chunky men joined the figure in black. They were the Shadow's Xincas.

Then all three were gone without a single glimpse on Andy's part. The lights of police cars were coming toward the museum. Remembering Cranston's injunction, Andy turned to go inside. More puzzled than ever, he was wondering what the next events would be. One person alone could have told him: The Shadow!

CHAPTER XVIII
THE CHANT OF XITLI

FITZHUGH SALTER was not at all surprised when Andy Ames entered his office. He took it for granted that Andy had heard from the police. A few minutes later the police themselves were stamping into the curator's office in a fashion that made Salter motion for silence.

"I have something to tell you," declared the curator. "Something which may be in the nature of a demonstration, though I am not quite sure. Meanwhile"—he glanced at the half circle composed of six detectives—"I must insist upon absolute silence."

The quiet was broken by new footfalls coming in from the outside door. Hurriedly, Salter went to quiet the newcomers. He came back with two more detectives and another man: Eugene Brendle. As soon as Salter closed the door, Brendle explained that the detectives had called him, to which Salter nodded.

"I asked them to do so," he said. "Odd things have been happening in this museum, Brendle. Matters which concern both of us, as well as others."

He turned a half-doubtful glance toward Andy. In Salter's gaze Andy recognized a revival of the curator's old feud with Professor Hedwin.

If Salter had known how Hedwin had treated Andy before coming to the museum, the curator's doubt would have vanished. However, since Salter decided not to protest Andy's presence, Andy simply followed Cranston's injunction to remain silent.

Andy was thinking about Yvonne, and his worry was increasing. He finally reassured himself that Yvonne could not have come to the museum, or Salter would have mentioned it. When Salter began to speak, Andy did not realize that the curator's own statement proved that Yvonne could have come without Salter's knowledge.

"Professor Hedwin believes in a cult of Xitli," Salter told the group. "In my opinion, such a theory was more than unproven; it was preposterous. Such, I say, was my opinion. I have modified it within the past few days. When Aztecs were reported in New Orleans, I began to wonder.

"Hedwin laid great stress upon the throne room of Xitli. He claimed that the basalt block which he brought back from Cuicuilco was the throne seat of Xitli. But, mind you, in all his talk of Xitli rituals involving a living fire god, Hedwin never declared that a real Xitli existed.

"He made it plain that someone, masked as Xitli, could control the cult. It would be possible, by Hedwin's own analysis, for a clever man to assemble Aztecs in the top floor of this museum and there give them orders which they would accept as law."

Opening a cabinet, Salter produced a phonograph record. Moving a screen from a corner, he revealed a recording machine. Running his fingers along a crack, he drew a thin, green wire into sight.

"I stayed in the museum purposely," declared Salter, "and on certain evenings I was sure of two things: that persons were moving about, and that someone was using the elevator. So I installed a microphone in Xitli's throne room and carried the wiring down here.

"Last night I not only heard all that happened in the throne room, but I recorded it. Unfortunately, my knowledge of spoken Mayan is limited. I was forced to play the record over and over to make sure of all that Xitli had said to his Aztecs. It would have been no use to call the police until my work was finished.

"By then the thing had happened. The Aztecs had done what Xitli told them. They had gone to the waterfront and murdered Pierre Laboutard. Fortunately"—Salter showed a relieved smile—"the loss of Laboutard was not serious."

"But they killed Talborn, too!" exclaimed Brendle. "If you had notified the police in time, you might have saved him, Salter!"

"Not at all," insisted Salter. "There was no mention of Talborn, or the Monseca crypt, in the recording. Xitli must have learned about the place where the treasure was hidden through Laboutard. This translation"—he placed typewritten papers on the desk—"proves that he told his Aztecs not to harm Laboutard until Xitli gave the word."

THE detectives were picking up the sheets, but Brendle was more interested in the phonograph record. He asked Salter to run it through, but the curator shook his head.

"Not yet," he said. "I have a new disk on the machine in case the cult meets again tonight. Though the Aztecs apparently can go in and out at will, I purposely left the museum open to encourage them if they came here. I was gone myself for a matter of fifteen minutes."

That statement was the one that should have impressed Andy. It meant that Yvonne could have come to the museum and entered unobserved. But Andy was thinking in terms of Professor Hedwin, who had stayed inside the museum after leaving Salter's office.

At this moment the professor could be up in the throne room, garbed as Xitli, ready to receive the killers who formed the Aztec cult!

Startling though the thought was, its realization was far more sensational. Almost in response to Andy's thoughts, a crackling came from the loudspeaker above Salter's recording machine.

Excitedly, the curator sprang to the corner and started the blank disk that promised to receive again the words of Xitli, to keep them as permanent evidence.

From out of the crackling came the voice of the masquerader; a muffled tone, yet startling. It was fluent, proving the speaker's knowledge of the strange tongue that he spoke. Salter, motioning for silence, was listening intently.

As the voice paused to receive a return babble from Aztec throats, Salter whispered excitedly:

"I can understand it! His words are more coherent since I improved the reception—"

The voice of Xitli interrupted. Salter was nodding, at moments excitedly, at others solemnly. He kept pushing back the persons who asked him to translate the things he heard. There were intervals when Xitli let the Aztecs reply, but Salter managed only to wedge in a few remarks.

"This is their last meeting," said the curator. "Xitli is telling them that their work is done. They are to disband and return to Mexico."

Again, after a necessary pause while Xitli spoke, Salter relayed the words of the fire god.

"He is speaking of a sacrifice," declared Salter. "The Aztecs are clamoring for one. He is telling them to wait until the time when—"

Xitli's voice had begun again, rising above the clamor of the Aztecs. Before Salter could say another word, a low chant began. Strange, discordant, it became a terrifying thing; into its weird cadence came the beat of drums.

At every break there was a word from Xitli, as though the fire god had picked up the burden of the chant and reduced the others to a mere accompaniment.

Turning from his corner, Salter started toward the door, moving mechanically, like a man in a strange dream. He was reaching in his pocket for a revolver. Moving after him, the detectives did the same.

At the door, Salter paused, listening to the swelling of the chant, which had reached a hideous, outlandish pitch punctuated by the sharp articulations of Xitli.

"Come," spoke Salter. "A few of you—no more. It would not be safe for many. But if we watch—"

At that instant the chant was broken; not by the voice of Xitli, nor the hammering of drums, but a shriek so ardent that it seemed the only human thing in all that vocal horror. To most who heard it, the scream was an appeal for help from some unknown person whose distress was so packed in the cry that words would have been superfluous.

To one, the shriek signified more. Andy Ames realized that only one person could have uttered it: Yvonne Carland. His worst fears had been realized. Yvonne had fallen into the power of the Aztec cult. She was the sacrifice that the fiends demanded from their monstrous leader, Xitli!

ONE man stood in Andy's path; that man was Fitzhugh Salter. He had sprung about, was waving his arms, apparently to tell his numbed companions that a mere venture to the throne room of Xitli would mean their doom. But Andy wasn't one to be convinced by Salter, though the detectives were willing to take the curator's advice.

Shoulder first, Andy bowled Salter from the doorway, sent him sprawling across the corridor. Andy had the gun that he had used in Mexico, and he tugged it from his pocket as he sped for the elevator.

His boldness influenced the rest. Brendle came from the curator's office with a flood of detectives that nearly trampled Salter in the rush.

As he ran, Andy could still hear the chant of Xitli coming from the loudspeaker in the office, above the surge of many feet. It was loud, discordant, still carrying a note of frenzy; but there was no repetition of Yvonne's scream.

All was a blur to Andy as he reached the elevator. Rescue was his motive, but over him had come the appalling thought that he might be too late to save Yvonne. Yet Andy's ardor did not fade. If he could not save Yvonne, another motive would inspire him; that of revenge upon Xitli, god of fire!

CHAPTER XIX
XITLI SPEAKS

THEY dashed into the throne room in the same positions as when they had left the curator's office,

Andy ahead of the detectives. But in the race along the corridor of the top floor, Andy doubled his lead on his companions. He had one thought: to reach the throne room in the least time possible and consider consequences later.

So ardent was Andy's dash that he lunged into the fateful room before he could stop himself. A fire was burning in the center of the floor; beyond it, Andy saw Yvonne, attired in Aztec costume, senseless on a slab in front of Xitli's throne.

In the throne itself was the green-masked, feathered fire god, his flame-hued costume blending with the flickering of the flames. Poised between the palms of Xitli's gauntlets was a stone knife, its handle against one hand, its point against the other.

The knife of sacrifice!

Too well did Andy know the practices of the ancient Mayas and their successors, the Aztecs; their way of sacrificing maidens to appease their mythical gods. But all that was summed in Andy's one desire—death to Xitli!

Rescue or revenge. It would be one or the other, dependent upon whether or not Yvonne still lived. By downing Xitli, Andy could end the curse of the fire god and the power that went with it. But Andy found no time to aim his gun, let alone pull the trigger.

He had precipitated himself into the midst of the Xitli cult, and Aztecs were upon him in a wave. Floundering, his revolver spinning from his hand, Andy saw the cleaving edges of hatchets brandished above him, ready to descend in time to the still persisting chant and the beat of the drums.

The thing that saved Andy was the voice of Xitli. At the fire god's harsh command, the Aztecs restrained their weapons. Then Andy found himself faced about, his arms pinned behind him. They had dragged him to the throne at Xitli's order

Other Aztecs had covered the doorway. They were flanking it, their stone hatchets at their fingertips. Stopped almost under the blades were a pair of detectives who were motioning back to others, telling the rest to wait. They had fallen into a trap almost as bad as Andy's.

They could have used their guns; in fact, they were still ready to do so if the Aztec hatchets budged. But it was better policy to wait, for no shots could reach Xitli. Aztecs were blocking off the path of aim toward the fire god. This frozen scene at least meant life, if no one disturbed the situation.

It was the voice of Xitli that all awaited; the one tone that could decide between life and death.

The words from the green mask were harsh, yet lulling to the Aztecs. The chant faded and a weird silence gripped the throne room, wherein the slight crackle of the fire seemed to grow in accompaniment to the tone of Xitli. Then the fire god did a most singular thing.

Gripping the knife by its blade, he proffered the handle to Andy. With his other hand Xitli gestured toward Yvonne, motioning for Andy to cut the thongs that bound her.

Numbly, Andy did so, and he saw the girl's eyes open. A moment later, he was lifting Yvonne to her feet, helping her past the fire where Aztecs stood immobile, their hatchets still upraised.

Andy heard the tone of Xitli, a voice that he recognized, speaking in English. As he reached the door, he told the detectives to put their guns away. Andy still could not understand the situation, but he knew that he had been spared by Xitli and that the fire god was a friend.

The detectives pocketed their revolvers, and Xitli's followers lowered their stone hatchets. They retired to the walls and squatted there, like patient lions obeying the mandate of a trainer. Then Xitli himself was coming from the throne room to meet the group in the hall.

He stepped toward the costume room where the Aztecs could not see him. There he removed his mask, to reveal himself as Professor Hedwin.

"BE careful," warned Hedwin in a low tone. "The Aztecs must not know that I am one of you. They cannot be blamed for the murders which they committed. They did those deeds through ignorance."

"You mean you aren't Xitli?" queried Andy. "That is, you weren't the man who brought the Aztecs here?"

"A correct assumption," returned Hedwin with a smile. "In fact, I actually doubted my own theories for a while. But when I realized that the Xitli cult must actually exist, I decided to disband it. There was only one way: to pose as Xitli myself."

Hedwin was taking off the headdress and the flame-hued robe. But his argument, though it appealed to Andy, did not go over with the detectives. They crowded in upon the old professor, then looked about for Salter. The curator had not yet arrived, but Eugene Brendle was on hand. He gave Hedwin a scathing look.

"It won't do, Hedwin," declared Brendle. "The proof is all against you. Smart business, trying to frame an alibi, but it won't go, under the circumstances."

"The proof is against me?" queried Hedwin. "You mean these?" He shoved the robe, the mask, into Brendle's hands, along with the headdress. "Bah! What do they mean? Put them back where they belong in the costume room. Let the real Xitli have them when he comes."

"The real Xitli?"

"Yes." Pressing Brendle aside, Hedwin pointed a bony finger toward a man who was coming from the corner of the corridor. "Here he is!"

The man was Fitzhugh Salter. He was still breathless from his spill outside the office. Before Salter could say a word, Hedwin had the floor.

"I watched you, Salter," cackled the professor. "Night after night you came to the museum, thinking that no one knew it. But I understood your game. While you pretended that my theories were worthless, you were gathering the Xitli clan.

"You knew that I detested Carland and Dorn. But so did you, Salter. You found a perfect way to murder them, for which I cannot entirely blame you. But it was despicable on your part to throw the guilt on me!"

In his harangue, Hedwin made no mention of Talborn's treasure, which in itself provided a profit motive for the crimes of Xitli. But the question of the treasure merely weighed each side of the balance between Hedwin and Salter.

Either of the two could have learned what Talborn had done. Hedwin might have looked over the shipments from Mexico, while Salter had such opportunity upon their arrival in New Orleans.

"Call Brendle," suggested Hedwin, turning to Andy. "Have him bring back the Xitli costume. Or better still, suppose we take Salter to the costume room and let him put on the regalia. We'll make him show himself as Xitli!"

His face thrust close to Salter's, Hedwin gave the curator a fierce glare. Quite undisturbed, the curator finally found his breath and turned to the detectives.

"Does Hedwin know about the recordings?" he questioned. "If he did, he might change his tune. Suppose"—Salter was smiling as the detectives shook their heads—"that I tell him."

A baffled look came over Hedwin's face. Then Salter was detailing the scene that had taken place in the office; how, on the night before, he had also listened in on a meeting of the Xitli cult and had kept a record of it.

Hedwin couldn't seem to find an answer; even Andy, whose leanings had turned toward the professor, was convinced by Salter's argument. Only Yvonne still had a plea for Hedwin.

"I shouldn't have screamed," she told Andy earnestly. "When Xitli held the knife above me, my nerves gave way. But he was only trying to quiet the Aztecs."

"Quite right," agreed Hedwin quickly. "I told them that the sacrifice should wait until they returned to Mexico. I had to go through all the drama of an actual threat to show them that Xitli could restrain his hand at the very moment of a sacrifice."

THE detectives were not restraining their hands. They had heard enough of Hedwin's alibis. They started to drag Hedwin toward the elevator, and the professor made no protest. Right then Salter inserted a single word:

"Wait!"

Surprised that Salter would intervene for Hedwin, the detectives halted. Facing the slumped professor, Salter spoke in a tone of marked apology.

"I believe your story, Hedwin," he said simply. "But first I had to prove my own. I was never Xitli; neither were you until tonight. Do you remember"— Salter had turned to Andy and the detectives— "how I tried to hold you back downstairs?

"It was because I understood the things that Xitli was saying when Yvonne screamed. He was telling them that there had been enough of blood, that they were to leave this land as they had come here. He said that Xitli would dwell alone within his temple.

"But that was not all. The voice of Xitli was more fluent than it was last night. Then he spoke only in forced phrases; tonight he used the language as if it were his own.

"I have satisfied everyone that I was not Xitli; now I declare Hedwin innocent, too. The proof is in my office. You will all recognize it when I play the records. You will hear the voice of the Xitli that we seek, the one who actually demanded murder—"

They heard it without going to Salter's office. It came from behind them at the very door of the throne room, which everyone had forgotten. Turning about, the startled group saw Xitli himself, come upon them so suddenly that he seemed actually to have materialized himself like a genuine god of fire.

Masked, feathered, in full regalia, Xitli was throating the order to his Aztecs, who still occupied the throne room—an order which, even to those who lacked all knowledge of Mayan, could mean but one thing. Death!

CHAPTER XX
THE FINAL DUEL

THE surge toward Xitli was immediate but hopeless. Before Andy and the detectives could bring their guns into action, the feathered fire god had swept into his throne room.

Hoping to stop him before he roused the Aztecs, the attackers swarmed through the door, only to be met by lunging men with swinging hatchets. Well did Xitli know the speed with which his Aztecs acted, how little they feared death themselves.

In one swift instant it seemed that doom was certain for Andy and the over-ardent detectives. Then, without a single gunshot, Aztecs were plunging headlong to the floor, tripped by two of their own companions—the men nearest the door. A pair of squatly blockers had literally flung themselves in front of the surging horde.

They were not Aztecs, those two, even though they had passed as such in the flickering glow of the throne room. They were The Shadow's Xincas, sent to the meeting by their chief with orders to thwart murder when the time came.

The fact that they had not intervened earlier was proof that Hedwin's story was true. All along the Xincas had known that Hedwin, garbed as Xitli, was trying to calm the cult.

But it was a different Xitli who now commanded. His attacking Aztecs had been slowed, but not stopped. Andy and the detectives were plunging into battle, unwisely giving the Aztecs the close range that the squatly fighters liked. Above all rose the triumphant voice of Xitli, with its loud command to kill.

Only a power more startling than Xitli's could turn the tide. Such a power did.

It began with a roar from the throne of the fire god toward which Xitli himself had turned. The roar was the splitting of the built-in throne as it spread in two parts, revealing a black passage behind it.

From the blackness came a challenging laugh, the mockery of an invisible foe. At that mirth, Aztecs turned, for they knew the fighter that it meant.

Xitli himself tried to drown the challenge with another cry to kill, but the tone of The Shadow, increased by the hollow behind the throne, still dominated.

Like blocks of stone come to life, The Shadow's Xincas rose and hurled themselves toward the door, bowling Andy and the nonplused detectives out into the corridor.

Starting to shoot at Aztecs, the surprised invaders did not see the Xincas until the pair hit them, below gun level, with the force of battering rams.

The Xincas were simply clearing the battleground, where only one combatant was needed: The Shadow!

Tongues of gun flame were stabbing lead from the sundered throne, clipping the Aztecs who tried to fling their hatchets. Others were dropping back, amazed by the broken throne, which seemed to spell an end to the power of Xitli.

But one thing more was needed to throw the murder tribe into utter confusion. The Shadow supplied the necessary deed.

Springing from the secret passage, he reached the seat of Xitli's throne and poised, crouched with his aiming guns, upon the basalt block that was the symbol of the fire god.

To the Aztecs, it was death to touch that stone. In The Shadow they saw a god of death, the only sort of being that could defy Xitli!

FROM behind the shelter of his followers, Xitli howled for a new attack that did not come. In desperation, he flung one of his fire vials. The Shadow saw it coming and swept his cloak over his eyes.

The thing burst with a blaze, and with the flare the Aztecs heard the shout of Xitli, competing with the laugh that The Shadow delivered through his muffling cloak.

Blindly the Aztecs charged. The Shadow side-stepped, letting them stumble toward the throne, from which they quailed as they felt its touch. Through the mass of blundering figures, The Shadow was looking for Xitli. He saw the masquerader beyond the throng, coming up from the floor, where he had stooped to shield his eyes.

Xitli saw The Shadow and gave another fling. This time his weapon was a stone ax that one of his followers had dropped. He lobbed it over the heads of the Aztecs and howled new triumph as he saw The Shadow make a desperate twist.

But in that spin The Shadow found the opening he wanted. With his sideward dive, he stabbed a shot between the figures of two Aztecs.

The Shadow's aim was perfect. Xitli never saw the finish of the ax fling as the stone blade sliced the brim of The Shadow's hat and harmlessly slashed the black cloak before clattering on the floor. For Xitli's heart had received a bullet straight from The Shadow's gun.

No longer could Xitli command. The only tone that echoed through the throne room was the laugh of The Shadow.

Thrusting Aztecs aside, The Shadow reached the throne. There his laugh ended; he was speaking commands that the Aztecs understood. His voice was in their language; it came from Xitli's throne. It was the word of a power greater than the fire god. Submissively, the Aztecs dropped their weapons.

They heard the clatter of the closing throne. When their blinking eyes could view the change, they saw that The Shadow was gone. But Xitli still remained among them, a dead figure on the floor. Death to Xitli meant the end of the fire god's cult. No longer would these Aztecs murder.

From the corridor, Professor Hedwin entered. He spoke to the Aztecs, and they listened, for The Shadow had told them to await another's order. Behind Hedwin came Fitzhugh Salter.

The curator stooped above the form of Xitli and removed the dead man's mask. He beckoned others to come and view the lifeless face of Eugene Brendle, the man who had covered his crimes, along with his identity, when he posed as Xitli.

A SHORT while later they found Lamont Cranston down in the curator's office, where he had just arrived. A mere spectator, Cranston listened to the details that the others pieced while detectives were marching the surviving Aztecs out from the museum.

It was easy to fit facts regarding Brendle once he had been identified as Xitli. He had been connected with the Mayan Museum from the start and had heard the Xitli legend. As the contractor who superintended the building, Brendle had easily installed the secret entrance to the throne room.

"Brendle suffered more than either of us, so far as Carland was concerned," said Salter to Hedwin. "The same applied in Dorn's case. But Brendle was clever. He kept up a friendship with Carland so that the blame would be placed on one of us."

"You mean on me," corrected Hedwin. "The throne room was my idea. But do you know"—the professor's eyes gleamed wisely—"I don't think that Brendle expected the Aztecs at all. He intended to use Laboutard for murder; then, perhaps, hold some brief masquerade to draw attention to the Aztec cult.

"The throne room was of my design; Brendle's addition of a secret passage would have been attributed to me, though I knew nothing of it."

"But when the Aztecs came—"

"Brendle used them, of course. He posed as Xitli and put the Aztecs to the task that Laboutard refused."

Silently, The Shadow admired Hedwin's analysis. It lacked a few details, but was otherwise correct. The Shadow could have supplied the missing points, for he had recognized them while many were still in progress. But when the story had been thrashed out, The Shadow had something to add, which he could do quite capably as Cranston.

"You speak of a double game," he remarked. "Talborn was after treasure. When Brendle learned it, he followed up the murders of Carland and Dorn by attempting to take Talborn's treasure."

"Quite right," agreed Salter. "The idea of wealth appealed to Brendle."

"He needed money," insisted Hedwin. "He was constantly worried over the fifty thousand dollars that Carland owed him."

"Then why," came Cranston's query, "did Brendle refuse sixty thousand that I offered him for the Carland property this evening? I actually gave him a check for it, but he tore it up and insisted upon this instead. You will find the duplicate in Brendle's pocket, along with the title deeds that still belong to Yvonne Carland."

The Shadow produced his copy of the written memorandum. At first sight Brendle's contract regarding the rice lands looked like a generous arrangement, but Brendle, exposed as Xitli, could no longer be regarded as generous. Cranston's lips formed a smile as his keen eyes roved the puzzled group.

"There must be a catch to it," he said. "Otherwise Brendle would not have made the offer. I think the catch concerns the term 'rice lands.' Brendle knew that the property was salt marsh, unfit for raising rice. All he wanted was a chance to survey the land and find something else, presumably by accident."

"What else?" queried Andy.

"I would say oil," replied The Shadow. "The land was Carland's to begin with, and oil was his business. His talk of rice was merely a blind. Having to borrow on the property, he did not want Brendle to know its real worth. But Dorn knew all about it. Carland talked to him in terms of oil, not rice."

The whole of Brendle's scheme opened wide. His double murder had been a quest for wealth, not a mere grudge against Carland and Dorn. It brought home another point, which the listeners heard Cranston supply in a matter-of-fact fashion.

"Laboutard knew the delta region," said The Shadow. "He is probably the man who informed Brendle that there was oil on Carland's property. Which made it all the more necessary for Brendle to dispose of Laboutard, the one man who could have blackmailed him later.

"I have heard that there are great possibilities in Louisiana oil land." The Shadow turned to Yvonne. "So allow me to congratulate you, Miss Carland, on the future wealth that you deserve. From what I have learned of Brendle, he would not have played for small stakes. If you need fifty thousand dollars to regain those title deeds, my checkbook is still available."

STROLLING from the office, The Shadow left the museum and returned to his car, where the faithful Xincas waited. They had kept right on through, after turning battle over to The Shadow.

As he started the car, The Shadow gazed toward the great museum, its piles of pyramiding steps leading to the topmost floor, where crime had risen to its heights, then fallen. From Cranston's lips came the laugh of The Shadow.

Those within the museum caught the echoes of that mirth. It was fanciful, weird, seemingly distant, yet as real as the vast bulk of the mighty pyramid above them. Real to those who had seen the fray in which that laugh had resounded from the lips of a black-clad battler who fought for justice.

They knew the parting laugh of The Shadow, the tone that symbolized his triumph over Xitli, god of fire!

THE END

Now on sale in DOC SAVAGE #63:
The Awful Dynasty, The Angry Canary and The Swooning Lady

THE BOWMAN WHO BECAME
AN ARCHER *by Anthony Tollin*

"I never intended to become an actor," John Archer recalled in 1984. "I was afraid to get up next to my desk in class to read a term paper. I fell into acting quite by accident." Born Ralph Bowman, he had originally intended to pursue a cinematic career on the opposite side of the camera. He'd studied cinematography at USC and had been working as an aerial photographer when he stopped off for lunch at a Los Angeles restaurant. "A man by the name of Ben Bard had a dramatic school next door and he was having lunch with an agent and another actor, Jack Carson. Bard was bragging that he could make an actor out of anyone. On a bet, he looked around the room and sent the hostess over to ask me if I'd come over to see him. 'Look,' he said, 'you have the look the studios are looking for...How would you like to be an actor?' Well, I wasn't getting anywhere as an aerial photographer, and I was willing to try anything. He offered me a full scholarship, and three months later I got my first acting job."

Ralph Bowman made his screen debut in *You Can't Cheat an Honest Man* (starring Edgar Bergen and W. C. Fields), before playing more substantial roles in *Dick Tracy Returns* and *Overland Stage Raiders* (alongside John Wayne).

A Bowman became an Archer when the young actor won a new name and an RKO movie contract on a CBS talent competition. "Hollywood producer Jesse Lasky had this big radio show, *Gateway to Hollywood*, with Wrigley's Gum as the sponsor. It brought guys and gals to Hollywood from across the country to audition over the radio. For a period of thirteen weeks they kept asking 'Who is going to be John Archer and who is going to be Alice Eden?' They had three segments of semifinals and those

winners qualified to compete in the thirteenth broadcast. Fortunately, I was the one who won the name and started my new career as 'John Archer.'"

The newly christened "John Archer" costarred with Ann Shirley in *Career* and went on to appear in dozens of films including *Scattergood Baines*, *City of Missing Girls*, *Bowery at Midnight* (alongside Bela Lugosi), *Guadalcanal Diary* and *Sherlock Holmes in Washington* (with Basil Rathbone). When a scheduled movie studio raise was not forthcoming, John and his wife Marjorie Lord moved east in 1943 to pursue Broadway careers.

"I had noticed that all the young actors who were getting all the good parts were out of New York. Of course, everyone wanted to be in the theater, but you had to start in radio because that was where the bread and butter were." Archer starred as Agent Andrews on *The FBI in Peace and War* and was also often heard in supporting roles on *Counterspy*, *Gangbusters* and a variety of soap operas. "We were just running from studio to studio all day long."

In 1944, John Archer was chosen from hundreds of actors to be the newest voice of The Shadow. "I auditioned for director Bob Steel and he hired me on the spot. Bob and I hit it off immediately, and he brought me over to meet the sponsors at Blue Coal." Archer portrayed Lamont Cranston in 29 episodes that season, with Hollywood transplant Judith Allen replacing the ailing Marjorie Anderson as Margot in December. "I had listened to the series as a young actor starting out in Hollywood, never dreaming that a few years later I would be playing the title role while also starring on Broadway." John also voiced Lamont Cranston that season in mystery segments on *Quick as a Flash*, a new

Jesse Lasky (center) with *Gateway to Hollywood* winners Alice Eden and John Archer

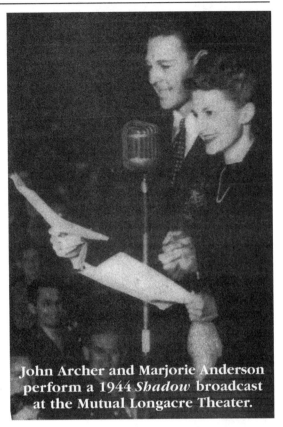

John Archer and Marjorie Anderson perform a 1944 *Shadow* broadcast at the Mutual Longacre Theater.

Mutual game show hosted by longtime *Shadow* announcer Ken Roberts.

A dozen *Shadow* scripts during Archer's season were written by Alfred Bester, who brought strong fantasy elements into the series, pitting Cranston against a strange visitor from another world, a radioactive man and a murderous medico who killed his victims through ultrasonically induced nightmares. The legendary science fiction author often reused his earlier comic book plots, including his 1944 Green Lantern comic script, "Heroes Are Born ... Not Made" (published in *The Big All-American Comic Book*), which he reworked for radio as "The Face of Death" (reprinted in this volume).*

Like his shadowy predecessor Orson Welles, John often encountered scheduling conflicts juggling his radio and theater careers. "I was rehearsing a Broadway-bound play called *One Man Show.* We were out of town doing the tryouts in Boston, New Haven and Philadelphia, and I'd have to take the train into New York every Saturday night after the performance so I could do *The Shadow* on Sunday." Archer's success as a Broadway leading man soon

led to a hiatus in his radio career. "When a new play came along, I said 'Goodbye' to the radio work, but when the play closed, it was 'Hello, radio!'"

After reinventing himself as a Broadway star, John Archer returned to Hollywood in 1939 under contract to Universal Pictures, where he costarred with James Cagney and Edmond O'Brien in the classic gangster film *White Heat.*

The following year, John received top billing in the landmark science fiction film *Destination Moon*, which altered his opinions regarding rocketry. "I'd previously considered space travel to be crazy Buck Rogers stuff, but *Destination Moon* scriptwriter Bob Heinlein and our Cal-Tech rocket scientist advisors convinced me that it was only a matter of time before a Moon landing would become reality."

Destination Moon made the *New York Times'* list of the year's ten best films. Robert Heinlein's screenplay was adapted as an early episode of NBC's *Dimension X* radio anthology, and Archer and the film were cover-featured on the first issue of DC Comics' *Strange Adventures.**

Cast as a G-men similar to his earlier radio role in *The FBI in Peace and War*, John Archer costarred with Bob Hope and *Shadow* radio veterans Bill

---

*Bester reworked his 1942 Starman story, "The Little Man Who Wasn't There," and his *Green Lantern* scripts "The Lizard of Fire," "The Man with the Missing Memory" and "The Man Who Wanted the World" as *Shadow* melodramas during his first year as a radio writer.

*Coincidentally, "Destination Moon" was appropriated in 1967 as the title of the final original Shadow paperback novel from Belmont Books.

John Archer in *Destination Moon*

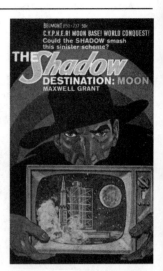

Johnstone, Arnold Moss and Luis Van Rooten in *My Favorite Spy*. After re-establishing his movie career, Archer shared the screen with Kirk Douglas in *The Big Trees*, enacted the title role in *A Yank in Indo-China* and became a familiar face in Westerns including *Santa Fe* and *Best of the Badmen*. A decade later, John delivered two of his final big-screen performances in *Blue Hawaii* (as Elvis Presley's uncle) and *I Saw What You Did*.

Archer was also frequently seen on the small screen during the Golden Age of Television, guest-starring on dozens of series including *Suspense*, *The Twilight Zone*, *Science Fiction Theatre*, *Perry Mason*, *Maverick*, *Bonanza*, *Wagon Train* and *The Frank Sinatra Show*, along with recurring roles on *Cheyenne*, *Lassie* and *The Bob Cummings Show*.

When Hollywood roles dropped off in the 1960s, he launched new careers as a restaurateur and sales rep, leaving acting to a new generation that included his Oscar-nominated daughter, Anne Archer.

Throughout his life, the star who had earned his screen name on a CBS talent show retained a special fondness for radio's "Theater of the Mind." Although he'd had a long career in Hollywood, it was his single radio season starring as The Shadow that attracted the most attention during his later years, and John Archer was frequently called upon to recreate The Shadow's famous laugh at old-time radio conventions. "I did not at the time realize that [*The Shadow*] was something special, that it would live forever and ever, which it will," John insisted. "People are always interested: 'Oh, *The Shadow*! We listened to it all the time!'

"An actor is lucky if he is able to play one role in his career that is memorable enough to be remembered years later. The Shadow has gone on to achieve legendary status as one of the most memorable characters from the Golden Age of Radio. I'm proud to have portrayed The Shadow and to be a part of that legend." •

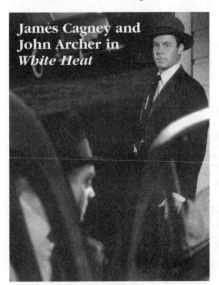

James Cagney and John Archer in *White Heat*

Former radio Shadows Bill Johnstone (left) and John Archer (right) in *My Favorite Spy*

THE SHADOW
"THE FACE OF DEATH"
by Alfred Bester
as broadcast February 11, 1945 over MBS

(MUSIC: "SPINNING WHEEL" - FADE UNDER)

SHADOW: (FILTER) Who knows what evil lurks in the hearts of men? The SHADOW knows. (LAUGHS)

(MUSIC UP ... SEGUE BRIGHT THEME)

ANNR: Once again your neighborhood 'blue coal' dealer brings you the thrilling adventures of the SHADOW... the hard and relentless fight of one man against the forces of evil. These dramatizations are designed to demonstrate forcibly to old and young alike that crime does not pay.

ANNR: The SHADOW, who aids the forces of law and order is in reality Lamont Cranston, wealthy-young man-about-town. Years ago in the Orient, Cranston learned a strange and mysterious secret ... the hypnotic power to cloud men's minds so they cannot see him. Cranston's friend and companion, the lovely Margot Lane, is the only person who knows to whom the voice of the invisible SHADOW belongs. Today's drama ... "The Face of Death."

(MUSIC UP ... SEGUE INTO NEUTRAL BACKGROUND)

ANNR: As a violent thunderstorm rages outside, three men sit comfortably around a blazing fire in the exclusive Savoy Club. They are Robert Adams, a well-known engineer, Greg Baker, wealthy banker, and Lamont Cranston ...

(THUNDER AND RAIN UP THEN DOWN. CRACKLE OF FIRE BG.)

BAKER: Listen to that storm, will you. How'd you like to be out on a night like this, Cranston?

CRANSTON: I wouldn't, Baker, but I'm afraid I'll have to be. Got to be leaving soon.

BAKER: Nonsense. Stick around. This is the time to sit by the fire and tell ghost stories, eh? Know any creepy yarns, Adams?

ADAMS: (TENSE) Don't talk like that.

BAKER: What?

ADAMS: I said don't talk like that.

BAKER: For Pete's sake, what's the matter with you?

ADAMS: Nothing.

BAKER: Look at him, Cranston. The man's actually trembling. Don't tell me you're afraid of thunder and lightning.

ADAMS: I am not afraid of thunder and lightning. I am not trembling. Will you shut up and leave me alone.

BAKER: For Pete's—

ADAMS: And don't say "for Pete's sake" again. You're a babbling meddlesome fool, Baker. You're a fat, thick-headed idiot and I don't like you. Do me a favor and die!

BAKER: Now listen, Adams ...

CRANSTON: Hold it! Hold it! This *had* gone just about far enough.

BAKER: Nobody's going to sound off like –

CRANSTON: That's enough! Suppose you drop into the card room, Baker .. See what the crowd's doing.

BAKER: The card room ...

CRANSTON: Go ahead.

BAKER: Oh … Oh, sure. I guess I can take a hint. Of course, Cranston…

(STEPS FADE OFF)

BAKER: I'd forgotten you were on the House Committee. (FADING) Got to reprimand a member for insolence, he … (LAUGHS)

(DOOR CLOSES OFF)

ADAMS: All right, Cranston. What's the fine?

CRANSTON: There isn't going to be any fine, Adams.

ADAMS: I've forgotten the house rules on my offense. Am I suspended or what…?

CRANSTON: Suppose you stop talking through the top of your head and tell me what's wrong. No … Don't try to fool me, Adams. I know something's bothering you.

ADAMS: You're crazy.

CRANSTON: Money trouble?

ADAMS: No.

CRANSTON: Woman trouble? There's a rumor you've broken off with your finacee..what's her name … the explorer girl …

ADAMS: Lucy Knight. No, I haven't broken off with her.

CRANSTON: You might as well spill it, Adams. A man doesn't sit around with a white face and shaking hands unless he's afraid of something.

ADAMS: All right … I'm afraid of …

CRANSTON: Of what?

ADAMS: I'm afraid I'll be turned to stone.

CRANSTON: Turned to what?

ADAMS: Stone!

CRANSTON: You'd better explain.

**Scriptwriter
Alfred Bester**

ADAMS: Ever heard of Medusa?

CRANSTON: Medusa? You mean the famous mythological woman …

ADAMS: Yes. That one. The tall beautiful demon whose face turned men to stone if they looked at it.

CRANSTON: Go on.

ADAMS: I received a threatening letter last week. It said that Lucy had desecrated the shrine of Medusa in her archeological work in Asia Minor. It said that Medusa would have to be pacified with an offering. It demanded ten thousand dollars.

CRANSTON: That's ridiculous. Surely you don't believe—

ADAMS: Listen. Three days ago I arrived home one night and found my English Setter … you remember Bobs … turned to stone.

CRANSTON: I don't believe it.

ADAMS: There was a note alongside. It said this was a warning. The price was now raised to fifteen thousand dollars.

CRANSTON: But Adams, you can't possibly…

(DOOR OPENS OFF SHARPLY. FOOTSTEPS FADE ON SLOWLY)

CRANSTON: Who's that?

ADAMS: Cranston! Look!

CRANSTON: What in blazes!?

ADAMS: It's she … The … The Medusa! The white Grecian Robes! The silver mask on her face!

(CUT STEPS)

MEDUSA: (ON) Robert Adams. You know me?

ADAMS: I … I know you.

CRANSTON: Now just a minute.

MEDUSA: Silence, mortal! Silence before the Gods! Now, my business is with this one, Robert Adams … later perhaps I may have words with you!

ADAMS: Wh-what do you want?

MEDUSA: Robert Adams. You have been warned twice…this is your third and last. The immortal Medusa demands a sacrifice! Medusa will have her sacrifice … or she will show you her face!

CRANSTON: Nonsense!

MEDUSA: You have one hour, Robert Adams! One little hour to pay … and pay you must or this silver mask will slip aside and you will look on my face…on the face of death!

MUSIC: (QUICK STAB INTO BRIDGE)
                (SLIGHT WIND BG. STEPS ON CONCRETE)

CRANSTON: The rain's stopped, Adams. Come on, I'll walk you home from the club.

ADAMS: What time is it?

CRANSTON: Twelve forty-five.

ADAMS: Then I've only fifteen minutes left.

CRANSTON: Don't be a fool. No one's going to turn you to stone.

ADAMS: Why did you let her escape, Cranston? Why'd you let her out of the club?

CRANSTON: Be reasonable, Adams. You fainted dead away after she threatened you, and pitched straight into the fire. If I hadn't grabbed you, you'd have been horribly burned!

ADAMS: Yes … Yes … I'm sorry.

CRANSTON: By the time I turned around she was gone.

ADAMS: She'll be back. I know it.

CRANSTON: Don't be an idiot. Medusa is only a legend … A legend, Adams!

ADAMS: I know … A beautiful woman … If you look at her face, you'll be turned to stone.

CRANSTON: No one believes in myths today; no one's afraid of them. So get a grip on yourself. Probably only a practical joke.

ADAMS: Y-yes … perhaps.

CRANSTON: Here's the park entrance … Come on, we'll take a shortcut through.

NEWSMAN: (OFF. FADING ON SLOWLY) Paper! Getcha morning paper! Whaddya read. Paper …

ADAMS: I … I suppose I've been a fool. (LAUGHS WEAKLY)

CRANSTON: That's better. Laugh at it. Think of how embarrassed you'd be if you took it seriously and found out it was a joke.

ADAMS: Of course … (TRIES TO LAUGH AGAIN.) It's a joke. Probably something Lucy's dreamed up. She knows all about those old Greek legends …

NEWSMAN: Paper … Getcha morning paper … (ON) Morning paper, gents? Whaddya read?

CRANSTON: I'll take the *Globe.* Anything for you, Adams?

ADAMS: No thanks … (FADING OFF) Seen 'em all at the club … Hurry up, Cranston….

CRANSTON: Be right with you. Here, boy, got change for a dollar?

NEWSMAN: Yessir. Half a second …
                (JINGLE OF COINS)

CRANSTON: Say Mister … did he call you Cranston?

CRANSTON: That's right. Why?

NEWSMAN: Ain't you that amacher detective that's all the time hangin' around with the Police Commmissioner?

CRANSTON: Yes.

NEWSMAN: Listen, Mr. Cranston. My brother is havin' an awful time gettin' a hack license. I wonder if you could put in a word with …

ADAMS: (SCREAMS WELL OFF MIKE)

NEWSMAN: Mr. Cranston!

ADAMS: (WELL OFF) Help! Help! (SCREAMS)

CRANSTON: That's Adams up ahead in the park! Come on!

    (RUNNING STEPS)

NEWSMAN: What's goin' on there, Mr. Cranston?

CRANSTON: I don't know!

NEWSMAN: Hey … Mr. Cranston! Take a look! There … There's a dame up there … See?

CRANSTON: Where?

NEWSMAN: Running through the trees … Look at her. She's all dressed in white….

CRANSTON: Good Lord! It's the Medusa …

NEWSMAN: The who?

CRANSTON: Adams! Adams! Are you all right?! Adams!

NEWSMAN: Th-There's someone layin' on the road, Mr. Cranston … He looks white too …

CRANSTON: It's Adams …

NEWSMAN: He looks all funny, Mr. Cranston….

CRANSTON: Wait …

    (SLOW STEPS THEN CUT)

NEWSMAN: Wh-What's the matter with him?

CRANSTON: I can't believe it. It's impossible! He's been turned to solid stone!

    (MUSIC BRIDGE)

    (DOOR OPENS. STEPS)

CRANSTON: Good morning, Commissioner Weston.

MARGOT: 'Morning, Commissioner …

    (DOOR CLOSES)

WESTON: So … you finally got here, hey? Sit down … both of you.

MARGOT: Why, Commissioner, you actually sound angry.

CRANSTON: For a change.

WESTON: Yes, I'm sore … Good and sore. Listen here, what's the big idea of tryin' to take my department for a ride?

CRANSTON: What do you mean, Commissioner?

WESTON: Don't act innocent, Cranston. I think that gag you pulled off last night was pretty low and unfunny. Reporting a murder to the police…Getting the squad out to the park in the middle of the night to find a stone statue there.

CRANSTON: I wasn't fooling, Commissioner. I saw that man turned to stone. That evidence I gave your homicide squad was no practical joke.

WESTON: Now lay off, Cranston. Don't push a gag too far.

MARGOT: Did you check on Mr. Adams, Commissioner?

WESTON: Sure I checked. Sure he's missing … but he's in on it too.

CRANSTON: Listen to me, Commissioner. You know I'm not the kind of person that goes in for practical jokes. I wasn't fooling last night. I'm not fooling now. That Medusa story is true …

WESTON: Now Cranston …

MARGOT: We're not fooling, Commissioner …

WESTON: You're not—? Oh, for the love of Pete … that makes it worse.

**Judith Allen and John Archer pose as
Margot Lane and Lamont Cranston**

CRANSTON: How's that?

WESTON: Am I supposed to take a myth seriously? Am I supposed to send out the dragnet for a goddess? Am I going to call in Cardona and say: Cardona … go out and arrest a dame who turns men to stone.

CRANSTON: You've got to do something, Commissioner. This is no joke.

WESTON: I'm beginning to wish that it was….

            (TELEPHONE RINGS)

WESTON: Wait a minute …

            (PHONE UP)

WESTON: Yes?

BAKER: (FILTER) Mr. Cranston, please.

WESTON: Who's this? How'd you know he was here?

BAKER: This is Gregg Baker. They told me at his home he'd be at Commissioner Weston's office …

WESTON: Okay … You can talk to him…But remember, Mr. Baker…this is the police commissioner's office … Not a telephone exchange … For you, Cranston …

CRANSTON: Thanks … Hello, Baker?

BAKER: Cranston! Was that true about Adams … The story in the paper this morning?

CRANSTON: Yes.

BAKER: Oh no … No! It can't be! It's got to be a joke …

CRANSTON: What's the matter?

BAKER: Listen … I … I found a warning from The Medusa when I got home last night … I … I was supposed to pay ten thousand dollars by ten o'clock this morning …

CRANSTON: Yes?

BAKER: Or else she threatened to turn me to stone.

CRANSTON: Did you pay?

BAKER: No … I laughed … thought it was a joke. And not it … it's ten o'clock and … (YELLS)

CRANSTON: Hello! Hello! Baker!

               (PAUSE THEN PHONE HUNG UP)

MARGOT: Lamont! What's happened?

CRANSTON: Get your hat, Commissioner … We've got a date to keep in a hurry.

WESTON: Wait a minute … What's the rush? What's happened? Who've we got a date with?

CRANSTON: I'm afraid it's with a statue!

               (MUSIC BRIDGE)

               (CAR COMES TO STOP. DOOR OPENS)

CRANSTON: This is Adams' house. Come on …

               (RUNNING STEPS ON PAVEMENT)

MARGOT: Lamont … Do you think he …

WESTON: Don't say it, Miss Lane. Please! Don't say it!

MARGOT: But Commissioner, you're not afraid of The Medusa are you?

WESTON: Only of the newsapapers, Miss Lane. I'm going to take an awful riding on this.

CRANSTON: Hello! That's odd! The front door's open.

WESTON: We might as well go in. Let's have the bad news now.

CRANSTON: All right … Come on!

               (STEPS FROM STONE TO WOOD)

CRANSTON: If I remember right, Adam's phone is in his study. It's this way …

               (SCREAM OFF MIKE)

MARGOT: Lamont!

WESTON: Hey! That sounded like a woman!

CRANSTON: It came from the study …

               (DOOR OPENS OFF)

LUCY: (OFF…WILD) Help … Help…Police!

CRANSTON: That's Lucy Knight … Adams' fiancée..

**Ted de Corsia, aka
Commissioner Weston**

WESTON: All right, lady … We're police! What're you blowing your top about?

LUCY: (ON) C-Come into the study … Quick! Gregg Baker … He … He …

MARGOT: Lamont!

WESTON: For the love of Pete!

CRANSTON: Yes … it's just about what we expected, isn't it.

               (CUT STEPS)

LUCY: Wh-what's happened to him? What's happened?

CRANSTON: I'm afraid Baker's looked at Medusa's face too. He's been turned to stone!

               (MUSIC UP TO COVER)

               (MIDDLE COMMERCIAL)

WESTON: All right … All right … Now, don't let's have any hysterics, ladies … This case is bad enough without that.

MARGOT: Please, Commissioner … Miss Knight is pretty upset as it is.

WESTON: Look, Miss Lane … Take her somewhere else for a while … into the kitchen for some coffee or something.

MARGOT: All right. Come on Miss Knight …

LUCY: (HYSTERICAL) I can't understand it…I can't … First, Bob … then Gregg Baker …

MARGOT: Come on … You'll feel better …

            (STEPS … DOOR OPENS AND CLOSES OFF)

WESTON: Well … This sure is a mess, hey, Cranston?

CRANSTON: It's the strangest case I've ever seen, Commissioner. Take a look at this statue … It's Baker in every detail … face … hands … clothes … everything turned to stone.

WESTON: Yeah … Just like Adams.

CRANSTON: It's simply unbelievable.

WESTON: Listen, Cranston … Exactly what is the Medusa Legend?

CRANSTON: Well … Medsua was a mythological creature. She was supposedly a beautiful woman. Her hair in some legends was a mass of snakes … poisonous vipers.

WESTON: Holy Smoke!

CRANSTON: The mere sight of her face was enough to turn any living creature to stone …

WESTON: Dogs too, hey? Like Adams' setter.

CRANSTON: That's right. Medusa was slain by Perseus, a legendary hero who approached her as she slept, watching her reflection in a steel shield.

WESTON: Oh, that's great. That's really great. Now, I suppose I'll have to have the force equipped with mirrors when they go after this Medusa. Let me have the phone …

CRANSTON: Here you are … Going to order the mirrors?

WESTON: Don't be funny …

            (PHONE UP. DIAL TURNED)

WESTON: I'm going to order action!

CRANSTON: Right! Will you excuse me a minute. I want to talk to Lucy Knight.

WESTON: Go ahead …

            (FOOTSTEPS ON MIKE)

WESTON: (FADING) Hello, Cardona? Send the homicide squad up here. Yeah … Gregg Baker..The address is …

            (DOOR OPENS ON AND CLOSES, CUTTING WESTON, STEPS CONTINUE, THEN SECOND DOOR OPENS)

MARGOT: (ALARMED) Who's that? (RELIEVED) Oh … Lamont … Golly … we're jumpy.

CRANSTON: I should think you would be. Feeling any better, Miss Knight?

LUCY: Y-Yes … I think so.

CRANSTON: Care to answer a couple of questions?

LUCY: Y-Yes … All right …

CRANSTON: You were engaged to Bob Adams?

LUCY: Yes.

CRANSTON: But you knew Baker.

LUCY: Yes … As a matter of fact we all went to college together. Gregg and I were even engaged once … That was after a Drama Club Production of *Romeo and Juliet* we played in … We t-took it seriously …

CRANSTON: But apparently you got over it?

LUCY: Oh yes…I began to major in archeology and started on field trips … That took most of the schoolgirl romance out of me.

CRANSTON: I see … Incidentally, who finances your expeditions?

LUCY: Gregg did.

MARGOT: Is that why you came over to see him this morning?

LUCY: No-No … I c-came over to see him about B-Bob and that ridiculous Medusa story in the papers. I thought …

MARGOT: Yes. We all discovered it wasn't any joke.

CRANSTON: One last question. Did you touch anything when you were in the study before we arrived? Anything at all?

LUCY: N-No. I just came in and saw Gregg and ... and screamed ... and you answered.

CRANSTON: All right. Thanks a lot Miss Knight. Come outside a minute, Margot.

MARGOT: Sure, Lamont ... Excuse me, Miss Knight ...

              (STEPS. DOOR CLOSES ON)

CRANSTON: Look, Margot, I think I've got a lead on this case. I'm going home now. I want you to run an errand for me ... .but fast!

MARGOT: Of course. What is it?

CRANSTON: Take the car and hustle down to my club at once. They've got a copy of Dun and Bradstreet there. I want you to bring it to my apartment.

MARGOT: For heaven's sake ... Why?

CRANSTON: Our friend, the Medusa seems strangely interested in money for a so-called immortal. I'd like to get a line on her financial rating. Maybe dollars and cents will spell ... murder!

              (MUSIC BRIDGE)
              (KEY UNLOCKS DOOR. DOOR OPENED. STEPS. DOOR CLOSED)

MEUDSA: Greetings, mortal.

CRANSTON: Who's that? Who's in my apartment?

MEDUSA: Do not move, Mr. Cranston. Do not attempt to turn on the lights.

CRANSTON: You're the Medusa.

MEDUSA: Yes.

CRANSTON: What do you want? How'd you get in here?

MEDUSA: There are no locks to bar the way of the immortals. I came to speak to you, Mr. Cranston.

CRANSTON: About what?

MEDUSA: About yourself.

CRANSTON: I'd rather talk about you.

MEDUSA: Listen and tremble, mortal. The gods brook no interference. Many and varied are the ways of the gods ... It is not for mortals to understand or try to understand. It is not for mortals to interfere ...

CRANSTON: I'm listening.

MEDUSA: I have a brother god ... His name is Juggernaut ...

CRANSTON: Yes.

MEDUSA: He is a jealous god well known on this Earth ... Do you know what happens to those who stand in the path of the god Juggernaut? ...

CRANSTON: What happens?

MEDUSA: They are crushed like flies ... .like vermin ... They are crushed as I shall crush you, Mr. Cranston ... in my own time.

CRANSTON: You're not frightening me one little bit.

MEDUSA: Yes ... yes ... So have many mortals spoken to Medusa in their time ... with brave little words. But I come to them. I remove the silver mask that hides my face ... I smile on them ... with the smile of death!

CRANSTON: Smile now, Medusa.

MEDUSA: Not yet, mortal ... Not yet. I have sent a message to you. In it you will find the amount of sacrifice you must make to Medusa. It is a small amount...for the wealth you own. You will play it gladly...

CRANSTON: I will pay nothing!

MEDUSA:	You will pay … and pay … and pay … lest the fate of Robert Adams and Gregg Baker overtake you. This is your warning, mortal…take heed! And now…farewell!
CRANSTON:	Oh, no … dear lady … this isn't goodbye, yet!
	(BEGIN AD LIB STRUGGLE)
MEDUSA:	Fool! Would you see my face?
CRANSTON:	I can't in the dark, my pretty killer! So don't threaten me…
MEDUSA:	Take your hands off me, fool! Would you soil the robes of the gods with your clay!
CRANSTON:	Keep away from that door, sister!
	(DOOR OPENS PARTIALLY)
CRANSTON:	Owww! So the gods can punch, eh? Well, let's see how they can take it!
	(QUICK STEPS FADE ON)
MARGOT:	(FADING ON) Lamont! Lamont! What is it? What's going on?
CRANSTON:	Look out, Margot! Keep away from the door!
MEDUDA:	You mortal fools!
MARGOT:	(ON) Lamont! The Medusa!
	(FINISH OF STRUGGLE. MARGOT SCREAMS)
CRANSTON:	Margot!
	(QUICK STEPS FADE OFF)
CRANSTON:	Margot … Are you all right?
MARGOT:	Y-Yes … I guess so …
CRANSTON:	I tried to keep you away from the door. I almost had the Medusa for keeps.
MARGOT:	I … I'm sorry. I didn't mean to come blundering in like that, Lamont. I guess I helped her get away.
CRANSTON:	That's all right. We'll get another chance at her.
MARGOT:	Y-You see … I couldn't help myself. I f-found something at your club that upset me pretty badly.
CRANSTON:	Come inside, Margot; try to calm down. It can't be as bad as all that.
MARGOT:	It … it's awful. Y-You've had a threatening letter from the Medusa. Unless you pay twenty thousand dollars … you're going to be the third victim on the list.
CRANSTON:	I know all about that. I also happen to know something else. The Medusa may be the three hundredth victim on THE SHADOW'S list!
	(MUSIC BRIDGE)
MARGOT:	Finished with the Dun and Bradstreet?
CRANSTON:	Just about.
MARGOT:	What did it tell you?
CRANSTON:	A couple of interesting things. In the first place … Robert Adams had a very low rating. Apparently Bob was not as well to do as we thought.
MARGOT:	What else?
CRANSTON:	Baker isn't listed at all.
MARGOT:	Then that proves the Medusa must have known Baker intimately. Otherwise how would she know Baker could afford to pay so much money?
CRANSTON:	Yes…that's true. However it also indicates that The Medusa did not know Adams financial standing …
MARGOT:	Of course! If she did … she wouldn't have tried to blackmail him.
CRANSTON:	She's showing good financial sense trying to blackmail Cranston … but bad common sense. Let's see that letter now …
MARGOT:	Here …

CRANSTON: Hmmm … Plain paper…Plain envelope … Printed in ordinary ink. Obviously our goddess tried to disguise her handwriting.

MARGOT: Read it!

CRANSTON: Hail, mortal! You have been honored by the gods and permitted to make sacrifice to Medusa. You will bring twenty thousand dollars in cash to the Fountain Plaza in the park by Midnight.

MARGOT: That's the giant fountain with all those stone mermaids and tritons … It's near the Mall.

CRANSTON: Yes, I know … (READS) Otherwise you will suffer the fates of Adams and Baker by one o'clock. The gods do not jest. See to the sacrifice…(NORMAL TONE) Pretty melodramatic, eh?

MARGOT: Please don't joke about it, Lamont. What are you going to do?

CRANSTON: Isn't it obvious? Keep the date of course.

MARGOT: You're going to pay?

CRANSTON: Yes … I'm going to pay … off!

MARGOT: Wh-What do you mean?

CRANSTON: I'm going as THE SHADOW, Margot. I'd like to see how Medusa will go about turning an invisible man to stone!

(MUSIC BRIDGE)

(BRING UP WIND TO B.G. FOR SCENE…ALSO SPLASH OF FOUNTAINS OFF)

MARGOT: This is it, Lamont…

CRANSTON: You know, I don't think I've been on the Mall in years. I'd almost forgotten that giant Neptune in the center of the fountain … Magnificent, eh Margot?

MARGOT: Lamont, this is no time for art appreciation. What are we going to do?

CRANSTON: Wait….

MARGOT: Just wait?

CRANSTON: Just wait.

MARGOT: What time is it?

CRANSTON: A few minutes to twelve.

MARGOT: The-The Medusa will be here soon.

CRANSTON: I hope so. It's a little chilly waiting here.

MARGOT: Chilly and spooky! Golly … It's so dark and lonesome ...

CRANSTON: I can thin of more cheerful spots…

MARGOT: Lamont …

CRANSTON: I don't think we ought to talk, Margot.

MARGOT: Why not?

CRANSTON: If Medusa hears Lamont Cranston speak and then THE SHADOW appears … She might put two and two together …

MARGOT: Oh … All right … I'll be quiet … (PAUSE)

MARGOT: (WHISPERS) Lamont!

CRANSTON: Shhh …

MARGOT: I think I heard something!

CRANSTON: Shhh … Listen … (PAUSE)

MARGOT: I … I guess I was hearing things.

CRANSTON: All right … let's wait some more … (PAUSE)

"The Face of Death" was a takeoff on **"Heroes Are Born … Not Made,"** a 1944 *Green Lantern* comic story.

MARGOT:	Lamont! Listen …
	(FOOTSTEPS OFF FADE ON VERY SLOWLY)
MARGOT:	Footsteps!
CRANSTON:	Yes … I hear …
MARGOT:	Th-They're so creepy!
CRANSTON:	Shhh …
MARGOT:	Is it … Medusa?
CRANSTON:	Quiet!
BOY:	(OFF. YELLS RAUCOUSLY) Hey, Charlie! Wait for me!
	(FOOTSTEPS RUN AND FADE OFF)
MARGOT:	Oh … Golly…Golly … A false alarm …
CRANSTON:	Shhh … We've got to be quiet now.
MARGOT:	Yes …
	(PAUSE. CLOCK CHIME TWELVE OFF)
MARGOT:	It … It's twelve o'clock. Do you hear the clock?
MEDUSA:	(FADING ON) Yes, mortal … The god's are always prompt … Prompt as Fate itself!
MARGOT:	Medusa!
MEDUSA:	You have kept the appointment for the sacrifice. It is well. Where is the mortal bearing the sacrifice?
MARGOT:	Y-You mean Lamont Cranston? He … He …
SHADOW:	(LAUGHS)
MEDUSA:	Who laughs? Who laughs at the immortals?
SHADOW:	Another immortal, oh mighty Medusa!
MEDUSA:	What immortal?
SHADOW:	Look up, fellow God … Look high. See me standing here … Standing amidst the sparkling waters.
MEDUSA:	In the fountain? Who? Where?
SHADOW:	I am Neptune … God of the waters. Standing here … an image of stone … but yet a god!
MEDUSA:	You lie! Stone cannot speak!
SHADOW:	Neptune speaks as he will. Guard your tongue, Medusa..Remember, Neptune is the father of Jupiter … the father of all the Gods …
MEDUSA:	No!
SHADOW:	You are all answerable to Neptune for your deeds … I am displeased with you, Medusa!
MEDUSA:	No … No! This is impossible!
SHADOW:	I am descending from this perch amidst the waters. I am coming to you for an accounting, Medusa! It is not wise for a God to turn immortality to the purpose of extortion!
MEDUSA:	You are not coming down! I see nothing! It is a trick! I will not be fooled!
SHADOW:	Feel the might hands of Neptune, then … Crushing you down … Ripping from you face the false mask that hides nothing but greed!
MEDUSA:	No! No! Let go … (SCREAMS) Gregg! Gregg! Help me!
BAKER:	(FADING ON) Helen! For God's sake, what is it?!
SHADOW:	Ahhh! So Medusa calls upon mortals for help!
BAKER:	Get back…Whoever you are! Get back …
	(GUN SHOTS)
MARGOT:	Shadow! Watch out!
BAKER:	Take your hands off me!

	(GUN SHOTS)
MEDUSA:	(SCREAMS) Gregg! What is it? I can't see it?
BAKER:	Let go of me ... Let go ... (CHOKES) Yaaaaaahhhhh!
MEDUSA:	What have you done to him? Who are you? What do you want?
SHADOW:	Your mortal servant lies unconscious on the cold earth, Medusa ... Now, may I remove that silver mask ...
	(LAUGHS)
MEDUSA:	No! No! Noooo ...
SHADOW:	The mask falls ... Turn us to stone, Medusa! Turn your baleful face upon us! You cannot? You are only human after all ... Human ... and helpless ...
	(LAUGHS)
	(MUSIC BRIDGE)
CRANSTON:	So you see, Commissioner, it was just a clever extortion stunt all along.
WESTON:	What gets me is that it was Helen Steel working in cahoots with Baker! I might have known.
MARGOT:	Who is Helen Steel, Commissioner?
WESTON:	She used to be a sculptress, Miss Lane. She turned crooked and served a term for fraudulent practice. Used to carve statues and sell them as genuine Greek and Roman marbles ...
CRANSTON:	Helen Steel worked with Baker. She prepared the stone statues in advance ... they were made of Stonite ... a preparation like plaster of Paris that sets like real stone but is light enough to be carried.
MARGOT:	I see ...
WESTON:	The way I see it ... they picked on Adams as the first victim to terrorize the rest of the victims.
CRANSTON:	Right. Adams was killed in the park...His statue left behind while Baker carried off the body. Medusa flitted around to divert attention so Baker could escape unnoticed.
MARGOT:	Then Baker pretended to kill himself?
WESTON:	Yeah. Pretty smart pulling that act on the phone ... That made the whole field ripe. Baker figured that after two people were knocked off by the Medusa, no one would dare to refuse payment.
CRANSTON:	But Baker made one bad mistake. He was supposed to have been turned to stone while he was phoning me, remember?
MARGOT:	That's right.
CRANSTON:	But when we got there, we found the phone back on the hook. Remember, you picked it up to dial Cardona, Commissioner?
WESTON:	That's smart thinking, Cranston. Of course ... The phone should have been dangling on the cord. He'd have dropped it if he was really turned to stone.
CRANSTON:	The other clue I had to work on was the fact that Baker's financial standing was not listed. For a banker, that's tantamount to an admission of bankruptcy. He's got to be listed if he wants to stay in business.
MARGOT:	Golly ... I never thought of that.
CRANSTON:	It was a pretty shrewd plan all around ... Everything seemed to point to Lucy Knight as the villain ... Probably they picked on Adams for the first victim for just that reason ... We were pretty lucky to stop them in time.
	(CURTAIN)
ANNR:	This story is copyrighted by Street and Smith Publications Incorporated. The characters, names, places and plot are fictitious. Any similarity to persons living or dead is purely coincidental. Again next week The SHADOW will demonstrate that ...
SHADOW:	(FILTER) The weed of crime bears bitter fruit ... Crime does not pay ... The Shadow knows! (LAUGHS) •